STONE

STONE

The Hellfire Riders' enforcer, Stone Wall, has just three weaknesses.

Dogs.

Little kids.

Damsels in distress.

But this time, the damsel isn't in distress. She's bait, luring him in with haunted eyes and a sad smile. And Stone should have known better, but he couldn't resist those soft, sweet lips. One kiss put him in a cage, fighting for his life. Fighting not to let winning rip his soul apart…and losing that fight.

So he played the hero. That's over with. The moment he's free, that damsel in distress is going to give him his pound of flesh. Kiss by kiss. Lick by lick.

It's payback time.

LOOKING FOR CONTENT WARNINGS? FLIP TO THE END!

To avoid putting spoilers up front where readers might accidentally see them, I've listed the content warnings on the very last page. If you are browsing through a "Look Inside" feature and can't flip to the end, please feel free to visit my website and look for the content warnings link in the menu. www.katiwilde.com

STONE

THE HELLFIRE RIDERS

KATI WILDE

STONE

The Dead Lands
Fantasy Romance

The Midwinter Mail-Order Bride

The Midnight Bride

Pretty Bride

The Midsummer Bride
(coming soon)

Wolfkin & Berserkers
Shapeshifter Romance

Beauty In Spring

High Moon

Teacher's Pet Wolf

Sheriff's Bad Bear
(coming soon)

Other Romances by Kati

Going Nowhere Fast[1]

Secret Santa

The King's Horrible Bride

All He Wants For Christmas

The Wedding Night

Evil Twin[2]

---

[1] Includes cameos by the Hellfire Riders
[2] Set in the same world as the Dead Lands

CONTENTS

...

FOREWORD

Finally! It's Stone's book!

Hopefully you are a new reader to the series, because if you began in 2014 with the first book, there was a four-year wait between *Gunner* and *Stone.* Bull and Duke helped to ease the pain, but for all of you who hung in there—I can't tell you how much I appreciated it!

But it did create a slight problem, because after four years...well, unless everyone went back to the beginning, they might forget details. And although I wrote *Stone* to stand alone as much as possible, that's a long time to expect readers to remember what happened before.

My solution before Stone's book released was to offer a recap of those books that directly preceded the action in this one—and since *Gunner* & *Stone* share relatively the same timeline and begin in the same place, that meant I needed to remind everyone what happened in *Saxon* and *Blowback.*

So I wrote a comic for everyone to recap those stories... and I'm including it here!

The formatting is a little strange, simply because the

individual panels were meant to be shared online—so they are square instead of book-page shaped. Add in the dark ink that some of the images need and that can only be printed on one side of a page, and the overall format is not ideal, but I hope the best compromise between mediums.

Thank you all so much for taking this journey with me! I have an author note at the end this time, so until then, happy reading!

—Kati

A NOTE ABOUT READING ORDER

IF YOU SKIPPED HERE FROM GUNNER'S BOOK, NO problem! You can go back and read *Bull & Duke* without worrying about this book spoiling those. And if you've recently read the other books in the series, you probably won't need this series recap...but you might enjoy it anyway!

And if you finish this book and still want more Hellfire Riders, I've got you covered! A few familiar faces show up in *Going Nowhere Fast*, a story featuring Anna and Stone's cousin, Aspen.

CONTENT WARNING

IF YOU'VE FOLLOWED THE HELLFIRE RIDERS SERIES TO this point, you probably have a good sense of the level of violence and my style. However, I need to point out that this book is darker than the others! So if you need spoilers, I've included detailed warnings on the very last page of this edition. Just flip to the back!

THE HELLFIRE RIDERS

A COMIC BOOK RECAP
BY
KATI WILDE

SAXON GRAY, THE HELLFIRE RIDERS PREZ,
HAS ALWAYS LOVED JENNY, BUT HER DAD
IS THE PREZ OF A RIVAL CLUB!

JENNY, DAUGHTER OF THE STEEL TITANS PREZ, HAS
LOVED SAXON EVER SINCE HE SAVED HER FROM THE
EVIL PREZ OF THE EIGHTY-EIGHT HENCHMEN!

OUR STORY BEGINS
WITH SAD NEWS...

MY DAD
IS DYING
AND
I'M IN
DANGER!

BUT SAXON ISN'T A
BIG, STRONG HERO
FOR NOTHING!

DON'T WORRY, JENNY!
I'LL PROTECT YOU AND
COMBINE OUR CLUBS,
AND ALSO F*CK YOU
REAL GOOD EVERY
NIGHT!

YAY!

THE NEW PREZ OF THE EIGHTY-EIGHT
HENCHMEN = MORE NEO-NAZI TRASH

AS SAXON AND JENNY BEGIN THEIR RELATIONSHIP AND THE CLUBS ARE COMBINED, THE EIGHTY-EIGHT PLANS TO DESTROY THEM WITH A SNEAK **ATTACK!**
I'LL PROTECT YOU, JENNY!
7/12

saxonnnnnn nooooo!!!!!!!!
Gun bang!
8/12

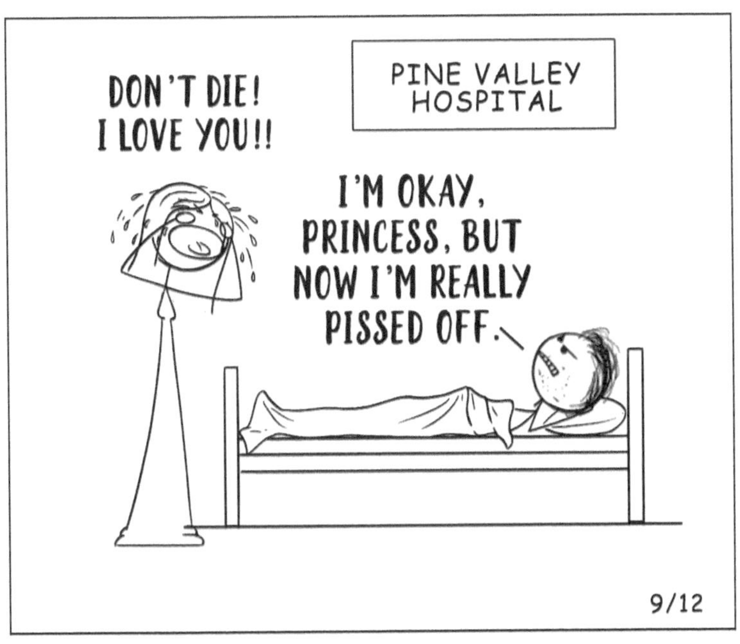

THE HELLFIRE RIDERS STORM
THE NEO-NAZI'S COMPOUND,
BURN THEIR METH KITCHEN,
AND FREE GIRLS FROM A
SEX-TRAFFICKING RING.

SAXON FIGHTS THE EIGHTY-EIGHT'S PREZ...
I'LL MAKE SURE JENNY IS NEVER HARMED AGAIN!
UNTIL FINALLY...
11/12
HAPPILY EVER AFTER 
THE END
NEXT: JACK & LILY

THE HELLFIRE RIDERS RUN OFF (AND KILL A BUNCH OF) THE EIGHTY-EIGHT HENCHMEN, A NEO-NAZI MOTORCYCLE CLUB.

JACK "BLOWBACK" HAYDEN IS THE HELLFIRE RIDERS' WARLORD. HE'S RUTHLESS AND SCARY, WITH A SAD PAST AND AN EMOTIONALLY DAMAGED HEART, AWWWW.

LILY "ZOOMIE" BURNS IS THE ONLY FEMALE PATCHHOLDER, AND HAS TO WORK TWICE AS HARD AS ANY OF THE MALE CLUB MEMBERS JUST TO BE RESPECTED.

HE LOVES HER AND HE CAN'T BEAR SEEING HER HURT

BUT HE'S ALSO KIND OF FUCKED UP IN THE HEAD AND HE'LL DO ANYTHING TO HAVE HER, SO...

HELLO! I'M A JUICY HAMBURGER AND JACK WOULD REALLY LOVE TO EAT ME, BUT ONE DAY LILY WAS DRUNK AND BET HIM THAT A VEGETARIAN RESTAURANT IN THEIR RURAL TOWN WOULD GO OUT OF BUSINESS WITHIN TWO YEARS. SHE SAID IF IT DIDN'T, THEN JACK COULD TIE HER UP AND HAVE HIS WAY WITH HER FOR A SINGLE NIGHT.

SO EVERY DAY FOR TWO YEARS, HE ATE AT THAT RESTAURANT, HOPING TO HELP KEEP IT IN BUSINESS... BECAUSE WHAT HE REALLY WANTED TO EAT WAS LILY.

YOU WILL REALLY MAKE ME FOLLOW THROUGH ON THAT DUMB BET?
WHY IS HE TRYING TO RUIN ME?
YEP!
YOU'RE SO FUCKED UP IN THE HEAD, JACK!
I KNOW I AM. SO HOW MUCH LUBE SHOULD I BRING?
BUT BEFORE HE CAN COLLECT...
5
THE DEVIL'S HANGMEN SHOW UP AT THE HELLFIRE RIDERS' CLUBHOUSE! THEY'VE TAKEN OVER THE EIGHTY-EIGHT'S TERRITORY. NOW THEY WANT THE HELLFIRE RIDERS TO GIVE UP THEIRS, TOO...OR ELSE!
SOME GUY JACK WILL KILL
SHERLOCK, THE VP
ANOTHER GUY JACK KILLS
THIS ONE WILL DIE IN STONE'S BOOK
CROC, THE PREZ
JACK KILLS HIM, TOO
CREEK
WE'RE GOING TO BEAT YOUR ASSES...ALSO YOU HAVE A GIRL IN YOUR CLUB?? HAHAHAHAHAHA!
REALLY AN UNDERCOVER FBI AGENT! AND JACK KNOWS HIM!!!
6

QUICKLY, THE HELLFIRE RIDERS HAVE A CLUB MEETING AND DECIDE TO KICK SOME DEVIL'S HANGMEN ASS! THEN THEY BEGIN TO SPEAK OF MUCH MORE IMPORTANT THINGS...
CAN IT BE TRUE? DOES JACK CARE ABOUT ME? I CAN'T BELIEVE IT. I'M GOING TO MAKE SURE OUR NIGHT IN BED IS THE WORST SEX EVER!
WHISPER JACK REALLY LIKES YOU, LILY! ....AND HE ALWAYS HAS!
WHISPER THAT'S WHY HE'S ALWAYS PROTECTING YOU!

LATER THAT NIGHT...
THIS HUNGRY MAN IS GONNA GET HIMSELF SOMETHING TO EAT!

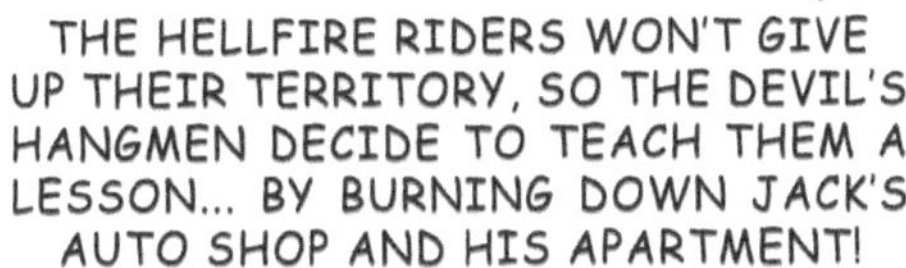

THE HELLFIRE RIDERS WON'T GIVE UP THEIR TERRITORY, SO THE DEVIL'S HANGMEN DECIDE TO TEACH THEM A LESSON... BY BURNING DOWN JACK'S AUTO SHOP AND HIS APARTMENT!

JACK'S AUTO SHOP
WHAT CROC DOESN'T REALIZE IS THAT JACK DOESN'T GIVE A SHIT! HE DOESN'T CARE ABOUT ANYTHING EXCEPT....
THAT'LL TEACH YOU TO DEFY THE HANGMEN! IF YOU DO, YOU'LL PAY FOR IT!

SHE'LL ALWAYS HATE ME FOR THIS, BUT AT LEAST I HAVE ONE NIGHT!
LET'S GET THIS OVER WITH, JACK! I KNOW YOU HATE ME AND HOPE TO RUIN MY PLACE IN THE CLUB, SO I DON'T INTEND TO ENJOY A SINGLE MINUTE OF THIS...EVEN IF YOU ARE REALLY SEXY AND HAVE A BIG DICK!

BUT AS HE'S BANGING HER, LILY LOOKS INTO HIS EYES, EXPECTING TO SEE THAT HATE...
DEEP THRUST!
HARD STROKE!
sexy squelch!
=MOAN=
=GASP=
SPURT!
AND INSTEAD SHE SEES HIS TRUE FEELINGS!
11
OMG! JACK LOVES ME! AND HE EVEN MADE ME COME DURING ANAL!
GOOD ANAL IS HOW YOU KNOW A HERO'S LOVE IS REAL!
12

BUT NOT ALL IS WELL, BECAUSE A BIG FIGHT IS BREWING BETWEEN THE RIDERS AND THE HANGMEN! AT A STRIP JOINT ON THE COUNTY LINE, THE TWO MOTORCYCLE CLUBS ARE ABOUT TO FACE OFF—UNTIL CROC PROPOSES A WAGER...AND THE WINNER WILL TAKE ALL!

LET'S FINISH THIS!
SHE'S MORE STUNNING THAN EVER BEFORE!
BUT WHAT IF CROC HURTS HER...? HOW CAN I STAND BACK AND LET IT HAPPEN?
WILL JACK TRY TO PROTECT HER AND DESTROY ALL THE RESPECT SHE'S EARNED?
15
GET READY TO CRY, GIRLIE!
WHACK!
WHOOSH
=WHAM=
BAM!
ZOOMIE ZOOM!
!!!!!SUPERASSKICK!!!!
16

AFTER SINGLEHANDEDLY SAVING THE HELLFIRE RIDERS' TERRITORY, YOU'D THINK A GIRL COULD GET A BREAK. BUT, ALAS...

THE DEVIL'S HANGMEN APPOINT **SHERLOCK** AS THEIR NEW PREZ, AND THEY ALL SIT IN THEIR CLUBHOUSE AND WHINE ABOUT HOW LILY HUMILIATED THEM.

SO SHERLOCK HATCHES UP A PLAN FOR REVENGE THAT WILL ALSO WIN HIM FAVOR WITH A CARTEL BOSS WHO BROADCASTS ILLEGAL FIGHTS-TO-THE-DEATH IN...

THE CAGE!*

*YES, THIS SHOWS UP IN STONE'S BOOK!

SAY GOOD-BYE TO EVERYONE YOU LOVE! YOU'RE GOING TO MAKE ME A LOT OF MONEY IN THE CAGE!
I HOPE JACK GOT MY MESSAGE!
RED EYE AND HIS GOONS!

I love you, Jack.
I love you, Jack.
I love you, Jack.
Jack.
I love you
I love yo
I love y
I love
I love yo
ve you, Jack.
I lov
I love yc
I love you, Ja
ve you, Jack.
I love you, Jack.
I love you, Jack.
ve you, Jack.
I love you, Jack.
I love you, Jack.
I won't fight. Not until I have to. I'll keep the phone with me as long as I can.
I love you, Jack.

I'M COMING, LILY!!!!

HAPPILY EVER AFTER!
I LOVE YOU, LILY!
THE END.

STONE

*To DiscoDollyDeb
and every other reader who hung in there
over the years. I wouldn't still be here without
readers like you. Thank you for every Kati
Wilde book you've taken a chance on, thank you
for every time you've recommended my work,
and thank you so much for your patience.*

*To my girls, Ruby and Ella, who began this
journey with me so long ago. You're the most
amazing of friends and I am the luckiest woman
to have found you both in this huge and crazy
online world. To Mel and Lea, who really really
really want Jack & Lily to have that baby…I
might have to write another epilogue again.*

THE CAGE

ONE

Every night, after I'm imprisoned in my stall, the sound I dread most is the soft *clunk* of the electronic lock releasing. Fear of an unlocked door might seem stupid, considering that I want nothing more than to escape this nightmare that I'm trapped in. But since I'm not free yet, the only place I feel safe is behind that steel-reinforced door—until six a.m., when the door opens and my daily duties begin.

So when the *clunk* wakes me just after midnight, terror instantly freezes me in place, lying on my side and with my back to the door. Two months ago, that emotion might have been hope instead of terror. Even a month ago, my first thought might have been *The FBI finally found us!* or *Matt took the guards by surprise and he's busting us out of here.*

But after three months in this hellhole, hope is hard to hold onto. So instead I lie motionless in bed and think that one of the guards must have gotten tired of jacking off in the control booth and decided to help himself to some forbidden pussy. Now I'll have to let him rape me or I'll have to fight him off, and both options are a death sentence.

Because I've only got a few rules to follow. Number one is, "Do as you're told." Number two is, "Keep your cherry"—at least until Papa decides to give it away.

No one ever explicitly *said* that I can't keep a scalpel under my pillow, but I don't have to be told that it's an unspoken rule. Having a weapon—especially one that I stole from a locked cabinet in the medical room—will get me in trouble. And around here, 'trouble' doesn't merit a hand-slapping. It means a bullet to the head. But only after I've been passed around to all the guards and other prisoners. So what's worse—one rape, or a few dozen rapes followed by death?

I know what's worse. But as footsteps stealthily approach my narrow bunk, I pretend to sleep…and my right hand creeps beneath my pillow.

My fingers curl around the scalpel's handle just as an urgent whisper hisses through the dark.

"Cherry, are you awake? Did Lissa get locked in here with you?"

It's Bravo. One of the guards. And he's looking for Lissa?

My mind races with the implications of that until he grips my shoulder and gives me a hard shake. "Cherry!"

I let go of the scalpel and simulate waking up, blinking heavily, looking at him in confusion. In the dark, the expression on Bravo's face is hard to make out, but the suppressed panic in his tone is easy to hear.

"Have you seen Lissa?"

"Not since she went into her stall at ten," I tell him in a drowsy voice, as if still not fully awake.

"She went in there before it was locked? You're *sure*?"

"Yes." And I am. Every night it's the same. Her quarters are across from mine and, just before the lights go out, we wish each other goodnight through the small windows in our doors. "Why?"

Bravo doesn't answer. Instead he mutters a curse and hightails it out of my room. The door automatically locks behind him.

I sit up, my body thrumming with tension, my heart racing. Lissa's gone. And Bravo's panicking because he's the one who unlocked her stall.

I know all about their hookups. The guards aren't supposed to touch either of us, but Lissa isn't forbidden for the same reason that I am. My virginity will be a prize to some lucky fighter in the stable—*if* any of them are ever lucky enough to make it through ten bouts in the Cage. But Lissa is the sexual bait they use to abduct those fighters in the first place, so the guards aren't interested in protecting her chastity. And when Papa decides that one of the fighters or a guard deserves a reward, she's the one to give it. Sometimes a blow job, sometimes more. But unless it's been sanctioned by Papa, the guards aren't supposed to fool around with her—because the guard in charge, Victor, runs a strict operation and he claims pussy is a dangerous distraction.

Victor's not wrong. Distracting a guard is exactly why Lissa began flirting with Bravo. He's younger than the others—not a boy, because none of the guards are—but probably not much older than me. Maybe around twenty-five or so.

My brother, Matt, thinks the guards are probably a local militia that turned mercenary. He believes that some of them—like Victor—were actually in the military at one point. But the others either washed out of basic training and have something to prove, or they just like to strut around and play soldier. I'm not sure which of those Bravo is, because they're careful not to tell us any personal information, but he has the 'strutting around' part down pat. He's always swinging his dick around, the kind of guy who thinks nailing a chick makes him more of a man and who can't bear anyone questioning his masculinity. So all Lissa had to do was coo at him and say that she loved the size of his cock, and Bravo was more than willing to risk unlocking her door so she could slip out and meet up with him.

Their hookups have been going on a few weeks now. Soon she plans to bite off his dick or whack him over the head or rip out his throat. Whatever it takes to incapacitate him and get away.

But apparently she didn't even meet up with him tonight. So after he unlocked the stall door—which can only be done from the control booth near the barn's main entrance—she must have found an opportunity to slip away. And if a bloviating prick like Bravo can't conceal the panic in his voice, then he must be fucking *terrified*.

Good.

I listen in the dark, trying to hear what's going on outside. Are the guards going from stall to stall, searching for her? If so, they're being quiet about it.

Sliding out of bed, I tiptoe to the door and peer through the small window. This building used to be a horse barn, and the original layout is mostly still intact. A wide aisle separates the rows of stalls where the fighters are imprisoned. The stalls all have sliding doors that are solid wood on the lower half, but with narrow bars on the upper half that can swing open independently of the bottom. My stall at the far end of the barn is different; my walls are all wood, not made partially of bars, and my door is just a regular door—as if the space originally served a different purpose than holding a horse. Maybe a tack room, maybe something else. It doesn't matter. The only purpose this room has now is to lock me up at night.

Lissa's stall is the same—but she's not locked up in there. And as far as I can tell, Bravo hasn't raised the alarm yet.

Probably hoping that he can cover his ass. Maybe thinking that when the questions start, he can pretend not to know how or when she escaped.

Which would give Lissa a six-hour head start before they begin looking for her.

Six *hours*.

A full-body shiver wracks through me, but it's not all cold. I *am* cold. The tight nurse's uniform that I wear during the day is the only clothing these assholes have given me. So I took a hospital gown from the medical supplies my first week here, but the thin fabric offers little protection against the freezing November air.

I hardly feel the chill, though. Excitement quivers through my tense form, and I strain to hear anything, anything at all.

There's nothing.

I watch for a few more minutes before slipping back into bed, but I know sleeping again will be impossible. Not while I'm filled with so much hope and anticipation, and mentally sending all my strength and courage to wherever Lissa is right now. Because if she escapes, this nightmare will soon be over.

TWO

Exactly at six a.m., Elton John's "Crocodile Rock" begins playing on the loudspeakers installed throughout the barn. When my door buzzes open a few seconds later, I'm already dressed and ready to begin my duties. I emerge from my stall sporting a full face of makeup and blown-out hair, along with the ridiculous outfit I'm required to wear, which looks as if it was bought during a Halloween sale. Not because my clothes are scary, but because it has that "adult female costume" look which turns every character into the sexy pinup version.

Since I fulfill the role of nurse around here—making

sure the fighters receive proper nutrition and exercise, and monitoring their overall health—I've got the corresponding costume. Comfortable scrubs are out, because Papa prefers "women to look like women should." To him, that means a tight white shirtdress barely long enough to cover my ass cheeks, white thigh-high stockings fastened with suspenders, and black Mary Janes with three-inch heels.

And a smile. I can't forget to wear my beautiful, womanly smile.

This morning, that smile isn't as hard to fake. Lissa's been gone for almost six hours. And although the barn is in the middle of nowhere, she's left the property often enough that she knows where to go for help and how far away it is. If not for her, I wouldn't have any clue where we were, because I arrived blindfolded in the back of a van and haven't gone anywhere since then. But she shared the info with me, drawing a map and making me memorize our location, just in case I was the one to escape. We've discussed the best way to reach the nearest highway without being spotted. After that, the plan is to hunker down until a semi-truck drives past. *Only* a semi-truck, because anyone on a motorcycle or in a car might be heading here to the stables, and we'd be screwed if we flagged down the wrong person. But a trucker is likely just passing through.

If Lissa moved at a quick pace throughout the night, she should be reaching that highway…right about now.

That's what I'm thinking of when Victor meets me outside the door to the doc's medical office, which means my cheery "Good morning, sir" isn't as forced as it usually is.

Like the other guards, Victor wears black army fatigues tucked into ankle-high boots and a black T-shirt as a uniform. He's got the same high-and-tight as the others do, his dark hair buzzed close to the scalp at the sides and slightly longer on top. That's where the similarities end, though. They're all in good shape, some bulky and some lean, though none exude the same strength that Victor does. But that impression of strength doesn't have anything to do with Victor's physicality, not really. Instead it's in the way he holds himself, like a trap waiting to be sprung. It's the way he looks at you, as if there's nothing you can hide from him. Line all the guards up, and anyone could pick out Victor as the smartest and most dangerous of them all.

The door to the medical office buzzes open, courtesy of a guard in the control booth, who's watching us through the cameras mounted along the central aisle. I notice Victor glance toward Lissa's door—she should have come out at the same time I did—and I quickly sweep inside the office, knowing that Victor will follow me in. He does, then unlocks the cabinet where all of the vitamins and medications are kept. Silently he stands watch as I prepare the individualized doses for the nine fighters in this barn, showing him each bottle of medication so he can check the label before I take any pills from it. They aren't going to risk that I'll poison one of their cash cows.

I wouldn't, anyway. None of the fighters are angels, but they didn't have any more choice about coming here than I did. They're all just doing the same thing I am—trying to stay alive long enough to get through this.

In three months, I've outlived twelve fighters, but I don't pretend that my chances are better than theirs. Papa won't set anyone free. All of us are going to die here, one way or another. Some of us will simply last longer.

Unless Lissa manages to send help.

Smiling again, I load up a tray with little paper cups full of pills, and exit the doc's office with Victor at my heels. The fighters in the barn know the morning drill as well as I do: as soon as Elton begins singing, they better get their asses out of bed. So the first is waiting in the center of his stall until Victor gives him the okay to approach the bars.

Of all the fighters, Crash keeps his stall the tidiest. He's already made up his bunk, the blanket precisely folded and tucked. His grooming implements sit neatly on the edge of the concrete sink in the corner of the stall, and he's already put the disposable razor to use. His square jaw is baby-smooth. He's dressed, too. Some of them don't bother putting on their pants while in their cells, but Crash always does. The guys don't receive much clothing—just a pair of gray sweats—but Papa doesn't require them to look pretty or keep their surroundings clean. He doesn't care if they take a dump in the corner of the stall or piss into the aisle. He doesn't care if they stand under the shower heads that rain into their stalls every night at nine p.m. or if they smell like an open sewer. They only have to do two things: stay strong and healthy, and fight when they're told to.

And when it comes to hygiene, some of these guys let themselves go. For a couple, it's depression and despair. For others, it's rage and rebellion. But either way, Papa doesn't punish them for it. Some have thrown feces at Victor's men—or at Lissa and me—and a few weeks back, one fighter got his hands around a guard's neck and snapped it. Papa blamed the guard for being careless, and that was that.

In the end, it all comes down to money. These guys earn Papa millions of dollars in the Cage. So the only time the tasers and the cattle prods come out is when the fighters don't follow their regimen of nutrition, exercise, and sleep.

Crash has never been tased, but it's not because he's afraid to break the rules. Instead, having a regimented schedule suits his personality. Heck, put him in a pair of fatigues and he could pass for one of the guards, because he's got that same clean-cut appearance and military bearing, as if he just stepped out of boot camp.

But I bet not one guard would want to go toe-to-toe with the big man. Not even Victor. Because Crash is a fairly quiet guy, somewhat serious, and self-contained… but I've seen what he's done to his opponents in the Cage. He sizes them up and zeroes in on their weaknesses. Then he kills them with terrifyingly brutal efficiency.

No doubt he's already sized up every guard, too. Probably calculated how he would kill each one of them. And I would love to let him out of his stall and see what he'd do to Victor—or to any of the guards. But except for the guard who got his neck snapped, they're too careful for that.

Too careful…unless they think with their dicks, like Bravo did. And now Lissa is *free*.

Soon we all might be.

With my heart light as a feather, I step up to the bars and chirp, "Good morning, Crash. How are you feeling today?"

"How the fuck do you think I feel?" he snaps back.

My heart dives back down to earth. Crash isn't a nice guy, but he's usually kind to Lissa and me, and never takes out his anger and frustration on us. Which means he isn't feeling himself this morning.

Smile vanishing, I ask him quietly, "Is your head hurting?"

"Yeah. Like there's a fucking bomb about to explode inside my skull."

Because there is—an inoperable, malignant tumor the size of a walnut. "Just a headache? Any dizziness?"

"No." Accustomed to the routine, he stands still as I shine a penlight into his eyes. The left pupil contracts. The right doesn't.

Shit. That is *not* good. "Any numb spots in your extremities or changes in your vision? Unusual sensitivity to light?"

"No."

He's probably lying. The way his pupil's blown, he likely has problems seeing out of that eye. But in his place, I'd lie, too—because Papa doesn't have any use for a man who isn't in peak condition.

So I go along with it and say, "I assume your motor control is still fine, because you didn't shred your face while shaving this morning."

"That's right." There's a slight softening in his tone. Because he knows I'm not fooled—and that by going along with his lie, I'm putting my ass on the line, too. "Everything's just fine."

"Just a headache, then. I'll note it on your chart. And I can give you a few aspirin now, but when the doc comes, I'll ask him for something stronger. I don't know if he will allow it, though."

Because any sort of doping is forbidden in the Cage. It's almost incomprehensible to me that an illegal fight organized by a bunch of criminals is regulated more tightly than the Olympics. But, once again, it all comes down to the money. And since they *are* criminals, they don't trust each other not to cheat. So each fighter undergoes rigorous drug testing.

"Aspirin will do," he says, but his gaze is on Victor— who just got onto his radio and ordered another guard to check Lissa's stall.

Crash glances back at me and cocks an eyebrow.

Asking what I know.

I'd love to tell him. I'd love to say that, right at this moment, she's probably near a highway and waiting for the right kind of vehicle to drive by—and that law enforcement might be here as early as noon.

But even if Lissa sends someone to rescue us, there's no real escape for Crash. The best he can hope for is dying free, surrounded by the people he cares for…and around here, hope is a precious, fragile thing. Giving him that hope now might be cruel—especially if nothing comes of it.

I can't promise that help is coming. I only promise what I can give.

"Doc wants me to consolidate the workout groups again." Because they exercise in groups of three, but if one of the fighters dies in the Cage, that group loses a member—and this stable had several losses lately. "So starting today, it'll be you and Handlebar at ten and four."

His breath catches. He stares at me for a long second—as if this is something he's afraid to believe in or hope for. As if he's afraid that in the next second, it might be taken away.

A few hours per day with Handlebar. Like many of the fighters who end up in the stable, they're members of an outlaw motorcycle club—but although most of the guys are from different clubs, Crash and Handlebar are from the same one. And all I know about motorcycle clubs is what Matt has told me. Mostly that they're tight-knit groups whose members call each other brothers.

Crash and Handlebar seem on another level entirely, as if they're not just ride partners or brothers. Maybe it's romantic—though double-teaming Lissa is how they ended up in here, so if there's a sexual component to their relationship, they're not only into each other.

But there's definitely love between them. And that love is what Papa used against them.

None of these guys voluntarily get into the Cage and fight to the death. Most of the time, their families are threatened. The choice is simple: Fight, or they'll kill your mother. Fight, or they'll rape your wife. Fight, or they'll torture your kid. Papa holds a knife against their hearts and forces them to decide—and most of them choose to fight.

With Crash and Handlebar, there was no need to threaten their families. All the leverage Papa needed was right there between them.

And the only positive thing about this whole situation is that—if the best that Crash can hope for is to die surrounded by the people he loves—at least I can give him a few hours a day with the person he loves the most.

His deep voice has a ragged edge to it when he says, "You're a good one, Cherry."

Not good enough. But I do what little I can. And since Victor's attention is on the guard who's about to enter Lissa's stall, I mutter under my breath, "Maybe this time don't encourage Handlebar to snap a guard's neck, so they won't separate you again."

His grin and swift glance at Victor say that, given a chance, he'd do the neck-snapping himself. "No third in our group?"

There's nine fighters left in the barn, and the groups are usually made up of three fighters. But one of them—Tusk—doesn't play nice with others. So he exercises alone.

"No third yet," I say. "But that'll change. They told Lissa that she'll be heading out today or tomorrow to bring in a new guy."

Unless we're rescued by then. Hopefully we're rescued by then. And without Lissa to use as bait, maybe it'll delay that plan.

We'll find out soon. The sound of her door buzzing open and Elton's "Tiny Dancer" accompany me to the next stall. Victor's close behind me, but his attention is on the guard entering Lissa's cell.

My attention is on the fighter waiting for us. Matt. Sheer emotion clogs my throat, as it does every time I see him locked behind those bars. Love and horror. Anger and fear. They all combine and form the blade that Papa holds against my heart.

Looking into his emerald eyes is like looking into a mirror. If his hair wasn't bleached to a pale blond, it'd be the same light auburn as mine. He's tall—not as overall big or as heavy with muscle as Crash is, but still strong and quick, and that's what has kept him alive these three months.

He's already dressed in his sweatpants, too. Not because he's modest. He just doesn't want his sister getting an eyeful of his junk.

His gaze searches my face as he approaches the bars. I keep my eyes on his face, too, but for a different reason. Swastikas and other white supremacist symbols decorate his neck and arms. It sickens me to see those emblems inked into his skin. Everything they represent is the opposite of who he is and what he believes in.

But they're a costume, the same way my nurse's uniform is. Four years ago, in an effort to help bring down a sex trafficking ring, Matt went undercover with a motorcycle club and began working his way up their ranks. Then something went wrong with one of the jobs he was in charge of—and before the FBI could pull him out, he got tossed into this stable as punishment.

And me… I'm here thanks to some really bad luck. Maybe that luck's about to change, though.

Matt's gaze narrows as I tell him cheerily, "Good morning, Hatchet."

I use the road name that he was given in the motorcycle club. He's got a fake identity to go along with it, and a name that he used while undercover—Billy Miller—but I pretend not to know it. Only Papa and the doc are aware that he's my brother. It's safer that way. These guys fight to the death, and if one of them tried to use me to gain an advantage against Matt…it might work. So we don't even risk it.

"G'morning, Furiosa."

Considering what 'Cherry' is in reference to, Matt refuses to use the name Papa gave me. But he also doesn't risk using my real name. Furiosa is as close as he comes to the nickname he called me when we were kids.

As far as Papa knows, my name's Christina Miller, because that's what Matt said it was. No one bothered to check if there actually is a Billy Miller with a sister named Christina.

I'd die before telling anyone my real name. Because if they looked me up online and saw I have a brother who's in law enforcement, that would be the end of us. He'd be dead within the hour—and I would be, too.

Instead we're fighting to keep each other alive, and as safe as anyone in this barn can be.

No doubt my safety is uppermost in his mind when he demands, "Why the hell was Bravo in your room last night?"

He doesn't keep his voice down. Immediately Victor swings his attention from Lissa's cell to me. "Bravo went into your stall?" he asks sharply. "Why?"

I tell him the truth, because the head start Lissa had is over whether I say anything or not. But if they try to get the story out of Bravo first, it might give her a little more time. "He wanted to know if Lissa was accidentally locked in with me last night."

"Was she?"

"No."

Victor's lean face hardens. His gaze shoots to Tango, who emerges from Lissa's stall and announces, "She's not in there."

I only have a second to catch Matt's gaze and see a gleam of realization, because he knows all about Lissa's hookups with Bravo and the escape plan. Then Victor grabs my elbow and marches away from Matt's stall, hauling me along with him.

The abrupt movement jostles the tray in my hands. Fighting for balance, I manage to keep the pills from spilling—then realize I'm not being steered toward my room. I assumed that I'd be tossed in there and Victor would put the entire compound on lockdown while they search for Lissa. Instead he heads down the aisle toward the barn's entrance, and I struggle to keep up with his pace, my heels clicking rapidly on the concrete.

Through clenched teeth, he tells me, "If something like this happens again, Cherry, you damn well better tell me straight away."

I'm not sure if "something like this" refers to Lissa going missing or Bravo entering my stall, but either way, I have no intention of following that order. Sometimes it seems as if the guards believe we're on the same team. Maybe because I take such good care of the fighters, getting them ready for the Cage, which helps Papa succeed. But none of it is for Papa's sake. The healthier my brother is, the stronger he is, the more likely he is to survive the Cage—and the more likely *all* the fighters I look after will survive. At least until we're found or until we break out of here. And if the only way to escape is by killing every last guard, I'd help them do it.

So I'm not on the guards' side. I never will be. By threatening Matt's life, Papa might be able to force obedience from me, but he can't force loyalty.

I'm not stupid, though, so that's not what I tell Victor. Instead I say, "I assumed Bravo already reported it to you."

Because Bravo *should* have. And that reminder puts Victor's anger where it belongs. His lips thin into a white line before he orders Tango to take another guard with him and to locate Bravo.

We pass Handlebar's stall. The bearded biker hasn't yet moved to the center of his cell. Instead he's still sitting on the edge of his bunk and slowly pulling on his sweats, his tattooed torso mottled by bruises from his last round in the Cage. His head jerks up as we go by, and I catch a glimpse of his frown—his eyebrows drawing low and shadowing his eyes, as if he's thinking there can't be any good reason that Victor is hurrying me past the fighters without stopping to give them their morning health check. But if Lissa's free, it's a *very* good reason. I flash him a reassuring smile before Victor drags me out of his sight, and then there's nothing ahead but Tusk's stall and the guards' break room with its mini-kitchen. So I'll probably be locked in there, performing Lissa's usual task of heating up the fighters' breakfasts while the guards search the compound.

But I'm wrong again. Instead of dragging me into the break room, Victor pulls me into the converted stall across the aisle from it.

The control booth. Lissa and I are never allowed in here...probably to prevent exactly what I'm doing now. My gaze skitters around the room, trying to take in everything—the security station's layout, the bank of monitors, the door-release panel—before I slow down and really *look*, just as Matt said I should if this opportunity ever came.

No weapons are lying around, unsecured. And I don't see any gun lockers that can be broken into. Which means stealing a stun gun off a guard is the best bet if the fighters ever try to arm themselves.

Instead of steel bars, a solid wall separates the control booth from the corridor that runs through the center of the barn, with a reinforced door as the entrance—probably so the attending guard can secure himself inside if the fighters break out. But that also means the guard in the control booth doesn't have a view into the barn and the fighters' stalls, except on the video monitors.

Oh, and there are *so many* blind spots. A half dozen cameras are mounted on each side of the aisle, and the way the camera angles crisscrossed, I thought for certain that they could see inside the stalls. But they can't. The aisle is covered from all angles. A fighter couldn't leave his stall without being seen. Yet within the stalls, the corners and the entire floor are hidden from the cameras' sights.

That's good to know. That's *so* good to know. If the

attending guard can't see a fighter in his stall, it won't raise an alarm—because the guards can't see *most* of the fighters on the monitors, even now. Only the ones who are standing near the bars are visible.

And those fighters could be freed with a single press of a button. The control panel appears so simple. It sits on the desk, the flat gray interface helpfully labeled in black Sharpie.

My gaze settles on one. *"#13"*—that's Matt's. One push and his door would open. But there's also a button with *"All"* written over it.

I don't know if I'd ever press that one. Not with Tusk right across the aisle. The giant fighter has survived eight rounds in the Cage—more than any other fighter in this or any other stable—and loves to remind me that in two more wins, my virginity will be his reward. But it's clear that Tusk thinks he's already earned that prize. If I free him, he'd take what he believes is his. So I'd hit every button except the one that opens his stall. It might be cruel to leave him locked up. But that cruelty could save my life—and maybe some of the other fighters' lives. Tusk hasn't saved his killing for inside the Cage. That's why he exercises alone.

"Pull up last night's video," Victor tells Charlie, the guard seated in front of the monitors, then looks to me. "Was Lissa in her stall at lights out?"

Trying not to be too obvious, I drag my gaze away from the temptation of those buttons. "She was."

"Start at twenty-two hundred hours," he instructs Charlie. "What time did Bravo enter your stall?"

"Around midnight," I tell him, watching the monitors as Charlie fast-forwards through the footage. The video isn't just of the interior of the barn. One camera outside covers the entrance, and another has a wide-angle view of the empty desert behind the barn. Nothing covers either side of the barn—also good to know—though they might have more cameras around the property. A farmhouse serves as a base for the guards and the whole compound. No doubt they have more security monitors there.

"There!" Victor barks. "Slow it down again."

The playback resumes normal speed. To my surprise, it's not at the moment Lissa emerges from her stall. Instead Victor focused on two guards standing in the aisle—Bravo and Hotel, who must have been on duty manning the control booth last night. No sound comes through the video, but it's easy to read their interaction via their gestures.

Or maybe it's easy to read because I already know how all of this happens. Lissa's told me. Bravo offers to keep an eye on the control booth if Hotel wants to go outside for a cigarette. Hotel always does. And there he is, giving Bravo a grateful fistbump before exiting the barn.

Hotel appears on the exterior camera, leaning back against the yellow vinyl siding next to the door, his lighter flaring through the dark. Bravo disappears into the control booth, but only for a moment. Even as Lissa's stall door inches open, Bravo races out of the booth and across the aisle, his hands yanking at his buckle. By the time Lissa arrives at the guards' break room, he'll have his pants down around his ankles and his dick ready to go, because Lissa has to return to her stall before Hotel finishes his cigarette. So Bravo always gets a head start with his hand.

"Goddammit," Victor mutters, and Charlie adds something like "That stupid fucker."

And there she is. I catch my breath as Lissa slips out of her stall, my fingers tightening around the edges of the tray. The monitors capture her from six different angles: a slender, painfully beautiful woman with long, flame-red hair, sneaking her way past the fighters' stalls, crouching as she passes their doors so the wooden panels along the bottom conceal her progress. Even without any sound available, I know she's moving silently—afraid that if one of the fighters discovers her deal with Bravo, he'll expose the arrangement to the other guards or force her to trade sexual favors for silence.

Anxiety grips my throat and I silently urge her on, as if I'm watching her escape in real time, instead of witnessing something that happened six hours ago. Outside the barn, Hotel exhales a cloud of smoke. My gaze flickers to that monitor before returning to Lissa, my heart thundering.

Hotel's the problem. If not for him, Lissa would have bitten off Bravo's dick weeks ago. But she has to get past Hotel, too. The current plan is to steal Bravo's stun gun and zap Hotel with it on the way out. But that plan can go wrong in a million different ways, so she's been reluctant to try it, hoping a better opportunity comes along.

And a better opportunity must have. Because if she had attacked Hotel, Bravo wouldn't have needed to ask me where she'd gone.

She slinks past the stall across from Handlebar's. I begin to shake, tension and excitement battling for control of my nerves. My gaze bounces from Lissa to Hotel. I keep expecting him to walk around the side of the barn for a piss or because he heard something that drew his attention, or any reason that allowed Lissa to slip past him. Because she's not far from the exit now and—

"What the hell?" Charlie sits forward in his chair, frowning at the monitor showing the security feed from the camera nearest the barn's entrance.

Confused, I stare at the same screen. Lissa's clearly visible. The view is at a downward angle, because the camera's mounted at about the same height as the top of the stall doors and on the same side of the aisle that she is. But although she's still crouching slightly, her knees half-bent, now her upper body is upright and she's not facing forward anymore. Instead her back is pressed against the stall door behind her, her head against the bars. Almost as if she's trying to make herself as unnoticeable as possible, flattening herself against the nearest wall. Maybe she heard something? She seems tense, straining—but I missed whatever alarmed her because I'd been looking at Hotel.

Charlie sucks in a breath. "Oh fuck fuck *fuck*."

I glance at another monitor and my stomach drops. The different camera angle reveals a thick forearm reaching through the bars, the giant hand clamped over Lissa's mouth, her wide, terrified eyes—and the huge shadow behind her.

Tusk.

Paralyzed by shock and horror, I watch her fight him. She claws wildly at his hand and wrist, drawing bloody streaks, but his grip doesn't loosen. Yet she must have gotten away from him. She *had* to have gotten away because he's locked behind those bars. No way to pull her inside his cell, no way for him to get out. So if Tusk had hurt her, they'd have found her there in the aisle, in front of his stall.

Abruptly she's yanked upward, off her feet. Then higher. As if he's hauling her to the top of the stall but nothing's there but more bars. The original stalls didn't have ceilings, just empty space up to the rafters, so the horses wouldn't hit their heads if they reared up. When they made these stables into prisons, they simply laid more bars across the top of each box stall. I've seen the fighters using them to do pull-ups. And I've stared up at them from my bed, thinking that even though the bars aren't as narrowly spaced as the ones at the front of the stall, they're still too narrow for my brother to fit through. But a woman with a small frame—especially one who is half starved, because Papa prefers girls who are model-thin—might be able to squeeze between them. I've just never tried it because I thought the cameras would catch me in the act.

But everything above the stall doors is in the cameras' blind spots. And Lissa's almost as scrawny as I am.

Unable to breathe, I watch Tusk drag her even higher. Lissa kicks wildly, trying to pull out of that grip, and my bright, hopeful certainty that she got away from him withers into cold, sick dread.

He hauls her over the top of the stall door. Her head and torso vanish from the cameras' view—and with that disappearance my frozen horror shatters into terrified desperation.

"Lissa!"

I bolt for the door, the tray of pills crashing to the floor. The image of her legs flailing from a half dozen different angles is seared behind my eyes, and it's the only thing I see as I charge blindly across the aisle.

"Cherry, stop!"

I scream again, this time in rage and frustration when Victor catches my arm and yanks me to a halt. Fighting him, I try to get closer to the bars, frantic to see inside the stall. Tusk's powerful, hulking form seems to fill his cell, a thickly muscled mountain of naked, hairless skin. On some level, I'm aware that Victor's hold is saving me from the same fate as Lissa, because Tusk could grab me, too, the moment I neared that stall door. But those six hours that I'd rejoiced over, thinking that she'd have so much time to escape this nightmare, have become six hours that she's been stuck in a terrifying hell. I can't bear the thought of delaying her rescue another second.

But even throwing my weight forward gets me nowhere. My high heels only slip and scrabble against the concrete floor. Victor's fingers are like steel clamps around my upper arm, but the pain of his tight grip and his bruising strength barely register over the dread and agony ripping at my heart. My breath comes in sobbing gasps as Victor draws his Taser and aims it into Tusk's stall.

"Back away from the bars." Victor snaps out the order over the commotion coming from the other stalls—the fighters yelling, wondering what the hell is happening. Matt's voice is mixed up in those shouts, an extra edge of fear in it. Fear for me. "Get into the restraints. Now."

Obediently Tusk turns around and backs up against the stall door, raising his arms straight up and placing his wrists into the manacles welded to the bars for this purpose. No one's fooled by his meek compliance. Victor's aim doesn't waver as he gestures Charlie forward. The younger guard approaches the bars slowly, cautiously—then, in a flash, he reaches out to snap the manacles closed, as if fearing in that instant Tusk will catch him and drag him through the bars, too.

With Tusk secured, I begin struggling against Victor again, trying to get closer to the stall. Victor still doesn't relax or let me go. "Feet."

The guards don't always bother with the ankle

restraints when they have to enter a fighter's stall, but they don't leave anything to chance with Tusk. A slot in the bottom of the wooden door slides open, giving Charlie access to the big man's ankles. It seems an eternity passes before he fastens the chain links with a steel carabiner.

"Go unlock the door," Victor tells him next—and releases my arm.

Jolting forward, I slam against the front of the stall. I grip the bars and my gaze frantically searches the small space…not seeing her. Not on the bed or under it, not on the floor.

Then I crane my neck and rise up onto my toes, so I can peer straight down. A cry breaks from me when I spot tangled auburn hair. She's crammed against the solid wood of the door, less than an inch from my knees.

"Lissa!" I shout but she doesn't move, doesn't respond. "Hurry, Charlie! She's here against the door, right here—"

The *clunk* sounds. I shove the sliding door open and Lissa slumps into the aisle, her red hair spilling over my feet.

And we're too late. I know it even before I see the bruises around her neck or press my fingers to her inner wrist, praying for a pulse.

"How is she?" Victor crouches beside me, holstering his Taser, but not even looking at the lifeless woman on the concrete floor. Instead his watchful gaze remains on Tusk. "Cherry?"

"She's gone," I tell him, my voice a broken rasp. "She's

already cold."

Tusk's grating laugh answers me. "Cold now. But you'd be surprised how long that cunt stayed warm."

My head jerks up, grief and horror lodged like a sharp, hot stone in my throat.

"Shut your goddamn mouth," Victor warns him.

But that warning doesn't mean a thing. We all know it. Victor won't touch Papa's prize fighter.

And Tusk is getting off on this. Papa didn't even have to threaten any family members before Tusk agreed to fight in the Cage. He *likes* killing. But until this moment, I didn't realize how much he relishes grief and pain, too. He's staring at me now as if my agony is an arousing feast, his eyes gleaming hungrily and bloodlust engorging his dick.

"But there's a downside to killing her so quick and keeping her quiet," he continues with undisguised glee, and I try not to listen to him, my hands shaking and tears blurring my vision as I attempt to straighten her torn clothes. "I didn't get to hear her scream—"

"Enough!" Victor snaps.

"—and without her heart pumping she didn't bleed as much as I'd hoped. Not like Cherry'll scream and bleed when I pop that—"

Everything seems to slow. It doesn't, of course. It's just adrenaline charging through my body and changing my perception, so that every step I take seems diamond-sharp and clear, as if formed by an eon of intense heat and pressure. Yet the change only takes an instant, a nuclear blast that transforms grief to rage, and action is the fallout.

I snatch the Taser from Victor's holster and launch myself at Tusk. In the split second that it takes me to close the distance, his eyes flare wide with surprise, his naked body tensing. But despite that involuntary reaction, no fear fills his expression—instead he grins, as if my attack amuses him.

Then he'll really enjoy this. I jam the stun gun against his testicles. "How about you scream for *me*?" I coldly suggest and pull the trigger.

He doesn't scream. He can't. His teeth snap together and his muscles contract as the electrical current surges through his balls.

Only a second passes before Victor rips the weapon from my hand, but the icy satisfaction of witnessing his agony seems to last for another crystalline eon—and I only pray that it feels like an eternity to Tusk. His body sags against the restraints as Victor roughly drags me back, then Tusk snaps back to enraged motion—roaring my name, fighting against the manacles, murderous intent in the gaze he fixes on me.

Victor shoves me through the stall door. I stumble over Lissa's body and renewed pain tears through me, overwhelming the burning rage that briefly cauterized the bleeding wound that her death had ripped open inside me.

"Jesus, Cherry." That disbelieving comment comes from Charlie, but I barely hear him as I sink to the concrete next to Lissa and lift her head onto my lap. I know I should be afraid of how Papa will punish me—or Matt—for what I just did to his most valuable fighter. I should be terrified. But there's no room for fear in me, not while I hold her as close as I can, my hot tears falling on her cold skin. There's only room for pain and grief. Then Tusk begins laughing and loudly singing along with Elton.

The circle of life. A song that I used to happily sing along with Matt when we were kids. A song that Lissa and I sang together here, trying to recapture a little joy and the memory of life outside this prison. A song that her murderer is singing along with as a joke.

Suddenly there's room for one more emotion within me: the despairing certainty that I'll die here, but it won't be a mercifully quick death. Instead they'll kill me little by little, destroying every bit of life and hope within me long before my body is dead. Only a few minutes ago, I'd been so sure that this nightmare was almost over.

Instead it has just begun.

THREE

I don't know what they do with Lissa's body. Probably the same thing that they'll do with Bravo's. The crack of the gunshot that marks his execution comes just before eleven that morning, a few minutes after Crash and Handlebar finish their five-mile run. Both bikers and the two guards who are serving as my escort go momentarily still and look in that direction, but I continue writing Handlebar's and Crash's pulse rates into their charts without a single hesitation.

The gaping hole that Lissa's murder has torn open inside me is empty now. Matt is terrified that I'll be executed, too, but I don't feel anything except numb. It's a form of shock, maybe. Or some other coping mechanism that kicked in. Whatever it is allowed me to get through the hours after we found her, because curling up in a ball and crying wasn't an option. Instead Victor dragged me to my feet, ordered me to clean up the pills I spilled, and continue the fighters' health checks.

So I did. Then I began the exercise rotations, and although the short walk out to the track is usually filled with jokes between the fighters—being allowed outside always puts them in a good mood—this morning they were distinctly subdued. Almost everyone liked Lissa. Even the guys who are here because they took the bait she dangled. I heard a couple of them swear to end Tusk if they ever got into the Cage with him. And almost everyone has congratulated me for getting the drop on Victor and laughed when they heard where I'd zapped Tusk.

Everyone except Matt. Each mention of it just makes him more afraid for me.

But not even once does he tell me that I shouldn't have done it. That's not who he is. What's done is done. So all that matters is what needs to be done *next*.

I've begun to regret my actions, though. Not what I did to Tusk—I'll never regret that, unless Papa decides to take his anger out on Matt. But I don't think he will. Fighters are too valuable, so whatever he does, it'll be done to me. And I just can't find it in myself to care all that much.

Instead my regret is focused in another direction. Because I did everything right. I kept my eyes open, the way Matt taught me to. I noticed that when Victor holstered his Taser, he didn't fasten the strap that secures the weapon. I knew that his gaze wasn't on me, but on Tusk. I knew that Tango had left the barn to round up Bravo, leaving only Charlie and Victor on duty.

So in that long, diamond-sharp time…I could have taken out Victor. I could have stunned Charlie when he came out of the booth. And I could have freed all of the fighters. Escape wouldn't have been certain. We'd have had to fight our way past the other guards up at the farmhouse. But we'd have had the advantage of surprise…and a chance.

Until I squandered that chance.

Lissa was killed because she'd been trying to find a way for us all to escape—and her death provided the one real opportunity that we've had.

But I fucked it up. None of these guys seem to realize how much my rage cost all of us. I know it, though. And the pain of that knowledge is almost enough to pierce the numbness as we return to the barn.

But I'm more aware of the subtle glances passing between Handlebar and Crash as they talk—not really saying anything, just a random conversation about some guy they both know, and loudly enough for the guards to overhear. But I swear there's an undercurrent, as if another conversation is taking place beneath the audible one. The same kind of conversation that took place right before Handlebar snapped a guard's neck.

As we enter the barn, though, the next look they share seems hot with frustration. Because they weren't going to take out a guard, I realize. They'd been hoping to kill Tusk, who has been locked up in his restraints—his back against the bars and his head vulnerable to anyone passing by his stall. No doubt one of them planned to rush our guards while the other got his hands around Tusk's head and broke his neck.

Except that plan won't work now. Two more guards stand outside of Tusk's open stall—not watching him, but watching over Doc, who's examining the big fighter.

Crash and Handlebar share a look that seems to say "next time" before heading toward their own stalls.

"Cherry." Doc's voice stops me before I can follow them. "When I've finished here, Papa wants to see us up at the farmhouse."

Where I'll receive my punishment, probably. Or be executed, too. Still numb, I only nod.

Not unkindly, the doctor adds, "Perhaps freshen up first?"

Because I didn't fix my makeup after finding Lissa and crying over her body. I only wiped most of the smudged mascara off.

Papa won't like that. And I don't give a shit what Papa likes…but my life isn't the only one at stake here.

"I'll take about ten more minutes here," he says, which

is just enough time.

Or not enough time. Because Matt's standing at his stall door, with tension drawing his face into harsh lines, his emerald eyes fiercely bright. His fingers are locked around the bars, but although I see his knuckles whiten, he doesn't reach for me.

"Whatever it takes," he whispers hoarsely as I slowly pass his stall. "Whatever you have to do, do it. Just stay alive."

"You, too." My throat aches as if the numbness is burning away. "I love you."

I say it so quietly, I don't know if he can even hear me. But he knows. Just as I know where that torment in his eyes comes from. My brother has been my best friend for my entire life—and we can hold conversations with simple looks, just as Crash and Handlebar do.

So it's that look Matt gives me, the one that tells me how much he loves me, that I hold within my mind as I repair my makeup and head back to the barn's entrance. Doc is waiting for me just outside, with two guards still serving as his escort—and probably to make sure he doesn't run off, too.

These guards aren't part of Victor's militia, but the more sophisticated, suit-wearing guards that travel with Papa. I don't know what hold Papa has over the doctor, but it's easy to imagine. He looks like the kindly, easily-befuddled father in a family sitcom. The roundness of his pale face is emphasized by his receding hairline and the mouse-brown combover he wears. He's not much taller than I am, and overall gives the impression of slender softness disrupted by the angular points of his elbows, knees, and nose. A white lab coat tops a blue dress shirt, necktie, and khaki pants, but I've never asked if the coat is a uniform, just like my nurse's outfit is. Maybe it's something he wears in real life and Papa drags him away from his medical practice on demand. I don't know. We don't share personal information. He knows the fake name that Matt gave him—Christina Miller—but calls me Cherry just like everyone else around here. He probably knows that I was a veterinary technician, because my medical vocabulary would give that away. But he hasn't probed for details and I haven't volunteered any. The doctor has been nothing but kind and helpful, but I don't know who or what Papa has threatened him with. And if it's a wife or kids, then Doc might decide to place their safety over mine—and I wouldn't even blame him. So I won't ever confide in him or ask him to help me, beyond what he already has.

Instead I keep trying to help myself—and Matt. I've only been up to the farmhouse once before. This compound is out in the middle of nowhere, surrounded by desert scrubland in every direction. The fighters' stables consist of two horse barns, and the farmhouse is an old white clapboard building. The house is older than the barns, which makes me think that whoever bought this place came into a little money racing horses—hence the track behind the barns—and made those improvements first before running out of money. My grandpa always said that the best way to make a small fortune racing horses was to start with a large fortune. Apparently whoever owned this place before Papa took it over never made enough to upgrade the house.

Parked near the house are two black sedans, along with the pickup that Victor's men use to make their rounds around the property. Nevada plates, but I'm not near enough to read the numbers. The truck has Arizona plates. I note the makes and models—just more information to give Matt later, to help him and the FBI take all these fuckers out.

All of them. There's more coming. A distant rumble and a dust cloud tell me that the Iron Blood is on its way. The motorcycle club serves as Papa's real muscle, at least when it comes to the stable and bringing more fighters in. I have no idea how deep it all goes. But for sure there's the Cage, drugs and guns, and sex trafficking.

That's how Lissa got here. She was given a choice: use her body to lure in fighters, or end up on her back with a needle in her arm.

Sudden tears prick my eyes. Oh God. *Lissa.* The grief is so hot and sudden that it blasts the numbness away, because the reason the Iron Blood are coming is to pick her up, so she can lure in new blood. But she's gone.

"Don't you dare cry for him," Doc says sharply.

Startled, I glance at him. But he's not watching me.

Instead he's looking out past the barns, where two of Victor's guards are digging.

Burying Bravo.

"I'm not," I say, my voice raw.

Doc's face softens. "Don't cry for Lissa, either. Her misery is over now. We should all be so lucky to have it end so quickly and painlessly."

Lucky? In disbelief I stare at him before pulling my gaze away. I would bet anything that Lissa would rather be miserable and alive than buried out in the desert next to Bravo. But maybe that's what Doc has to tell himself to keep going. We probably all lie to ourselves all the time, just to keep a spark of hope alive.

Maybe what I'm doing now—pretending that license plates will ever make a difference. But I have to do *something*. I have to believe it'll help, one day. So I look each of Papa's guards in the face, in case I ever need to identify them later. I try to memorize every distinguishing mark, listen for accents, strain to hear names.

And I don't dwell on the fact that I don't get much. These guys don't waste words. In silence, they wave Doc and me through the front door of the farmhouse. This is where Victor's guards come to sleep and relax when they're off duty, but no one seems relaxed today. Maybe because they were all forced to witness Bravo's execution—which served as a warning not to make the same mistake.

Papa's waiting for us in the parlor, which I suspect is a room used solely for this purpose. Nothing about the other rooms I've been escorted through suggests anything other than a country farmhouse, with floral curtains and over-stuffed furniture, but the parlor has a completely different vibe, as if specifically decorated to Papa's taste. Leather and wood abound, reminding me of an elegant study or library—except with no books. Two guards in black suits flank the parlor door as we're waved in. Another covers the French doors that lead out onto a porch. Victor stands at rigid attention in front of Papa, who's the only one in the room looking at ease. Wearing a suit without a tie, the neck of his white shirt open, he sits on a wide Chester-field chair with his legs crossed at the knee and casually holding an unlit cigar.

I don't need to memorize his features. Everything about him is indelibly seared into my brain by the terror and desperation I felt during our first meeting.

Salt and pepper hair. An angular face, tanned and lined but not like my grandpa's was after working outside for decades. This might be a man who spends his days in a field, but he'd be observing the people working for him and not working himself.

Papa lights his cigar, observing me through a puff of smoke before asking, "No smile for me, Cherry?"

I manage an expression that must have satisfied him—or maybe it's just my obedience that does—because he nods and gestures toward the leather sofa across from his chair. "I understand that you've had an emotional morning. Please, have a seat."

I comply, making certain to arrange myself in as ladylike manner as possible, with my back straight, hands folded in my lap, my knees together. Doc sits with far less grace, feet braced apart on the floor and leaning forward to pour himself a coffee from the carafe centered on the low table between us. Shortbread cookies form a neat semi-circle on a silver tray.

Oh my god, those cookies look so good. My mouth waters, imagining the sweet, buttery crumble. But I don't dare reach for them.

"He suffered minor electrical burns on his testicles," Doc says.

"No permanent damage?"

Shaking his head, the doctor sips from his coffee, then adds, "It wouldn't have been a pleasant experience for him, but aside from a little discomfort over the next few days, there will be no lasting effects." His lips twitch. "Though he might step more carefully around Cherry."

"Yes." Papa's answering smile holds no amusement, but his gaze doesn't move toward me. Instead it hardens and lands on Victor. "I think everyone would do well to be more careful around Cherry."

A dull flush climb's Victor's neck. Because it was his Taser that I'd stolen. So Victor won't be dropping his guard around me in the future. Which means nothing will change, because he never really dropped his guard in the past, either. This morning was a fluke. A singular opportunity that I'll never see again.

The only real surprise is that I'll be seeing anything again. If Papa's saying that the guards will need to be more careful around me in the future…that means I'll have a future. Which wasn't so certain before now.

It probably wasn't certain until Doc said that Tusk wouldn't have any lasting damage.

Not that it means I get a pass. With Victor properly chastened, Papa's gaze settles on me and he rises to his feet. "A lady never loses her temper."

A million angry replies fly to my tongue but I swallow every one. Wearing a smile, I say pleasantly, "Yes, sir."

You fucking sadistic asshole.

I tense as he comes closer, the lit cigar dangling from his fingers. I hate everything about our positions when he stops in front of me, my face on level with the front of his trousers. It's not a relief when he grips my chin and tilts my head back to meet his eyes—the cigar still scissored between his fingers, the smoke curling past my eye, that burning tip so near to my cheek. "You're a good girl, Cherry. And I understand that you might feel as if I've broken a promise to you."

I don't respond because I don't know how to answer that. Disagreeing and agreeing both seem dangerous. Tension holds me in a breathless grip as I wait for him to continue.

"You must be disappointed. A gentleman keeps his word, and I said to you that you only had to do as you're told, and you'd be safe. Yet Victor tells me that Tusk was boasting of his eventual prize when you attacked him. Was it temper or fear that propelled you forward?"

I know what this answer should be, because women are allowed to be weak and terrified. Never angry.

"Fear," I lie softly.

He nods as if that was what he expected and gently pats my cheek before returning to his seat. "You are not wrong to blame me. Truthfully, I never expected any fighter to win ten rounds. So you were to be a tease—an incentive for them to win, one that they saw every day but could not touch." Briefly he purses his lips, then shakes his head as if in regret. "Though I will not deny him the prize if he wins, I will see that you emerge from it as unharmed as possible."

My response is ashes in my mouth. "Thank you, sir."

He sighs. "That does not sound genuinely grateful."

Fear spikes through my stomach. "I truly am, sir—"

"No, Cherry." He holds up his hand to stop me, regarding me with a pitying look. "You think I do not understand? In these immoral times, it takes great effort for a girl to remain chaste, as you have, and you are to be commended. But there always comes a time when a girl's role evolves into that of a woman's, and she must relinquish the prize that she's guarded so carefully. In this past month, I have comforted my own daughter as she shared the same fears before her marriage, uncertain of the man I had chosen for her. Yet she has adjusted very well to her new role and to all of the duties demanded of her. As will you."

Oh my god. There's nothing to say. Absolutely nothing to say that won't get me in *so* much trouble. "Yes, sir," I whisper.

"And perhaps it is for the best that you will be rid of your virginity. With Lissa gone, you will need to take over her duties in the barn. But that is something we will discuss further when you return."

Her duties in the barn. Which means that after Tusk is done with me, I'll be the one to give the fighters their 'rewards.' That new duty might be a punishment for zapping Tusk or might have happened to me after I was no longer a virgin, regardless of today's events.

I should have expected it. But to hear my fate spelled out so casually still sends me reeling, so that the rest of what he said makes no sense to me. "When I return?" I echo stupidly.

Papa doesn't answer me. Instead he looks to one of the suited guards flanking the door. "Please show our guests in."

Members of the Iron Blood. Only three, though I heard far more motorcycles than that arrive.

But I can barely focus on them. I don't know why Papa's announcement slaps me so hard. It truly wasn't anything I couldn't have guessed. But it's as if I can't wrap my head around it. Maybe it's shock finally catching up to me. Maybe it's the horror of realizing how easily they plan to replace Lissa. I *know* we are nothing to them. Not me, not the fighters—we're just meat with no value beyond what we help Papa earn in the ring. Intellectually, I've known that. But this is the first time I've *felt* it, and it's as devastating as it is enraging.

But ladies don't lose their tempers. No. Ladies smile prettily and make themselves memorize as much as they can about the members of the Iron Blood who just came in, because one day this lady will tell a bunch of nice policemen exactly what these bad men did.

I haven't met them before. They come for Lissa regularly but I'm never outside of the barn when they do.

Helpfully, they put their names and ranks on their leathers vests. It seems stupid for criminals to make it so easy for someone to identify them, but I suppose that's part of the whole outlaw motorcycle gang schtick. They don't fear the cops or being caught; they're above the law or outside the law or simply a law unto themselves—and so certain that they can either silence or threaten anyone who might identify them—that they'll wear their road names openly and proudly.

Two men follow close behind the first—the club's president, Rattler. He's big and barrel-chested, with a shaved head and graying, scraggly beard. One of the guys behind him is even bigger. He's bearded, too, but it's shorter and bushier. They're all wearing long sleeves, so I can't see if they have tattoos on their arms, but the bigger guy—the enforcer, Chef—has letters inked across his fingers. *RIDE FREE.* The third biker is shorter and more wiry than the other two, with a narrow face and close-set eyes. Paladin.

He doesn't have a rank patch below his moniker, so I guess that means he's just a regular club member.

But I suspect that in usual circumstances, even a regular member would be one of the alpha dogs in the room. Because there's a strange vibe between Rattler and Papa from the moment the other man enters. As if the biker's used to entering a location and taking it over. As if he's the one who usually makes people scramble. As if he doesn't defer to anyone…but here, in this room where he clearly doesn't fit, he has to.

I never get that sense from Victor. But maybe it's because of the guard's military background. He's used to taking orders.

Rattler is used to giving them. Yet it's Papa who calls the shots here.

"You are ready to ride out?"

Rattler nods. "Two days' travel. A day or two to scope out the fighters. We'll have your new man by Sunday. Where's the girl?"

"I'm afraid Lissa has had an accident," Papa tells him, then gestures to me. "So Cherry will be taking her place."

What? I can't keep the shock from my expression.

"As bait?" Rattler looks me up and down, then bursts out with a laugh. "You got anyone with tits?"

"She has a lovely figure," Papa says without inflection.

The biker seems to realize how close to danger he's riding. He stops laughing and pulls at his beard. "She's pretty enough. But your last girl was smoking hot and had some curves on her. A man could imagine grabbing a few handfuls of her—or of that red hair. The only thing a man can grab there is a few bones.”

“Cherry will do just fine as a replacement this time.”

“Cherry?” That stops him for a second. “She’s a virgin?”

“She is. And I expect her to return in the same state.”

“A fucking virgin, trying to lure—” Rattler takes a deep breath, pinches the bridge of his nose. “We’ll take one of our own girls. They know how to suck a dick, at least.”

“One of your own girls…who can be traced back to your club? Who might go for help? No.” Papa’s voice has turned to steel. “Cherry has reason to do what she’s told. Don’t you?”

I don’t expect to be a part of this conversation, despite it being about me. So a second passes before I find my voice.

“Yes, sir.”

“You see? And Victor will be traveling with her in the van. He’ll watch over her and see that she stays on task.”

No surprise from Victor. Perhaps Papa already informed him. Maybe to prove that he won’t be outsmarted by a girl again.

“Whatever floats your boat, boss.” As if shrugging away the whole business, Rattler turns toward the door. “We’ll be waiting outside. We gotta long ride ahead.”

If Rattler leaving without being dismissed pisses Papa off, he doesn’t show it. Instead he glances at me thoughtfully, but speaks to Victor. “Perhaps a few enhancements are in order. Rattler does know the sort of men who will be lured. And if the men being enticed are men of his calibre… Well. Some men enjoy a perfect filet mignon, and others love ground beef smothered in ketchup and mustard. So give them ground beef."

And I'm the ground beef. Or the filet. The past ten minutes have been so surreal that I'm not completely certain what I'm supposed to be.

But it's clear what's happening now: I'm leaving the compound. Where I'm supposed to lure in a fighter…but where I also might find another opportunity. One I won't mess up again.

I suppose it just means that I'm a complete and utter fool…but I begin to hope again.

FOUR

I come around to a hard shake of my shoulder. "Wake up, Cherry."

Oh my god. I feel like I've been run over by a freight train made of pillows. My brain and body seem slow and muffled.

I just want to go back to sleep.

"No more sleeping." Another shake jars me away from that plan. "Time to get to work."

Work. Which isn't the work I should be doing, in Dr. Singh's office. No more mewling kittens or sweet old hounds or mean parrots. No drinks after work with the girls. But that had been over even before I flew to Las Vegas to see Matt.

"Cherry!" Victor snaps.

"I'm up," I say groggily, and try to make it at least half true by pushing up onto my elbows. My hair's in a tangle around my face and my mouth… God. My tongue feels swollen and dry, and tastes as if something crawled in there and died while I was sleeping.

Not sleeping. Was unconscious. Drugged.

Because I'm not in the barn anymore.

Victor tosses a towel at me and points across the room. "Piss and shower. Leave the door open. No funny shit."

No funny shit. "Roger that." I drag myself off of a stained, bare mattress. "I promise that whatever you find in that toilet when I'm done will be deeply unfunny shit."

Or nothing at all. Judging by the state of my skin and my shy bladder, I'm badly dehydrated. I have vague memories of Hotel spilling water down my chin and chest, telling me to drink while the entire world rattled around me. And of Doc with a syringe, telling me that I'd be okay, that this would make it easier.

I find that injection site on my inner elbow. And another next to it, less expertly done, so it looks like a mosquito bite. As if after making sure I got some water down me, Victor drugged me again.

So that's how they made sure I wouldn't alert anyone while we were driving to…wherever we are now. A rundown house with a bathroom floored with cracking linoleum, sporting a Pepto-Bismol pink sink and tub, rusted stainless steel fixtures, and a boarded-up window.

Bending over the sink, I fill my cupped hands with tap water and drink—three double handfuls, then make myself stop so that I don't puke it all up—and struggle to fill in the gaps.

I remember Papa saying that I'd be bait. Then returning to the barn to get the makeup I'd need—

Get free. Any way you can. Don't worry about me. Just get to Harris or Martinez.

—and talk to Matt. I must have told him what was happening, because his voice rings clearly through my head.

And then…almost nothing. Just that faint recollection of Doc.

"Get a move on, Cherry," Victor says from the next room.

Into the shower, where grimy soap scum darkens the anti-diarrheal pink. But the water is hot, something I haven't enjoyed in months—our showers are two-minute lukewarm streams that spray into our stalls every night—and at least the moldy shower curtain offers the luxury of privacy. I wash as quickly as I can and then simply wallow in the delicious heat, letting it wake up my still-groggy brain.

Get free, Matt told me. But after getting free, I still have to be careful about who I contact. Matt's boss suspects that there's a leak in the Bureau, because Papa and the others who run the trafficking network always seem to be two steps ahead—and a few agents have been killed after their covers were blown. But there are two men that Matt trusts. Harris and Martinez. So I'm supposed to go directly to them, because anyone else might be dangerous.

But if I have to, I can seek the protection of local cops, because the chances that some random police officer is connected to any of this is slim. And that means getting their attention any way I can. Screaming, shouting bloody murder—or even attacking someone. Because as soon as I'm arrested, I can get a message to Matt's boss, telling him the location of the stables. Then they'll rescue Matt.

Whatever it takes.

It won't be easy, because I suspect Victor will be on my ass the entire time. But I got the drop on him once. I can do it again.

Filled with purpose, I dry off behind the shower curtain and wrap myself in the towel. Victor's standing in the bathroom door, waiting for me. "Get that dress on and come out."

That dress is one of Lissa's. Grief clogs my throat as I pull on the skintight sheath, and I wonder how many times she put it on and planned the same thing—of making a scene, of desperately trying to find a way to escape—but I channel both grief and despair into determination.

The scent of pizza hits me as I follow Victor down a hall and into a small kitchen. My stomach growls but Victor didn't bring me out here to feed me, I realize.

Instead a member of the Iron Blood—Paladin—is sitting on one of the folding chairs around the cheap card table, holding a bloodied towel to his brow.

His foxlike gaze cuts to me. "You're the nurse, yeah? This shit won't stop bleeding."

Then he can bleed out, for all I care. But as he lifts the towel away from his face, I see that wouldn't happen, anyway. The wound isn't deep—just a split over his eyebrow—but hardly life-threatening.

Unfortunately. "Do you have any superglue?"

I ask Victor, but he doesn't need to answer. Hotel strides into the kitchen carrying a first-aid kit. I don't remember Papa mentioning that he'd join Victor, but I'm not really surprised. If this trip is punishment for the guards, then Hotel must be paying for leaving his post to go smoke. He's probably glad he wasn't given the same punishment as Bravo.

I don't thank him when he gives me the kit, but I end up enjoying the hell out of tending to Paladin, because it gives me a close-up view of how someone beat the shit out of him. I've tended to enough fighters after their bouts in the Cage to recognize the damage that fists and feet can do, and someone worked this asshole over good.

That's someone I'd like to thank. Instead I only ask Paladin sweetly, "Did you win?" and his glower answers that.

I finish up and set the first-aid kit next to the stack of pizza boxes. Only two slices left, but I'm not asking permission. I take them both and slide them onto a paper plate, then sit on the chair across from Paladin.

The slices are cold and greasy and the best thing I've ever eaten. I force myself to go slow, though I'm terrified that Victor will drag me away from the first real food I've had in ages. But he doesn't order me to put down the pizza or to go finish up my makeup and hair—because of what Paladin is telling him, I realize after a moment.

"He left town?" Victor asks, frowning.

"Yeah, but they left their shit in the motel room." Paladin twists the cap off a beer—and realizing that there are sodas in the fridge, I grab a Pepsi and take it back to my pizza.

Nothing *ever* tasted so good.

Through my fat and sugar and caffeine high, I listen to Paladin tell Victor that someone is coming back—the fighter they want me to lure, I slowly figure out.

Victor scrubs his hand over his face. "Why not just get another one?"

He shrugs. "Usually we would. But someone called in a favor."

Because most of the fighters are chosen for their performance in the underground matches that these motorcycle clubs participate in during their bike rallies. But not all of them. Like Matt. The club he was under-cover in had been working *with* Papa. But when a job went wrong, the Cage was his punishment. So it sounds like the guy they're looking at now fought like many of the others…but that's not the reason he was chosen. Instead he pissed off the wrong person.

My stomach draws up tight. Though I know that doesn't mean this target is a good guy…well, I can't help it. Anyone who pisses off these assholes is someone whose side I'd rather be on.

"This town is full of bikers," Victor says. "How do we recognize him?"

We. Because Victor will be watching me do this.

"You won't be able to miss him. He's a big, scarred fucker and wears a Hellfire Riders kutte. But I think we got pictures." He raises his voice, calls out, "Hey, pretty boy! Get your ass in here for a minute."

Pretty boy. Paladin's not kidding. The biker who walks into the kitchen is hands-down the most beautiful man I've ever seen—in real life or in movies or an Instagram feed. Near-black hair, a square jaw, and pale blue eyes. His rumpled shirt is half unbuttoned, and he's zipping himself up…because he was just having sex in the other room, I realize. He's not wearing a vest but it hardly seems to matter—I won't need a name to identify him. He's so gorgeous that it's like a kick in the gut, stealing my breath for a second.

Then utter disappointment follows, because if he's friends with these guys, then all that beauty is a lie and he's an evil piece of shit.

A pretty, blue-eyed devil.

And a creep. He hands his phone over to Victor, and

while tinny sounds of cheers and a fight come from the speaker, his glacial blue eyes look me over appraisingly.

"This is the virgin pussy that's supposed to reel him in?"

"Yep," Paladin confirms.

"Not bad," the man decides after looking me up and down. "What's your name, girlie?"

"Cherry."

"'Cherry?' Like one of the girls out of Luc's stable?" He addresses Paladin, not me. "Is she branded? Because this bastard'll notice that shit."

Branded like Lissa was on the back of her neck, as if she was nothing more than a cow.

Paladin shrugs. "I dunno."

"She's not marked." Victor strides over to the table, then slides the phone onto the table in front of me and pushes play on a video.

I don't want to look. I don't want to see the guy whose life they want me to destroy. But as soon as I look, I can't look away.

The fight isn't in a proper ring, or even a cage. Instead it looks as if the audience creates the ring, surrounding the pair of fighters in a big warehouse. I recognize Paladin as the opponent—so here's the man who pounded his face in.

He's stripped to the waist and barefoot. Sweat gleams over tanned, tattooed skin. His hair's short, and so wet with sweat that I can't tell if it's brown or dark blond. But Paladin was right: he'd be hard to miss. Not because he's stunningly beautiful like the creep here—or because he's a big, scarred fucker, like Paladin said—but because even in this short video, he seems to burst through the screen with the sheer force of his vitality. He dodges a jab from Paladin's fist, takes a kick to the ribs that sends him stumbling back, and then laughs—loud enough to be heard over the cheering crowd—before charging back in.

Victor clicks off the video when he's mid-swing, and I make myself breathe again. I don't like watching fights. I've seen too many end in screams of agony, or with men pleading for their lives, and death. But I'd have liked to see this one slam his big fist into Paladin.

He's not so amused, scowling as Victor tosses the phone back. "This is a waste of a favor. That fucker's not so good. He barely won our match and only because he got lucky. He won't last a single round in the Cage."

"Yeah, he will," Victor says. "He went easy on you."

"Bullshit," Paladin denies, but Victor dismisses him. Instead he looks to the blue-eyed devil.

"You see that tattoo on his shoulder? He was Force Recon. If you think he'll be easy to take out, you're a fucking idiot."

The devil grins, a gut-clenchingly gorgeous smile, not the least bit insulted. "Every man's an idiot when you put pussy in front of him. And a virgin?" His eyes go hot and lazy as they settle on me. "Just let him get a taste of what's between her legs. There's nothing sweeter than a girl with a cherry, especially if you make her come. It's the best fucking drug in the world."

Yeah, super creepy. And stupid. Body chemistry doesn't change based on a hymen. The pizza probably has more effect on the taste of bodily secretions than my virginity does.

But I suspect that he's not really talking about anything biological, anyway. Instead it's all some mental shit that's the equivalent of what played out in that video. Just some guy trying to beat another guy, but instead of in a ring it's beating another guy to a girl's vagina. Which isn't about the girl at all, but just some sick male superiority over other males.

"I'll put my trust in another drug," Victor says, and something in his tone pulls my gaze.

He doesn't give much away. But I've got a feeling that he's disgusted by this whole setup. Not the part where we'll be abducting a fighter, but the rest of it—that he thinks we're under-prepared and that the others aren't taking this operation seriously enough. And what was the difference? Seeing the guy. As if that tattoo really rattled him.

As if he's thinking that a girl and a roofie might not be enough. As if he's thinking this guy will see straight through me, then fight his way past anyone who tries to take him down.

I hope he's right. But with luck, I'll flag down a cop before that, and it won't even get that far.

Too bad my luck is pure shit.

FIVE

As we walk down the street, with my heart pounding and my stomach roiling with tension and fear, Victor warns me again.

"No tricks. You spike his drink, then you persuade him to go outside. And I'll be listening to every word you say."

Though a microphone in my wig. I didn't know he was going to make me wear one. Nothing is going like I hoped it would. My plan to get the attention of law enforcement by any means possible was destroyed before we even left the house, when a man in a sheriff's uniform showed up… and the Iron Blood handed him a wad of cash.

I'm still reeling between rage and despair as Victor ushers me toward the Ponderosa tavern, where my target is supposed to be drinking. The streets are lined with parked motorcycles. There must be thousands of them. And thousands of bikers, too, crowding the sidewalks of this small town. Every restaurant and bar we pass is packed to the rafters and with dozens more milling around outside the entrances. Desperately my gaze searches so many faces, young and old, bearded and shaved—and their women, so many women with them—but don't know if I can trust any of them. They can't all be outlaw motorcycle clubs but how can anyone tell the difference? If there's a secret, Matt didn't tell me what it was.

But there must be someone who can help me. I know there are good people in the world. I just need one person who'll stand up for what's right.

Just one.

Victor's fingers tighten on my arm. "You make one wrong move, I'll shoot your brother myself."

My shocked gaze flies to his.

"You think I can't see the resemblance?" A grim smile twists his mouth. "So you just do what you're told. You deviate from your orders, first I'll kill you, then I'll kill him. And I'll bring this guy back to the Cage anyway."

Wordlessly I nod again, my throat a solid aching lump of pain and fear, my breath wheezing too hard to work up a scream—if a scream would even make a difference. The noise inside the bar is deafening, with the Black Keys competing with a crowd of people shouting to be over-heard. I don't know how they expect me to find anyone in here. But I have to, if I want to save Matt.

To save my brother, to save myself…I have to lure a man to his death.

Because that's what the Cage is. Even if he wins once, he'll have to win again and again to survive—each time, killing someone else.

That blood will be on my hands.

I can tell myself that it's not. That this is all because of Papa and Victor and the Iron Blood and a corrupt sheriff. That they're all trading lives for their own greed and self-interest. I'd be trading a life for a life—and I was given little choice.

But I *have* been given a choice. And the choice isn't between Matt's life and this man's life. I know that. Victor's full of shit. Handlebar killed a guard and suffered no consequences. Tusk killed Lissa and I was the only one who did anything to him. Whatever I do here, Victor won't touch Matt. My brother's too valuable.

I'm not. So if I sacrifice this man, I'm really sacrificing him to save myself. Then what will change? Nothing. Matt will still have to fight in the next Cage round and might die anyway. Soon enough, Tusk will rape me and probably kill me. And this guy will likely die in the Cage, too.

I might be able to change that, though. Because I've been desperate to find one decent person to help, to stand up for what's right…

And that person will have to be me.

"There he is!" Victor has to raise his voice over the din. "Up at the bar!"

I still can't see him through the crush of people. I can't even see past the person in front of me. But the decision I've made settles into my very soul, steadying my nerves.

Tonight I'll probably die. But before I do, I'll warn this man and make certain Victor and the Iron Blood can't touch him. Then, somehow, I'll slip away from Victor through the crowd. Maybe just long enough to borrow a phone or beg someone to send a message to Matt's boss.

Maybe I'll find some way to tell my brother I love him, one more time. To tell him this was my choice.

But I think he'll know.

"I'll be listening!" Victor reminds me one more time, then gives me a little shove.

I stumble forward only half a step before jamming up against the back of another biker who's as wide as he is tall. Not my target. The crowd around the bar is about six or seven people deep, everyone shouting at each other and at the bartender, trying to get his attention. I force my way between two gray-bearded bikers who smell like whiskey and smoke, and swing an elbow when one of them gropes my ass.

And there's my target, even bigger in person than he appeared on the video. I get a quick glance of the *Hellfire Riders* written above an emblem of fiery wheels as he turns away from the bar, tucking a wallet on a chain into his front pocket—but if he managed to buy a beer, it's not in his hand.

Good. The plan is to roofie his drink. So if he doesn't have one yet, that gives me a little more time.

He scans the crowd as he turns, his gaze sliding right past me over my head, as if looking for someone taller... then skipping back and down. His eyes lock with mine.

Probably because I'm staring at him. I can't read his expression as he stares back—the only thing clearly written on his face is the damage that Paladin did. A busted lower lip gives him a pout. His left eye is partially swollen shut and he'll be lucky to see anything out of it by tomorrow. Nothing permanent, though. Not like the scars that cut through his right eyebrow and carve a ragged trail across his cheek, as if whatever slashed up his face barely missed his eye.

Slowly that eyebrow rises. The corners of his mouth tilt into a crooked smile and he gestures me closer with a curl of his index finger.

My heart pounding, I force my feet to move. This is it, then. These are the steps that will light the match that burns the Cage to the ground.

I wish I didn't have to burn with it.

He bends his head when I'm a step away, which brings him down a few inches, but he still has to half-shout across the distance and over the noise. "Does it scare you?"

Dying? Of course it does.

But was I that easy to read? "Does *what* scare me?"

"My face."

Oh. "No."

"You sure?"

I think of the blue-eyed devil, of how beautiful he was, and of how grossly creepy. I think of Papa and his elegant cruelty. "I'm sure," I say—probably not loud enough for him to hear, but he's watching my face so intently that he seems to get the gist, anyway.

"Good," he says and grins, which is so bright and sudden that I can't stop my grin in return.

Until blood starts dribbling from his lip. "You're, uh… bleeding."

"Shit." Without any apparent effort, he turns and pushes aside three massive bikers crowded up to the bar and snags a paper napkin, then tosses me a wry look. "You should see the other guy."

I laugh, remembering Paladin's face—and his petulant insistence that this man only got lucky. "I have!"

His brows shoot high.

Oops. "I saw your fight!"

About thirty seconds of it.

He grins again and presses the wadded napkin to his mouth. "So you saw me win?"

"I did. And I'd love to buy you a drink and toast your victory." Because Victor is very deliberately edging into the corner of my vision. "But maybe you'll buy me one, instead? In a dress this tight, a girl can only carry money so many places—and pulling anything out of those locations in public might get me arrested."

That earns me a laugh. "You know I will, darlin'. Come on."

His big hand engulfs mine, lacing our fingers together. We don't have far to go, just a few steps to the bar, and in his wake I don't get jostled or groped. Somehow he even secures a barstool and quickly lifts me onto the seat, then spins me so that I'm facing him.

I try to catch my breath as he shouts to the bartender, lifting two fingers. All this time, I haven't looked away from his face. His black vest covers a plaid flannel shirt. I take a second to check out his rank—Enforcer—and his name.

Stone.

"It'll probably be an hour before we get those beers," he says. "That all right?"

"I'm not in a hurry. Are you?"

"Not even a bit," Stone replies, and everything about his posture echoes that statement. He appears completely at ease, even as his big body forms a barricade against the shoving crowd. A barricade that protects me, I realize— and creates a tiny, private bubble in this crush of people.

For the first time in months, I feel…safe. But it's a safety that's no more real than the safety of my locked cell in the stable.

All that matters is that I keep this man out of a similar cell. His eyes are hazel and flecked with green, and despite his easygoing smile, his gaze is piercing as he studies my face. "You aren't here with a club."

"Is it that obvious?"

"Only because if you belonged to someone, he wouldn't let you out of his sight." His gaze sweeps down to my hips before zooming back up. "You local, then?"

I'm a terrible liar, so I try to stick with the truth. "I'm staying at a place nearby."

"Staying with someone who took you to that fight? Or you just like watching them?"

"Only in action movies." I take the wadded napkin from him and press it to his lip when it starts bleeding again. "Not so much in real life."

"You see a lot of fights in real life?"

Too many. My throat tightens, and I force a careless shrug. "A couple."

"So you'd have preferred going to a movie over going to my fight. Even though I was stripped to the waist, looking goddamn sexy, and busting a fucker's head."

I can't stop my smile. "But there wasn't any popcorn."

"Shit. Okay, serious question." Stone catches my wrist, stopping me from tending to his mouth. My gaze flies up to his. That narrowed hazel stare bores down into mine. "You like action movies. So tell me—where do you put *Die Hard*?"

"Uh-oh. The question itself says that you want me to put it in first place. But I can't."

He looks pained. "Don't hurt me like this, girl."

"Sorry. But I've got to go with *John Wick*. Sure, saving

your wife from thieving terrorists at Christmas is great. But John Wick lost everything when his wife died—and then they killed the dog she gave him." I shake my head, then tug on my wrist until he lets me go. I apply pressure to his split lip again. "So watching him make everyone pay is just so, so sweet."

"Aw, shit. I forgot about the dog. You're right. That's hard to beat."

"You have a dog?"

His eyes soften in a way that makes my heart clench. "Yeah. A boxer, Daisy."

"Here in town with you?"

"Back home."

"Where's that?" Hopefully somewhere he can get to easily after I warn him about what's coming for him.

"Oregon."

Crap. I'm not exactly sure where we are now, but I think it must be Arizona or New Mexico. "You're a long way from home, then."

"Yeah, I am."

"What do you do there when you aren't fighting?" I check his lip for more bleeding…it's stopped for now. But he needs to quit smiling.

"I'm a lumberjack."

My eyebrows shoot upward. "That's still a thing? I thought Paul Bunyan was the last one."

That makes him grin, but he doesn't start bleeding again. Yet. "It's still a thing."

"Oh. I thought you might be enlisted." Hoped he might be. The military could provide him some protection, surely.

His eyes narrow, though not in the same playful way as before. "What made you think that?"

"As you pointed out, you were stripped to the waist and damn sexy. So I looked hard." Because they wanted me to recognize my target. But it wasn't his face or his thick muscles that made the biggest impression—instead it was the same intensity that he focuses on me now. "I saw your tattoo."

"I'm surprised you knew what it meant. You've got family in the service?"

I didn't know what it meant; Victor did. That this man had been in special forces. I wish that was enough to protect him. But several of the other guys currently in the stable came out of the military, too. Crash has a tattoo similar to this man's, though I'd never asked what it meant.

"A friend of mine was," I tell him now.

"Does that friend happen to be the bastard who hasn't taken his eyes off you?"

"What?" My heart stills. "Who?"

"To your left, a little farther down the bar," Stone says without glancing away from my face. "Six-two, white, a high-and-tight, got 'drill sergeant' written all over him. And dressed like that, he sure as fuck didn't come on a bike. So I'm thinking another local. You know him?"

Victor. Not once have I seen Stone take his eyes off

me, yet he'd noticed the guard watching us. Pulse thundering, I glance that way now, as if trying to be casual about it. But there's no casual. Thanks to this microphone in my wig, Victor knows he's been made.

The guard meets my eyes, then lifts a hand as if in greeting before turning his back to me. Because he doesn't need to watch. He can still listen.

"Oh, *him*. No." I return my gaze to Stone's, find him watching me closely. "That's my boss. He probably just saw me here and is making sure I'm okay."

"And what about the asshole in that direction?" He tilts his head slightly back and to the left.

Utterly confused, I scan the crowd—and don't see anyone through the mass of bodies. Though I know who it must be.

Hotel. Probably looking as out of place here as Victor does.

But I genuinely don't see him. I don't understand how Stone did. "I…don't know."

"All right. So just tell me straight out—is he your pimp? Because I don't mind paying. But I like to know up front if that's what this is."

My mouth falls open. "You think I'm a prostitute?"

He shrugs those massive shoulders. "No insult intended. It's honest work."

If a woman chooses it, maybe. "I'm *not*."

"Fair enough." A brush of his thumb beneath my chin gently closes the outraged gape of my mouth. "Have you got a name, then?"

"Cherry," I tell him, and when his deep laugh rolls out, my face goes hot and I push at his chest. "I'm not a hooker."

Just a virgin in the wrong place at the wrong time.

"Okay, okay." His laughter settles but amusement still dances in his hazel eyes. "What are you, then?"

"Most recently, a nurse."

"Yeah?" His brows arch and he gives me a once over, as if trying to match everything he sees—from the flaming red wig to the skintight dress to the platform heels—with what I just told him. "So that explains what pulled you in my direction."

"What does?"

"A care-taking streak." He gestures to his battered face. "You saw my fight, and here you are trying to patch me up."

What else am I supposed to do when someone's bleeding in front of me? "Or maybe you just seem like a nice guy."

"I'm not." This time his smile doesn't hold any humor. "So if I seem like one to you, the men you know must be real assholes."

I huff out a laugh. "You have *no* idea."

"You want to tell me about it?" His voice deepens, his gaze steady on my face. "I'm real good at making trouble go away."

Oh god. My heart twists up so tight. Because I wanted just *one* person who would help, before realizing I would have to be that person. But here this man—a complete stranger to me—is offering to make my trouble go away.

And he's the one person who can't help me. Because he needs *my* help.

I'll be killed for this. But I'm suddenly glad that this man—Stone—is the one I have to die for. That it's not someone like Tusk or Papa.

So I force a smile though my entire chest is aching, and continue flirting. "You look like you're really good at causing trouble, too."

"Guilty," he admits. "So is that why you came over? Looking for someone to cause trouble?"

"No. Just…looking for someone who takes good care of his dog."

"How do you know I do?"

"Because you're trying to take care of me."

"Well, fuck." His big hand cups my cheek, his gaze searching mine. "That sounds like you don't expect anyone to treat you better than a dog."

I try for a bright smile and am pretty sure I fail miserably. "I'm just glad it was you who I ran into."

"Yeah, girl." His thumb rubs the wavering curve of my bottom lip. "I'm glad you did, too."

And he kisses me. Just lowers his head and kisses me. In a crowded bar, with a million people around us, and while my head is filled with thoughts of saving him and dying painfully. I'm uncomprehending at first, eyes wide open and staring into the blurry image of his too-close face, while his firm lips brush over mine, back and forth.

Gently. Not taking. Just teasing.

Or maybe soothing. Because the crowd fades away, and so does any thought of Victor, or dying, or the horrible reason I'm here. There's just Stone, kissing me so tenderly. As if he thinks a harder kiss will break me.

It won't. After all that I've been through, how could a kiss break me?

But maybe Stone's kindness will. His offer to help me. Because suddenly, I want this kiss. I want to feel something sweet and good before I die.

And this is *so* sweet. And he's *so* good.

My eyelids fall closed, shutting out everything but Stone. I say his name against his lips before fisting my hands in his flannel shirt and dragging him closer. A sigh of pleasure escapes me when his mouth coaxes mine open. Still tender, but not holding back now. He tastes like peppermint and the faintest coppery tinge of blood, his tongue slicking over mine in a way that makes a shiver race over every inch of my skin.

"Fuck." The curse is nearly a growl as he breaks away, then comes back in to nip my bottom lip. "How the fuck are you even real? Looking like you do, but kissing like that."

"Like what?"

"Like you've never been kissed by someone who wants you." His long fingers tighten around my nape and he tips my head back, his gaze scouring my face. "Like you need to be kissed by a man who's dying to get inside you. Do you?"

Breathlessly I nod. "Yes."

God, yes. Because Stone takes my mouth again, and if this is how a man kisses when he means it, I don't ever want to do anything but this, don't ever want to feel anything but this. As if he's consuming me with every hot stroke of his tongue, as if there's nothing else in the world for him, either. No bar, no fight, no pain. Nothing but me, and his need for me.

His hand grips my ass and he drags me to the edge of the stool, his hips forcing my thighs wide. And oh god. God. He's big and hard and when was the last time I felt like this? Fumbling around in the backseat of a car when I was sixteen? Dry humping a guy at a frat party? I remember the excitement of those encounters, the frantic heat, the wonderful sense that there was so much more to come, so much to look forward to. My entire life seems as if it's been divided into before and after the Cage, and not once in the *after* has my blood surged hot, not once has sex been about pleasure but instead a horrible and frightening inevitability. Not something to look forward to.

And although this kiss won't go that far, I love Stone in this moment for giving that feeling back to me. For making me remember a time when my body wasn't going to be a prize, when rape wasn't my only future, for *asking* what I want and letting me have that little bit of control again.

Yet even those fumblings and dry humpings weren't like this as he leans in, so solid and strong. His erection grinds between my legs like he knows exactly what he's doing, knows exactly what spot will send sparks flashing behind my eyes, my inner muscles tightening. Knows exactly how to make me pant against his mouth and help-lessly rock against his thick inches, how to make my pussy damp and eager for him.

Damp? No. I'm *so* wet. Oh my god. Slick and hot and if he unzipped right here, I wouldn't even say no. Instead I'd use him to fill this empty hollow ache. I'd wrap my arms around his neck and my legs around his hips and take that big cock inside me, let his body finish what this kiss started. Let him consume me completely with every hard thrust, let him burn away the horrible here and now.

"Christ." He groans against my mouth before taking another taste, then lifting his head to gaze down at me with heavy-lidded eyes. "You look like you need to be fucked. You need to be fucked, girl?"

My breath shudders wildly. In answer, my hands go to his belt buckle.

He suddenly laughs, catching my fingers. "Not here. Shit. No matter how hot tugging aside your panties and getting into your pussy would be."

I can't do it anywhere else. This is my only chance.

But even as I think it, that chance is fading. Reality is returning. Because I'm not here for this.

I'm here to save him. And to light the match that burns the Cage down…hopefully. Though I don't yet have a plan about where to go from here until Stone rubs his thumb across my lips and says gruffly, "I just need to find my brother, tell him we're heading out."

His brother. Someone's here with him. Relief rushes through me.

This will be so easy, then. I'll go with Stone to find his brother. And then, as fast as I can, I'll tell him what's going on. Victor will rush in and grab me, but Stone should be safe if he's not alone. Because I'm supposed to drug him, but our drinks haven't even—

"Fucking finally." He reaches past me, steps back with two foaming pints. "Here you go, darlin'."

Crap. I take my glass, doing my best not to look in Victor's direction. I know he's watching to see if I roofie Stone's drink.

The longer I play along, the longer Victor will let me be. "Getting through this crowd won't be easy. Do you need me to carry that beer for you?"

In answer, Stone drains the whole thing as I watch in wide-eyed amazement.

"I guess you were thirsty," I say when he slams the empty back to the bar.

He laughs and wipes his mouth with the back of his hand. "Let's just say that I'm looking forward to eating something a little sweeter, but using what I can to hold off. C'mon, then."

Taking my hand, he pulls me off the stool. Almost immediately I'm bumped from the side, half of my beer sloshing over the rim of my glass. "Oh shit!"

The biker who bumped into me—and whose jeans just got soaked—looks as if he'll break my neck before his gaze lands on Stone, who turned back when I cursed. And it's like a magic trick, how fast the man's expression becomes apologetic. "My bad. Should have watched where I was going."

"It's all good, brother," Stone says and lifts the glass out of my hand, holding it up out of the danger zone as we begin threading through the crowd.

"You can have that, if you want!" I call ahead to him. "I'm not much of a beer drinker!"

But Stone must be, because his glass is empty again by the time we reach the back corner of the tavern. A hand-written sign with 'Private Party' scrawled across a sheet of plain paper is slapped up against a wooden post. A popular party, by the looks of it, with more people crowding this area than were up at the bar—maybe because there's plenty of liquor here, too, and what looks like a free-for-all on pitchers of beer.

Stone pulls me in closer again, voice raised over the noise. "Normally I wouldn't introduce you to my brother, because he's real fucking pretty! Women see him and suddenly I'm dog meat or they're into a threesome. But I won't risk losing you in this mess!"

"No worries either way!" I cling to his side, steeling myself for what's coming next, trying to think of how to explain it quickly and believably. Because Stone's life depends on it. "I don't trust pretty, and I'm not interested in sharing you with anyone!"

"Good, because I'm not into sharing, either."

He keeps pushing his way through the bodies, forging a path for me in his wake. Everyone's taller than I am, so nothing's visible except a forest of shoulders and vests and beards. Abruptly the forest clears and I'm facing the most beautiful man that I've ever seen.

Except I've seen him before, in the house where I woke up today. It's the blue-eyed devil who called in the favor from the Iron Blood—the one who's setting up Stone to be taken to the Cage.

And Stone says *this* man is his brother? But he isn't safe here with him.

Panic thrums through my veins. What now? *What now?*

I barely hear Stone greeting the man and introducing me. Only see the devil's icy gaze on me when Stone's arm circles my waist. He must be wondering why I haven't already drugged Stone. Why I haven't already taken him stumbling outside, where he'll be easy pickings for the Iron Blood. That cold stare locks with mine and I begin shaking, because I wasn't expecting this. Now I don't know what to do.

Except stall. And keep playing along.

I glance up at Stone. Who's been so sweet to me. So good to me. And I *will* save him.

But I need time to think. Pasting on a smile, I take his empty glass. "You want me to get you a refill before we go, baby?"

"I sure would, darlin'." His gaze is hot on mine and he doesn't immediately let me go as I move away. His fingers drift across my hip as if he doesn't want to be separated even by the ten feet to the nearest table for a refill from one of the pitchers.

Oh god. Oh god *oh god oh god*. I don't know if the blue-eyed devil is watching me, but Victor and Hotel probably still are. So I have to make this look good. While my back is to Stone, I not-so-surreptitiously slip a vial out of my bodice. They'll see me. They'll think that I'm drugging his drink like I'm supposed to.

I take my time at the table, pretending to slyly dump the roofie into a glass while also being so completely obvious about it that I'm waiting for someone to call me out at any moment. For someone to shout that I'm putting a date-rape drug into someone's drink. But apparently no one sees me.

Or maybe in this crowd nobody gives a fuck.

Despite the show I'm giving, not a single drop of the drug makes it inside the glass—and the table's such a mess, no one could possibly tell that a few milliliters of dissolved Rohypnol are mixed in with the puddles of spilled beer.

My racing heart trips over itself as I make my way back to Stone. His eyes are still eating me up, yet there's something more…guarded in the way he's looking at me. As if he suspects what I was doing with his drink.

Was my pretense *too* obvious? Am I going to lose his

trust before I even get a chance to help him?

Stomach roiling with nerves, I hand him the glass—and he takes it. Thank god. Whatever put that look on his face, it isn't the beer.

So maybe it was something the blue-eyed devil said. "Are you all right?"

"Better now." As if he'd rather have me close than ten feet away. He tilts his head toward the other man. "Just discussing the perils of defenestration."

"Being thrown through a window?" That's…a strange topic. Or maybe it's not. The scarring on Stone's face might have been caused by broken glass. "Is that what happened to you?"

His eyes narrow. "Don't you be pretty *and* smart."

Is he intimidated by smart? If so, it's good to know there's *something* that intimidates a man his size. With a laugh, I tell him, "I'll try." Though not very hard, because I need to be smarter now than I've ever been before. "I'd rather be something else, anyway."

"What's that?"

Alive. Free.

But I'll settle for keeping Stone alive and free, instead.

Chest suddenly tight, I shake my head. Because the blue-eyed devil is watching me closely, and the only way to help Stone is to get him away. So I gesture at his beer. "Why don't you finish that up and we'll head out?"

Maybe that was too pushy. Because Stone frowns but downs the beer, and I can feel his gaze on me as I desperately plan. His chugging the drink should give us a few extra minutes. Surely Victor and Hotel will hold off until they think the drug has started working. That'll give us a head start.

I'm not even sure where they are. My gaze searches the crowd, trying to see them. But it's impossible.

"Ready, then?"

I nod, and Stone slings his heavy arm around my shoulders, begins guiding me through the mass of people.

"You all right?"

I glance up. Stone's watching me with that guarded look again. Probably because I'm terrified and not hiding it well.

But everything I say might be picked up by the microphone in my wig. So I have to be careful.

Swallowing hard, I curl my finger so that he bends his head closer. I go up on my tiptoes, my mouth near his ear. "I'm just overwhelmed by all the people. Do you think there's a back way out of here?"

He nods and changes direction, heading for the bar. I keep searching for Victor or Hotel, or any of the Iron Blood that I might recognize—but I'm not tall enough to see beyond my immediate surroundings. But Stone is so big that anyone watching him must be able to follow his route easily.

Shit. Heart thundering, I cling to his arm as he pushes through a swinging door and into a brightly lit kitchen that smells of grease and onions. Almost immediately, it's easier to breathe, easier to hear. A harassed-looking man in a hairnet calls out that we can't be back here, but Stone simply continues on, his stride long and easygoing.

Too easygoing. We don't have any time to lose. Gripping his hand, I begin moving faster, getting ahead of Stone and pulling him along.

He grins. "In a hurry?"

That grin dissolves when I rip off my wig and toss it aside. "Come on. Come on, come on."

"Hold up."

We can't. "Where's the exit?"

Even as I ask, I see it. Stone doesn't put up any resistance when I drag him in that direction, but something in him is changing. Or something hidden in him is emerging. Something sharp and deadly.

"What's going on, Cherry? Who are you running from? Is someone after you?"

The steel in his voice tells me that if I don't give an answer quickly, he's not taking many more steps.

"They're after *you*," I tell him, then ease open the exit door. The back lot is empty, deserted. A huge dumpster sits to the left. "I'm supposed to drug you and then hand you over to some guys who will make you fight to the death."

"Are you talking about the Cage?"

I glance back at him in shock that he knows about it—and am even more stunned when I see his broad grin. As if he's *glad* to be targeted. "You know it?"

"Yeah, I know it." He laughs before his eyes narrow.

"Who the hell sent you in here after me? The fucker you called your boss?"

"Yes, but he's not in charge. He's just a guard." And is probably looking for me right now. I pull on Stone's hand. "We have to go. We have to run."

This time he pulls back, shaking his head. "Nah. We need to head back inside, rope my brother into this, and hole up somewhere while you tell us everything."

"We can't go back in." Desperately I haul on his wrist, trying to get him outside with me. "Your brother was the one who set you up. He pointed the Iron Blood in your—"

One second I'm pulling on him. The next, my back is shoved up against a wall and Stone looms over me, his hazel eyes burning with fury, his face a lethal mask.

Terror closes my throat. Because this man...*this* man isn't the one who kissed me at the bar. This is someone who might kill me in an instant.

"Don't you even *suggest* that Gunner did this," he snarls. "Not for one fucking second. That man has saved my life a million goddamn different ways. So give me a choice between him and you, and it's him every fucking time. You understand?"

Mutely I nod.

His burning eyes watch me for another long second as I tremble wildly and desperately try to keep myself from crying. Because I'm not mistaken. Who could forget a face like that man has? But if what Stone says is true, of course he'd believe his brother over me. Just like I'd believe

Matt over everyone else, too.

And Matt is why I have to keep trying. No matter what the cost.

"Please," I whisper brokenly. "Don't go back in there. I don't know him, so maybe there's something I don't understand. But *please* don't go back in there."

His gaze softens and he sighs. "All right. We'll head out, get you somewhere safe. Then I'll send him a message and we'll..."

He blinks. Then blinks again, pulling back away from me, and I can't stop my cry of dismay when I see who's standing behind him.

Victor. With a hypodermic needle that he tosses aside, his gaze on Stone as the biker turns...stumbling a little.

"Ah, shit," Stone says, slurring.

Oh god. Whatever Victor injected the big man with is moving fast through his system. And I'll never be able to carry him. There's just one decision left to make—to run. As fast as I can. To find a phone, to get help, anything. With a sob, I fly through the exit.

And slam straight into Hotel.

SIX

STONE

WELL, SHIT. IF I'D KNOWN THAT FINDING THE CAGE WAS as easy as kissing a redhead, I'd have kissed a few more.

Or maybe just kissed that one. *Cherry.* Fuck, her mouth was so sweet and hot. Maybe the rest of her was sweet and hot, too. I can't remember much beyond her bringing me a beer while I was talking to Gunner—while he was warning me away from her, because the girl was obviously a fucking mess.

But I like messes. So that wasn't going to slow me

down.

Now Gunner's probably laughing his ass off. For sure he's going to come at me with a smugfucking 'I told you so,' because I woke up about a half hour ago feeling like absolute shit. Like a hangover, but worse. Probably from whatever Cherry slipped into my drink.

I should've known. That girl had trouble written all over her. And she looked real nervous the whole damn time.

Except when I was kissing her. So I hope she's here, so I can find her and kiss her again.

Wherever the fuck *here* is. Some kind of cell, with bars at the front and overhead, but the walls are made of wood. An aluminum roof forms a peaked ceiling, with ductwork and pipes going every which way. Lights are off, but there must be more cells like this one. I can hear other men snoring and shuffling around on their beds.

I'm buck naked on my own bunk, which doesn't bother me much. Except I don't know where my kutte is. I don't give a shit about the rest of my clothes. But my Hellfire Riders vest, yeah—I care a hell of a lot. Knowing someone took that off me gets my blood going.

But no worries. Because I'll get it back.

And suddenly it's playtime. The halogen lights pop on overhead, flooding my cell. Some golden oldies start up, shit I haven't heard since my dad gave me rides to pee-wee football practice. From all around me come the sounds of men getting their asses out of bed—and that throws me about ten years ahead of pee-wee football and straight into boot camp.

I hated boot camp. Loved everything else about my time in the service. Fucking *hated* boot camp.

But I know how this works. And the important thing to learn from boot camp isn't the basic training. Nah, what really matters is getting to know the men around you, figuring out what the people in charge want from you— and how hard you can push back.

Gray sweatpants wait for me by the sink. I drag them on, swallow a couple of handfuls of water, and head over to the front of my cell.

And holy fucking shit. A laugh busts out of me, because straight across a concrete aisle is one of the assholes I've been looking for. "Handlebar, you stupid fuck! You've got every brother in the Butchers searching for your ass."

The big biker glances over. A grin spreads across his bearded face and he heads for the bars—moving not quite as easily as I'm used to seeing him move. Got beat up some, then. Either here or in the Cage.

But if it was in the Cage, all that matters is that he won.

"But it was a Hellfire Rider who found us? We're completely fucked, then." He smirks, shaking his head. "What brought you looking?"

"They tried to snatch our girl Zoomie a little while back."

His face darkens. "Did they get her?"

"Nah. But it made us start looking for anyone else who went missing." And we reached out to the Bedlam Butchers in that search. "Figured out they were nabbing bikers who were winning rally fights."

"Hold up. You're telling me that you knew this Cage shit was going on and you still got taken? And *I'm* the stupid fuck?"

"What the hell can I say? The bait had big red hair and a sweet little ass."

"Yeah, the red hair did us in, too. One minute I've got her choking on my dick while Crash is plowing her pussy from behind, the next we're here."

Goddammit. I'm not a possessive man. I don't give two shits about a woman's past. And jealousy is a waste of time. Yet the way my gut tightens up, something in me isn't too thrilled that they've had a taste of Cherry, too.

But I knew the girl was trouble before I ever kissed her. So I'm still into it.

"Crash here?" I'm guessing he is. Because if Crash isn't here, then he's dead—and Handlebar wouldn't be smiling or joking. Those two Butchers are as tight as Gunner and me.

"Yeah. Four boxes down." Handlebar tilts his head to my left, his gaze boring into mine. "He could use some fresh air."

To get out of here. So Crash is alive, but not doing so good. "There's no windows to open?"

Holes in their security. No doubt Handlebar's been

assessing it from the beginning.

"A few small ones," he says. "But they don't open easy from inside. Maybe they'll open up from outside."

Asking if the cavalry will be coming. "I'm basically one of those rancid farts that leaves a trail of stink—a trail that's real easy to follow. After they get a whiff of me in here, I figure they'll open up those windows fast."

Satisfaction gleams in the other man's eyes. "You always have smelled like you're full of bullshit."

"And I call that my greatest natural talent." Another talent is knowing when to pay attention—which I've been doing. While Handlebar and I are yapping, a shift change takes place to my right. Not in a cell, but a closed-up room. Security station, probably. Manned by only one guard.

To my left, past five more cells is another closed-up room. A guard stops in front of it—not carrying any weapons except a stun gun, seems like. I recognize that guard. The bastard who looks like a drill sergeant, the one Cherry called her boss. But that bastard isn't a boss. Might be in charge here, but he's not a boss, and that's a real important distinction.

Drill Sergeant signals to one of the cameras and the door unlocks. The fucker's carrying keys on a belt but there's nothing to unlock on these doors except some restraints they've got set up on the bars. So it must be all automated and they need someone in that security station to open the cells.

And they've got a girl locked up behind there, wearing

a wet dream of a nurse's uniform. She doesn't turn in this direction but heads straight down the aisle to another door. Drill Sergeant's right on her ass, though he's not looking at it. He's scoping out the other guards on duty. I've already pegged them as militia—well-funded, by the look of them. Except for Drill Sergeant, though, I'd bet my left nut that none of them were in the service, and their training was most likely a souped-up, chest-thumping parody of real military training. The way Drill Sergeant's eyeing them now suggests that he doesn't one-hundred-percent trust them to be doing their jobs right.

Might not trust the nurse, either. When the next door unlocks, Drill Sergeant follows her in.

Cherry said she was a nurse. The woman I just saw didn't have flame red hair down to her ass, but a light auburn that falls past her shoulders. Body sure looked like Cherry's, though—all long legs, and not much in the way of curves. Her thighs and ass were still soft as hell, though. So were her lips.

I get a flash of—*what the fuck, tossing a wig?*—before the memory skitters out of reach. And a lingering image of Cherry looking up at me, mouth trembling and her emerald eyes filled with fear...and of me, feeling real fucking pissed off at her.

Because of something she said? Or because I figured out that she drugged me?

I can't remember, goddammit.

"Stone." Handlebar's grave tone brings my gaze

swinging back to him. "You got family?"

I know why he's asking. It was damn near impossible to get straight answers out of the family members of the missing fighters, but their fear spoke for them. Some had merely been threatened. Others had gotten worse than threats.

So I wasn't going to take that risk with my parents or sister. "Not that these fuckers will find. They'll be looking for ghosts."

My wallet held fake identification and nothing that links me to home. My kutte only tells them my road name and which club I belong to. But if they're stupid enough to go asking the Riders about me…well, shit. I hope they do.

The other man nods, his face grim. "Best that way."

It *is* Cherry. She comes out of the room carrying a tray, smile bright and hips swaying—and except for her facial features, in no way resembling the vulnerable, jittery woman I met at the tavern.

My chest tightens up. Because I *liked* that woman. What I'm seeing now, though, tells me that woman was nothing but pretend.

Maybe I'll like this woman, too. Fuck knows I can't take my eyes off her. She heads over to one of the cells on my side of the corridor, so I don't have a good angle on her. Handlebar does, though.

"What's the story with the girl?" I ask him.

"Cherry? She's a fucking angel. Though she's got claws,

too." Abruptly he grins, raising his voice. "Ain't that right, Hush Puppy?"

Laughter comes from the other cells. Some fucker yells out, "I thought we agreed to call him 'Donut Hole'?"

"My vote is still on 'Falafel'!"

"I don't give a fuck what you all call him. Fried balls are fried balls," Handlebar says loud enough to carry, then settles down and focuses in on me again. "A few boxes to your right is Tusk, who's the sickest fucker you've ever met. Watch your six around him. He pulped some poor bastard's skull in the weight room, and I don't *ever* want to know all of what he did to Lissa. But if I get a chance to kill him, I intend to kill him. I suggest you do the same."

Fair enough. "Who's Cherry with now?"

"Crash."

Dispensing pills, it looks like. And making notes on a clipboard.

Handlebar continues, "Every morning, we get our multivitamins and general health check. Then a healthy balanced breakfast, then cardio. I hope you like to run, fucker. Five miles a day, minimum—and Cherry records our times, along with our pulse rate and blood pressure."

"You shitting me?"

"Not even a bit. Then a healthy balanced lunch, followed by weight training. Healthy balanced dinner, lights out at ten. We're also expected to spend our down time with the heavy bag in our stalls. Because if we go soft, we die in the Cage. Yeah?"

Fucking hell. Except for the 'healthy balanced meal' shit, none of what he's saying is any different than what I do on the regular at home. But I don't like the idea of doing it on command and on someone else's schedule.

I watch Cherry head across the corridor. Christ, those legs. Did she wrap them around my waist while my cock was up inside her tight little cunt? Or maybe she never got further than a blow job. Not being able to remember if I had her on my dick bothers me more than her drugging me does.

But no doubt that as soon as the roofie kicked in, there was someone ready to swoop me up. Now that guard never lets Cherry get too far away from him. "Who's the drill sergeant?"

"Victor."

"He runs the security crew here?"

"Yep. Right now you've got Mike in the control room, and Charlie who just came out of it. The others who are usually at this stable are Delta, Hotel, Bravo…oh, hold up. Bravo's toast. Rome's toast, too, because he"—Handlebar makes a neck-snapping motion with his hands—"got a little too close to me."

"Are you fucking around with those names?" All of them letters in the NATO phonetic alphabet.

Handlebar snorts. "Hand to god, brother. That's what they call themselves."

Maybe to preserve their anonymity but mostly just proving they're a bunch of assholes playing soldier. "So who's in the cell?"

Because more than just Handlebar and Crash have disappeared from the clubs the Hellfire Riders are friendly with.

"Hatchet." The other man's lip curls. "From the Eighty-Eight."

Not a friend of the Riders or the Butchers, but a piece of neo-Nazi trash—and someone who must have fucked up and was sent here for punishment, because the Eighty-Eight Henchmen's noses are all up in the ass of whoever's running the Cage.

"Who's up top?"

"Some slick fucker they call Papa."

"Who's he with?"

"Fuck knows. Never got close to him, never talked to him personal. He uses the Iron Blood to bolster Victor's crew but comes in with his own security. Private and real fucking professional. Other than that...?" A shrug lifts his broad shoulders. "No goddamn clue."

Which means this Papa doesn't give much away, because Handlebar wouldn't miss a thing. And the asshole who tried to grab Zoomie had private security, too. Lots of money. The Hellfire Riders probably should have taken a closer look before blowing them up and burying their remains out in the boonies, but we didn't know then how big this operation was.

Handlebar gives me a rundown of the other men filling the stalls between him and Hatchet. First there's

Flack, who he calls an asshole. Airbag, who's all right. Abyss, also all right. On my side there's Crash, then Log Cabin, who's an asshole, and Bullethole, who's all right. Both stalls to either side of me are empty, then the last one holds Tusk. Room for fourteen fighters, but they only have ten—though Handlebar says there's another barn on the property with the same setup, and that there must be other stables owned by others like Papa nearby, because they don't travel far to the Cage on the nights they fight. And they don't fight anyone from the same stables.

Then he stops talking, because Victor and Cherry arrive at his stall—and it's easy to see why he called her an angel. Her voice is so sweet and cheery and bright, she's like a sexy beam of sunshine.

Then she turns my direction. For an instant, that brightness falters and I get a glimpse of the jumpy girl who first caught my eye in that tavern. Then her wide smile returns, those full lips so luscious and red and sultry, her gaze almost shy as she hangs back and looks up at me through her lashes.

I guess she's not giving me vitamins or a health check right away, because instead Victor steps closer.

"As you're new here, I'll go over the rules with you one time. Lights come on, you wait in the center of your stall until we tell you to come forward—"

"Yeah, Handlebar already filled me in on your rules. I just don't give a fuck."

Cherry bites her lip, her smile dissolving into a fearful

expression as she glances over at Victor. But that asshole isn't going to do anything. Handlebar just told me he snapped a guard's neck, and he's right over there in that stall instead of in the ground somewhere, so that means the guards don't do shit to the fighters.

Not that I'll be fighting.

Victor's eyes narrow. "These rules are for your own good. The healthier you are, the longer you live. And what we expect of you is—"

"Mad Max, yeah?"

Cherry's head snaps up, eyes going wide, her face pale. "Wh– what?"

"What you've got is basically the Thunderdome. Two men enter, one man leaves. Except I won't be fighting."

"You'll change your mind soon enough—"

"No, I won't. So get the fuck out of my face and let me talk to my girl." Who's looking shocked, terrified, uncertain. "So, action movie fan—which one's your top Mad Max? The original? Or *The Road Warrior*?"

Her wary gaze darts to Victor again before a hint of a curve returns to her mouth. "It used to be *Beyond Thunderdome*. Until *Fury Road* came out."

"Aw, shit. I haven't seen that one." I'm lying my ass off. "So how about you curl up with me in my cell tonight and tell me what happens?"

"Cherry will be in her own stall, Mr. Stone. Because she's a good girl. And she follows the rules. Isn't that right, Cherry?"

Like a light blinking out, her wide and beautiful smile returns. "Yes, sir."

"And you, Mr. Stone—"

"I'm not fighting in the Cage." All the amusement drops from my tone. "Not now, not ever."

"Not right away, no. The next match is in ten days, and you won't have a clean blood test by then. But soon enough, you'll change your mind."

A clean blood test? "Is that because of whatever you slipped into my drink, darlin'?"

Those emerald eyes meet mine, the green shadowed and dark. Like she's swimming in guilt.

"It's all right, girl," I tell her. "I ain't mad."

I won't forget. But am I angry? Nah.

The drill sergeant tries again. "Mr. Stone—"

"But *you*, Vic. I'm going to kill you." My broad smile tells him just how much I'll enjoy it. "So go ahead. Make your threats, tell me how you'll torture my family and friends, get it all over with. Just don't block my view of Cherry, because the sight of her is the only thing that'll keep me awake through all the jabbering you're about to do."

I can practically hear his teeth gritting. Because that's my other natural talent. Pissing off tight-assed fuckers and making them lose their shit.

Though Victor doesn't lose his. Instead he shakes his head and gestures Cherry forward, and she begins asking me how I'm feeling.

And, hell. Truth be told, I'm feeling pretty damn good.

Because I've got no intention of playing along with this Cage shit. Instead I intend to tear this operation down. And ride off into the sunset with the girl.

Just another day at the office.

SEVEN

Stone *should* be mad. He should be mad at Victor, at the situation he's trapped in—and especially mad at me. Because I was supposed to save him. And I didn't.

I wasn't the one who ended up drugging him, as he seems to believe, but a detail like that hardly matters. The way it all turned out, I might as well have slipped him the roofie like I was supposed to. Because nothing I did made any difference. Except now I'm in even more trouble.

Victor hasn't punished me for my rebellion yet, because he's leaving that to Papa. But he's watching me more closely. Reminding me to keep my smile on.

And although I was ready to die that night, I'm not ready to die now. It's one thing to be killed for saving a man's life. I don't want to be killed for not smiling wide enough.

So I smile through the health checks. I smile while the first group runs around the track, and smile while Matt gives me a look that asks whether I'm truly all right.

I'm not. Because everything in the whole world is wrong. And I tried to do one thing right…and failed.

That failure hurts so bad. And it hurts to see Stone so determined not to give in. Almost every fighter who comes in is defiant, at first. Yet Stone's defiance is on another level entirely. As if he truly believes they won't get to his family. That they *can't* get to his family.

But they always do. Which makes me even more worried for Stone. Because Papa won't damage the fighters. But he'll often make the fighters pay in other ways, and the longer and harder they resist, the more it'll cost them. The more Papa will hurt them by hurting whoever the fighter loves. I don't want to see that day come for Stone.

And today, it probably won't. It might not for a week or more. So it's with mixed emotions that I watch two guards escort him outside to join Crash and Handlebar at the track—my heart aching because he's been thrown into this mess. But genuinely smiling again when he greets Crash like a long-lost brother, pulling him in for a back-thumping hug.

"No contact unless you're in the Cage!" Delta calls out.

Stone ignores that order. He draws back but grips the other man's shoulders, grinning at him. "We're a long fucking way from Afghanistan."

"Not that you'd know by looking at this place," Crash says, gesturing to the desert scrub around us, then to the turret where a guard watches over the track with a sniper rifle.

So they know each other from the military. I want to tell them not to reveal that connection, to pretend they aren't friends. Because if Papa truly can't find a family member to use against Stone, he might use that friendship with Crash.

But Crash is ahead of me on that. In a low voice, he says to Stone, "Handlebar tells me your family are ghosts. So if they pull some shit and try to use me—don't let them. I'm already a dead man."

Stone frowns. "What the hell does that mean?"

"NO CONTACT!" Delta bellows.

"They *will* tase you," I tell them softly.

That draws Stone's attention to me, and his frown darkens. "They couldn't give you a fucking coat?"

Because we're in the high desert, but it's the middle of November. This outfit doesn't do a thing to protect me from the cold. Since the fighters have nothing but sweatpants and running shoes, they aren't covered much better. But as soon as they begin their run, they never seem to feel it as much.

I pretend not to feel it, either. "I'm used to it."

"Are you?" His voice lowers. My breath stops when he catches my wrist and flattens my hand to his bare chest. His pectoral feels like heated steel beneath my palm. "Your fingers are freezing."

"Yo, fucking new guy!" Tango shouts. "Don't touch the nurse!"

"She's checking my heart rate, asshole!" Stone's gaze never flickers away from mine. "How's it seem to you?"

Deep. Strong.

"A little fast," I whisper, though that's just my own frantic pulse, racing as his warmth seeps into my hand. He's flirting with me as if nothing has changed—as if we're still in the tavern, where he kissed me and made me remember a time when I still had a future. When I still had hope.

But we're not at the tavern anymore, and hope isn't as sweet as a kiss here. Instead it hurts so much. Like a blade through my chest, like the *clunk* of a locking stall. And my throat aches when I tell him, "You should be more careful than this."

"She ain't lying, brother," Handlebar says. "And they won't care if they take her down with you."

Stone's jaw clenches and he releases my wrist. I curl my fingers, trying to hold onto his warmth. But it's gone before they finish their first mile.

* * *

As they're walking off the track, Handlebar calls out to me, "So, Cherry—did you stash the prize money somewhere?"

"What prize money?" I hold up a battery-operated blood pressure cuff, and he extends his arm so that I can fasten it around his wrist. "What are you talking about?"

"Stone's prize money."

They think I stole it? Hurt fills my chest. Which is stupid. Because after luring Stone into the Cage, where he's probably going to die, what's a little theft?

"That's why they picked him up, yeah? He won a rally fight." Handlebar flashes me a grin and leans his head in, adding in a low voice, "Tell me where you stashed the cash, and I won't tell anyone else."

Oh. They don't really think I stole it. They're just teasing me.

It's hard to laugh, though. Because I did wrong Stone. And his winning a fight wasn't why they picked him. But the last time I told him why, that the blue-eyed devil had set him up, he didn't believe me. And all his easygoing good humor vanished into lethal fury.

He's in good humor again now. "Christ, man. I can barely fit my dick into a pair of jeans. I sure as hell couldn't stuff ten grand into my pocket, too."

I glance up in surprise. Was he carrying around that much? "You won ten thousand dollars in that fight?"

"Yeah, I did." His gaze narrows on me. "Just like they announced before and after the match. I thought you watched me kick that little prick's ass?"

Throat tight, I shake my head. "They only showed me a video."

"So you'd know who to pick up," he says flatly.

Mutely I nod, not meeting his eyes. He's not angry that I drugged him, but his tone tells me that my lie doesn't go over so well.

Until he shrugs. "Eh, it wasn't much of a fight, anyway. Broke more of a sweat out here on the track."

Which obviously wasn't much of an effort for him, either. A light sheen of perspiration glistens over his bare skin but, even after running five miles, his breathing is deep and even. Crash's is about the same, and Handlebar's more heavy and ragged, but easier than in his first week here. A lot of these big guys are strong and muscular, but never put the time into cardio before arriving. Some don't put in the time after, either. Like Tusk—he gets out on the track and just walks, and the guards can't really do anything about it.

Just like they don't do anything to stop the chatter here. The fighters aren't supposed to talk to each other. But the guards don't even bother warning them anymore. Not unless Victor's around.

Crash grunts. "The Iron Blood took it, then."

"Nah," Stone tells him. "I left it in the motel safe. Gunner's likely got it now, so it'll be waiting for me when I get home."

When he gets home. I force myself not to think about

how unlikely that is. Instead I try for optimism, too. "It's a nice amount to have waiting for you."

"Yeah, it's not as much as it sounds like. Not after I pay club taxes on it. And I stuck a K into the toy drive box."

My heart stutters. "You donated a thousand dollars to a kids' charity?"

Then I helped kidnap him.

Crash snorts out a laugh. "He probably did. I can't tell you how many times he nearly ended up in the shit after helping some kid who was only there to lure us in so their daddies could light us up. Or, fuck—that time a fucking flea-bitten stray ran into the kill zone, and he nearly blew the whole fucking op."

"But did I blow it? I did not, motherfucker."

"Yeah, well—we oughta called you Nearly instead of Stone." Crash looks to me as I remove his blood pressure cuff, checking the numbers on the digital readout. His voice hardens. "And he's one of the best men I know, Cherry. A good man. So you take care of him, yeah?"

I pull in a painful breath. "I'll try."

"All right."

"Yeah, and Crash is full of shit." With a lazy smile that the scarring on his face pulls crooked, Stone holds his arm so I have to step closer to remove his cuff. "To him, all a good man has to be is loyal to his club. To stand up for his brothers. By that definition, I might be a good man. But if you go by any other definition of good, I'm a real bad man."

Crash laughs. "Yeah, right. You saved a fucking flea-bitten *stray*, brother. And if you're trying to flirt with Cherry, you gotta go good. She's not into the bad boys."

"Shit. That true?"

"I'm not into anyone right now, good or bad." I can't afford to be.

"No?" His teeth scrape over the bottom of that lazy smile and he leans in, voice low and gruff near my ear. "Funny. One thing I remember real clear is how eager you were to take my cock, right there on that bar stool. That was no lie. You were so fucking hot and ready for me."

My breath shudders. "Maybe."

"Step back from the nurse!"

"Ain't no maybe about it. And sometime soon, I'm gonna get my mouth on that hot and ready pussy. Gonna suck on your little clit until you're grinding that wet cunt all over my face and chasing your come. Is it a good man or a bad man who does that to a woman?"

What kind of man can do *this* to a woman? He didn't even touch me and I'm hot and aching, my skin no longer feeling the tight cold but shivering with the thrilling image he just put into my head.

"Look sharp, brother."

At Handlebar's warning, Stone steps back. His burning gaze still holds mine. "Which one?"

"Both," I tell him breathlessly. "Good and bad."

"I'll take that." His crooked grin sends another shiver running all over my skin, and I hide my flush by lowering my face and scribbling numbers onto the charts.

This is the last cardio session of the day, so I return to the barn when the fighters do—though I'm not allowed to walk with them, but slightly behind. Still I hear Stone ask Crash, "What the fuck did you mean, you're already a dead man?"

Their voices go low after that. Not so that I don't overhear—because Crash already told me about his tumor—but so the guards don't. I watch with an aching throat as Handlebar's back and shoulders stiffen up, as he shakes his head. As if trying to deny what Crash is telling Stone.

And I know what Crash is saying. That there's no help for him, here or anywhere else. But Handlebar's convinced that his friend can be saved if they can just get out of here. If they can get to a real doctor.

Crash has told me that he's been to those real doctors. And Handlebar has told me that they were all quacks who didn't know what the fuck they were talking about.

I suspect they're both right. That there's not much Crash can do about the tumor. But that he also needs to get the fuck out of here.

And I… Well, maybe I've stopped hoping.

But I can't stop trying.

I COULD NEVER DO MORE than one or two pull-ups in gym class. And I want to believe that sheer grit will let me pull myself up and through the bars over my stall, but that doesn't happen. So I switch strategies, hanging from one bar and swinging my legs until I can hook my feet on the next. When I finally manage to contort and squeeze my way through the gap, I lie across the steel rods, panting as quietly as I can, the muscles in my shoulders and arms burning.

I'm on the same side of the aisle as the control booth, so I could crawl over all of the stalls and make my way there. But tonight, I only shuffle silently to the next stall—Matt's.

Then I don't know what to do. I can't risk making noise to wake him up. Crash is in the stall across the aisle and he'd never expose me to the guards, but he might wonder why I made so much effort to talk with Hatchet, a white supremacist who claims his only use for females is between their legs.

And too many undercover agents have already been outed and killed while trying to take down the Cage. So I can't ever expose my brother.

Who's…looking up at me. I don't know if he was already awake or just felt me staring down at him, but I can see the gleam of his eyes through the dark—then the gleam of his sudden grin.

He can do a pull-up. Easily, and using only one arm. A show-off move that makes me huff out a little laugh when he lifts himself up so his head isn't far from mine. In truth, there's nothing remarkable about his being able to do that. Not here, where these guys often exercise in their stalls like this.

Except it's utterly remarkable that he's doing it, and

I'm here to see him. My stifled laugh becomes a stifled sob when he reaches up with his free hand to hug me as best he can. It's the first time in three months we've been able to really touch or show affection, and I can't stop my tears, can't stop myself from clinging to his arm.

His voice is thick as he whispers, "How you doing, sis?"

I can't answer. But my tears are raining all over his head, so he has to know.

He lowers and pulls himself up again, keeping up the pretense of exercising. This time when he comes up, he says, "You're like a ninja up there. How'd you think of this?"

My throat tightens unbearably. "It's how Tusk got Lissa into his stall."

"Aw, fuck." His fingers hook my dangling hair behind my ear. "I'm so sorry. I liked her, too."

I fight to swallow the tears that start up again. Because there's more that needs to be done. "The control booth doesn't have bars on top. If the guard leaves for the bathroom or something, I can open the stall doors."

Slowly Matt nods, but doesn't answer right away. Instead he takes his time, lowering and raising himself through five reps before coming back up. "You'd have to go over these other stalls."

Over Flack, Airbag, Abyss, and Handlebar. I'd be safe with three. Flack...I don't know. He can be pushy and scary. Not like Tusk. But not a good guy, either.

But maybe the promise of freedom would bring out

the nice in him. "If they saw me, I could simply tell them what I was doing."

Nodding again, he doesn't say anything but performs a few more reps while wearing his thinking face. Finally he comes up and says, "After what went down with Bravo, the guards are going to be on their best behavior for a while—and won't leave that station unmanned. It'll probably be a few weeks before they get careless again."

We don't have a few weeks. "The next fight is in ten days."

"And I'll make it through again."

By tearing out a piece of his own soul. Because 'making it through' means killing his opponent. I know how it affects him. I know how it affects most of these guys, though some are better than others at hiding it.

My brother's good at hiding it from everyone else. But he can't hide it from me.

"Matt," I whisper.

"I know." His eyes close, his expression tormented. "But what's the alternative—you jump the guard in the control booth? You spend every night risking yourself by crawling over all these stalls and hoping no one notices, praying a guard has to take a piss so bad he doesn't call in the other one to cover him? We have to wait for them to get careless."

"What about a distraction? Something that brings the guard out of the control booth?"

His gaze sharpens. "You got any ideas?"

I shake my head.

"I'll think on that one. Chances are, protocol is they don't leave the booth unmanned if there's an emergency or a commotion caused by one of the fighters. Instead at least one will lock himself up tight inside."

So it can't be an emergency. "What if…they're sick? Like what if it's not piss that they can't hold. What if they both have the shits?"

Matt pushes his fist against his mouth to stifle his laugh. For a long minute he simply hangs from the bar, shaking. Then he lifts himself again. "They'd have to get sick after the shift started, or else they just get someone else to cover."

"So maybe dose the coffee in the kitchen."

"Good thinking. Can you get access to a laxative?"

"I should be able to. But…" Oh no. "I have to wait until Doc comes again."

And that will likely be on same day as the next fight in the Cage. Which means the first chance to use the laxatives will be *after* that fight.

Matt must see my dismay, because he pulls himself up close. "Hey, hey. I'll get through. And this is better, trust me. Gives us time to plan, to work out the angles. Who'll be on duty, what they drink, how you'll dose them. We rush, we make mistakes—and we might only get one shot at this. So we'll take it slow. Okay?"

Though the thought of waiting through another bout in the Cage is terrifying, I nod. "Okay."

"All right. Now you better get back. And practice climbing up here, sure—but stay above your own stall and keep the Spider-Man shit to a minimum. The first rule of being a superhero is keeping that mask on."

"Tell that to Iron Man."

"Get a suit of armor and I'll change my tune. Because the first rule of being my sister is that you stay alive. No matter what. All right?"

"You, too." My vision blurs again. "And I love you."

"Love you, too." And even here, he's my big brother. "Now get your ass to bed."

EIGHT

STONE

You know your life's in the shitter when you look forward to a five-mile run simply because there's nothing else to do. And because it's one of the few times each day you see the girl you're working on.

Not talking to her much, though.

I fucked that up by pushing in and touching her on the first day. Since then, the guards hover close to Cherry while we're outside. They don't stop me from talking to Handlebar and Crash, but unless it's regarding run times and pulse rates, Cherry doesn't say much. If she does, the guards shut it down. Same goes for the morning rounds. That drill sergeant stays right on her ass.

The fucking music they're always blasting through the barn doesn't help, either. That's another reason to look forward to the track. Because that's some goddamn torture right there.

Not Elton. He wouldn't be my choice—give me T-Pain any day—but that shit's catchy as hell. And that's the problem. It gets into your brain, lulls you in with familiarity and repetition, until you're singing along in your head.

And if you're singing along in your head? Then you're not thinking of other shit. Like how to break out of this fucking place.

If the music's catchy enough and the volume's high enough, then you can't tune it out or ignore it. You also can't hold conversations, except by talking loud enough for everyone to hear. Then when the lights go out and the music goes off, the silence is so golden, you just fucking wallow in it. All that sudden quiet also makes you believe that every sound is louder than it really is. So you don't risk making any noise, such as whispering to the man in the next stall and planning an escape.

It's all straight out of a 'how to keep dangerous prisoners docile' playbook. So I don't know who the hell Papa is, but either he's got experience with prisons, or he's got some smart fuckers working for him. Because they aren't just relying on steel bars and stun guns and greenhorn guards to keep us in. They went for the psychological shit, too.

Lucky for me, the training the Marine Corp put me through in case I ended up imprisoned in a terrorist camp taught me about that shit. And ways to combat it, to keep focused.

Cherry's good for that. Picturing her smiling at me—not the bright toothy smile she wears here, but the sweetly nervous one from the tavern. The one that said she was in trouble and maybe a hard ride on my dick would help her out. Then I'll think of the softness of her lips, the heat. The way she didn't seem to know what to do with a man who was kissing her, and her little shuddering breath when she figured it out.

I don't even care that it was an act. That's a damn fine memory to focus on.

The rest of the time, I'm picturing what Gunner must be doing now. I've been gone four days. The first day, maybe he spent a couple of hours thinking I was in bed with Cherry somewhere. But after I missed our flight home, he'd have spent the rest of the day tearing apart the town where that biker rally was held. First searching for Cherry. Then realizing what happened.

I won a rally fight. Then I was gone. Just like every other bastard who ended up in the Cage.

That's when shit would have kicked into high gear. A hell of a lot of clubs were represented at that rally and he'd have started looking at every one—including the Iron Blood. As soon as Gunner gets a bead on them, maybe a few days more will pass where he's gathering intel and searching for this compound.

At home, other parts will be in motion. First one will be setting up protection for my sister, my parents—because the Hellfire Riders know threatening family is how the fuckers who run the Cage roll. The club would do this for any brother, but they'd do it for my sister and parents even if I weren't a member. My sister, Anna, slings drinks at the bar the Prez owns and is best friends with his woman. The Hellfire Riders also just folded in a smaller club to our ranks, and the man who used to be the Steel Titan's president is someone who's practically an uncle to me—and longtime friends with my mom and dad. So if these fuckers somehow figure out who I am, my family will be looked after.

Knowing that is what makes these days pass as easily as they do. Sure, I'm focusing. I'm not letting any of this shit get to my head. But I can only do that because I'm certain Anna and my parents are safe.

Because I'm something of an anomaly among bikers. I mean, shit—we all love our families. Some more than others. But a whole lot of bikers join up with a club because they're looking to belong to something. They're looking to build another family. Because the one they've got isn't quite right. They don't fit or some shit. A bunch of them don't come from real happy homes.

I do. My family's fucking amazing. My mom, my dad, my sister—I love the shit out of all of them. And know they love me right back.

So I'm not looking for family. I've found some in the club, true. Gunner's closer to me than a true brother. The Prez, Zoomie. They're right in there. The other brothers—I'd kill for any one of them, too. It's a family that grew on me but it wasn't why I joined up.

Nah. I joined up because I can get shit done.

That's why the military was a damn good fit, too. I could take care of shit. Then once I was out of the service… I needed the same thing.

My mom—who is real good at reading people—figured I'd go into law enforcement. And I saw the appeal. But I also saw how often my hands would be tied. Sometimes that's a good thing. Too much power goes to a fucker's head.

Other times, it's just bullshit. Like when the local chapter of the Eighty-Eight Henchmen were after my sister's friend Jenny. Our local sheriff's a good guy. But there wasn't a damn thing he could do until the Eighty-Eight did something to Jenny first. By then, his help would have come too late.

So the Hellfire Riders took care of the Eighty-Eight. By the time we'd finished, half were dead and the rest were on the run.

That's what I fucking love about the club—we take care of our own. No matter what it costs. If something needs doing, we get that shit done. And as the club's enforcer, I'm right at the forefront of the doing. So it suits me real well.

Sitting in a cell doesn't suit me as well. But I trust that Gunner and the others are getting shit done. So that gets me through this.

So do Handlebar and Crash. Those fuckers are my brothers from a different mother, too. First our Force Recon unit. Then the Bedlam Butchers. We aren't members of the same club, but I'd lay down my life for them.

And then there's Cherry. Six in the morning, the Rocket Man starts burning out his fuse over the speakers, and out of her stall she comes—looking like the angel Handlebar said she was. A sweet, sexy angel whose bright smile and cheery voice make all this shit a little more bearable.

It's a damn good thing these assholes don't know much about me and where all my soft spots are. Because it's not just my family they could threaten. It doesn't even matter that what happened between Cherry and me in the tavern was faked, that she was just dangling bait. I'm a sucker for a girl in trouble. So all they'd have to do is threaten to put a bruise on her, and I'd be in the Cage so fast their heads would spin.

Hell, if they brought a dog in here and aimed a gun at its head, I'd hold out for maybe half a second.

Probably not even that long.

Lucky for me—and for Cherry—the guards here

must figure my interest in her is just careless flirtation to pass the time. And it *is* a way to pass the time, true. But I still can't remember if I fucked her before I passed out on whatever she slipped into my drink. Can't remember if I got up in that hot little cunt—or if I got my mouth on more than her lips. Christ knows, eating her pussy would have been the first thing I did. I was craving a taste from the moment I saw her. While talking to Gunner—and while she must have been spiking my drink—all I could think about was spreading her thighs and making her come on my tongue. But whatever happened after that…I don't know. I've only had a few flashes of her throwing a wig and of her looking up at me, those soft lips trembling.

I still want a taste. But next time, there won't be any roofies involved. And I'm sure as hell not going to forget everything I do to her.

She won't forget it, either. Because she didn't fake everything when I was kissing her. I'm certain of that. Just like I'm certain she won't fake a thing when I'm with her again.

And she knows it. Yeah, she does. Like now, when she turns away from Handlebar's stall holding her tray of vitamins—only two little cups left, one for me, one for Tusk. There's a moment every time her eyes meet mine when that emerald goes so dark, when she bites her lip before remembering to smile bright and wide. When her gaze slips down over my chest, and for an instant she looks so damn hungry that her mouth might as well already be on my dick, it stiffens up so quick.

That's not just her being a good nurse and giving me a visual examination. That's want. That's need.

So maybe I *did* give her something to remember that night. Maybe I licked her pussy like she was made of sugar. Maybe I fucked her real good.

All I know is, we'll be doing it again. Soon.

"You're looking well today," she says—and I love her voice. A little sweet, a little husky, it finishes the job that her eyes started, bringing my dick to full mast. Not that she can see her effect on me now, while I'm standing close to the bars. But I'm so damn hard, I could drill a hole through the wood making up the bottom half of the door. "How are you feeling?"

"Like I won't be sorry if I never hear 'Candle In The Wind' again. But also real glad they don't play the Princess Di version, because that shit makes me cry like a baby."

Her smile compresses into a little grin, as if she's trying not to laugh. "And how are you feeling physically?"

"Damn good." Gripping the bars, I let my gaze slide from her eyes to her mouth to her tits. "Like if I had a nurse in here with me through the night, I'd probably make her come four or five times."

"Only four or five?" Her eyebrows arch. "So you're feeling weak, then? I'll make a note in your chart."

Shit. I *do* like this girl. And I fucking hate the bastard who steps forward, making the amusement in her smile vanish into that bland, bright curve again.

I don't look at him. "I don't need a wingman, Vic."

"Just answer the nurse's question, Mr. Wall."

Mr. Wall.

So he knows my name.

That shit shrivels my dick, but I don't even blink. "Pretty sure I already did answer her. Since I'm not playing in your little Cage, all that matters to Cherry here is whether I'm in fine enough shape to fuck. And I am, darlin'. Any time you like."

But I can't even get a smile out of her now. Not a real one. Just the one she gives everyone else—and even that falters when Victor starts talking again.

"Anna Wall lives on Newberry Road outside of Pine Valley, Oregon. Paul and Clara Wall on Walnut Street, also in Pine Valley."

Just hearing those names out of his mouth wraps barbed wire around my heart. Cherry's eyes squeeze shut, her expression a picture of dismay.

But me? They aren't getting anything out of me. Because the one thing I'm certain of is that the Hellfire Riders are looking out for Anna, for my parents.

Carelessly, I shrug. "Is that supposed to mean something to me, Vic? Because it don't."

"You need to change your mind, Mr. Wall. Our associates do not take refusal lightly."

"Yeah, and you need to stop this cockblocking shit and move out of the way so my girl can give me some vitamins."

"You have two days to give a different answer. Think it over."

"I'm not real big on thinking. So how about taking a 'no' right now. And tossing a 'fuck no' on top, just for shits and giggles." I look to Cherry, whose eyes are dark emerald pools. "So come on up here and give me some of that sexy Vitamin C, girl."

She moves closer, her voice a trembling whisper barely discernable over the music. "I'm so sorry."

"Nah. You ain't got nothing to be sorry for." My family's just fine. I pluck the little paper cup off her tray. "And when I bust out of here, I'm taking you with me. How about that?"

That sweet, nervous little smile appears again. "You're a good man, Stone."

I'm not.

But I like it when she looks at me as if I am.

NINE

Apparently no one cared enough about Lissa's death to pass on the news right away that she was dead, because a week goes by before they stop sending her meals. We don't cook here in the barn. Instead the meals are delivered daily from the farmhouse in neatly wrapped individual trays, each one labeled for each fighter, the macros and calories calculated according to their weight.

Mine and Lissa's portions were never as large as theirs. Papa has stringent ideas about how much a woman should eat. So our calorie count is barely enough to cover what we actually need.

When the fighters die, maybe a day or two passes before the meals stop. Lissa and I used to split the dead fighter's extra meals. It was the shittiest, most horrible feeling in the world. But I remember her telling me once it could help us stay strong.

Staying strong. That's why I eat hers along with mine.

It never, ever stops tasting like ashes.

But the next delivery only includes my lunch and dinner. So I heat up the last one of hers along with mine, then grab my spork.

Tango comes in as I'm finishing up, because it's time to escort me back to my stall. He doesn't say anything about the two trays in front of me. He knows I'm only supposed to have the one each night, but none of the guards have ratted me out. All of these guards are pieces of shit, but they can have their nice moments. All week, I've been doubling up my meals and they all know it.

But it's over now, anyway.

With a sigh, I dump my tray and wash my spork. The utensil always has to be in a particular spot when the kitchen is checked. Lissa's is right there, too. I think about taking it—they might assume it disappeared along with her meal deliveries—but decide not to risk it.

Not now, at least. I've got another plan to put into motion.

To Tango, I say, "I need to check in with Crash, because he was having stomach issues this morning."

He nods. "You'll get a minute."

Good. My heart beats a little faster as I head out of the kitchen—veering all the way over to the opposite side of the aisle as soon as I come out, as far from Tusk's cell as I can walk. More than once, he's been jacking off as I pass. A few times he's let his semen drip from his fingers as I go by. Like the weird guy out of Silence of the Lambs. But there's no Hannibal Lecter in the next cell to make him eat his own tongue.

There's just Stone. I glance into his stall as I go by. He's working the heavy bag, muscles flexing beneath tanned skin. For all that he doesn't intend to fight in the Cage, he doesn't stay inactive in his cell. Instead he's always working out. Maybe keeping busy, or to stave off boredom. I'm not sure, and I don't get much chance to ask.

But it's been three days since Victor gave him the ultimatum. In the months I've been here, that two day warning has never passed without Victor coming back with evidence that the worst has happened. Not once. But we're on day three and still nothing. Maybe Stone's confidence wasn't misplaced.

Which doesn't mean everything will turn out all right. If they can't make him fight, they'll kill him.

But they won't waste their investment right away. So they'll try for a while first.

Hopefully by then we'll be out of here.

Crash is the key to that plan. Because I can't just get the medicine I need—the doc will want to see documentation leading up to it. And I can't ask Matt to make up a story of constipation, because the Doc knows our relationship and he might be rightly suspicious. But Crash is a good guy. And he feels as if he owes me for putting him in the exercise group with Handlebar and for helping to conceal his tumor from the doc and Papa. Still, he might have played along even if he didn't owe me.

I halt in front of his stall. Tango stops a few feet away. Crash looks over at me, eyes narrowing as I say, "Any improvement on the, uh, bowel situation?" I glance at Tango as I ask the question, lowering my voice slightly, as if trying to keep patient confidentiality. "Are you still blocked? Or have you been able to...you know?"

One of the things I like most about Crash is that he's smart. And quick. "Take a shit? Not yet."

"Okay. Well, let me know in the morning if you're having the same problem. In the meantime, I'll ask them to add more fiber to your meals."

Laughter passes over his expression, then is gone. "Just what I fucking need. More of that whole grain bullshit."

"Sorry. If that doesn't work, I'll ask the doc for something stronger."

"All right. Thanks, Cherry. You always take real good care of me."

I give him a bright smile. "That's what I'm here for. You should also drink lots of water. Sometimes that helps to get things moving."

"I'll do that."

I wish him goodnight. Not looking over into Matt's

stall is *so* hard, but I don't dare because I might burst out laughing. Yet there's a little skip in my step as I continue on—then stop dead when the music suddenly goes silent.

Before ten p.m. What in the world…?

I look back down the aisle. Tango is looking that way, too. Victor comes out of the control booth—though he's not usually in the barn so late. My stomach sinks as he heads straight to Stone's cell.

"I have a message for you, Mr. Wall."

Oh no. No, no, no. Dread pulls me back down the aisle. Because I've seen this before. When the Iron Blood threatens or beats anyone, they take a video as proof. I've never seen Victor make such a production of it, though, turning off the music first and announcing that he has a message.

He stops in front of Stone's stall and holds up a tablet—and whatever Stone sees on the screen turns his face white. His hands come up to grip the bars, his burning gaze fixed on the image before him.

I can't see what it is. But I've seen them before. People beaten, bloodied. Crying and begging.

Victor taps the tablet to start the video playing. The volume's up so high everyone in the barn can hear. At first nothing but a faint, frantic barking in the background.

Then a man's voice. *"Say something to your brother, Anna."*

"I'm okay. Don't freak out," is a woman's quick, hoarse reply. *"I'm all right."*

"A little roughed up," the man agrees cheerfully. *"But it could be worse. This could be my fist."*

A sharp crack follows—a slap hard enough that the sound echoes through the barn.

Stone flinches but doesn't take his gaze from the screen. His jaw is like granite. The barking in the background continues.

The man in the video says, *"Now, Stone, here's the deal. You fight, you win, and you'll get to call your pretty sister and hear how alive she is. In fact, you can call her after every fight you win. Anna—do you know what happens if your brother doesn't call?"*

"It means he lost," she chokes out on a sob.

"It means something else, too. Because for everyone else, the threat to their family is enough to make them fight. Then we leave the family alone, even if he loses. And they keep their mouths shut so it's a win-win for everyone. Yeah? But with your brother, and because he's so fucking stubborn, we'll be doing something different. Because as soon as you lose, Stone, I'm coming back here to finish what I started. I'm going to fuck your sister's sweet ass, I'm going to tear that pussy apart with my cock, and then I'm going to put a bullet in her brain. So as soon as you lose, motherfucker, your sister loses, too."

Victor lowers the tablet. And the way Stone stares at him—I've seen that look before. All humor gone. Only a promise of death left.

Neither man says a word before Victor heads for the barn exit. But I hear Handlebar telling him quietly, "I'm so fucking sorry, man."

I am, too.

As if he hears me think that, Stone's deadly gaze slices in my direction, cutting me open with all the hate and anger that I deserved from him at the beginning.

"Let's be clear, girl," Stone tells me in a voice that I've never heard from him. So cold. So lethal. "*Now* I'm mad."

At me. Because I'm the reason he's here. Because I'm the reason his sister was beaten. Probably raped. Maybe worse.

With a burning knot in my throat, I nod. Stone turns away from me as if I'm nothing to him now. A second later, the pounding on his heavy bag starts up again.

"Come on, then," Tango says. "Show's over."

And no skip left in my step. Just a heart so heavy, I barely make it to my stall before I begin to cry.

TEN

STONE

Three days later, I'm ushered into a van, chained to a seat, and headed for the Cage. Not to fight. Cherry must have slipped me one hell of a roofie because I don't pass their drug test. They still bring along all the fighters in the stables to watch, so that we can study the men we might be up against next time.

And I'll do that. I'll watch them. Because I can't afford to lose.

Though on the way there, it's real fucking hard to see

anything but Anna. For three days, whether my eyes are open or closed, my sister is *all* I've seen. Stripped naked and strapped to a chair with duct tape. Tears streaking down her cheeks and blood dripping from her mouth, her jaw swollen from where that bastard hit her. And only one question keeps pounding through my head.

How the fuck did he get to her?

Is Gunner dead?

The Prez?

Blowback? The Hellfire Riders' warlord knows just about every thing that needs to be known, sees just about every threat that's coming. And they all knew this one would be coming. So how the hell did that bastard get past all of them?

I should have been there. I should have fucking been there. Instead of jerking my cock in a cell, pretending everything would be hunky-dory swell. Anna needed me to do what I do best. To get shit done.

But I didn't do a goddamn thing.

I still can't do a goddamn thing—except exactly what these bastards tell me to do. Roll over, play fetch. Turn into a mad dog when they eventually put me in that ring.

After about three hours, the van stops. There's nothing to see yet. They've got the vehicle set up like a prisoner transport, with no windows in the cargo hold and no access to the cab, no view out the front. Six of us are shackled to the benches. At the barns, four other vans were loaded up at the same time, along with most of Victor's guards—and

I'm guessing that's the real reason every fighter gets a free show. Not so we can get a look at the competition, but because they need the guards here, not at the compound.

They don't take any chances moving us all as a group. Instead we're escorted out one at a time.

I don't give them any hassle when my turn comes. Despite all the money these bastards rake in by streaming these fights over backass channels on the dark web, the facility they've got us in is a rundown piece of shit. It's an old abandoned warehouse, with what I'm pretty fucking sure are bats flying around in the rafters. The Cage itself is just a big box of chain link fencing that might take a couple of workers a half hour to erect.

They probably put it up today. An operation like this will stay mobile, harder for the authorities to track down. Most likely, they haven't used this location before and won't use it again. So even if the cops get their hands on one of the broadcasts, even if someone recognizes this warehouse, they'll be chasing after ghosts.

And those broadcasts are where the bastards are putting their money. The cameras they've set up sure as hell didn't come from Walmart. Thick cables run along the floor toward a van mounted with a satellite dish—a van that likely serves as the mobile heart nestled deep within onion-like layers of code hiding the broadcast's source.

At the other end of that signal are all the rich fuckers around the world who get their jollies watching men kill each other—with a buy-in of a million bucks just to see the fights. There isn't an audience on location. Just the guards, the fighters. Probably a few video technicians in the van.

After they chain me to another bench, I scan the faces of the fighters around the Cage who were brought in from different stables. A few of them I recognize from rally fights up and down the west coast. All of us lured in by some sweet ass bait.

All of us stupid assholes with our brains in our dicks.

Cherry's here, too. But I can't even look at her without seeing my sister strapped to that chair, bleeding and crying. Without feeling like I'm rotting from the inside, because I fell for a sad smile and sent those bastards straight to Anna's door.

And how the fuck did they get to her?

But that's the wrong question to ask now. It's a question with an answer, but not an answer I can get while I'm here.

That's the real issue—I'm still here. Which means the Riders haven't found a link between Cherry and the Iron Blood that'll lead them to the Cage. Yet the Iron Blood found a link from me to my family.

But how the everloving fuck did the Iron Blood figure out who I was?

Supposedly the reason they picked me is because I won a fight. But they found Anna, so that doesn't track. I didn't give them anything to go on. No real identification. Just my kutte. But nothing on my vest would lead them to my family.

I didn't give Cherry anything to tell them, either. She knows I'm a lumberjack, but I work for Widowmaker, another Hellfire Rider. He wouldn't offer that information to anyone. I told her that I had a dog, but they didn't track down my family using a dog's name. Especially a name as common as Daisy.

But winning a rally fight isn't the only reason men end up in the Cage. Some are targeted. Either to punish them or to send a message. I can imagine what the message was—to stop looking for the missing fighters, which was why Gunner and I were at the rally in the first place, trying to dig up info that would lead us to the Cage.

Yet that doesn't tell me who aimed the Iron Blood in my direction. Who knew my real name and told them I was at that rally?

Another Rider would know both. But no fucking way did one of my brothers betray me. That I'm sure of. I have no clue who it was, though.

There's someone who might know. I glance to my right, where Cherry's checking in with Crash, who isn't fighting tonight either. That tumor's got his balance fucked but somehow he and Cherry spun it as an ear infection. She did right by him on that. But it's the very fucking least she can do after using her pussy as bait to capture him and Handlebar.

Now she's going to do right by me. "Cherry."

Surprise rounds her red lips as she glances over. Probably because I haven't said a word to her in days. Now the expression tightens into a bright, wary smile when she makes her way to me.

"How are you feeling, Stone?"

The cheery note in her voice grates right over my teeth. "Sit the fuck down."

They left a few feet of room between each fighter—maybe to prevent us from killing each other before we get into the Cage. Cherry hesitates a moment before sitting gingerly on the bench between me and Crash.

Not because she's following the order, I realize. But because they're getting started. A big, bearded asshole wearing an Iron Blood kutte and a president's patch steps into the Cage, begins walking the perimeter while calling out the rules to the fighters chained to the benches.

The rules are simple. Get into the Cage when your name is called, or they put a bullet in your head. If one fighter isn't dead by the end of the fifteen-minute time limit, both fighters get bullets in their heads.

So I can't look forward to a Hunger Games ending. Defiantly refusing to fight won't end in victory.

You fight and you kill, or you die. That's it.

This part must not be broadcast, because the Iron Blood's prez is showing his face. I appreciate that. Gives me a good look at one of the bastards I need to kill as soon as I'm out of here. Rattler. But I don't know yet if he's the one I really want.

As Rattler leaves the Cage, I ask Cherry in a low voice,

"Who went after Anna?"

She steals a glance at my face before returning her gaze to the ring. The guards aren't paying much attention to any of us on the benches—they're focused on the Cage. Probably will stay focused on it unless we cause some kind of commotion.

Still, her pleasant expression never wavers and her response is as quiet as mine. "The Iron Blood."

I figured that. "Which one?"

"What did he look like?"

"Never saw his face." Just my sister's.

In the Cage, some fucker in a fancy tuxedo and wearing a green nylon mask starts talking into a microphone. A goddamn emcee, as if we're in a real fighting ring—and that mask is probably so they can digitally overlay his face with any image they want. He's not talking to us but to the bastards out there tuning in and placing their wagers on the fighters' lives, so I ignore him and focus on Cherry again.

"Did you recognize the voice?" Threatening to rape Anna. Threatening to kill her.

That rot in my gut spreads.

Cherry bites her lip before whispering, "He sounded like Chef…maybe? He's the enforcer."

Same as what I am for the Hellfire Riders. The man who gets shit done. But I sure as fuck don't rape and kill women.

"How'd they know who I was?"

Her hands are folded on her lap—fingertips picking at that short hem of her dress. The only tense, nervous gesture I've seen her make amid all her pleasant blandness. Now she spreads those hands in a faint "I don't know" gesture.

Maybe that's true. "Who picked me out as your target?"

She goes still, her gaze darting to my face. "I already told you."

The hell she did. "When?"

"When we were leaving the bar."

Fucking memory gaps. "Tell me again."

She shakes her head. Her gaze blindly returns to the Cage. "You didn't believe me. And you were…angry."

I remember that. Being pissed off at her. And that flash of her looking up at me, fear darkening her emerald eyes. "Tell me again."

Her fingers begin worrying her hem again. "It was that guy you were with. You said he was your brother."

Gunner? She's going to try to tell me *Gunner* did this?

No surprise I was pissed at her that night. I'm pissed off *now*.

"Don't you fucking lie to me."

"I'm not," she whispers fiercely. "He was at a house with us earlier that same day—"

"Bullshit. Gunner was with me *all fucking day*."

"Then what do you want me to say? I *saw* him. And I couldn't exactly mistake his face for someone else's!"

Oh…fuck. Oh holy fuck.

Not Gunner, but one of *his* brothers. They're all as pretty as he is. They're also hard to tell apart. And the poor bastard grew up in a motorcycle club that was more like a cult. His family's been trying to get him to come home for a while.

Problem is, Gunner doesn't like them much. The other problem is…*me*. The man he'd rather call his brother.

So what was his family's plan? Solve one problem by getting me out of the way—but make it look like they had nothing to do with my disappearance, so that Gunner wouldn't go home and kill them all?

Cherry glances at me again. Maybe sees the realization on my face. "You believe me this time?"

Yeah. Though it's not Gunner. Instead I've got four of his brothers to choose from. Not the oldest. He's in prison and will be for a while. So probably the second one—who's also prez of their motorcycle club.

Strawman. He's got a few years on Gunner, but anyone could mix them up. It's easy to believe Cherry did.

She's gone rigid in her seat, staring past me with fear glassing her emerald eyes. Farther down, they're unchaining Hatchet. The Eighty-Eight Henchmen's eagle and death head are tattooed on his back. White nationalist symbols are inked all over his torso.

Fucking trash. It'll be no loss if he doesn't walk back out.

I don't recognize his opponent. Some poor bastard

from another stable. They push Hatchet into the Cage with him and snap the door closed.

A small noise has me glancing back at Cherry. Her face is completely white. Her fingers are shaking—though she rolls them into tight fists when she notices me looking at her.

I remember what she said about seeing fights. That she prefers the ones in movies and not real life.

I'd prefer a movie to this shit, too. Because there's nothing entertaining about watching two desperate men beating each other to death. A bell rings and they start circling, sizing each other up. Shouts erupt from the benches, all the fighters rooting for the man on their side. Except there's no sides, because we're all on the same one—under the boot of the bosses. Papa and whoever owns their stables.

I haven't met Papa yet. Don't care to. Except to see the face of another fucker I'm going to kill.

"What do you know about Papa?"

Eyes glued to the fight, lips pressed tight, Cherry doesn't answer.

"How much is he paying you?"

That gets her attention. Barely. She shoots me a distracted frown before looking back at the Cage. "What?"

"What are they paying you?"

This time disbelief fills her sideways glance. "You think I signed up for this?"

"Maybe. Maybe you get off on this shit. The blood, the

killing." Some people do, and they pay a million to see it. "Maybe you enjoy watching a man take a beating."

A beating like Hatchet's taking now. He and his opponent are fairly evenly matched in height and weight, but I've seen a lot of fights. After a minute, I'd have put my money on Hatchet. He's a bit faster, a bit smarter. But he also seems to be holding back, as if waiting for the other bastard to tire himself out, and that decision just caught him some hurt. He reels into the chain link fence, spitting blood.

With her fists clenched in front of her lips, Cherry watches with her whole body trembling, looking like a woman on the verge of screaming.

Yeah, she's not here for the blood. "Who've they got on you?"

In the Cage, Hatchet has finally turned on the juice, feet and fists flying. She shudders and closes her eyes, relief smoothing her face.

"Cherry." I shouldn't even care. But I can't stop myself from asking. "Who've they got on you? Parents, sisters… kids?"

Her eyes open again. She's still staring into the Cage, where Hatchet's got the guy in a headlock. Game over. But I don't know if she's seeing anything. That emerald is dull and her voice is hollow as she says quietly, "No one. I don't have any family."

"So you're following orders to save your own skin?"

Hands folded in her lap again, she nods.

"So you save your own skin, and just don't give a shit about anyone else's." Like my sister's. And Christ, this fucking rot in my chest hurts. "Fair enough."

She shoots me a glance full of green fire. But just a glance, then she's watching the fight again. There's no smile on her face as Hatchet puts the guy into a sleeper hold. Instead she looks stricken when he tightens his arm and knocks the poor bastard out cold.

No blood. No broken bones. Hatchet's killing the other man in about the nicest way possible. Squeeze just right, and the chokehold puts an opponent to sleep within seconds. Then it starves him of oxygen, and he doesn't wake up. So he dies quietly, painlessly.

But dying takes a while. And it goes silent around the Cage while it happens. Cherry's not looking anymore. Her eyes are closed again, her breath shuddering like she's silently crying.

Hell, maybe she fucked the guy who just died. Maybe she's losing a boyfriend or some shit.

Hatchet lets go of the body and heads for the Cage's door, spitting more blood. The masked emcee starts jabbering away as a couple of guards drag the dead fighter out and toss him into the corner of the warehouse.

Cherry gets to her feet—then stops when Hatchet snarls at her, "Back off, female. Just get me a towel."

The guards do that. She sits again, spine straight, chin high. Then her head whips around when I ask her, "Did you dangle bait for that neo-Nazi trash, too? Maybe flash him your pussy while telling him how much you admire Hitler?"

She looks horrified—then pissed. "No!" she snaps. "I didn't."

I laugh. Because that's fucking rich. *She's* angry now? "Do you ever feel even a little guilt over what happens to the men you lure here?"

For a moment, she stares at me like I've slapped her, her emerald eyes big and wounded. And…fuck. I can't stand the sight of her. But that sick rot inside me burns and aches when she looks at me like that.

But those big, haunted eyes fooled me once. Never again.

Harshly I tell her, "You fucking *owe* me. And one day, I'll collect."

Her chest heaves as she stares back at me. Her soft lips tremble before she firms them again—and nods.

Then she turns away from me, scooting closer to Crash. I don't like that any better.

Don't want her near me. Don't want her anywhere else.

Flack is up next. Sitting beside Crash, Cherry appears so damn tiny. They're whispering together while the emcee does his thing. A word here and there reaches me. Something about chocolate candy and the control booth. And something that makes Crash silently laugh so hard the entire bench shakes. He gives her a thumbs-up, then the bell rings and they go quiet.

Flack loses after a long, bloody battle. From one of the other benches comes the sound of puking. Jeers follow. But probably every fighter over there is grateful for that vomit because it gives them something to look at besides the broken body in the Cage. He's dragged out and tossed on top of the other corpse. Like they're nothing but pieces of dog shit.

Then the guards begin to unchain Handlebar. Fuck. Tension sews steel wires through the muscles of my back.

I glance over at Crash. The big man's jaw is locked, eyes fixed on his partner—his hand crushing Cherry's. She doesn't make a sound, but the pointed heel of her left shoe twists against the floor, like she's trying to bear the pain of that tight grip by stabbing the concrete.

"Ease up, brother."

Crash scowls at me, eyes blazing, then seems to realize what he's doing to her fingers. His hold lets up and she pats his hand like it's all right. Trying to make this easier for him.

Nothing will make it easy. Not a soft hand, not a single word. Still I tell him, "He's got this."

"Yeah, he does," Crash agrees, then lifts his chin in an encouraging nod when Handlebar glances back at him through the chain link fence.

Handlebar *will* get through this. He's got fists like sledgehammers.

Knowing that doesn't make it any easier to watch him walk into the Cage. Never has been easy, no matter how many times I've seen a brother walk into a situation that might get him killed, and I've got no way to help him. In the Marines, it happened all the goddamn time. As a Hellfire Rider, not so often, because I'm usually right there in the fray—but often enough that I never lost the taste of hating it.

I barely look at the other guy beyond sizing him up and getting a sense of his fighting style. Trying to see him as a person will just fuck a man up. I've killed a lot of people in my time. But I don't regret any of them. Either they were a danger to the country I'd sworn to protect or a danger to the people I care about, which made them the bad guys.

The guy in the Cage with Handlebar, though…I've got no issue with him. Handlebar likely doesn't, either. Fuck, maybe the guy's the same as Handlebar or me— maybe with a partner on one of the other benches, or a sister at home who'll be raped if he doesn't fight.

Can't think of that. Can't think about how Handlebar's opponent has been given no real choice. The guy's trying to kill a brother. So he has to be the one who dies.

But there's nothing good about it when Handlebar wins. Except that my brother's still alive. That *is* a thing to celebrate. There's nothing but relief in me when he snaps that neck.

This whole goddamn situation, though—it's just sick, sick shit. All my life, there's been lines I don't cross. Don't hurt kids, women, animals. Don't hurt anyone who hasn't threatened me or mine. Only go after the bad guys.

The Cage shoves a man across every line he's ever drawn. Makes him fight with no honor. With no dignity. With no real victory.

And I figure there's two ways to die in that Cage. Either you lose and are killed by another man, or you win and it kills the man you were.

The man that Handlebar is hasn't been killed yet. But the Cage just gave him a hell of a beating. That's likely why Handlebar doesn't do a damn thing after winning, doesn't look our way or even pump his bloodied fist, despite the adrenaline that has to be racing through his veins. He just returns to the bench and stares at the ground.

I glance at Crash, who knows Handlebar best. "He all right?"

"He will be tomorrow," he says. "But you say anything to him now and he'll rip your head off."

That must be why Cherry doesn't make a move to go clean up Handlebar's cuts and scrapes. She does after Airbag is done—after he practically has to crawl out of the Cage. That fight went down to the wire, and looking at him, I'd say he needs a hospital. Not a nurse in a tiny skirt. But I have to give her credit. As she works on Airbag, then on Log Cabin, she's as good as any field medic I've ever seen—at least for the injuries that I *can* see. She patches up what's bleeding, splints any broken bones. Anything worse gets handed over to the doc in the morning, Crash tells me.

Then I hear him say, "Thank fucking Christ." His attention's on the next fighter they're unchaining—the giant they call Tusk. I've barely seen him, never talked to him. But I remember Handlebar saying to kill him if we can.

Maybe someone else is about to get that chance. "You think he'll go down?"

Crash shrugs. "All I know is, they always save him for last."

Which means this shit's about over. And must mean Tusk is the main show here, the one the online audience is waiting to see fight—and a hefty part of the reason they spent all that money to watch.

As they lead Tusk toward the Cage's entrance, Cherry backs away from the benches, putting a hell of a lot of distance between them. The smile on her face never wavers but her wary gaze doesn't stray from his hulking form for a second. Not even when shouts begin rising from the other side of the ring.

"Get in there, you fucking pussy!"

"You can take that sick bastard!"

"You're going to let these motherfuckers win?"

Because Tusk's opponent is refusing to go in. Christ. They jeered when someone puked but these insults are different. They're encouraging him.

I'd be shouting the same damn thing. If you're going to go down, then at least go down fighting.

But Crash shakes his head. "I don't blame him. If I

didn't think I could beat Tusk, I'd take the bullet."

No one's taking a bullet. A raucous cheer breaks out when Tusk's opponent finally heads into the Cage. A big guy. Solid. Not as massive as Tusk, but close. No slouch in the ring, either. The emcee calls him Draft—and says he's already got six wins under his belt.

Tusk has eight wins. So that's why this is the main event. They've got two heavyweights who've already proved themselves. And tonight, one will die.

The bookie taking bets must be jizzing in his pants from excitement.

"This shit's about to get real ugly," Crash mutters as Cherry comes back to sit between us again.

Closer to him.

And the ugly shit is what's in my head, my chest. I shouldn't give a fuck where she sits.

Jaw clenched, I stare ahead into the ring as the fight starts. Not seeing a damn thing.

Until Tusk bites a big chunk out of Draft's cheek.

Oh, fuck no.

Fuck no.

There are no rules in the Cage. But there are still *rules*. And unless you're real fucking desperate, you *never* take a bite out of someone during a fight.

Tusk isn't desperate. He's enjoying it.

Tearing the other man apart. Piece by piece. Breaking bone by bone. Making him scream and beg. But Draft's not dead yet—he doesn't even get that mercy—when Tusk shoves him face first into the chainlink fence right in front of us and begins raping him.

While staring at Cherry.

She's not watching. Her fingers are in her ears and her eyes are closed, trying to shut it all out. I wish to fuck that I could shut it out, that I couldn't see Draft's face—or hear him.

That poor fucker. That poor goddamn fucker.

He should have taken the bullet.

There's more puking coming from somewhere as Tusk grunts and finishes up. I'm not far from it myself. All that sick rot in my gut boils with rage. That Tusk would do this. That people pay to see this. That the bastards who run this place set it up to happen.

One way or another, I'm burning this goddamn place to the ground.

The whole place is quiet when Tusk drops the other man to the floor. Then he just stands there until Cherry glances up—fingers still in her ears—as if looking to see whether it's over.

His teeth bloody, Tusk grins at her. "One more."

She squeezes her eyes shut again. Tusk's got one minute to finish the kill, so he starts stomping on Draft's head.

I don't watch that. Instead I look over Cherry's bowed head at Crash. "What the fuck did that mean? 'One more?'"

He looks real grim. "You win ten fights, you get a prize."

"Her?"

He nods, then nudges her with his shoulder until she looks over at him. "We're not going to let it happen, you understand? We fucking swear it."

Her lips tremble. "Okay."

Like she appreciates him saying so but doesn't really believe it.

Crash narrows his eyes. "I mean it. Either your plan will get us out of here or it won't. But Tusk won't get to you. Not if we can help it. Right, brother?"

"Sounds right." I'll make it my fucking mission in life to bring Tusk down. All this shit needs to burn. And that sick fucker needs to burn with it.

Her lips are pressed together but her chin's wobbling as she thanks him, then turns to me. Her eyes are bright.

"Thank you," she whispers shakily.

"Don't thank me. I haven't done shit yet."

"It still means something. Especially since…"

She trails off there and averts her eyes, but I know what she's not saying. That she owes me.

But this is different. And not really for her. After what I just saw, I'd kill Tusk no matter what.

That she's a prize simply gives me a timeline: it needs to be done before the next fight. Or *during* the next fight.

If there is one. "What plan to get out of here?"

She blinks and glances at me again, her eyes wary. But she only hesitates for a moment before she opens her mouth—then shuts it.

Because the guards come over and begin unchaining Crash and me.

Crash grunts. "Back to the van, then?"

"No," the guard says. "You two are going into the Cage."

Cherry abruptly frowns, shaking her head. "They aren't cleared for it. Their bloodwork doesn't pass."

"Doesn't matter. This isn't part of the broadcast."

Dismay widens her emerald eyes. "A demonstration?"

"Yep. On your feet, new guy."

On my feet. While Cherry looks from Crash to me, all that dismay melting into horror and fear. Me, I'm still trying to fit this shit into my head. Supposedly, fighters from the same stables don't ever face off against each other. We're valuable assets, owned by Papa. So Papa might put us up against a fighter with a different owner, because although there's a risk of losing that asset, there's also a chance of winning big money—which is what this shit is really all about.

If Papa puts two of his own assets up against each other, though, there's no real winning. Only losing.

So it doesn't make any goddamn sense. Unless Papa decided that one of his assets isn't worth much, anyway. Like if Papa found out an asset doesn't really have an earache, but a tumor.

That better not fucking be what this is.

But Crash must be thinking the same. He confidently bumps fists with Handlebar while swaggering past his partner—then mutters, "I'll take the bullet," as we continue toward the Cage's entrance.

"The fuck you will."

"I'm already dead, brother. And you've got…" He trails off, looking into the Cage. "Hold up. Is this some tag-team shit?"

Because two men are coming in through the other entrance. One meathead who appears on the verge of shitting his pants. The other's got his chin up, wearing an aggressive, cocky expression on a face that's real familiar.

"Holy fuck," I tell Crash. "That's Sherlock—the prez of the Devil's Hangmen. He's the one who nabbed our girl Zoomie."

And passed her over to the slick cartel fucker who would have stuck her in the Cage, too.

"Then why's he still living?"

The slick fucker isn't. But the Hellfire Riders didn't want to draw attention to ourselves by taking out the Hangmen, too. Instead we stayed real quiet, so it looked like the Hangmen were responsible for losing Zoomie and killing the cartel's man. "Blowback figured their higher-ups would take them out."

Crash rolls his shoulders, loosening them up. "Looks like Blowback was right."

Yeah, he was. Cherry called this a demonstration, and the guard said the broadcast was over. But the cameras are still filming. Because they'll throw the two Devil's Hangmen in the Cage as punishment for their fuckup— and use the video to make sure any other associates know the consequences of failure.

Which is pretty much what the emcee says during his introduction. I ignore the fucker, because he's not telling me anything I need to know.

I say to Crash, "I'll take Sherlock."

And won't be a bit sorry. The Devil's Hangmen were bad fucking news the second they moved into the next county and began running meth and girls and guns. The drugs and weapons, I don't really give a shit about.

But those girls. I've seen how some of them ended up.

So I'm looking forward to this.

Crash nods, his face all business. "Who's the other one?"

"Pretty sure he was named the Hangmen's enforcer after Blowback got rid of the first two."

Got rid of. As in, tiny pieces buried all around central Oregon.

"So I'm up against a third-stringer? Fuck me. I'll take yours, instead."

"Over my fucking corpse." It comes out lightly, but I mean it. The third-stringer helped snatch Zoomie, but Sherlock gave that order and took the lead. So the only people I'd step aside for are Zoomie herself, or the Hellfire Riders' prez. "Our girl wasn't wearing a Bedlam Butchers vest when he took her."

"Goddammit." Because Crash knows he can't claim any right to Sherlock over me—though he's not really trying to, either. With his balance shot and his wonky right eye, even a third-stringer might give him some trouble. But we both know that, so neither of us is going to bring it up. "All right. Only because yours looks as if one hard smack will turn on the waterworks."

Maybe. Sherlock's daddy was prez of the Hangmen's mother chapter in Vegas. So it might be that he was coddled his whole life and always got the smooth ride, but believed it was his own steel balls and badass attitude that got him where he was going. I've seen plenty of boys in boot camp break like that. Men who thought they were tough, but learned that they'd just always had it easy. Then they cried like babies.

Sherlock doesn't cry. As soon as that bell rings, he begins putting up a decent fight. Taking a few hits. Then getting a few in while I take his measure. He's all right. Strong, fast. But I outclass him by a fucking mile—and given the rage building in me ever since I saw Anna's bloodied face, I'd have loved to take the full fifteen minutes to beat the shit out of him.

But I'm not the only one here. And Crash isn't fighting at one hundred percent.

So I'll finish this quick. But not before I tell Sherlock, "Remember when Zoomie beat the holy fuck out of your first prez? That should have warned you. But you had to go and touch her anyway. And that makes you one stupid piece of shit."

A dead piece of shit. Face red, he lunges at me. I snap his neck and drop him like the trash he is.

Crash has got the other Hangman backed up into a corner. Even with his balance fucked and his vision half gone, the brother's holding his own. All the money that Uncle Sam put into training him didn't go to waste.

"Need a hand?" I call out.

He grunts. "Fuck off."

I glance at the clock. Thirteen minutes and twenty-five seconds left. Outside the Cage, Handlebar appears more at ease. Though it's not over yet, the quick look he gives me says it all. He knows I've got Crash's back. That makes all the difference.

And a little ragging isn't amiss. "You're about to hit two minutes on a third-stringer! Maybe spend a little less time choking your dick and more time choking the dickhead?"

Nah, not choking. Crash is like me. He'll go for quick and clean.

And he does. Neck snapped. Done.

Though the chainlink, I see Cherry on the bench, looking like a sweet mix of one scoop sickened and two scoops relieved. She meets my eyes and gives me a sad little thumbs up, then her worried gaze is all over Crash—maybe afraid the hits he took rattled his head.

But he seems steady when he turns. "All right?" I ask him.

"Peachy keen."

He raises his fist and I bump mine against it. This one, we can call a win. Every other fight in the Cage was some sick shit. But not this. This is what I *should* be doing. Taking care of the Hellfire Riders' business. For the first time in days, the rot isn't eating at me. And I feel all right. Because I got shit done.

Now to get even more shit done. Like killing that sick fucker Tusk. And burning this place to the ground.

"You gonna unlock this before Christmas, or are you waiting for Santa to bring you a brain first?" Crash says to the guard standing outside the Cage's entrance.

The guard darts an uneasy look over to Victor, who's wearing a flat stare and regarding us with his arms crossed over his chest.

Bluntly he says, "You aren't done."

"Yeah, we are." Crash glances over at the two bodies, then at me. "They look pretty fucking dead to you?"

"Hard to tell," I say easily, though my gut's knotting up real tight. "Could be they fell asleep with their heads on crooked."

That flat stare doesn't flicker. "Only one fighter walks out of the Cage. Those are the rules."

I push in closer to the fence. "That's fucking bullshit. It's also against the rules to put in anyone who doesn't pass your drug tests. This was a demonstration. The bastards were taught their lesson. We're done."

Victor's jaw clenches. Everyone on the benches is absolutely quiet. But not the same silence as when Tusk killed Draft. Instead it's a stunned, intense quiet—as if they can't believe what they're hearing, either. As if they figured the same as we did: two teams enter, one team leaves.

The bastard looks to the clock. "You've got eleven minutes, gentlemen."

Fuck no. Oh fuck no.

"*Bullshit!*" With a roar, Handlebar lurches up halfway out of his seat, his chains clattering as he fights against them. "Fucking bullshit! They killed the fuckers, they got their win, so unlock the fucking door!"

Other fighters are joining in the cries of *Bullshit!* and *Unlock the door!*—except for Tusk, whose laugh booms out and doesn't stop. The whole warehouse is suddenly filled with noise.

But it's nothing. All of it's gone. There's only Crash, turning to meet my gaze. His right eye's reddened and watering, the pupil blown, and isn't focusing in on me like the left eye is. But the message in them is clear.

Hoarsely I tell him, "Don't you say it."

"I'm already—"

"Fuck your already-a-dead-man shit." We're all dead men, sooner or later. My time was already pushed out to 'later' thanks to Crash. "You remember Goat Ridge? Because I do. You saved my ass. It's my turn to save you."

He goes right for my jugular. Not with his fists or feet. With one statement. "They'll kill Anna."

Ah Christ. Ah fuck. The image of her bleeding flashes in front of my eyes. But I shake my head. "Gunner won't let them near her."

He's crazy in love with her. Has been for years. He'd die before letting them hurt her again.

"You'd bet her life on that?" Face hard, Crash leans in and his next words stab a knife into my gut, releasing the poisonous rot. "They got past him once. They got past your whole fucking club."

The sour poison boils up my throat. Jaw clamped shut, I stare at him. My brother. My friend. I *won't* do this.

Except I will. We both know I will. Because Crash tossed Anna into the Cage with us.

"You goddamn fucking asshole." It's thick and raw, as if my throat's bleeding.

"You know it's right," he says simply, then faces the fence.

Faces his ride partner, who's still yelling at Victor to unlock the door. My chest becomes a black hole as Handlebar must see in Crash's eyes what I saw. Every goddamn thing inside me feels as if it's collapsing in on itself when Handlebar's voice tears apart like steel through a shredder.

"Don't you fucking do this," Handlebar grates out. "Don't you fucking do this. You fight. You can beat that bastard."

I'm the bastard now. And he's right. Only a bastard would let a friend sacrifice himself instead of throwing in with him and going down together. Only a disloyal piece of shit who deserves to be in that pile of corpses—and who doesn't deserve to be called brother.

But they got to my sister once. And I want to believe that the Hellfire Riders are protecting her now. But for all I know, the Iron Blood never let her go after making the video. They might have her locked up in a stall somewhere, ready to kill her if I refuse to fight—or if I lose a fight.

Jesus, I can't breathe. Crash is trying to say his goodbyes, but Handlebar's in denial, telling him to shut the fuck up, to kick my ass, to fight. On her bench, Cherry looks from Crash to me, tears silently spilling from her emerald eyes, fingers laced tightly together in front of her trembling lips.

Suddenly I want those fingers touching me, because all I see is the memory of how she held Crash's hand through Handlebar's fight. As if she could make him feel better.

But her touching me couldn't make any of this better. It couldn't make what I'm about to do feel *right*, like Crash said it was.

Nothing will ever be right again.

And I can't look at her now. Seeing her cry rips the hole in my chest open wider. I don't even fucking know why. She's nothing to me. Just some sweet girl I kissed in a bar. And that girl was a lie.

"Ready?" Crash says from behind me.

Never. A cluster of razors lodge in my throat when I face him. He looks resolved—and calm. Though his eyes close when Handlebar's next hoarse words reach him.

"I'll never forgive you for giving up, you fucking

bastard. You *fight*, goddammit."

Expression pained, Crash gestures me closer, grips the back of my neck and presses his forehead against mine. His voice is thick as he says, "That stubborn bastard didn't listen to me. So you tell him. My last words are that I love him, yeah? And I couldn't have asked for a better ride partner."

Fuck me. I can't fucking breathe, can't fucking see. "I'll tell him."

"And tell him to feed my cat. I know he hates that mangy little shit, but she's his now."

This time I can only nod.

"All right, then. Except for one other thing." He grins and backs up a step, raising his big fists. "You'll have to work for it, fucker."

ELEVEN

The first match I ever saw in the Cage taught me the difference between real fights and movie fights. Yet as Crash grins and raises his fists, nothing about *this* fight seems real.

Instead it looks like something out of a movie—two big men circling each other. Their physiques are evenly matched, down to the tattoos they wear on their shoulders, like two action stars about to face off in the climactic fight that ends the show.

For an instant, my gaze lands on the two men already lying dead in the Cage. That fight had seemed unreal, too.

Because that's also a movie thing—the idea that breaking someone's neck kills them instantly. Most of the time, it's simply not true. Damaging the spinal cord might cause paralysis, but the person doesn't immediately die. More likely they'd suffocate. And it takes a while.

Someone only goes quickly when there's massive damage to the brain stem. That's the kind of damage Crash and Stone know how to do.

And they seem evenly matched. But they aren't. Not just because of Crash's tumor and how it's affecting his coordination. He's also wearing a grin. But as Stone circles around and I see his face, there's nothing like a grin mirrored there. Only resignation. Only emptiness.

But everything's different. So unreal. They begin trading blows, and it's almost like watching something choreographed. I've seen Crash fight before. It was *always* like how he took out the first man. Quick. Efficient. Brutal.

This isn't. Instead it's like they're playing. Or practicing, with Crash on the offense and Stone on defense. Stone keeps moving back. Taking hits he could have avoided.

Like maybe Stone thinks he deserves them.

Handlebar keeps shouting encouragement with every hit. But I think he knows what I know. That Crash already told the other man to kill him.

And in movies, I know how this goes. If it's a bad guy versus a good guy, the good guy will be on the brink of defeat before pulling out a win. And if they're two good guys, they'll square off and fight to a draw—then team up to take out the villain.

But this is real life. And in the Cage, when two good guys square off, they both lose.

And they don't have much time. The clock's counting down.

Crash glances over at it. "Two minutes, fucker! I'm not going easy."

Handlebar shouts, "No! Stone, don't you—"

Unleash whatever he'd been holding back. Like he does now. With sobbing breaths, I watch as everything changes, as Crash goes on the defense. But he's still laughing, grinning. Egging Stone on.

The other man isn't hurting him. There's not a single bruise on Crash. Stone's just...moving him around. Getting him into position. I don't even realize it until Stone whips forward so fast, almost like he's going for a head butt, but there's no connection. Even as Crash is recovering his balance, Stone darts around behind him and locks his arm around Crash's throat.

Then Stone just holds him. Almost sweetly. Stone's eyes are closed, his jaw against the side of the other man's head. His lips move, but I don't hear what he says. Just see Crash's slight nod. Just hear Handlebar roaring a denial as the muscles in Stone's arm flex.

Compressing the arteries. It's the same thing my brother does. Makes it quick and painless.

Crash's body goes limp. Agony contorts Stone's face

as he slowly, slowly lowers him to the ground—going to his knees, holding Crash against his chest, never letting up on that choke. He presses his lips to Crash's temple and says something else. Maybe he's sorry.

"Let him go, brother." Handlebar's voice is broken and pierces the quiet that's fallen. "You can still let him go."

Stone could. It isn't too late. Crash could wake up now and be okay. Or maybe Victor will have a sudden change of heart, or the fighters will suddenly revolt and break their chains. Or the FBI will bust in to save the day.

In movies, that's what would happen. A last minute twist and a happy ending.

"Fifteen seconds," Victor announces.

Stone's teeth clench. Then a sound rips from him. The agonized scream of a man's soul tearing away.

He wrenches Crash's head to the side.

Handlebar's roar of denial echoes the silent scream that fills my head and my heart. This can't be real.

But it is. I know it is.

Sobs hitch painfully in my chest as Stone rises to his feet with his arms wrapped around Crash's torso, his heavy muscles straining under the weight. The Cage unlocks and two of the guards head in.

"Back off," Stone snarls and carries Crash's body to the exit—toward Handlebar, who's raging against his chains. "Take him, brother. Take him."

A keening sound comes from the bearded man as Stone lays Crash in his hands. Then Handlebar's hoarse,

"You're no brother to me. I'll kill you. First fucking chance, I kill you."

Jaw set, Stone nods and backs up a step. When the guards start closing in, Victor at the lead, he tells them, "You're not throwing Crash's body away like trash. You're going to let this man bury his brother. Or about five of you are going into the ground tonight, too. You'll eventually get me down, but not before I can do a lot of fucking damage."

Victor stares at him a long second before nodding. "We'll bury him back at the compound."

When Stone gets that agreement, all the aggressive fire and steel seems to vanish. He moves back to the bench like a man still carrying a heavy body with him. With silent sobs tearing at my chest and throat, I pick up my first aid kit and head over. He didn't put a mark on Crash, but Crash got in quite a few hits on him. Blood streams from a cut in his scalp, his left eyebrow, his mouth.

I can't help Crash. But I can do this. It's one of the few things I can do for any of these guys. Keep them healthy. Patch them up.

"Don't you fucking touch me. Don't you *ever* fucking touch me." His harsh voice freezes me in place and he snatches the antiseptic pad from my hand. When he looks up at me, his gaze isn't cold and lethal. Not tormented or grieving. Just dark and empty. Soulless. "And don't you dare cry. Not when you're the reason I was in that Cage with him. Your skin is safe."

Grief and anger lock my throat. The urge to shout that Crash was my friend, too. But it wasn't the same as Stone's bond with him. I know it wasn't. And whatever blame he places on me, it can't be close to what he's putting on himself.

I nod and back off, but his next question stops me.

"What was the plan?"

Renewed grief stabs through my heart. My plan to slip the guards chocolate laxatives and get them out of the control booth. I'd filled in Crash tonight for the first time—and he'd loved discovering why I'd had him playing along and pretending to be constipated for days.

But he's gone. And I can't just switch the symptoms over to someone else.

"It's impossible now," I tell him in a thick voice.

"Then you're useless to me, aren't you?" His empty gaze moves back to Handlebar, who's clutching Crash close. "So get the fuck out of my face."

I do, and the tears that keep falling aren't elegant or pretty. Because this isn't the movies.

And there won't be any happy ending here.

TWELVE

STONE

IT'S A SILENT RIDE BACK TO THE BARNS. NO CONGRATU-lations come from the other fighters in the van, though most say something to Log Cabin. But to me, nothing. Probably because of what they see in my face.

Or don't see. Because I've got a big fucking hole inside me. Where the man I was used to be.

And right now, something my mom once said is echoing around inside that hollow space. She's a high school counselor now, but wasn't always. Back in the day, she was some hotshot psychiatrist up in Portland. That was before Anna got sick with childhood leukemia, before the long cure and recovery meant my mom wasn't putting in as many hours in at the office, before our family moved to a little town in Central Oregon. My mom gave up the flashy job, but didn't give up her calling. Growing up, Anna and I got all kinds of shit drilled into our heads, my mom teaching us all kinds of lesson—sometimes so subtly we didn't know what she was doing until it was done.

But most stuff, she just said flat out. One of those things was that some people have big fucking holes inside them. So they fill them up with something else. Drugs, sex, violence, television, kale—whatever makes them feel like less of a big, empty piece of shit. And some go overboard and it ends up killing them.

A lot of people don't end up choosing what fills them up. They just fall into it. A drink here, a puff there. But sometimes, she said, they choose what fills them up. Knowing it can't get them through forever. But it can get them through long enough that they can make it out the other side.

I'm choosing mine. Two goals to focus on.

Killing Tusk. Burning down the Cage.

And if I don't come out on the other side… Fuck. I don't really give a shit.

As long as I get those two things done.

*　*　*

We get back to the barns, and it's the same routine as before. The guards lead us out of the vans one at a time under Victor's supervision. Except this time they leave the van's back doors open and facing the other vehicles, and I can see what's going on while I'm waiting for my turn. Handlebar comes out of one, carrying Crash, and that hole inside me goes so ragged and bloody that I can't fucking breathe again.

The guards don't escort Handlebar to the barn. Instead they head around it. Where he'll bury Crash.

I lost two brothers tonight. And if Handlebar still wants to kill me for it…I'll let him. After Anna's safe.

They lead Tusk in, and watching him helps that ragged hole start filling up. Not going to be killing him tonight. But I will. I would have anyway, for what he did to Draft—and what I suspect he did to a hell of a lot of other fighters, considering the way Crash knew some ugly sick shit was about to happen.

But also because Crash made that promise to Cherry. He can't follow through now. So it's one thing I'll do for him.

She comes out of the van, hovering over Airbag as he limps toward the barn. I don't know what plan she and Crash cooked up to get out of here. Something she needed him for, a plan that won't work anymore.

But Cherry might have given all of us another way out.

It's just Abyss and me left in the van when the guards come for me.

"I want my phone call," I tell the guard unlocking my wrist shackles.

He laughs. "This ain't a jail, new guy. You don't get a lawyer."

Yeah, and this asshole is useless to me. To Victor, I call out, "That bastard on the video with my sister said I'd be able to call her after winning a fight. I won a fucking fight. I want my call."

Victor's eyes narrow. "That promise didn't come from Papa."

"Then who runs this fucking place? The Iron Blood? They can go around making deals for Papa that he doesn't have to follow through on? That's who you're working for, too?"

His jaw clenches. Well, that's real damn interesting. Not a fan of the Blood? To the guard he says, "Leave him there a minute. Take number seven."

Abyss. Calling him by his stall number. And leaving me here with my wrists unshackled, and only my ankles still locked down. But two more guards stand by ready with the stun guns.

So I'll take my chances with Papa right now. Victor sends a text. Everything's quiet. Out here in the middle of goddamn nowhere. The cold's settling in through the open doors. Sweatpants aren't shit in the desert in November. The guards who took Abyss in are heading back to the van when the phone rings.

"Victor." A pause. "Yes, sir. I heard Chef make the promise. After every win."

Chef. So Cherry was right. The Iron Blood's enforcer. One more asshole to kill.

By the way Victor's nodding along to whatever Papa's saying now, the boss must not be too happy with the deal that fucker made. Probably Chef should have stopped at promising to kill Anna...but I wouldn't be surprised if she had something to do with that promise, too. Because without it, I'd never have fought. I'd have assumed Chef killed her after that, anyway. She probably saved herself by saying that the only way to make me fight is by giving me proof that she's still alive after.

Saved herself. Just like Cherry is.

My gut fills up with rot. Then satisfaction rushes in when Victor nods and says into the phone, "Yes, sir. You are always a man of your word."

Papa is a man of his word? What a fucking asshole. There's nothing worse than a self-righteous bad guy. He's a goddamn flesh-peddler, trading in death and entertainment. But keeping his promises makes him an honorable man?

More likely, he's just rich. And rich fuckers have a habit of justifying all the ways they crush the little guys under their boots. *I keep my word, you keep yours, and we're all equal and in this together—and we'll just ignore the fact that I didn't give you much of a choice when we made our deal.*

Yeah, it's bullshit.

But this time, I'll take it. And use it.

With the phone still against his ear, Victor glances over at me. "I would say that Mr. Wall proved himself a valuable addition to your stable."

And I would say they're all dead men walking. I'm not a valuable asset. Instead I'm the liability that'll bring them down.

"Yes, sir." Victor gestures to one of the other guards, who moves in and begins locking my wrists up again. "And the girl? She hasn't yet been punished for her disobedience."

What girl? Cherry?

Did they know about the plan she cooked up with Crash? Or that she lied about his earache?

Whatever it is, the reply is so short that Papa must not care too much about whatever rebellion it was. Probably because whatever she was doing didn't mean a damn thing in the end. Crash is dead.

"Yes, sir. I'll see that he gets his reward." Victor ends the call, looks to me. "You'll get your call."

That's one reward I'll take. Though I wish to fuck it had come at a lower cost.

"Get us out onto the 395 and start driving. I'll tell you when to stop," Victor tells the guard as he steps into the van's cargo hold. Not bothering to hide the name of the highway, even though I'll be making a call and might leak the location—probably because he knows any trace on the phone might give away the general area, anyway. "I'll ride back here and make sure Mr. Wall behaves."

Yeah, probably better do that.

No fool, Victor double checks my shackles before sitting across from me, like he knows the sight of his drill sergeant face will make this drive feel a million fucking times longer. "Papa asked me to convey his congratulations to you. He was pleased to see that you are a man of considerable skill."

Congratulations. For killing a friend. Papa can go fuck himself.

And that hole goes ragged again. Because now I get it. A demonstration. That wasn't just about teaching the Devil's Hangmen a lesson. Though it was probably that, too. But most of their money comes from gambling—and I'm the new guy, an unknown and more of a risk. But they've got a baseline on what I can do now.

But they knew Crash couldn't fight again. So they sacrificed him to get that baseline. Sacrificed one of the best men I know. In a demonstration.

My chest is real fucking tight as I ask him, "Who'd you serve with, Vic? Army, I figure."

Victor doesn't answer.

I don't need him to. I know a soldier when I see one. "That man Handlebar is burying now was a sergeant with Second Reconnaissance Battalion, Second Marine Division, a team leader, and a real fucking good man, too. Has a whole fucking collection of bronze stars. Don't give me your congratulations. A decorated Marine died in your Cage today."

A muscle in his jaw twitches. "He wasn't a Marine when he died."

Oorah, he's *begging* for me to beat his ass. "Once a Marine, always a fucking Marine."

"Bullshit," he snaps back. "You stopped being anything when you put on that vest you were wearing, declaring loyalty to your club instead of your country. You put your-self above the law and betrayed every goddamn thing you fought for. So did he."

That's real fucking rich. "You're a militia boy now, aren't you? That's the same fucking thing as a motorcycle club. A bunch of brothers who just want to live free and to take care of our own. But instead of protecting a man's freedom, you're helping to put them in cages."

"You *should* be in cages. You bikers have no respect for the laws of this country. Your clubs are running drugs, selling girls, bringing illegals across the border. We're just doing what the law can't. Or won't."

Christ. The only thing worse than a self-righteous rich fucker is a self-righteous hypocrite. "You think the Iron Blood and all their associates aren't running girls? The roads to the Cage are paved with all the needles your boys stuck in their arms to keep them on their backs. The people you're working for are telling them to come to the promised land and then turning them into whores."

"They should have known that if they come here illegally, they'll get into trouble. Just like you and your clubs. You break the law, you pay for it."

"Since when did the courts say that the proper punishment for a woman coming over the border is rape? Since when does a judge tell some asshole selling dope to get in a cage and beat another prisoner to death? And you talk about respect for the law?" A hard laugh escapes me. "You don't stand for a goddamn thing. You're just a fucking traitor to anyone who ever wore a uniform."

That got to him. His jaw clenches and he stares at me for a long minute. Then quietly, "I suggest you sleep, Mr. Wall. We've got a long ride ahead, and if you open your mouth again, I might change my mind about letting you make that call."

Bullshit he will. He's already proved himself to be Papa's little lap dog. But since I've got no interest in conversing with a goddamn traitor, I close my eyes.

Only one thing's in my head. Burning this place down. And I'll do it with one word to Anna. Because the Hellfire Riders haven't shown up yet, so that means they need a lead. A link to the Cage. And Cherry gave it to me.

Strawman.

PROBLEM IS, I CAN'T JUST say the name. Not because of Anna. I say "Strawman" to my sister, and she'll wonder what the fuck I'm talking about—but then she'll tell either the Prez or Gunner or Zoomie. And the name will do the job it needs to do. It'll give them that link.

But if I say it and Victor hears it, then it'll blow that link apart. Everyone who set this shit up—Gunner's family and whoever they know in the Iron Blood—must believe that there's no damn way the Riders or anyone else will ever track down the Cage or find this barn. They must think they've covered their asses that well.

And they *have*. Because after Zoomie was taken, the Hellfire Riders were looking hard for the Cage and we didn't see a damn thing until I tripped right over it.

So if I expose that link, it'll get covered up again quick. And then this phone call won't be worth shit.

The trick will be saying "Strawman" without saying it. And without saying anything close to it. I'm pretty sure that Gunner's brother being called "Strawman" has something to do with a scarecrow. But that won't help, either, because Victor's no idiot.

But "strawman" has another meaning—one Anna will put together. Because that's another thing our mom drilled into our heads.

Look out for strawmen.

It's a shitty tactic people use when they're in an argument they can't win. Instead they build up a strawman that resembles the other person's argument, then they knock it down and claim a victory. But the strawman is just empty bullshit that lets the person avoid addressing the real argument.

But I have to word it just right. And be quick, because Victor's not going to let me have a conversation with Anna.

And make sure she tells Gunner—not the Prez and not Zoomie—because even if she figures out what I'm getting at, it won't mean anything beyond that to anyone except him.

About an hour passes before Victor bangs on the forward wall of the cargo hold, telling the guard in the cab to pull over. Reception must be shit inside the van, because he opens up the back doors, unlocks my ankle shackles, and shuffles me out.

Middle of nowhere again. A two-lane road stretches through a whole lot of nothing. And it's fucking freezing.

The guard from the cab hands Victor a shiny new phone—probably an untraceable burner, because these assholes are damn good at covering their asses. "What's her number?"

I tell him and he dials it in, then hits the speaker-phone. Not letting me get my hands on the device.

I wish to hell they weren't so good at this.

The phone rings. And rings. And rings. Fuck, if the Riders have Anna hidden out at the clubhouse, the call might never get through. Reception out on the ranch is shit.

And that would be just my goddamn luck.

Then I hear a hesitant, "Hello?"

My stomach hollows out with relief and my throat closes up. Shit. Ah shit. All that planning to say just the right thing and the sound of my sister's quavering voice just knocked the wind out of me.

A sharp *"Stone?"* follows a second later.

No wavering this time. Only fear and worry.

I can't bear to hear how afraid she is for me. "How you doing, pipsqueak?"

There's a sobbing breath and then a quick, "I'm all right and I love you. Daisy's okay, too."

"Good." Damn good. And I didn't realize how badly I needed to hear that. Emotion burns in my throat, but I can't waste more time. "Now tell Gunner that me and Crash had a real bad argument, so I had to knock him down."

Even before I finish speaking, Victor drops the phone to the blacktop, then stomps on it. Fuck. How much got through? Enough? *Tell Gunner. A bad argument. Knock him down.* That's enough to tip her off, as soon as she starts to think about it. And she *will* think about it. Because they'll expect me to try and get a message through. But did she get it all?

I just don't fucking know.

THIRTEEN

STONE

It's nearly dawn when we arrive back at the barn. Sitting in a van for hours has stiffened up every muscle that took a hit last night.

Every hit that Crash laid on me.

And he keeps laying more on me. Every time I think of him, the hole inside me tears open wider.

I've had one good thing to fill that emptiness with: the realization that Anna had her phone with her. She's not locked up or being held by the Iron Blood, because there's no fucking way they'd let her keep a device like that with her.

So she's safe. There's no doubt of it now.

But it's knowledge with a sharp, jagged edge. Because she's safe. And if I'd known that, if I'd been as certain in the Cage…I wouldn't have let Crash sacrifice himself for me. I'd have gone out with him.

It doesn't matter that means we'd both be dead. Better dead than betraying a brother. But it's too fucking late now.

And a part of me is dead anyway. The part of me that used to be worth something.

But at least she's safe. Now Papa has no leverage to make me fight again. Except I *will* fight at least one more time. Not for Papa, though.

I've got a goddamn hole to fill—and a promise to keep.

In the barn, it's too early for Elton. It's dark except for the recessed lighting that offers enough illumination to walk down the wide aisle between the stalls.

First cell on the left is Tusk's. He's awake, doing pullups using the bars over the stall with his dick hanging free. The sick fucker doesn't look over and I don't try to get his attention, don't give him any reason to look at me. Better if he never sees me coming, never realizes I'm a threat.

Farther down the aisle, Cherry and a guard come out of Airbag's stall. Even in the dim lighting, I see the way her eyes widen and relief fills her expression. Like maybe she thought they'd taken me out to put a bullet in my head instead of letting me make a phone call.

"You done in there for now?" Victor asks. When she nods, he says, "Then see to Mr. Wall's injuries."

Fuck that. "They don't need seeing to."

"The nurse will determine that," the bastard says. "Get into your restraints."

Goddammit. This is the last thing I want—Cherry touching me. Trying to heal me, to make me feel better.

Nothing could make this feel better. Nothing *should* make this feel better.

But I don't have much of a choice. I step in the restraints, hands over my head, manacles on my wrists. Chains securing my ankles. They don't let her come in until I'm locked up. She sets a little medical kit at the foot of my bed and comes to stand in front of me.

"Bend your head a little, please."

Because even in those heels, she's about six inches shorter than me. And standing so damn close, reaching up to skim her fingers over my scalp as if searching for lumps.

"Any tender spots?"

Not in my skull. And Christ, she looks like hell. Makeup mostly gone. Cried off, probably. The skin around her eyes looks tender and swollen, her face pale with exhaustion.

I've never seen her like this. Not even the first night at the tavern. She looked vulnerable then—but this is another level entirely. As if she's not just vulnerable but fragile, on the edge of breaking.

And I'm such a sucker for it. Even now.

But the empty stall across from mine reminds me why I shouldn't be. "Where's Handlebar?"

"In the other barn." She rips open an antiseptic pad and begins dabbing a deep cut over my eyebrow. Quietly she adds, "They thought it best to separate him from you."

After his threat to kill me. That pit opens up in my stomach. But not as deep. Because she's looking up at me with those big eyes, tending to my wounds just like she did in the tavern. And despite the sting of the antiseptic, her hands are so fucking gentle. That softness seeps in, tending to the ragged wounds inside me, too. Filling me up with her sweetness.

But that's not what I want in me. When she opens up a butterfly bandage, I tell her, "Don't close it up. I want to wear these scars."

The marks Crash put on me. I want to wear these wounds for a long fucking time.

Her hand stills, her sad gaze searching my face. Then she nods like she understands. "All right."

Even her fucking voice is gentle. So goddamn sweet. I don't want that.

"I'll add them to my collection—all the scars I've got because a woman was saving her own skin."

Her expression tightens. But her touch never roughens. Neither does her voice. "Is that what these others are?"

"Yeah."

Antiseptic burns my lip as she says, "You said that you went through a window."

While telling her not to be smart *and* pretty. Because all that wounded vulnerability already got its hooks into me. Throw in the rest and I knew that I'd be fucked.

Got fucked anyway. "There was a window. But first there was a gorgeous girl who took me home. Back then, you might say I was real handsome myself."

Her lips twitch. "Still might."

"Only if you're a fucking liar." The way her amusement blinks out deepens the hole again, fills it with rot instead of her softness. But it only takes another second for her warmth to start seeping in again. "Long story short, her abusive asshole of an ex showed up with some friends, she got scared and saved her own skin by telling him that I'd slipped something into her drink. Cue a brawl, me going headfirst through a window, and leaving her bedroom not nearly as handsome as I went into it."

She bites her lip. "That's shitty. I'm sorry."

A harsh laugh escapes me. "Yeah, she said sorry, too. A few years after, that ex was locked up because he took his temper out on someone else, she said sorry and maybe we could try again. Thing was, her face hadn't changed—but she looked a lot uglier to me than she had before. So I passed up on that offer."

"Yes," she whispers. "Someone fucks you over once, you're not going to let them do it again. No matter their reasons.”

“The reasons matter. Because I get it. Being afraid. Saving your own skin. But *no one* comes out looking prettier than they went in.”

Her breath trembles. “I just want to get out of it. Pretty or not.”

“Do you? Funny. That’s what Crash wanted, too.”

Grief slashes across her face. Like I slapped her with it.

Because I did. She might have been the bait who brought us here, but nothing in that Cage was her fault. I was the one who betrayed a brother. And it was playing real dirty, hitting her with that.

Because I want her to hit me back. To put some hurt on me. Because it’s hurt that I should be feeling.

But she just continues tending to my wounds. Standing there drowning in grief and sorrow while smoothing the sharp edges of my pain.

I can’t fucking take it. “We’re done,” I tell her hoarsely. “I don’t want you touching me.”

She freezes before nodding. Lips pressed tight, she tapes on another bandage, then begins packing up her kit. “I’ll leave you an ice pack for your jaw.”

From the open door of my stall, Victor says, “You’re not done.”

You’re not done. It’s like a punch to the gut. For an instant, I’m back in the Cage and feeling so goddamn good, because I got shit done, and grinning while Crash asks the guard whether he's waiting for Santa to bring him a brain. Then realizing what's coming when Victor tells us, *You're not done.*

But there's only two of us in here now. Cherry and me. And there's not a fucking thing in this world that will make me lay a hand on her. I'll just lie down and let her take me out. She'll probably do it real gently.

More gently than I deserve.

"Did I miss an injury?" She's looking me over, her brow furrowed. "Do I need to look at your back?"

So Victor hadn't been talking to me. Now he tells her, "Papa was pleased with Mr. Wall's victory. He decided that it earned him a reward."

As if in confusion, she blinks at him, then glances back at me. I don't know what the fuck he's talking about, either. I heard him say something about a reward, but figured he meant the call to Anna.

But there was something else. Punishment. For disobedience.

Fucking hell.

Realization widens Cherry's eyes, then her face goes utterly still. "You mean…?"

"Give Mr. Wall his reward, Cherry."

Panic sharpens her voice. "But Papa says I'm not supposed to—"

"Not in his bed." Victor gestures to the floor in front of my feet. "On your knees."

Fuck no. "I don't want her touching me."

Not to heal me. Not as a reward for killing Crash. And sure as fuck not because they're punishing her.

Relief lightens her voice. "He doesn't want—"

"Then you'll give Tusk the reward."

That sick fucker must have heard his name. He calls out, "You'll give what to me?"

Her face goes white when Victor adds, "Considering where his cock was earlier tonight, I don't think you want to suck that off."

Horror fill her expression. "No."

"Number thirteen also won." Victor's eyes narrow. "Maybe we'll make you reward him."

The neo-Nazi. And Cherry's reaction to that suggestion seems more frantic and horrified than her reaction to Tusk, shaking her head wildly as she backs up a step. And Christ, my stomach's all twisted up in sick knots. I don't know how much of that rot is the thought of this being a punishment or because I can't stand the idea of her touching someone else.

"I'll take the reward," I grate out and her frantic gaze shoots to my face. "I'll take it."

Gratitude fills her expression. Fucking *gratitude*. And sheer relief. She starts toward me, then halts when I tell her, "Grab the pillow and put it on the floor."

Or else she might be kneeling on that cold concrete for a long time. Because I don't want a blowjob. Not tonight. Not after Crash. And not while chained upright in a freezing cell, my wrists and ankles in restraints.

Except my dick doesn't give a shit. I watch her bend over to snatch the pillow off my bunk, that tiny nurse's uniform riding up to give me a glimpse of tight little ass and all that smooth skin above the lace tops of her stockings. The weight between my legs grows heavier, thicker.

Christ. I glance over at Victor. The fucker must be made of ice. He's not checking out her ass. Instead his watchful gaze is still on me.

Where he'll see more soon. "This reward ain't a fucking show," I tell him.

He shrugs. "I've got to see it done."

"I'm sure as hell not going to come with you watching me. My dick's tiny, so it's real timid." And I don't share. Another man looking is too damn close to sharing. I don't want anyone to have any of her. "And it's going to shrivel if I have to look at your face."

Fucker doesn't leave, but he turns sideways so we're only in his periphery. Good enough.

Cherry all but runs back to me, drops the pillow to the concrete and sinks down—as if afraid I'll change my mind and send her off to blow Tusk or Hatchet.

She's shaking all over. Her hands as she reaches for the front of my sweats. Her every rapid, shallow breath. Her soft lips as she looks up at me.

Shaking like she's never done this before. Like she hasn't lured in a million guys with that mouth.

Maybe even me. "Did we get this far that night?"

"No," she says softly. Her trembling fingers curl over

my waistband.

"But you would have, yeah? You were so wet and hot for my cock when I was kissing you."

Her pale face pinkens. That sweet blush surges straight down the length of my dick, leaving me hard and aching. Without her even touching me yet.

"I would have had you on your knees that night. After I'd eaten your pussy. And after I'd fucked you good and hard, stretched your hot little hole with every inch of my dick."

Those were my priorities. The blowjob could have waited until round two.

Her blush deepens but she still doesn't do anything else. Because she's waiting for permission, I realize. Looking up at me, her bottom lip trapped between her teeth.

"Go on, then," I tell her hoarsely. "Give me a hot, wet hole to fill."

Freezing air surrounds my cock when she drags down the front of the sweats, but I don't feel the cold. Not while watching her eyes go wide as her gaze measures my erect length.

Her tongue darts out to wet her lips before she whispers, "You're not tiny."

"And you look like a greedy girl who likes them long and thick," I rasp. "Now show me how you use that pretty, pretty mouth as bait."

That makes her lips press tight again. But her hands

come up and take hold of my shaft, and that's…ah fuck. Awkward. Her palms are soft and dry, but her fingers are freezing in the cold air, and her grip is so damn light. I can barely feel the stroke of her skin over mine—yet it's also *all* that I feel. Like a tease of sensation that my entire body craves more of. More of this sweetness, more of this softness.

Ah Christ. I clench my teeth against a groan, everything in me focused on the slight pleasure of that touch.

Those emerald eyes meet mine, shining with a light I haven't seen in them before. Something bright and hopeful. "You like this?" she asks breathlessly.

I laugh. "Fuck no. As hand jobs rate, this is the worst I've ever had. No wonder you have to drug them."

That light blinks out and her gaze drops.

That rot rolls back in. But for the best. For a moment there, I forgot what this was. Because she was making me feel so fucking good. Chasing after the pleasure of her touch. Pushing away the pain.

But it's a reward. For killing Crash.

I can't let the pain filling me up vanish. Because I know now what would replace it—what I'd *need* to replace it. Cherry. And all her softness.

"You call this a reward?" I throw at Victor. "She's got hands like a dead fish."

She releases my cock like it burned her, bowing her head.

"For fuck's sake, Cherry," Victor snaps. "Just suck him

off and get it done."

"Cherry's sucking *who* off?" Tusk's demand cuts through the quiet in the barn. "That pussy's *mine*! That mouth is *mine*!"

"Is it, Tusk?" Cherry says softly and laughs, but when her head comes up there's no amusement there. Instead there's just…rage.

Oh fuck. I like that. So much better than wounded. Better than sorry.

I like that rage a hell of a lot.

Sparks fly through emerald as she calls out, "You think this pussy is yours, Tusk?"

"I *earned* it!" he roars.

"But he's the one who got the reward!" she calls back, then leans in to rub her cheek against my cock, moaning loudly, "Oh, Stone. Your dick tastes so good. *Mmmmmmmm.* I just want to slurp up your cum again and again."

Oh shit. A laugh rolls through me as an enraged bellow echoes from the rafters. The fucker sounds as if he's losing his mind.

Smiling viciously, Cherry moans again. "I need this big dick in my pussy. Please, Stone. Hold me down and make it hurt so good."

A crash comes from Tusk's stall, as if he just slammed his bed against the wall. And I can't stop laughing. I *really* like her when she's angry.

"Oh god, yes!" She gives a breathy little cry. "Push it in so deep!"

Then she raises those furious eyes to mine and sucks my cock all the way to the back of her throat.

The groan tears from me before I can stop it, because *her mouth*. Her sweet goddamn mouth. Her hands were cold and awkward but her mouth is so fucking wet, so fucking hot.

So fucking good.

She takes me in until she gags, her throat convulsing around the fat head, sending me straight to heaven. Then she begins sucking, drawing on my shaft so hard, it almost hurts.

Almost.

"Harder." Teeth gritted, I watch her furious struggle to take more than she's already managed. Not even a third of my length but all that anger is stroking every inch of me. "Suck me harder."

She does and Christ almighty, I've never felt anything like it. No finesse, nothing but fury scorching my dick, like she's determined to make me come through her sheer fucking will. I drag air into my heaving chest when she pulls back and sucks me down again, again, again, harder and harder.

But it doesn't hurt. Nothing ever felt so good.

Bliss boils at the base of my spine and rises the length of my cock. "Holy fuck," I groan raggedly. "You're about to suck the cum right out of me."

Heat flares through her eyes. Not just rage. Arousal. Satisfaction. Either she's turned on by sucking dick or loving what she's doing to me.

I'm loving what she's doing to me, too. I shouldn't. Christ, this is a reward for Crash. It's a punishment for her. But the hot pull of her mouth, the burn of rage in her eyes are destroying everything else in their path. Destroying me. I'd beg for those cold hands to stroke me now but I can't do a damn thing except grit my teeth and hold on as she works my dick so good that I helplessly begin fucking her face, thrusting shallowly past her lips, desperate for her to take all of me into her. Into her softness, her heat, until there's nothing else left that isn't hers.

Then one long, hot suck blows me apart. Head thrown back against the bars, I come so goddamn hard that stars burst behind my eyes. Cherry makes a choking sound, like she wasn't expecting a load of cum to shoot down the back of her throat. She backs off quick, coughing, her face flushed and eyes shining.

But not filled with so much rage now. There's some satisfaction, as if she's pleased that she made me come so fast. Then bemusement as my cock jerks a final time, and she wipes away the spurt that lands on her chin.

Her bright gaze meets mine. "You're all right?"

Better than I should be. "How the fuck do you think I am? The woman who fucked me over to save her own skin just sucked me off as a reward for killing a friend."

She bites her lip and averts her face, and the whole world dims.

Tusk is still shouting. The bars behind my back rattle

with the force of whatever he's doing in his stall.

"Bring her down here! Bring her the fuck down here! I earned that pussy! I earned it!"

A guard stops near my stall door. "Are we going to have to hear that all day?"

Victor doesn't answer him. Instead he says to Cherry, "You done yet?"

Without meeting my eyes, she pulls my sweats back into place and tucks me in. Her voice is thick. "We are."

"Then go clean up. Lights on in fifteen."

Silently she gets to her feet and grabs her kit. No longer touching me. Not even looking at me. And the second she's gone, all the pain and rot pours back in.

And fucking drowns me in it.

FOURTEEN

WHAT HAVE I BECOME? *WHAT HAVE I BECOME?*

I leave Stone's stall and race down the dimly lit aisle. Matt stands near the bars of his cell, his face lined with worry and fear. I only slow down long enough to choke out, "I can't," before stopping in front of my door.

I wrench it open when the clunk of electric lock sounds. *Go clean up.* That was the order. Instead I stand in the center of my stall, gasping sobbing breaths.

I used to be a good person. I used to be. But I'm not anymore.

Not after what I just did.

Stone didn't want me to touch him. He only offered because the alternative was so terrible. But I knew he didn't really want it.

I knew that and accepted Stone's offer, anyway. I should have left him alone. Should have just taken my punishment with Tusk. Instead I chose Stone because I wanted him. Not then. Not like that. But I can't deny his physical effect on me. So going down on him made a punishment seem like less of one.

But the worst part of it is…I loved so much of it. Loved seeing his response. Loved hearing his groans. Loved making him come.

Not only because I wanted him. But because I was so *angry*, and so tired of feeling helpless. So I took out all my rage on a man in restraints. A man who didn't want me touching him. A man grieving for his friend.

No one comes out looking prettier than they went in.

I knew I wouldn't. I knew this place would change me.

But I never thought I'd become so ugly.

BY THAT EVENING, I'M SO exhausted that squeezing my way through the bars above my stall takes everything I have left. Despair and grief are a constant burn in my throat—emotions that only thicken when I glance across the aisle at Crash's empty stall.

Matt pulls himself up. "Hey, sis."

He sounds as torn up as I feel. Though he doesn't know what I did to Stone. Maybe he knows what I was ordered to do—give a reward—but not how I became so angry and took my rage out on a helpless man.

I wish that anger had lasted. Instead only grief and despair are left.

"Hey," I whisper.

"You all right?"

No. But I nod.

He knows I'm lying. His face hardens. "It was Stone?"

I nod again.

"Did he hurt—"

"No." I stop that train before it goes any farther. "He's a good guy."

A humorless laugh shakes through him. "No, he's not. But if it makes you feel better, keep thinking that."

Knowing he's a good guy doesn't make me feel better. The knot in my throat thickens. "It's my fault he's here."

"No." It's flat, unyielding. "No."

"But I should have tried harder to—"

"*No.*" His fierce whisper cuts me off. "You remember when we first got here, you told me that it wasn't my fault that you got caught up in this—that it was all on Papa and the Eighty-Eight? This is the same damn thing. So if Stone's being here is your fault, then you being here is my fault."

I'm trapped by that argument. Voice thick, I tell him, "It still *feels* like it's my fault, though."

"Yeah." His face softens. "It never stops feeling like that."

And might get worse. I whisper raggedly, "With Crash gone"—my throat closes for a long, long second before I can continue—"and Flack gone, they've got too many empty stalls. They'll send me out again as bait. But after last time, they'll watch me even more closely. I won't get a chance to escape."

He sighs heavily. "Probably not."

"But I've got another plan." Breath shuddering, I tell him, "I'll get into the control booth and kill whoever's on duty, then I'll open all the doors."

Matt's lips twitch. "Will you?"

I nod. "I'll tell the guard that I want someone to take my virginity before Tusk wins his tenth fight. Then I'll slit his throat."

"With what? Your fingernails?"

"I've got a scalpel hidden in my stall."

The amusement flees his expression. Because he hadn't thought I was serious. Now he shakes his head.

"Hold up—"

"It's a good plan."

"Except for the part where you kill someone. That shit has consequences."

"No jury would convict me." Not after everything we've been through.

"I'm not talking about that. I'm talking about what killing does to the person you are."

Sudden tears fill my eyes. On a sobbing breath, I tell him, "I don't know who I am anymore. I'm not the person

I thought I was."

"Because you've had some extreme reactions to some really extreme shit?" Gently he brushes my tears away. "That's just called being human."

"A bad one."

"You couldn't be bad if you tried. And what you're doing is the best you can do—you're owning up to the shitty stuff you're doing to survive, how it affects other people…and how it affects you." He draws a deep breath. "Killing someone *will* affect you. Especially killing in cold blood like you're talking about. And I don't want what happened to me to happen to you."

After the Cage? "I don't see you any differently."

He's still the brother who does everything in his power to protect me.

"I do. I fucking hate myself," he says, his face tormented. "For getting you into this. For not finding a way out of it. For falling in line every damn time. And the only reason I'm holding on is because I've got you to love me."

My tears fall faster. "Nothing you did could change that."

"You couldn't change how I love you, either. And if it comes down to you being Tusk's prize and killing a guard, then you kill the guard. But wait until you have no other choice. Wait until the night before the next fight, before Tusk gets in that ring again. And all the time in between, keep looking for another way out. At least then you'll know you did everything you could."

Whatever that's worth. "Everything I do turns into shit."

Every single plan.

"No," he says softly. "You do everything right. It's the world that's shit."

But it isn't shit now. In this one moment. Reaching through the bars, I hug him tight.

He hugs me even tighter. "I love you so damn much, sis."

And that's what keeps me holding on, too.

FIFTEEN

STONE

Every day that passes is exactly the same. Wake up to Elton. Run on the track. Work the heavy bag. Jerk my cock to the memory of Cherry's mouth when it's lights out.

And every day that passes, I'm thinking that Anna didn't get enough of my message. Not enough to connect them to Strawman. Or maybe those wheels are turning. They just aren't turning fast enough.

Because every fucking day that passes, the hole in

me deepens. And I just gotta keep filling it up, reminding myself of what's important now. Kill Tusk. Burn down the Cage.

Don't fill up with Cherry.

Though I couldn't help myself, if she let me. I keep looking for that rage I liked so much. Maybe hoping that it'll rub off on me, give me some of my own anger to fill me up instead of this aching rot.

But there's nothing to see, because in four fucking days, she hasn't even met my eyes.

For the best. Just gotta focus on what oughta be filling me up. Focus on getting whoever's in charge of the Cage to put me in that ring with Tusk.

One of the guards raps on my stall bars. "Ready?"

That's one thing that's changed—no Handlebar, no Crash. And with Flack dead and Airbag mostly confined to his bed while his broken ribs heal, our exercise groups got shifted around. Now I'm first to go out, with Cherry and Hatchet.

She's waiting now with him, wearing that bright red smile and her emerald eyes averted away from me.

Fuck, this rot in my chest. The door buzzes open.

Hatchet's frowning at the two guards. "What the hell are you fuckers coming down with?"

The guard frowns back. "What are you talking about?"

"You aren't supposed to be on duty until tonight." Hatchet points to the other one. "And he's already pulled a shift. So are half of you all laid up with some crap? Because

I don't want to catch your fucking germs if you are."

Huh. The neo-Nazi's watching shifts as closely as I am. And apparently he's been here long enough that he's lost track of the days.

But he's got a point.

I head back into my stall and rip the blanket off my bed. The guard frowns at me. "You can't take that."

"It's not for me. It's for her." I nod to Cherry, whose gaze darts to mine. "Because you all might not be sick, but if she's out there freezing like she usually is, it ain't going to be long until you've got a goddamn plague passing around this stable."

The guard glances at his partner, then says into his shoulder radio, "You all right if Cherry takes a blanket out so she doesn't get sick?"

Victor's voice comes through. "Do it."

There's no rage when she looks at me now. Gratitude comes through as she turns and lets me drop the blanket over her slender shoulders. She should be fucking pissed, the way these assholes have her freezing out there.

"We set, then?" the other guard says irritably.

Hatchet's giving me a look that I can't interpret, and don't fucking care to interpret. But it's to the guard he says, "So what are you all passing around?"

"They're not sick. It's Thanksgiving," I tell him. "So some of these assholes are on holiday leave."

"Not all of us," a guard mutters.

The neo-Nazi turns disbelieving eyes on him. "Are

you fucking shitting me with that whiny bullshit? To us?"

The guard flushes and ushers us ahead, with Cherry between Hatchet and me, but that fucker Tusk is up against his bars and after her as we pass by. In four days, he hasn't shut up about earning his reward. Just seeing her sets him off.

She puts her head down and draws that blanket tighter around her shoulders.

Outside, the cold air slaps at my chest. The sun's bright but there's no warmth coming from it.

Hatchet's looking at her. That's one fucker I can't read, despite the racist shit inked all over his skin. He's always looking at her. But not like Tusk does. Or even like I do. Stealing glances. As if making sure she's all right.

Maybe he's like some of the other guys in here. Like Handlebar, calling her an angel. Because she takes care of them. Though at the fight, he was an asshole to her.

Just a goddamn asshole in general.

Then he says, "You think we'll get some turkey and stuffing in our healthy shit meal?"

Cherry smiles slightly. "Maybe the turkey. I'd rather have the pie."

"Yeah, me too." He tilts his head back. "My grandpa used to make a pecan pie that would knock your ass off."

Her voice turns wistful. "That sounds really good."

"Yeah. And then we'd eat the whole damn thing while watching the game."

Christ. "Did you watch the game before or after you

took your hood off?"

He looks over at me, eyes narrowing. "You got a problem with me exercising my freedom of speech, cuck?"

"I got a problem with everyone who rides with the Eighty-Eight. Though I find it real damn interesting that you're in here, since the Eighty-Eight are neck deep up the Cage's ass. You came here as a demonstration?"

"And won."

"That's a damn shame." Real damn shame. "What were you being punished for? Maybe the supply of meth you were in charge of dried up?"

His eyes widen. Just a flicker. "What do you know about a fucking supply?"

I know the Hellfire Riders took out the local chapter of the Eighty-Eight Henchmen not too long ago. But we don't go around boasting shit that'll come back on us. We just protect ours.

"I heard a clubhouse got hit and the meth kitchen got torched. And that they found a bunch of girls the Henchmen intended to sell." Because every single one of those assholes is trash. "So yeah. It's a real fucking shame you won."

Cherry's head is down again, biting her lip so hard that she's scraping off the lipstick.

Hatchet lets loose a grating laugh. "Yeah, just feel damn lucky you went up against that pussy, Crash. If you'd—"

"Stop it," she hisses at him. "Not that."

He looks at her, eyes narrowing. "Don't tell me to shut my mouth, female. I'll shut yours up so hard you'll be shitting teeth out your ass."

I swear to fuck she almost laughs at him. Her mouth presses tight and her eyes glitter, not with anger or humor but something trapped in between.

"What else would I shit out of? My toes?"

He blinks and his lips twitch, then a commotion from the direction of the barns has us all pivoting. The guards are already turned around, one of them chanting *"Oh shit, oh shit."*

A naked mountain races toward us. Tusk. Coming for Cherry.

"Fucking hell." Hatchet grabs Cherry's arm and shoves her back. "Get behind me. If he gets past the guards, I'll take him down. Then you run like hell for the barn."

Get him down? Yeah, I'll let Hatchet do that. She's wide-eyed, stumbling back—then looks to me in shock when I take her blanket.

"Gonna need this," I tell her. Because the fucker likes to bite.

The guards don't even try to slow down the charging bastard. Goddamn assholes. Hatchet gets right in front of her. Whoever's in front of Tusk is going down hard. Best thing to do when a fucker's charging is to whip to the side, let that momentum carry him through. But that'd take him straight into Cherry. So there's no other place to go.

Tusk hits him like a charging bull. Hatchet's no slouch,

that's for goddamn sure. He drops just at the right second and takes Tusk's feet out from under him, but the sick fucker's low enough to grab on and they both go down, rolling and rolling—and Tusk comes out on top.

Bad fucking place for Hatchet but good for me. I haul Cherry out of the way when she screams and lurches for the struggling pair, like she's going to take the fucker out with her tiny little hands.

Then I'm on Tusk, pulling the blanket over his face and hauling back. He roars and tries to tear it away, but I've got it tight. Fucking hell, it's like wrestling a mammoth. Can't break his neck. Shit. He's got muscles like steel. But everyone needs oxygen in their brain. I get my arm around his throat while he's bucking under me, and I start squeezing. His roars start wheezing. But Christ, he fights. His head jerks with fleshy thunks and I realize Hatchet's pounding his face in through the blanket from below.

And he's slowing. Getting sluggish. Real fucking sluggish. The muscles around his neck loosening up just a little bit. Gritting my teeth, I lock my arm tighter.

"*No! Not Stone!* Get Tusk—!"

Cherry's shout comes a second before agony rips through my shoulders and back.

Fucking tasers.

But shocking a guy's the wrong thing to do when you want him to let go of something. The muscles in my arms contract, and I sure as fuck don't let go when the stream stops.

They tase me again.

Again.

I scream through the third one, hear Cherry screaming for them to stop, but I'm not letting go. Not until this fucker is dead.

I'm getting there. He's limp. Now just got to make sure he doesn't get up again. I get a grip on his chin, ready to snap his neck.

Pain explodes through the side of my head.

STARS SWIRL BEHIND MY EYES. I'm lying on the cold ground with my face in the dirt. From somewhere nearby I hear Cherry's soothing murmur. And Victor ordering someone to check the restraints.

The restraints on Tusk. Because he's not moving. But he's still breathing.

Fuck.

With a groan, I sit up. Cherry's kneeling next to Hatchet, who's bent over and cradling his arm while she ties a torn strip of that blanket around his neck like a sling. At the sound of my groan, she glances over at me.

"Don't move yet," she says.

Not quickly, anyway. My vision swims.

"I'll be right back," she tells Hatchet, then scrambles over to me. "Don't move yet. Let me…"

Put her hands on my face, feel her way around my jaw and up the back of my neck, then forward over my scalp. I suck in a breath through my teeth when a gentle touch above my ear sends pain shooting through my skull.

Shit. I've felt this before. "Got a boot to the head?"

"Victor's." Her hands slide away. "I don't think it's fractured. But it'll be tender for a while. And we'll keep an eye out for a concussion."

Fair enough. "What's the other damage?"

"Electrical burns on your back." Her lips tremble. "And Hatchet's arm is broken pretty bad."

I don't give a fuck about any of that. "What damage did Tusk do on his way out?"

"Oh. He killed all three guards on duty, I think."

Didn't kill Tusk. But at least that sick fucker's good for something, and he got a little start burning down the Cage.

"Good," I say. "Fewer to put down later."

Her gaze lifts to mine. And there's that sweet, sweet rage. She doesn't say anything. Just nods, then goes back to Hatchet.

No longer touching me, no longer near me. I swallow the rot that pushes up through my chest, then look to Victor. The drill sergeant's mask is there, but he's pissed.

No need to guess why.

He glances at me, then to one of the guards. "Take him back to the barn."

No running today, then. I get to my feet. Thanks to Victor's boot, the change in elevation makes a few stars flash behind my eyes. But I don't even care about that.

I slow my stride as I'm about to pass by him. "Three

men, Vic," I say quietly. "So maybe you put in a word to your boss about putting me in the ring with Tusk. I'm still an unknown. Papa can make a fuckton of money with a good point spread and everyone betting on this asshole. But you've already seen me get close to killing him. You know he's a bad bet, but a whole lot of suckers will still throw in with him. So Papa'll get his earnings, and I'll take out the sick fuck who offed three of your boys."

He gives no response. Just looks to the guard, who shoves at my shoulder so that I get a move on. But I bet those wheels are turning.

They just need to turn fast enough.

SIXTEEN

It's two days before the doc arrives and can take a look at Matt's arm—and with him comes the Iron Blood and three new fighters.

So they found someone else to be bait. I don't know whether to be relieved that I wasn't forced to do it or horrified that some other girl got dragged into this. I don't know who. Probably someone the Iron Blood picked out, because they don't bring her here to stay like Lissa did.

But maybe it's like Matt said. Extreme situations cause extreme reactions. Emotions that don't seem right, but that you can't help feeling. Because I *am* relieved. *And* horrified. And terrified for Matt, because his arm's a mess. The best I could do was splint the break, then use ice packs for the swelling and aspirin for the pain.

In the medical stall, Victor watches over us while Matt sits up on the examination table. There the doc confirms what I feared. "It'll need surgery."

Which they don't do here. One of the other fighters needed surgery, too, for a fracture in his lower leg. Then they brought him back, he healed up—and died the next time in the Cage.

Because they give the guys time to heal, but not a lot of time to strengthen up again. Still. It's better than the alternative. And Matt won't have to fight again for a while.

"Okay." I grip Matt's good hand in mine. Both the doc and Victor know he's my brother, so I don't have to pretend anything in here. "So that'll be a few weeks he's gone?"

"More or less," the doc says, strapping the splint back on. "He'll be at my private clinic. Sedated and restrained, of course. And when I'm confident the arm is healing as it should, I'll send him back." He looks to Victor. "You'll take him? I understand that you are about to leave for your holiday. If you can make a detour to the clinic, that will make arranging transportation simpler."

Victor nods. "I'll do that. And you won't give us any trouble, Mr. Miller, because your sister's safety depends on your cooperation. Understand? You'll go real quiet and won't put up a fight."

Mr. Miller. Because they still don't know his real name. So he's Billy Miller.

Jaw hard, Matt nods. "Understood. I'll go quiet."

Both worry and relief fill my chest. Worry because I'll be alone. Relief because he'll be okay.

And the sick realization that Tusk's next fight will probably come before he's back. Before we can escape.

But I smile up at him. Because there's nothing else to do. "Be good, okay?"

His throat works but he smiles, then pulls me into a tight hug. Against my ear, he whispers urgently, "Don't wait for me to come back. Use the scalpel, then get out, contact my boss."

So the FBI can track down the doc's clinic and free Matt, too. I nod, hold him tight.

"Let's go, then," Victor says. "I want to get a move on."

Reluctantly, I let him go.

"You'll be all right, sis." Matt slides down from the examination table, cups my cheek. "Just keep on loving me, okay?"

Tears blur my eyes. "Always," I swear to him.

SEVENTEEN

STONE

ANOTHER DAY, STILL THE SAME—EXCEPT WITH Hatchet injured, my exercise group is down to one. And since Cherry's helping the doctor with the new guys, there are just two guards watching me.

And Victor, walking Hatchet out behind the barn. I see them as I head into the backstretch of the track, slowing as I realize where they're going. *Why* they're going.

Fuck.

Cherry said Hatchet's arm was broken bad. I've got

no love for any of the Eighty-Eight, but the asshole went to the mat for her. Now they're putting him down like a horse with a broken leg. So this is some fucking bullshit.

Hatchet's trying to talk Vic out of it. I can't hear a word he's saying but the body language is clear enough. Maybe the asshole doesn't know that the Eighty-Eight is everything Victor says he hates about motorcycle clubs. Maybe Hatchet's so desperate he'd say anything.

He's still talking even as Victor urges him onto his knees and points a pistol at his head. I round the curve that'll take me into the final stretch, and lose sight of them behind the barn. Then there's a long fucking delay. Maybe Victor is feeling generous enough to let the guy say his last words. But in the end, whatever Hatchet told him must not have made any difference.

The gunshot comes just as I hit five miles. Both of us crossing the finish line at the same time. But there's no winning here.

Only losing.

I'm wondering where they keep the guns when Cherry checks in on me, like she has each night before bed ever since I got kicked in the head. A guard stands a few paces behind her, but not paying close attention like they do when Victor's around. Their whole operation went slack as soon as he went on leave.

I'll take advantage of that, if I can. Either to get to Tusk or to get the fuck out—and take Cherry with me.

She asks her questions about whether I'm sleepy or dizzy or any of that shit. I'm not. And I've got my own questions.

"How much new blood came in?" There's someone over in Handlebar's stall. I haven't seen him yet, but he's spent most of the day crying.

A shadow moves through her eyes. "Three," she says quietly.

"Not lured in by your pussy this time."

She doesn't say anything to that. Just shines her little penlight into my eyes.

"Still pretty empty in this barn," I say. "And I saw another stall already opened up."

"Hatchet's?" She shakes her head. "He'll be coming back. They sent him out for surgery."

Surgery? Is that what they told her?

And she believed it?

But…hell. The asshole broke his arm helping save her from Tusk. So I won't lay that guilt on her. If she wants to believe he's out for surgery, I'll let her go on believing it.

"They put the third one in the other barn?"

"Yes."

"How's Handlebar holding up?" I know the answer, but I ask anyway.

Her gaze meets mine, worry darkening that emerald. "He's giving the guards a lot of trouble. And says he won't fight in the Cage again."

Of course he won't. Crash is dead, so he doesn't give

a fuck anymore.

I don't either. Except for two things.

"When's the next fight?"

Her lips tremble. "Four days."

Four days until Tusk's tenth win. "What are the chances they'll put me up against him?"

The look in her eyes says it all. *Zero chance.*

"On the benches, then."

They unchain us before we're ushered into the Cage. But Tusk will still be chained. I'll do it quick.

Alarm sparks in her eyes. After a quick glance back at the guard, she whispers tautly, "You can't. The guards will shoot you."

They probably will. Not that it makes any difference. I was a dead man the second that I laid eyes on this woman.

Urgently she leans in closer to the bars. "I can't let you do this for me."

"You think it's for you?" It's not. Not all for her. "I promised Crash that I'd do this."

And the days are going by so fucking fast, I'm running out of time to keep it.

EIGHTEEN

I didn't want to do this alone. But Matt isn't back yet. And I'm out of time.

Either I kill someone tonight…or Stone dies tomorrow. Whether he manages to save me and kill Tusk doesn't matter. If he attacks Tusk, the guards will shoot him. I might survive a rape. But Stone won't survive a barrage of bullets.

I tried to save him once, and failed. I can't fail again.

I *won't* fail again.

But oh my god, Matt was right. All the horrible things I've done so far are nothing compared to psyching myself up so that I can murder a man. I'm not even sure who is on duty tonight. But I've got to crawl across the top of the stalls, persuade him that I'm terrified and want to lose my virginity before Tusk rapes me, then while we're making out…slice his throat.

A part of me knows that it's not *wrong*. Not right, but not wrong. In some ways, it's no different than the men in the Cage—and I don't blame any of them for killing someone to save their families or to survive. I've been tossed into a cage, and killing someone else is my only way out, the only way I can save people I care about.

So I slide out of bed around midnight and change into my nurse's uniform, complete with stockings and heels—partly because I need to look sexy and partly because I might end up walking across the desert tonight. But I can't stop gagging on the vomit that climbs up my throat. My hands won't stop shaking. I don't know how I'm going to look sexy and lure the guard in. Instead I feel like I'm dissolving into bloody chunks from the inside out.

But I can't wait any longer.

Carefully, I clamp the handle of the scalpel between my teeth. When I'm at the control booth, I'll hide the scalpel in my dress, but don't dare crawl around with a razor-sharp blade against my skin.

Standing on the bed, I jump up and catch the bar overhead—and my hands are so clammy, I slide right off. I barely muffle my scream before hitting the mattress and knocking the wind from my chest.

Oh god, that hurts. Oh god.

At least I didn't land on the scalpel. Because it would be just my luck to have another plan go to shit and accidentally stab my own face.

Trying not to laugh hysterically, I lie there until I can breathe again. This time I wipe my hands on my skirt first.

I wince as my heels click against the bars when I swing my feet up. Heart pounding, I listen for any reaction. Nothing.

As silently as I can, I wriggle my way through the bars and lie flat across them. None of the guards are walking the aisle, though ever since Lissa was killed, three are assigned to night duty instead of two. But I don't see any of them. Light spills from the control booth and onto the opposite wall—which means the door's open. Maybe all three of them are in there. Or maybe two are in the break room.

I hope two are in the break room. If not, I'll be begging for a threesome.

But I bet they're in the break room. Victor returns tomorrow. And since he's been gone, Charlie's been in charge. None of the other guards respect his authority as much, and the continual grumblings from the ones who didn't go home over the holiday have sowed tension between them all since the others came back.

Crossing over to Matt's stall is old hat by now. But as soon as I'm there, I hesitate. Soft snoring comes from up ahead.

If the fighters are all sleeping, and aren't ready to rush the remaining two guards when I open the doors, this might all be for nothing.

One of the new guys is in the next stall, where Flack used to be. I don't know him well. As it is, I'm a little freaked out that this plan will fall apart when I try to cross his cell. I think he's the one I hear snoring, though. Airbag's in the next stall after that, and I'll be okay with him. But he's injured, so he can't be the one to lead the charge against the guards.

I need to get Stone's attention. I can do that from the stall across from his. Another new guy is in there. But when I went to check on Stone's head injury earlier tonight, the new fighter was already asleep. Hopefully he still is.

On my hands and knees, I carefully move forward. I'm just about to reach the new guy's cell when a distant *thunk* freezes me in place.

Pulse pounding, I wait. My panicked breaths sound so loud, rushing wetly past the scalpel clamped between my teeth. The metal against my tongue is making my mouth water, but I can't completely close my lips and so I'm drooling. Another hysterical, silent giggle shakes through me when I imagine my drool dripping onto the new guy and waking him up. Or trying to seduce a guard with spit all over my chin.

No other sounds. Just the rustle of a blanket and the creak of a bunk. And—

A thunderous *BOOM!* shakes the entire building. My muffled shriek is lost in the rattle of the roofing overhead and the shouts suddenly coming from each of the stalls, echoing through the stables. *Oh my god, oh my god.* I flatten myself to the bars, desperately trying to see what happened.

Did a truck hit the barn? Or was it an explosion? Whatever it was, it came from outside.

The guards don't know what it was, either. At the far end of the barn, Hotel and Tango burst out of the break room and into the aisle. I still can't see who's in the control booth but a shadow tells me he's standing at the entrance to it, shaking his head as if to tell the others that he doesn't have a clue what happened. One of their radios squawks but it's impossible to hear what's coming out of it over the noise the fighters are making. Most of them calling out, a few of them laughing. Tusk's banging on his bars and Stone—

—is staring at me. Though everything else in the barn has descended into chaos, it's as if he doesn't hear it. He's standing at the door to his stall and staring straight at me, eyes narrowed and jaw clenched.

Ice slips down my spine. Because I've seen that look before. Cold. Lethal.

Let's be clear, girl. Now *I'm mad.*

But why this time? Does he think I was trying to escape without taking the rest of them? Saving my own skin?

My throat tightens, then a splintering crash jerks my gaze back toward the guards and my heart nearly rockets out of my chest.

A man strides through the barn's open door—that he just kicked open. Light glints on a weapon. The guards pivot toward him.

What happens next is so fast that it's over before I can comprehend what happened. The three flashes from the muzzle. The sharp, snapping reports of gunfire. The guards falling to the ground.

Dead.

They're dead.

I lie atop the stall, shock and horror wiping every coherent thought from my brain. Still trying to understand everything I'm seeing. The orange glow of a fire outside silhouettes the gunman at the door. The light inside is too dim to make out his features but he can't be a cop or FBI. Law enforcement would have yelled out what they were before shooting the guards. Now someone else is coming in after him. A woman, her blond hair in a buzzcut. For an instant, she steps into the light spilling from the control booth, then heads inside that room. The first gunman starts down the aisle, glancing into each of the stalls.

Stopping in front of Stone's.

The fighters are in an uproar. Over all of the noise, I barely register the familiar *clunk* of a stall door unlocking.

No, no. Not *a* stall door.

All of the doors.

Oh my god.

Tusk's triumphant roar echoes through the rafters. Panic sends me scrambling back for the safety of my stall—but it's *not* safe, because now it's unlocked and the first place he'll look for me. I crawl past my cell and frantically squeeze myself through the bars over the doctor's office, trying to calm myself enough to think.

I've just got to get past him. How do I get past him? *Think.*

Forcing my breaths to slow and deepen, I drop from the bars and land next to the examination table. Quickly, I kick off my high heels. As soon as Tusk's inside my cell, I can sprint down the aisle. I'll be running toward the gunman. I don't know who he is, but I'll take the risk of being shot. Better than being caught by Tusk.

And if Tusk does catch me…I have a weapon. The scalpel's slippery from my drool. I wipe the handle dry on my skirt while creeping silently across the concrete floor. He probably couldn't hear me in here, anyway. Not with so much shouting echoing around inside the barn.

At the door I pause and crouch out of sight below the small window that'll give me a view of the aisle, gathering my courage. Just peek through. Watch Tusk go into my stall. Then run like hell.

Okay. I can do this. Holding my breath, I peek through the window.

And he's there. Tusk is right there. Looking back at me.

He grins.

Screaming, I stumble back. The door crashes open and his giant body blocks all the light from the aisle. His *naked* body. He's already hard, his eyes gleaming like his teeth, as if in anticipation of ripping me apart.

He stalks inside. Scalpel clutched in my fist, eyes locked on his, I circle around behind the examination table, trying to put *anything* between us. Oh my god, but he's fast. So fast. One second he's just walking and the next he's charging. Blind terror grips my heart. I turn to run and slam into a tray of medical equipment, sending it crashing to the floor.

Then he's on me. Screaming, I slash at his chest. I cut him, I know I cut him, but it's like he doesn't feel the blade at all. But one shove sends me flying and I hit the back wall so hard that stars flare behind my eyes. The explosion of air from my chest leaves me dizzy—then horrifyingly aware when he drags me down under him, shoving my thighs apart, ripping away my panties. Sobbing, I slash at his throat and only cut his shoulder before he grabs my wrist and pins my hand. Thunder cracks in my ears and he's all over me, crushing me beneath him, heavy between my legs and I can't breathe, I can't breathe.

But he's not moving. Not moving at all.

Because that thunder had been a gunshot.

And Tusk is dead.

On top of me.

With a shriek, I shove at his massive weight, scrabbling my way out from beneath him. The shadow of another huge form crosses the room, the dull metallic gleam of a weapon in his hand. New panic tears through me. Because this nightmare can't end like this. It can't.

"Please," I beg frantically as he comes closer. "Please, I don't care what you do to me. But please first let me find my b—"

Hard fingers shove fabric into my mouth, cutting me off. And it's *Stone*. Relief staggers through me, then vanishes again.

Because he's so angry. So savage as he hauls me close.

"All this time, you had a way out," he snarls viciously. "And a fucking *knife*. You could have escaped and went for help. *All this fucking time*."

No, I didn't. I *couldn't*.

Wildly I shake my head, try to tell him. I try to pull out the gag but he rips my stocking from my leg and ties it around my head, securing the wad of fabric between my lips. Fighting, I pull at the silk and a second later he binds my wrists behind my back. Movement to the left catches my gaze and I realize there's someone else in here with us.

The gunman. Oh god, oh god. But not just any gunman. The blue-eyed devil. The one called Gunner. Stone's friend.

The one who betrayed him. The man who put him in here.

But now Gunner came to free him?

Confusion and terror tangle in my chest. Then the world upends, and I cry out in surprise as Stone tosses me facedown over his shoulder. All I can see is the concrete floor and his gray sweats as he carries me down the aisle. Blood rushes to my head, my stomach hurting from panic and dread, my spit saturating the gag in my mouth.

We're getting out of here. I should be filled with relief but I don't know where we're going now. And I'm obviously not free.

Because I owe him. I remember Stone saying that. I owe him.

And that he'll collect.

A strange calm settles over me. Because I *do* owe him. So I'll pay up. As fast as I can. Then I'll go to the police and get help for Matt. He's safe for at least a few weeks at the doc's clinic. Papa isn't going to tell my brother that everyone at the stables escaped. They'll never admit that I'm gone. They'll just keep telling him to fall in line or they'll hurt me.

But I'll be out of their reach. And there's nothing, *nothing* that Stone will do to me that compares to what Papa might. I know Stone's angry. But I don't think he'd ever really hurt me.

I'm not so sure about his friends. And terror fills me again as I remember how, in my panic after realizing Tusk was dead and I might be next, I almost revealed that I had a brother.

Stone might not hurt me. But I can't risk *anyone* discovering who Matt really is. Especially anyone who's a member of an outlaw motorcycle club.

Heat flares against my side the moment Stone steps outside. Craning my neck, I catch an upside-down glimpse of the farmhouse engulfed in flames—and the other barn, too.

Horror crawls through my gut. Did his friends get the other fighters out first? Or are they in there burning? Desperately I twist and fight Stone's hold, trying to dislodge the gag.

"Settle the fuck down." His grip tightens, his fingers clamped on my thigh. "Unless you want me to march you over to Handlebar and tell him that Crash didn't have to die in that Cage. That if you didn't wait until you were saving your own goddamn skin, his brother could have been in a hospital weeks ago."

Handlebar. If he's out, then they must have freed the men in those stables, too. Relief fills my chest even as my throat tightens unbearably. I *did* try to get Crash out. Tried to get all of them out.

But that plan was too little, too late.

Abruptly Stone halts. The world spins again, the blood rushing from my head. Freezing cold metal bites into my bare skin as Stone sets me down in the bed of a pickup.

He leans in and grits out, "Don't fucking move or I'll round up every single man you caged up and bring them over here to use your pussy."

So…all one of them. Stone's the only one I lured in. Because that plan went wrong, too. And he thinks that I was just saving my own skin.

But until Matt is free, I'll go on letting him think it.

Defiantly I stare back. Daring him to follow through on that threat. Even though he told me once that he doesn't share. His jaw clenches, then he draws back and orders someone to make sure I don't move before stalking away.

I don't watch him go. Instead I watch the stables and farmhouse burn, while a riot of emotions storms through my chest.

Matt said my plans aren't shit; instead, the world is. And although tonight's plan went to shit…so much went right. I didn't kill a guard and free the fighters. But the guards are dead and the fighters are free, and it doesn't matter who did it. All that matters now is keeping Matt's identity safe until he's free, too.

Which is the same thing I've done for months. So everything has changed…but also nothing has.

Because Matt's life still depends on my silence. Because I've still got so much to hide.

And because with my luck, the world will keep on turning to shit.

NINETEEN

STONE

"Maybe not the best time, brother," Gunner says, his voice wary.

As if there will ever be a good time for this. A time when my chest isn't a rotted and ragged hole, a time when I don't feel Crash's body going limp against me and his spine popping apart with a twist of my hands, a time when I'll be a brother worthy of the name again.

There's no good time or bad time now. There's just a time to get shit done.

And this needs to get done.

It wasn't only the Hellfire Riders who made up the rescue cavalry. The Bedlam Butchers joined them. Handlebar's with a group of them now. No one's wearing a vest—won't give anyone a chance to point fingers later—but I know them. All of them dangerous fuckers, slapping Handlebar's back and laughing and celebrating his return.

Yet all that laughter stops when they see me heading their direction. Because I killed one of theirs. But I don't owe them a damn thing.

Handlebar, though. I owe him a hell of a lot more.

"I'm so fucking sorry, man," I tell him hoarsely. The heat of the fire's burning in my eyes, scorching down my throat as I spread my arms wide, welcoming what's coming. "I'll take whatever you got. Fists. Bullets."

I want the fists. I want the bullets. Either one is better than the agony ripping through my chest as Handlebar closes in on me, the grief in his eyes exposing a hole as dark and ragged as mine.

If he wants to fill that up with my blood, I'll let him. But I owe him something else, too.

"He gave me some last words for you." Though I don't know how I'll choke them out when I can barely speak past the raw ache in my throat. "If you want to hear them first."

His jaw clenches, the flames from the barn glinting in his eyes. Then he nods, his big hand clasping the back of my neck, pulling me in to rest his forehead to mine.

Just like Crash did when he told me this. "He loves you. You're the best ride partner he ever had." Fuck, I can't breathe again. "And you have to take care of his mangy cat."

A choked sound breaks from him. Then nothing for a long damn time.

His voice is real thick when he finally says, "I kill you now, we start a war between our brothers. But this ain't about them."

"No, it's not." And I'm not worth dying for. "When?"

"I've got shit to take care of first. I need to pull Crash out of the ground, lay him to rest where he ought to be laid. Then there's this fucking Cage. Because that killed him, too."

"We need to burn the whole fucking thing to the ground." Not just these barns. The whole goddamn operation. Because I've still got shit left to do, too. And I still need something to fill me up. Something that isn't soft and sweet, but as raw and as bloody as I am.

"Yeah." His grip tightens on my neck. "We take down Papa. We take out whoever the fuck owns the other stables. Then you and me…we settle up."

"Fair enough." I pull back, locking my hand with his, sealing in that promise. And fulfilling another. "Tusk is dead."

"Good. You've got Cherry?"

I nod. Yeah, I've got her. And I intend to keep her.

I should drop off her sweet ass in the nearest town

and never look back. But Papa and all the fuckers running the Cage will be searching for her.

Instead of them finding her, though, Cherry's going to give me what I need to find them.

But that's not the purpose in front of me as I head back to the truck. Instead I'm still seeing Tusk, pinning her beneath him. Instead I'm hearing Cherry scream. Instead I'm remembering the moment I realized that he'd gotten to her, and feeling like my whole world was about to end.

My whole world. If I needed a measure of how fucked up my head is, that's it right there. Because she's not even a fraction of my world.

She's just a girl I kissed in a bar. A girl who couldn't ever be anything more to me than that. Because she's a girl who's all about saving her own skin—and trusting a girl like that, a man not only risks himself but all his brothers, too.

I thought she did right by Crash? Nah. She did the bare fucking minimum.

That's the thought I hold onto as I jump into the back of the truck. The memory of Cherry out of her cell, with a fucking blade that she could have used at any goddamn time. The memory of Handlebar choking up.

Still gagged, she's sitting where I left her, back braced against wheel well and watching the barns burn. I crouch beside her.

"You're going to pay for every fucking lying word that came out of your mouth. You understand?"

Tusk's dead. But I've got one thing left to keep me going. And I know this girl now. She'll do what it takes to save her own skin.

Except she's not even listening.

I grip her chin, bring her emerald eyes around to meet mine. "You understand?"

Quickly she nods.

Yeah. She'll agree to any goddamn thing, and knowing that curls more rot through my stomach. I search her eyes, looking for the rage that I liked so damn much. Looking for any sign that she'll push back—like she did only a little while ago, when I threatened to let the fighters pull a train on her. Even gagged, she all but dared me to. Like she knew it was bullshit. But now there's nothing.

I shouldn't want her to do anything but fall in line… but fucking hell, I want to see something more in her than this. But the only flames in her eyes are flickering reflections from the flames consuming the compound. Jaw clenched, I let her go.

My head's so fucked up. And my heart, too. Because it took until now for me to ask Gunner, "Anna?"

"Safe."

A knot loosens in my chest. "And the fucker who touched her?"

"Taken care of."

Dead. The unwinding knot moves up into my throat as Zoomie climbs into the truck. Spiral's behind the wheel, Blowback's heading our direction. More trucks are being loaded up with fighters and getting the fuck out of here. Just about the whole club showed up to break me out. And it looks like it went off clean. No brothers lost.

But they'd have risked their lives for me. That's fucking everything.

And it's too much.

"I love a goddamn bonfire." Grinning, Zoomie takes a seat on the opposite tire well. "But we forgot the fucking marshmallows."

My throat's so damn tight. "Next time."

"Aw, look at you, you big asshole, promising to get kidnapped again just for me." She reaches over to playfully shove at my head before nodding to the woman beside me. "Who's the nurse?"

In that tiny outfit, still gagged by the panties I shoved into her mouth and the stocking that I tied around her head. The little skirt hardly covers her bare ass, and she's got her legs folded and tucked in so she isn't flashing everyone.

"Cherry," Gunner says.

She's staring at him. Not like girls usually stare at his pretty face. I'm the one who threatened her but she looks more afraid of him.

"Cherry?" Eyes narrowing dangerously, Zoomie says, "So why aren't we roasting her instead?"

"Because I've got something else in mind for her." That pulls her emerald gaze to me, and she draws in on herself when I add, "And I'm going to take a real long time to do it."

There. A little spark. A defiant lift of her chin. Just like when she was sucking my cock, making me come. When she was making the rot stop hurting so goddamn much.

But the hurt's what I deserve. So I focus on what I should be doing, instead—and that's what comes next.

Blowback vaults over the tailgate just as the truck starts pulling out. So almost everyone who makes decisions in this club is here. Thorne's not, but I figure the VP is holding down the fort at home, ready to bail us out if shit goes south.

But that means we're still missing one. "Where's the prez?"

I assumed Saxon would be one of the first through that barn door.

"With Jenny," Zoomie says quietly.

With his woman. But he wouldn't have stayed away for some small reason. Something in Zoomie's voice tells me this isn't a reason I want to hear, though.

And I realize there's someone else missing. "Red?"

Jenny's father. And a man who is like an uncle to Anna and me. A man who's been fighting lung cancer for months.

His face grim, Gunner nods. "He took his final ride."

Not going out the way the cancer would have gotten him. Going out on his own terms.

My throat closes up. "Who was with him?"

"Thorne and Saxon, and all of the old timers."

I should have been there. I should have fucking been

there for him. Should have said goodbye.

But the Cage took that from me, too. "When do we hit the Iron Blood?"

Blowback says, "Soon."

It can't be enough. "We'll have to keep a few alive so we can get to Papa. Fuckers who will talk. Maybe pick up some of the Eighty-Eight, too. Too bad there's too many of those Nazis to put them all down." The sound of a sharp indrawn breath has me glancing over at Cherry. I tug her gag from between her lips. "Who's Papa?"

Her throat works before she replies with a rasping, "I don't know."

"Don't lie to me."

"I'm not. I only ever heard them call him Papa."

"Handlebar said he had professional security. Who were they?"

"I don't know. I kept my head down and tried not to look at any of them."

"But you know what Papa looks like?"

She bites her lip, her gaze searching mine. Then she shakes her head.

A lie for goddamn sure. And since what she's saying is useless to me, I shove her gag back into place. She's still saving her own skin. Right now, she's more scared of Papa than she is of me.

That'll change.

She glances at Gunner again—just a swift, wary glance before averting her gaze. Ah, fuck. I bark out a laugh.

I know why she keeps looking at him like that. "Cherry thinks you're Strawman."

"My brother?" He frowns at her. "Why?"

"She saw him with the Iron Blood. Then saw you later—and never realized there's more than one asshole with such a girly mouth."

Cherry makes a sound, an explosion of breath through her gag. Wide-eyed, she looks from Gunner to me, then back again. Then her face crumples like she's about to sob, but it's choking laughter that comes out instead.

She buries her face against her bent knees, shoulders shaking. And continues laughing, a hysterical edge rolling through it.

Shit. I've heard laughter like that before. That's someone at the end of their rope. Months in this damn place—then in one night, witnessed guards being shot though the head, was attacked by Tusk and got her panties ripped off, then was gagged and thrown into a truck.

And some of that shaking seems more like shivering.

I grit my teeth, the urge to pull her into my arms and provide her with my own warmth a physical fucking *need*. But I won't. She's nothing to me.

A rolled-up sleeping bag and an insulated cooler tell me Gunner spent a day or two surveilling the compound before riding to the rescue. I drape the sleeping bag over Cherry's legs and front, and as her shivers begins to ease, that hysterical laughter starts quieting into small hiccuping breaths.

As if she's silently crying.

Fuck. *Fuck.*

I haul her sweet little ass into my lap. Her slender body stiffens against me, until I tell her gruffly, "We've got one blanket, and as soon as we hit the road and pick up speed, it'll be freezing back here. So just settle down."

She settles, laying her head against my chest, her warm breaths trembling across my bare skin. I tuck the sleeping bag in around her. This won't be for long. We're not riding to Oregon in the back of a pickup. Most likely we'll rendezvous with rest of the club at a staging area somewhere within a fifty-mile radius of the barns.

Only fifty miles of holding her like this. Too damn long to be sitting here with all of her softness seeping into me. And not nearly enough time.

But we've got time enough for something else. A little storytime.

I look over to Gunner. "So what the fuck took so damn long?"

TWENTY

I wake up when everything seems to sway to the left and strong arms tighten around me. I'm warm. *So* warm. I can't remember the last time I was. Disoriented, I don't move.

Then it comes back to me. The dead guards. Tusk. The burning barns.

Stone hauling me into his lap so we can share a blanket.

We're still in the back of the truck, though driving more slowly. I must have woken when we turned off the highway. No one's talking now. Apparently Gunner finished telling Stone about tracking us down, though I don't remember hearing the end of it.

I don't remember Stone removing my gag or untying my hands, either. But the bindings are gone.

Despite everything, I must have fallen asleep. Or maybe it's *because* of everything—my body's defensive reaction to too much stress.

Though I was holding it together pretty well until I discovered that if I hadn't mistaken Gunner for his brother, Stone would have never been in this mess. That I could have saved him, like I'd intended to. And then he'd probably have protected me, too. Found out what I knew about the Cage, and swooped in like his friends did tonight.

If I'd just looked a little closer at Gunner, Crash might still be alive—at least for a while longer. Stone wouldn't have killed a friend, Handlebar wouldn't have lost a brother. And Matt might have been free, too.

But *could have* and *might have* don't help me now. And they don't help Matt.

I don't think the Hellfire Riders would help Matt now, either. Not while believing he's a member of the Eighty-Eight. And I can't tell them the truth. He was certain that we'd both end up dead if his cover was blown because so many other agents have been killed.

Maybe the Hellfire Riders wouldn't do anything to him. They're obviously ruthless killers but I don't know if they're like the Eighty-Eight. The way Gunner and the blond woman came into the barn, so fast and deadly, the way they all interacted afterward, they seem more…like a SEAL team. Scary. But also organized, efficient. If they all came out of the military, a part of me wants to believe that they wouldn't jeopardize a federal agent's life.

But Victor's crew was military, too. So that's not a risk I'm willing to take.

The truck slows more. Gravel crunches under the tires. The road roughens, jostling me against Stone as we bounce over a rut and then come to a stop. Immediately there's a scramble of boots as the other Hellfire Riders unload.

I can't pretend to sleep anymore. When I open my eyes, I'm sideways on Stone's lap, facing the tail of the pickup. Everything's dark except for the headlights from a handful of vehicles. The bright glare from one prevents me from seeing much of our surroundings, but I get the impression of tall trees, catch the gleam of a few RVs. A campground, maybe.

Gunner's walking away from the truck. "You coming, brother? Your gear's in the fifth wheel, your bike's this way."

"My kutte?"

"Never found it."

"Fuck." Stone's hard fingers grip my chin, bring me to face him. In the harsh lights from the other vehicles, his face is all stark planes and angles, cut through by the white lines of his scars. "What'd they do with my vest?"

"I don't know." As soon as they loaded him into the van, Victor injected me with a sedative to knock me out again. "I don't know when they stripped you—at the barn or somewhere before that.”

A muscle in his jaw twitches. “If my kutte was at the barn, it probably burned.”

“Probably,” I say softly.

His eyes close, throat working as if he’s grappling with a strong emotion. Then he says flatly, “I’m handing you over to Spiral and Scarecrow for a day or two. You’re not going to give them any trouble, are you?”

I might. “Don’t hand me over to anyone. Just let me go.”

His eyes harden. “Let you go?”

“Yes.”

“Why the fuck would I do that?”

Why the fuck *wouldn’t* he? “Because you don’t need me. I don’t have answers.”

“Bullshit.”

“I don’t. But even if I did, I don’t know anything that you won’t get from any of the other fighters who were imprisoned in the barns.”

His soft laugh is devoid of amusement. “And I’ll have maybe a day or two to ask them. Those fighters are going to get to their families and hole up as fast as they can. You think Papa won’t come for them? And for *you*?”

Fear shivers down my spine. “I can hide.”

His eyes narrow. “Or run straight to the cops.”

That’s exactly what I’d do. “I wouldn’t. But even if I did, I wouldn’t say anything about you or your club. If that’s what worries you.”

His gaze goes *so* cold. "To save your skin, you'd open your mouth the second they put a bit of pressure on you. But that's not what worries me. What fucking worries me is that, after you tell them everything they want to know, they'll get to Papa before I will."

I *can't* let Stone get to Papa first. Not if it also takes the Hellfire Riders to the doc and Matt first. And anything I give them probably would.

Pressure builds in my chest, my throat. "What if I pay you what I owe? Will you let me go then?"

He goes still. "Pay me?"

Biting my lip, I nod. "You said you'd collect. So collect. Then let me go."

"I'll collect some fucking answers."

"I don't have any," I insist.

"Then how do you figure you'll pay up?"

"However you think is fair."

But I know what it'll be. And I don't care. My virginity has been a commodity for months now. At least I'd get to choose how to spend it. And choose who to spend it on.

If I'd met Stone in any other way, if that night at the tavern had been real instead of a lure…judging by my reaction to him, I might have chosen Stone, anyway.

He gives a harsh laugh. "You think that just because your little ass snuggled in against my dick gets me hard, I'll take a fuck in exchange for what I really want?"

Is it hard? Eyes wide, I stare at him. Paying attention now. And feeling the erect length pressing against my hip.

Oh. My breath shudders, my gaze flicking down before meeting his again. Heart thundering, I lift my chin. "I think it *is* what you want. You don't need me for info. You don't care about protecting me from Papa. And you plan to get more answers from the Iron Blood. So I think what you really want is your pound of flesh. Just take it, then—and let me go."

Expression suddenly feral, he grips my hair in his fist. "You think your pussy will make up for all that shit that went down?"

No. Nothing could make up for it.

But although I tremble, I don't waver. "Not Crash. And not your sister. But if making me pay will make you feel better…then I'll do what it takes."

Through clenched teeth he grits out, "All I want from you is information."

"I don't have any to—"

I gasp as his hands clamp over my hips and drag me onto his cock. My underwear's gone. Through the heavy material of his sweatpants, I clearly feel his erection, so hot and hard and long.

Harshly he says, "Since you're offering, maybe I'll just fuck the answers out of you."

Oh my god. My pulse rate skyrockets even as my inner muscles clench. "You can try," I tell him breathlessly. "But I don't have any."

That cold gaze sweeps my face again. A colder smile tilts his mouth. "We'll see."

We'll see. My heart is about to pound through my chest. "Go ahead, then."

"Now?" His big hand pushes between my thighs and I gasp when his fingers slick through my intimate flesh. His voice roughens. "Christ, you're so hot and ready. Did arguing with me do this?"

I don't know. But I *am* hot and ready. I can't believe it, but I am. And hotter when his fingers teasingly circle my clit. Biting back a whimper, I barely stop myself from rocking against him, seeking more of that light touch.

Barely stop myself from begging for more when he withdraws his hand. Eyes gleaming, he sucks my arousal from his fingertips before he stands, lifting me with him.

"Paying what you owe will cost more than a quick fuck in the back of a truck," he says, then looks to a man waiting nearby. "Take her to the ranch, put her in one of the cabins. No one touches her or talks to her until I get back."

"Will do."

Stone catches my face in his big hands, his eyes still cold as they search mine. "You think about what you just offered up. And about whether you want to change that deal. Because I'll take it, you understand? I'll make you pay—but I'll also make you talk. I'll have you *begging* to talk."

Nothing will make me talk. Not when it risks Matt's life. "And then you'll let me go?"

His jaw tightens and he stares at me for a long, long time. "Yeah," he finally says gruffly. "Then I'll let you go."

THE RANCH

TWENTY-ONE

STONE

Now that I'm out of the Cage, I ought to be getting shit done. But in four days, I haven't done shit.

None of the fighters from the barns knows a goddamn thing. At least not anything more than we already knew. So all the time I spent talking to them was a complete fucking waste.

And I can't get to the Iron Blood yet. I spent two days with eyes on the property in northern Nevada where they've got their clubhouse, but after the raid at the stables—and after Chef wound up with a bullet in his head and his house torched, courtesy of Gunner—their club goes into lockdown. Probably shitting their pants, thinking that whoever took out the stables is coming after them.

We *will* come after them. They can't stay in lockdown forever. Then we'll take their asses out. For that, I can be patient. Because putting the Iron Blood down is only secondary. They're just the muscle for the whole operation—and I want the head.

I want Papa. And since info isn't coming from the Iron Blood yet…I'll get answers out of Cherry, instead.

Whatever it takes to get them.

And sweet Christ, I've imagined all the ways. Four days of hurry-up-and-wait gives a man more time to think than is probably good for him. My dick's been a hot, heavy weight ever since she told me to collect what I owe. Ready at any minute to thicken up and follow through, fed by a steady stream of scenarios running through my brain. Getting those answers while I'm balls-deep, not letting her come until she's screaming what I want to know. Or making her come so many goddamn times that she's begging to tell me everything.

But that's just the *good* shit in my head. Because there's also the stupid shit that creeps up. Where she's not under me begging, but cradled sweetly in my arms. Confiding in me while I'm holding her tight, filling me up with her softness and smiles. The shit that makes my chest ache.

That's not what I need from her. I just need answers. Just need to get to Papa.

But something more important than him needs doing first.

I roll through Pine Valley just before noon on a Sunday. The town's about as dead as dead can be—and since Anna's car isn't at the Wolf Den, I head for home.

Head for home in a cage.

That's what I used to call any vehicle that wasn't a bike. Doesn't mean the same thing anymore, that's for fucking sure. But early December ain't the best time to be riding icy mountain roads between Nevada and central Oregon, so I'm driving Gunner's truck with my bike strapped to the motorcycle mount in the back.

Anna and I share a farmhouse a few minutes out of town. Pooled our cash and bought it together—though in truth, it's her house. The previous owner converted the second floor into an apartment that she could rent out, and that's where I live. But one day, I'll move out. Anna will stay, because she's made that farmhouse hers, renovating and decorating the rooms to her liking. To me, it's just a place to keep my stuff.

And although we bought it together, my name's not even on the paperwork. Supposedly that'd help protect her from anyone who might ever have a grudge against me or the Hellfire Riders. They wouldn't have an address.

That didn't work out too fucking well. Because it was here that Chef got to her. It was in the living room where she was taped naked to a chair.

Because I fell for a sweet smile and sweeter kiss.

My chest's a thick ugly knot when I pull into the drive. Truth is, I don't fucking deserve to come back. I should go to Handlebar now, let him settle up.

But I can't. Because there's still shit to do.

It's too late to turn around now, anyway. The truck has only just stopped when Anna's flying out of the house, leaping down the steps of the front porch with Daisy barking wildly at her heels. She's on me a second later, throwing herself at me and laughing as her arms squeeze me tight.

Thank fuck. She's all right.

She's all right.

I pull back to look down at her elfin face. She looks just like she always does. Like some delicate fairy. But that's only how she looks. She's a banshee under all that.

A banshee with tears in her eyes. Happy tears, but the sight of them rips my heart out.

"Aw, pipsqueak. Don't cry."

Her laugh is thick and watery as she wipes at her eyes. "I was just so happy to have the house to myself. I'm sad I have to share it again."

There's the banshee, making me smile. But fucking hell—she should never have been alone. Daisy's still barking, and all I can hear and see is her barking in that video while Anna's bruised and bleeding.

I take Anna's pointed chin in my hand now, examining her jaw, her mouth. Only the faintest sign of what Chef did to her. But even that faint sign is too fucking much.

She grabs my wrist. "I'm all right," she says softly. As if she knows that I'm still seeing her hurt.

And she's quietly telling me that it's not my fault.

It is. But I won't upset her more than my fuckup already did. This is my burden to carry. She's borne enough.

With a boulder lodged in my throat, I nod and let her go.

Her gaze searches my face. "Daisy's all right, too."

I know. She's dancing around my feet. But I can't even look at her. Both of them are out here and so damn happy to see me. Because they don't see what I am now. Everything on the outside's still the same, so they don't see the ragged hole filled with rot and shame.

I won't ever let them see it. Because here they are, shining with their love for me. I feel it, feel all that warmth sneaking in. But one day when they aren't blinded by their relief, they'll see what's beneath my skin.

I can't bear to think of that day. Can only think of what I need to fill me.

Getting to Papa. Burning down the whole operation. "You might be by yourself a little longer. I've got some business at the clubhouse that I'm going to be taking care of for a while."

Business with a hot cunt and a lying mouth.

Anna nods, still watching me so carefully. "Have you

seen Mom and Dad yet?"

Mom and Dad. Who'll take one look at me and see the corpse walking around inside what used to be their son.

"Not yet," I say and head past her. Because I can't fucking do this. I shouldn't be here. It was selfish to come here, to see for myself that she's all right, even though I'm the reason she was hurt.

I just need to get my shit and go.

"I told them you were coming back." Anna follows me toward the side entrance of the house. "But maybe you should stop by."

"I'll get around to it."

Some day when I can look them in the eyes. Some day when Mom won't pull me aside and get past my defenses with a few words, until I'm blubbering against her chest and telling her exactly what I've done.

I've got a feeling that day is never going to come. Better that way. They'll remember the son I was. Not the rotted and empty thing I am now.

Anna stops at the base of the porch. "Was Gunner with you?"

"No. He said he had some shit to take care of."

Like buying her an engagement ring. That's the one positive bit to come out of this entire fucking ordeal—that he and Anna got together while they were searching for me. That after ten years, the two people who I love the most in the world finally pulled their heads out of their asses.

But I should be happier for them. Should be over the fucking moon. But I'm just...numb. When I'm not hurting, I'm not feeling anything.

Except glad that my sister has Gunner to look after her. And that they'll have each other when Handlebar and I settle up.

Uncertainty tinges her voice. "Did Gunner say anything about...me and him?"

Just that he loves her. And that she loves him. Which I already knew.

But I shake my head. "Not a thing."

Because so much shit's gone bad. I'm not touching what they've found, not when I might poison it with the rot inside me. And I won't ruin the surprise of the ring he's buying for her now.

Her uncertainty deepens. Like maybe she's doubting Gunner now. But they'll work it out.

I open the screen door. Daisy's going wild, so fucking glad to have me home, her tongue lolling out of her doggy smile and dancing in circles around my feet.

And, Christ. I don't want anything more than to just kneel right here, let her slobber me with all her kisses. Dogs are so damn simple. They just love you. Just love you. They don't give a shit that you can still feel your friend's spine popping apart in your hands.

But Daisy deserves better than a man who'd kill a brother. Throat thick, I tell her, "Stay with Anna, girl. I'm no good anymore."

And that damn dog. Even after I slam the screen door in her face, she's still staring after me through the netting with her doggy grin, waiting to welcome me home, wanting me to pet her.

And I want to. Want to let that simple affection in every wild wag of her tail sweep all this pain away. But I've got shit to do.

I just shouldn't have come home.

I unload my bike and leave Gunner's truck at Anna's. It's cold as hell but the roads are dry, no ice or snow. About twenty miles on the other side of Pine Valley, an old dude ranch serves as the Hellfire Riders' home.

Another home I should stay away from. Riding a bike without wearing my kutte feels like riding with my skin peeled away, but as symbolism goes…it's real spot on. I've been wearing that vest since I patched in. Since I became part of this club and swore loyalty to every brother.

Now I'm returning to the clubhouse without my kutte. Seems like that should clue some of these assholes in, but every Rider I've met up with has greeted me the same way, real glad I'm alive and welcoming me back.

But they didn't know Crash. He wasn't any different to them than some other random man in the Cage. Gunner knew him, but we've been through so much shit together that I could probably shoot Gunner's mama and he'd give me a pass.

The other Riders, though…they ought to be looking

at me like the Bedlam Butchers did. Because Crash wasn't in our club, but he'd been my brother in the Marines, another man I'd sworn loyalty to. And I betrayed that loyalty, that trust. A fucker who does that doesn't deserve to wear a kutte.

The Riders are better off without me. But I need them to finish this shit. So here I fucking am.

The ranch sits about a mile off the main road. Dead grass blankets empty fields until a cluster of pines appears up ahead. The old lodge near that grove serves as the Riders' clubhouse. A string of what used to be guest cabins were built farther back. Cherry's stowed away in the last of them.

My gut clenches with the urge to head straight there, my cock stiffening as I imagine sinking into that hot and ready pussy. I barely touched her the other night and she got so damn wet. If it was arguing with me that had her dripping…fuck knows, I'll push her into fighting me again.

Maybe fighting me while I'm inside her. Staring up at me with that defiant lift of her chin, rage burning in her eyes, her tits bouncing as I pound my thick cock into that drenched little slit. Fighting, her pussy tightening up with every rough stroke, until she comes and her hot little cunt sucks me off like her mouth did.

I'm about to go off right now, just picturing it. The hard spike of my erection threatens to rip through my jeans.

But business first. And paying respects that ought to

be paid. Red's buried not too far from here.

I park my ride in the clubhouse's lot. This early on a Sunday, not too many brothers are here yet. There's the prez's bike and Blowback's. I expected them. A few others who are likely sleeping off whatever they were up to last night, a couple more on watch and serving as the clubhouse's security. Then Duke's and Bull's bikes—because they're always the ones on babysitting duty, watching over whoever we've got in the cabins.

Usually we're providing protection, and that's how the club makes most of its money. We could have gone the way of other outlaw clubs, running drugs or weapons or girls, but none of us have a real high opinion of fuckers who do that. Luckily, there's enough fuckers who do it— and enough bastards who run afoul of those fuckers and need protection from them—that we pull in a good sum. Usually the people we protect are pure garbage, but their cash smells the same as everyone else's.

It's not real often that we hold someone in the cabins to get information. The more expedient route is a sledge-hammer.

But Cherry'll be screaming for another reason.

I head into the clubhouse. Bottlecap's standing at the door—prospects always get shit duties until they're patched in as members. Duties that include fetching whatever a patchholder orders them to fetch.

I bump the fist he raises in greeting. "Did you pick up the shit I told you to get?"

"Food is in the kitchen just waiting to be warmed up, the other stuff is in a sack behind the bar," he says. "I had to hide them, or they might not have gotten to you still in their shiny packaging."

Because it looks like there was an orgy in here last night. Most of the owners of the bikes outside are sprawled half naked over the leather couches, legs and arms tangled up with miles of smooth skin belonging to club pussy.

Maybe celebrating the raid on the stables. Maybe just for the hell of it. Don't fucking know, don't fucking care.

Once upon a time, I might have been tangled up, too. Or might have responded to the texts I've received since I got my phone back, instead of deleting the messages and blocking the senders.

Hooking up used to be real damn easy. But I can't stand the thought of touching anyone now. Or the thought of anyone touching me. Not when I know they wouldn't really see what they'd be touching.

Cherry sees it.

She knows real well what's inside me now. And what *isn't* inside me now. Because she's willing to pay for the part that she helped tear out.

But I still won't let her touch me. Because I know what happens then. That sweetness, that softness starts filling me up. The pain starts easing.

And what would be left without the pain, the rot? Just emptiness. Just the numbness I can already feel moving in. If that fills me up, I won't give a fuck if I ever get to Papa.

Won't give a fuck about anything.

So I'll be touching her, fucking her. But she won't be touching me.

I take the stairs two at a time up to the second level. The main floor is the heart of the clubhouse, but executive meetings and the prez's office are upstairs. The door's open. Blowback's inside with Saxon, who's standing at the window, looking out over the trees. Despite the chair behind his desk, Saxon doesn't spend much time relaxing on his ass.

He glances over when I rap my knuckles on the door. He's a good-sized man, about an inch taller than me and thirty pounds heavier—every bit of it muscle— and a tough motherfucker. A few months back, he caught a shotgun blast in his shoulder and chest. Wasn't even healed up before he was out at the Eighty-Eight Henchmen's compound and taking out some skinhead trash. That injury's got to twinge hard now and then, but you'd never think it to look at him.

But then, he's always hard to read. Even right now, when he's staring right at me with those eyes made of pure fucking steel. He's not the smartest man in the Hellfire Riders—that's probably Gunner or Widowmaker. And he's not the deadliest—that's Blowback, no question. Not the most stubborn, either—that's likely Zoomie. But Saxon's right up there in every single category, and he's got something the others don't: the way he can look at a man and see everything that makes him up. Sees everything weak and everything worthy.

My chest tightens as Saxon steps forward. And he must see a sliver of something still worth having in the club, because he reaches out, locks his big hand with mine. A welcome back.

But he didn't miss the rot. Quietly he says, "Crash served in the same Force Recon platoon as you, yeah?"

Fuck. Throat too raw to say it aloud, I nod.

"Is killing these Cage fuckers going to help?'

This time I can speak. "Might be the only thing that does."

"All right, then." He sits back on the edge of his desk, folds his arms over his chest. "Where are we at?"

That's to Blowback, the Riders' warlord and Saxon's right hand man. There's a pretty good chance that he sees the rot in me, too…but just doesn't care. In a battle of 'who's the most fucked up,' Blowback might still win. Because I've got a big jagged hole in me, but I don't know if Blowback ever had anything inside him to start with. If maybe he was just born empty.

Empty, and deadly. In the Cage, I might have lasted a minute against him. If he was going easy.

All of which makes him real fucking scary, except he's got lines he won't cross. So the only people who need to fear him are those who threaten Saxon or the club.

I used to have lines, too. Until I threw Crash's body right over them.

Blowback lays it out for the prez. "I've got Spiral

and Picasso keeping eyes on the Iron Blood. Hashtag's running down a lead that the Butchers dug up on some girls who were being moved the same way their two men were moved up to the Cage. Might be another stable owner, might just be a money trail. But he's following it."

Since I've spent the past few days with Blowback, there's nothing he says that's a surprise. "In other words, a big fucking nothing."

"Until it's something," the prez says. "What about the girl? What'd she give you?"

I shake my head. "Another fucking nothing."

So far.

My stomach curdles when Blowback says, "Says her name is Christina Anne Miller. Twenty-five years old, born in Santa Fe. Doesn't know who her parents were, was raised in the foster system. Gave me the name of her nursing school, all the foster parents that she can remember, and her last address—which she says is probably rented out to someone else now that she's been missing so long. And says she doesn't know anything about Papa."

Christina Miller. "When the fuck did you talk to her?"

No one was supposed to talk to her. Or touch her.

"Saxon sent me in a couple of hours ago." Blowback shrugs, maybe knowing that going in pissed me off but there's not a damn thing to say when the prez tells him to. "Not a word was true."

Hold up. "What?"

"There's no Christina Miller. No one with the birthdate she gave me registered at that school or in the New Mexico foster system. Every other piece of information that I checked also fell through. But it was a good story. Might have held up if someone didn't know how to dig under the first layer. Consistent, too. I bet if you ask her, she'll give the same details."

Like something she practiced over and over. Maybe for three months.

Saxon's eyes narrow. "Why's she still hiding?"

"She's afraid of Papa," I say. "And not afraid of us."

"I led by saying we'd protect her," Blowback tells us, lips quirking. "Might be she didn't believe me."

Didn't believe the scary fucker with dead flat eyes. "I might get more headway in that direction."

The prez nods. "Try that. But I don't give a fuck who she is. Just what she knows, even if it's not about Papa. Because every string we pull might lead to him. So how did she get picked up? These assholes snatch a girl, usually the girl ends up being sold. So how'd the nursing angle come into play? Was that even legit?"

Yeah, it was. "She's got medical training of some sort. Maybe a nurse, maybe a paramedic. Might be a link to the doctor."

"Anything there yet?"

I shake my head. "I never saw him. And every fighter who did describes him as a whole lotta medium topped by pervert hair. Medium coloring, medium build, medium height."

"What the hell is pervert hair?"

"A combover."

"Ah. Yeah. Fuckers just need to shave that shit when it starts falling out." The prez's gaze sharpens. "But this girl spent more time with him?"

"She did." And must have picked up more than just 'medium' from him. "The drill sergeant, too. Victor. He had Papa's direct number and my sense is that Papa hired his militia as a separate deal from the Iron Blood. But I figure he'll be the hardest to pin down. He's smart enough to go to ground and stay hidden for a long time—unless he plans to come gunning for revenge over what we did to his boys."

Saxon frowns. "You think him gunning for revenge is likely?"

"Hard to judge. He hates bikers. But he's not stupid. Maybe fifty-fifty."

"So look for him and watch for him coming." The prez nods. "Anything else?"

"Might be," Blowback tells him. "I'm setting up a meet. Someone who used to be with the Devil's Hangmen, might have info to trade. You want in on that?"

That last part was directed at me. "Yeah, I do."

Because Crash and I killed two of the Devil's Hangmen in the ring. Those assholes used to be friendly with the fuckers who run the Cage, until the powers-that-be decided the club screwed them over. Now the Hangmen are pretty much scattered to the wind. Probably running scared.

But I'm not surprised Blowback dug someone up. And I won't be surprised if 'setting up a meet' turns out to be that he's got the man up on a meat hook somewhere.

"That it, then?" the prez asks.

"Yeah. I'm gonna go work on Cherry." Work on her real damn hard. "But heading out to pay my respects to Red first. How's Jenny doing?"

Red's daughter, Anna's best friend—a woman I've known my whole life, and who is the prez's woman now.

"She's hurting, but she's holding up," Saxon says, his jaw clenched. Because he's hard to read…but not when it comes to Jenny. Worry is written all over him. "She's already back to work."

Of course she is. That's Jenny, and how she deals with hurt. She finds something to keep herself busy.

And me…I find a hole to fill.

TWENTY-TWO

For four days, I don't do anything but sleep and eat, then sleep some more. I still wake up before six, my body's alarm clock set to get ready for the day. But there's no Elton, no *clunk* of the unlocking door. So I just close my eyes and sleep again.

Maybe it's just another reaction to stress. Maybe it's because I feel so safe.

And that's probably the greatest danger in this place—thinking it's safe. Getting too comfortable, because I'm warm and no one's telling me to smile, and they bring me more good food than I can eat. But the truth is...I'm still in a cage.

So on the fourth morning, I begin looking for a way out.

It quickly becomes apparent that there's not supposed to be one. It's just a single-room cabin with a small bathroom that holds a toilet and a shower. There's one door—with a deadbolt that can only be unlocked with a key from inside or outside. The window beside the door is shuttered closed. On the back wall is another window, but with bars over the glass—which isn't glass at all, I realize, but a thick plastic. No doubt chosen so that it can't be broken or shattered. Outside, a few trees grow by a stream. No one to signal to for help, unless the deer around here are super smart and can talk. But the one deer I see just stares at me with big soft eyes before wandering off.

In the main room, a full-sized mattress—thick foam, no box springs—rests on a simple wrought-iron bed frame...with all the joints welded together. So no taking it apart and whacking someone. A small electric stove keeps everything warm, and I'm not messing with that. Not when I'm locked in here with no escape route and not really sure if anyone will hear me screaming 'Fire!' In the corner of the room, two wooden chairs are tucked under adjacent sides of a small square table.

In the bathroom, there's not much more. Just a toilet, which doesn't give access to the flush mechanism or offer any easy way to muck up the workings—the same kind they had in the stables. Like there's some kind of prison supply warehouse for toilets.

But there's a vent in the wall over the toilet. The slats in the vent are tiny, but when I stick my fingers through, there's nothing blocking the other side. Just cool, fresh air. The vent itself is a rectangle that's maybe eight inches by eighteen inches. Narrow, but so were the bars over my stall. As long as I can get my skull through the opening, I should be able to squirm the rest of me through. And if I can't, then the rest of me is breakable.

I stand on the toilet rim to study the metal frame, and hope lifts through my stomach. Screws fasten the frame to the wall, the screw heads flush with the metal surface.

Not easy to remove. But removable.

I spend the next hour looking for something to use on those screws before giving up. Obviously they don't leave anything in here that's pointy and metal. I'm ripping my fingernails to shreds, trying to get the screws to twist even a little when I hear a key scraping into the lock.

Shit.

Hurriedly I get my ass out of the bathroom. The sound of my door unlocking isn't as scary as it was in the stables. But I don't want anyone to know what I'm doing. I don't think they'd hurt me. They'd probably make sure the vent was no longer an option, though.

Until Blowback came today to ask questions, the only visitors I've had were Duke and Bull, who check in on me and bring me food. Not that they told me their names. I had to read their vests.

But this has been different from the stables, too. Though some of the fighters gave me shit—some literally—most were okay. Some were friendly.

No one is friendly here. And I can't expect them to be. In the stables, we were all in the crap together.

Here, I'm the girl who helped kidnap Stone.

But this time...it's Stone who comes in.

He shoulders open the door, carrying in a few bags and a canvas duffle. I stand stock still in the middle of the cabin, with a storm of emotions building into a hurricane in my chest. The urge to run to him, to jump into his arms as if greeting a long lost friend. The surge of heat over my skin as I remember the last discussion we had. *Maybe I'll fuck the answers out of you.* And sheer relief, because it's been four days and no one has told me what he's doing or where he's been, even though I knew that he might be going after the Iron Blood.

But he looks...okay. Most of his injuries from the Cage have healed, no matter how much he wanted to keep them. That's just what injuries do. They heal.

On the outside, at least.

And on the outside, he's dressed like the first night I saw him. Casually, simply. Jeans, boots. A thick faded hoodie instead of a thick worn flannel. No vest, though. Maybe because he didn't find it.

Or maybe because he doesn't intend to wear anything for very long.

He turns and locks the deadbolt again. Tucks the key

into his right pocket. Not leaving again right away. With my breath coming unsteady and fast, I glance at his bags. One is a plain paper sack the size of a grocery bag and the other looks like takeout.

But that duffle suggests something more.

I swallow hard. "If those are clothes, it looks like you're moving in."

"Maybe for a few days." His voice is low and gravelly, his eyes skimming me from head to toes, as if taking in the messy bedhead, a face without makeup, and the giant T-shirt that replaced my filthy nurse's uniform and serves as my only covering. "That depends on you."

"Does it?"

Slowly he nods. "And whether I need to use what's in the fun bag."

"Which one's the fun bag?"

He reaches into the paper sack…and pulls out a ball gag. Still in the clamshell container. As if purchased just for me.

I'll make you pay—but I'll also make you talk. I'll have you begging to talk.

There's other stuff in there, too, though I can't see what. Just the impressions of more containers against the sides of the sack.

Heart thundering, my gaze flies to his again. I clasp my fingers together to hide their nervous shaking. "I hate to point out the obvious, but if you use that gag on me, I won't be talking very much."

And he grins. Oh my god. Just turns on that crooked, laughing smile that he wore so often before Victor showed him the video of his sister. My stomach clenches, longing tearing through my veins.

I've missed that smile. So much. And didn't even realize it until this moment, when that grin warms and opens everything within me.

He drops the ball gag back into the sack, then heads over to the table and sets down the takeout. "But like I said, that depends on you. So let's talk a while first—and share something that we missed."

That storm of emotions swirls through me again as I watch him pull out containers of turkey, mashed potatoes, stuffing. Thanksgiving dinner. Not just sharing a meal but sharing a missed holiday.

"I couldn't escape before that night," I blurt out, my chest aching. "I had the scalpel but I also knew that I'd only have one chance. And that I'd have to kill the guard. But I didn't even know if I could follow through. The whole time that I was preparing myself to get up there and do it, I almost kept puking. That's why I waited. Because I didn't know if I could kill someone. And I was afraid of how it would affect me after. So I kept hoping for some other option."

His steady gaze is on me through that rushed speech. "How it would affect you after...like how it affected me?"

"No," I tell him, my throat raw. "I knew it wouldn't be that bad. You had to kill a friend. I would only be killing a guard I knew. But…every other plan had fallen through. Like the one with Crash. I wouldn't have needed to kill anyone at all—just make them sick on laxatives so they'd get out of the control booth and I could free everyone. But that didn't work. So I was afraid of failing again."

He regards me quietly. Then nods. "All right. But tell me—are you planning to escape again? Maybe watched to see where I put my key? Maybe thinking of bashing me over the head and grabbing it?"

"If I can," I tell him. "Because I'm tired of being locked up."

"Fair enough. And if you get past me, you're free to go."

I stare at him. "Really?"

"Sure. If I get bashed over the head by a girl who weighs in at maybe a hundred and ten pounds soaking wet, I deserve to be the laughingstock of this club." He pulls out a chair. "Now, sit."

Oh god. I shouldn't really laugh about whether or not he'll free me when he's the reason I'm imprisoned. Biting my lip against a smile, I sit and grab a paper plate. "Shouldn't you be sharing this with your family, instead? I can't imagine they celebrated while you were gone."

And in that respect, I was luckier than he was. Because it wasn't a dinner, but I did get to spend Thanksgiving with my family. Not that it was a good holiday—it was the same day that Tusk attacked me and broke Matt's arm. But I spent a lot of time with Matt that day and the next.

"They didn't." He scoops out a load of potatoes. "But

if I sat down with them, that wouldn't be celebrating the holiday, either. Instead they'd either spend the whole damn time asking how I was, or spend the whole damn time *not* asking how I was but still wondering. And I'd spend the time insisting that I was all right. So instead I'll spend the time with someone who doesn't need to ask, and who I don't need to lie to."

Because he's not all right. Hesitantly, I say, "Are they okay? Your sister and your family? I know it's not right for me to ask but…I'd like to know."

His jaw clenches. "So you can share some guilt, too?"

My throat tightens and I nod.

"Well, take a load off. Because they're fine."

"Like you are fine? Or for real?"

His mouth quirks. "For real. Now eat your fucking meal."

"Okay." But I don't go for the potatoes, though they look buttery and delicious. I drag the pumpkin pie in front of my plate, cut out a slice, then see the look he gives me. "If I've learned anything these past months, it's not to wait around for the good stuff. So I'm eating dessert first."

That grin flashes again. "Then cut me a slice, too."

I do, carefully scooping the pie out while he shakes a can of whipped cream.

He waits for me to dig in, lets me enjoy a few bites before asking, "Who made the meals in the stables?"

I shrug, because I truly don't know. "I assumed it was someone up at the farmhouse, because the guards delivered the trays to the stables every day—and who is going to make daily deliveries to the middle of nowhere?"

"So maybe one of the militia? Or the Iron Blood?"

"Or someone they hired specifically for that purpose. Planning and cooking that many meals had to be almost a full time job. Whoever it was, I never saw them or talked to them."

He nods, eyeing me speculatively. Maybe surprised that I answered at all.

But in the past four days, I've thought a lot about this—about how much I'll say. There's some things I can't give to them. Like Papa or the doc. Not without risking Matt. But the other stuff? I don't see how it would hurt. And if I give them as much as I can, maybe they'll let me go earlier.

Because four days have already passed. And I'm not panicking about the time yet, because either one of two things has happened: after the raid, Papa decided to destroy everything connected to him and that might draw the attention of the authorities. In that case, Matt's already dead. But I *can't* think that. So I have to believe in the second scenario—that Papa won't tell Matt what happened at the stables at all. Matt's supposed to be in the clinic for a few weeks. So he'd stay quiet there. After that, Papa might move him to another stable, if there is one. Or sell him to another stable boss.

Right now, though, I kind of know where Matt is. And I'll know for a few weeks.

But why doesn't Stone already know about the meals?

I finish my pie and consider having another slice before reaching for the stuffing. "I know your friends killed the three guards in our barn…but did they kill *all* of the guards at the compound?"

"Yeah."

"So there's no one left to ask?"

"Unless we find Victor. What do you know about him?"

"Nothing. Truthfully," I say when he eyes me in that speculative way again. "He didn't give *anything* away."

He nods. "I believe that."

"But he recognized your Force Recon tattoo."

"Did he?"

I nod. "When we watched the video of you. When… Strawman showed it to us."

Who isn't the same man as his friend. I'm still trying to accept how that one fact could have changed everything for Stone…and for me.

"Where'd you watch the video at?"

"I don't know. I don't even know which town we were in. It was a yellow house with a pink sink and bathtub."

"Maybe I can get that out of Strawman."

I snort. "The same way you'd get it out of me?"

He gives me a slow, slow smile that curls heat through my stomach. Oh god. Maybe I shouldn't remind him.

Or maybe I should. Because I *do* owe him.

Though I don't know why I'm so okay with the idea of him collecting.

Heart pounding, I ask him, "What about the Iron Blood? Were you able to get anything?"

He shakes his head. "They're on lockdown. So you're all I've got."

"But I don't have much to give."

"No description of Papa at all?"

Torn, I swirl my fork through my potatoes. But this is just like everything else. I can give him a little. And maybe he'll let me go.

My chest lifts on a deep breath. "Well…he looks rich."

"Rich?" A laugh rumbles from him. "How do rich people look?"

"He's got rich-people hair."When his laughter deepens, I lift my hands helplessly. "You know what I mean, right? I'm not around a lot of rich people, but all the older men cut their hair the same way. Like presidents do."

"I know what you mean," he agrees, amusement deepening his voice. "What color?"

"He was white. But tanned."

"And his hair?"

"Dark brown with some silver in it."

"So fifty, maybe sixty years old?"When I agree, he asks, "Build?"

"Healthy. Tall. Not as tall as you. Maybe six feet. And although he was in shape, not big and muscular. Not like you. More like he plays tennis. Or spends a lot of time on a yacht."

Stone grins. "Like a rich person."

He's teasing me. I flush, but I'm laughing, too, as I nod and take a small bite of potatoes.

Then my laughter dies when he says, "And the doctor?"

Fear twists in my belly. I don't dare lie. Other fighters saw him, too. So I won't give Stone anything that he doesn't already have if I describe him.

"He's just…regular. Receding hairline and a"—I sweep my hand over my head to illustrate a combover. "Kind of a round face, but otherwise just average in every way. Just like your average neighborhood doctor. His manner, too. Mostly pleasant and kind and helpful."

"Helpful, how?"

"Well, like…" I push my sleeve up to my shoulder, show him the matchstick-sized implant under the skin of my upper arm. "It's birth control. He inserted it when I arrived at the stables, because he knew that eventually…"

I'd be raped. Or used as a prize or bait. Or forced to give a reward.

Stone's gaze hardens. "So you were grateful to him?"

"I was," I admit. "I knew he wouldn't stop any of it—if Tusk came after me, he wouldn't have stepped in front of him, just cleaned me up afterwards—but it was like he tried to make the things we couldn't avoid easier for us. And I figured he was there for the same reason as everyone else, that Papa threatened him somehow. But he never said anything personal, if that's what you're wondering."

"I'm more interested in his skill set. Did it seem like he specialized in anything?"

I've been thinking hard about this, too. Trying to figure out what kind of private clinic he might have. But my answer is truthful. "Nothing that stood out. He seemed like a general practitioner, to me."

"If we downloaded photos of licensed doctors in that area, could you pick him out?"

Excitement crackles through my stomach. Because I *could*. "Probably." Then conceal what I find until I go to the police. Or if I get to the cops first, suggest the same thing. "Though I don't even know what area we were in."

"Nevada. North of Reno." He unzips his hoodie and shrugs out of it. Because it *is* warm in here. Since I'm only wearing this shirt, I've got the heat up high. But it's even warmer now. He's wearing a T-shirt underneath, the cotton stretched across his broad shoulders and clinging to every heavy muscle. "That where you're from?"

Not even close. I shake my head, biting my lip and setting down my fork. "I really don't have any more to tell you. Can't you just let me go?"

"I could. But here's the problem." Expression hard, he leans back in his chair. "My brother Blowback came in to talk to you earlier, yeah?"

"Yes."

"And he's real good at digging up information. So he found out that everything you said to him was a lie. Your name, your birthday, everything. Christina Miller doesn't exist. You made it all up."

My heart rate spikes. "I didn't. Just because I'm not

active on Facebook or online doesn't mean I don't exist—"

"I'm not talking about Facebook. I'm talking about public records—and some not-so-public records. Every damn thing you said." A muscle works in his jaw as he stares at me. "So I've got to wonder if everything you just said to me now is a lie, too."

It wasn't. "It was the truth. It was all the truth."

"Maybe." His eyes narrow. "But if what you said is true, then I think what you're lying about now is claiming that was *all* you know."

My throat closes up. And I just stare at him. Because there's nothing left to do.

He reaches for the whipped cream, squirts a mound onto another piece of pie. "How about we start this again. What's your name?"

"Christina—"

"No." He cuts me off almost gently, setting the can aside, leaning in with his gaze searching my face. "You think I don't get it? You were locked up. Now you're locked up again. But the difference between here and there is that the second you get out of here, Papa will get you. And maybe you're thinking that you can run to the cops, but that's a real bad idea, because a man like Papa will have dirty cops in his pocket."

I know he does. That's why I have to go to Matt's bosses. But I *can't* say that.

"But we'll protect you here," he says, his voice strong and steady, his gaze unwavering. "You give us Papa, and we'll take him out. After that, you'll be safe anywhere you go."

Oh god. I believe him. And I would do what he said in a heartbeat…if Matt wasn't still out there. If I didn't think that Stone and everyone in his club would put a bullet in a member of the Eighty-Eight if they came across him. Even then, Matt is probably safer being known as a Henchman than known as a cop.

My voice is nothing but a strained whisper. "I just don't have anything more to give you."

"Maybe you don't think you do." Still gentle, he asks, "Where'd they grab you?"

"Las Vegas," I tell him truthfully.

"Why were you there? Visiting or working?"

"I…" Oh my god. I don't have a story for this. Because the only people who might have looked at Christina Miller knew exactly how I'd been taken. And they never cared why I was there. But this should be simple. Why do people go to Vegas? "I was with a bachelorette party."

"Were they nabbed, too? Is that why you fell in line—Papa threatened your friends?"

"No. It was…just me."

"So there will be a missing person's report out on you. In Las Vegas, about three months ago."

Oh my god. Would there be?

But…no. Who would have reported me missing? Who knew I was in Vegas? Only Matt.

So if Stone wants to search down that road… "Maybe,"

I tell him.

"Only maybe?" His eyebrows arch. "Nice friends you have there, not caring that you disappeared."

Shit. "Yeah, they're all bitches."

"And you're lying to me again."

"No—"

"*Why*, though? To save your own skin? You'd be better off putting yourself in my hands than in Papa's." His eyes narrow. "Are you protecting someone? A friend? Someone at home? We'll protect them, too."

And put myself into his strong, capable hands. But that can't be what he's really offering. I believe Stone wants Papa. But he has no reason to protect me—and has every reason to hate me.

But this is the danger, isn't it? Feeling safe here. When I shouldn't.

"So that's what this really is," I say, my heart a heavy and aching lump. "You come in here with turkey and pie, and say you'll be my friend if I'll just stop lying. But I'm not the only one who is lying here. Because I'm the last person you'd want as a friend."

"It's a shame that you're so fucking smart." Those eyes go cold. So cold as he sits back again, spreads his hands. "All right. You want the truth? *I've got nothing left.* Nothing but finding Papa, putting him down. And I don't even care if it kills me. As long as he's dead first. So there's nothing, *nothing* that'll put me off getting answers from you."

A clog burns in my throat. Nothing left. Though he

does. I've seen how much he has. He's told me how much he has. A family who loves him and friends who will burn down the world to find him.

"Don't take this the wrong way, because I'm not being facetious," I tell him thickly. "But you need to get help. A therapist or someone."

He barks out a laugh. "Yeah. So they can sit me down and tell me where my life went to shit? But I already know that one. It was when I fell for all the lies that a girl with a sad smile was telling me."

My breath hitches painfully. "I'm sorry."

"Sorry." Teeth gritted, he sits forward. "That's the only thing you say that sounds true. And I just don't get you. Papa locked you up. Would have given you to that sick fuck as a prize. Made you play bait and punished you by making you suck my dick. Aren't you pissed? Don't you want him dead, too?"

I do. So much. But I want Matt alive more.

I shake my head.

"I see it, you know," he says gruffly. "All the rage that peeks out. And I think I'd like some of that for myself. Better than rot. Or nothing."

But it's not better. Anger's only gotten me into trouble, like when I went after Tusk. Or made me hate myself, like when I took it out on Stone.

He's watching me again, reaches forward to cup my jaw, thumb sliding over my trembling lips. "You're real scared, aren't you?"

Not for myself, as he seems to think. But scared for Matt. Scared that another plan will go to shit.

"Yes," I whisper—then gasp as he hauls me forward out of my chair, then sits me on his lap, straddling his heavy thighs.

Heart thundering, I brace my palms on his chest. His big hands are clamped around my waist, his thumbs slowly rubbing circles on my belly. We're face to face like this, our eyes and mouths on level. And so close.

"How about we start over one more time?" His voice is a low, gravelly rumble. "Not to where I started asking you questions, but all the way back to that tavern, and the moment I turn around to see a girl staring at me. And I stare right back. Because she's so damn pretty. Even with that ridiculous hair."

"The wig?" A surprised little laugh shakes through me. "The Iron Blood said I wasn't sexy enough to lure someone in."

"Yeah, you were. Especially in that dress that hid absolutely nothing." His hands coast up my sides, molding the cotton of my shirt to my skin as closely as the dress did. "But that wasn't what hit me so damn hard. Instead it was the look in your eyes. Like your whole world was pure shit. Like you were searching for a way out, and maybe I was it."

"That sounds about right," I whisper past the unbearable ache in my throat.

"Was it? Then you found the right guy. Because I've got a few soft spots."

None that I can feel. Quietly I ask, "What are they?"

"Dogs. Kids. Girls in trouble." His hands come up to cup my face. "You were obviously in a hell of a mess, and I decided right there to get you out of it. Hopefully while you were riding my dick," he adds wryly.

Another laugh shakes through me, but I can hear the thick and watery tears that I'm barely holding back beneath it.

"So I'd already decided to help you. Just because of that sad look in your eyes." His jaw tightens. "Then you start talking to me. And I'm thinking, 'Fucking hell. I *like* this girl.' Because you're ticking all my boxes. You're funny, smart, sexy—and while I'm planning to take care of whatever put that look in your eyes, *you* are taking care of *me*. Trying to fix me up, make me stop bleeding. So here's this girl, obviously needing something from me, but not making a big show of what she's doing. Like she's a girl who would take care of anyone who needed it. Not because she wants something but because she's just…kind. And good."

His face swims in front of mine, my eyes burning. "No," I whisper brokenly.

"Yes. So when I first saw you, my plan was to help you out. Get you a ride out of town, maybe some money if you needed it. But it wasn't long before I realized that I'd be an idiot to let this girl go. That maybe I should take her home and clean up whatever trouble she's in. Because a girl like that—so sexy and sweet and good—I'd do anything in the world to protect her."

Chest hitching with silent sobs, I shake my head. Because I sensed this then, too. What he was. What could have been.

What can't be. Not after what I did.

"But you know when I was sure?" His voice deepens, and I go still when I feel the warmth of his breath against my mouth. "When I kissed her. Because she kissed me as if I was all that she wanted, too. As if she'd never met someone like me before. And as if she wanted more of me so fucking bad."

So bad. So much. When I feel the gentle press of his mouth to mine, my lips part and I taste cinnamon and sweetness and salt—and Stone. Everything I want, everything I need.

"Just like that," he says huskily against my mouth. "I'd fucking love to go back to that with you. To where we were before all this rot got into me, before all the lies. You want to start over, too?"

Longing spills through me. My breath shudders as I nod.

He gently lays a string of kisses along the line of my jaw. "So tell me what to call you."

Grief freezes me in place, ice that immediately cracks into painful sharp pieces. Because nothing is the same. But nothing has changed. And I can't go back.

"Cherry," I lie.

His body tenses. His hand fists in my hair, and I gasp

when he pulls my head back, forcing to meet his cold, cold gaze.

"That was the wrong fucking answer," he grits out, and surges up out of the chair. Carrying me with him—and snatching up the fun bag. "Because that girl, I figure she was trapped in a bad situation and in way over her head, but trying to do the best she could. That girl doesn't owe me a damn thing. But Cherry, she was just saving her own skin. And she owes me everything."

I do. I know I do. So I'll pay.

He sets me on my feet in front of the bed, stares down at me. I stare back, chin lifted and jaw set, determined to see this through despite the trembling wracking my body.

His eyes narrow on my shaking fingers. "Sure you don't want to try again?"

"I'm sure. I'll pay what I owe. Then you let me go."

"Let you go?" Lips whitening, he bends closer to snarl into my face, "I'll let you go when I get answers out of you."

"Then good luck, because I don't have any!" I snap, then shove against his chest. "So just get on with it!"

He does, shoving me back—not even hard, but I go sprawling across the bed, my shirt flying up and thighs splayed wide. Oh my god. Getting me right into the perfect position for a fucking. But then he just stands there.

Trying to open the clamshell packaging on the ball gag.

I snort out a laugh, closing my legs, pulling my hem down. "You can't get answers with that anyway. Remember?"

"Just take off that damn shirt." Frustration hardens his face as he grips the edge of the package, and the plastic tears between his big hands with a horrible screech. He tosses the gag to the bed, pulls off his own shirt. "And spread your legs."

"Why?" I pick up the red ball, the straps dangling. "Since you need my mouth to make me talk, are you gonna gag my vagina, instead? But how will you fuck me, then? God, I'm starting to think you're not very good at this 'making me pay' thing."

His hands go still on his belt buckle, head bowed and teeth gritted as if trying not to laugh. The he shakes his head, opens his belt and tears the leather from the loops. "You think you have any fucking idea how I'll make you pay? You think you know what's coming?"

I chortle. "Probably not me!"

He lunges toward the bed, eyes feral. I shriek when he's suddenly on top of me, denim-covered knees planted on either side of my hips, hands cupping my face.

"God fucking damn your fucking mouth." His chest heaving, he bends his forehead to mine, his eyes closed. "I don't know what's worse. You lying with every word, or how you keep making me *like* you."

My heart squeezes into nothing. "Probably that you like me," I whisper, releasing the gag to skim the backs of my fingers down his whisker-roughened jaw. "Or the lying wouldn't matter."

"Luckily, I've got a solution to both." Hard fingers

grip my wrist. "And don't touch me."

With my dead fish hands. Hurt spearing through me, I push at him—then struggle more when I realize what his solution to the problem of my mouth is. Because I'll pay what I owe but it's still not easy to let him gag me. I jerk my head to the side when he attempts to fasten it, pushing at the smooth rubber with my tongue, trying to dislodge the ball.

"Fuck yeah, girl," he groans harshly, pinning me down with his weight. "Keep fighting me."

Thorny need scores my senses at that rough command. He wants me to fight? I'll fight. Wildly when he pulls straps out of the fun bag and ties my wrist to the wrought iron bedpost, and I use my left hand to yank at the gag. Then I'm pinned beneath him again while he fastens my left hand. I squirm and buck, his erection a solid rod behind his zipper and lodged right between my thighs, and the fighting feels so good.

Until he backs off the bed, breaths harsh through clenched teeth, his cock a giant bulge straining the front of his jeans. He snatches my ankle and winds another strap around it, my screams muffled by the gag as I kick futilely at him. By the time he's got my other leg tied, my thighs spread wide, we're both flushed and sweating, and I'm so, so wet.

Stone stares down at me, eyes burning. "Where'd you get that shirt?"

Which I never took off. Too late now that I'm tied to

a bed. My only answer is a laugh into the gag.

"It looks big enough to be Bull's." Fiercely he grips the wide neckline. "But all I know is that it's not mine."

Cotton shreds, then burns across my skin as he yanks the entire thing away from me. Leaving me naked. Exposed.

His gaze hungrily moves from my wide eyes to my heaving breasts, then lower. "Christ help me," he mutters. "You're already soaked."

So I am. And fuck him. I strain to close my legs even a little. I can't.

With a rough laugh, he moves in closer to the side of the bed, shucking his jeans down his hips. Oh my god. I've seen him so many times without clothes—and have seen him erect before, up close and personal. But on my knees in his stall, with Victor looking on and rage swirling through everything else, Stone's cock was something that I'd be doing stuff *to*. It wasn't doing stuff to me. Not filling me up. Not fucking me. So it looked big then but now it's just *huge*, veined and thick and flushed an angry red.

He looks down at me, gaze half-lidded, his big hand stroking. "So you think you know what's going to happen now, yeah?"

Need clenches my inner muscles. Because I know.

With a soft whimper, I nod.

"Nah. I don't think you do. Or you'd already be talking." He licks his bottom lip, gaze between my thighs. "I'm going to use that wet little fuckhole real good. Until you're either screaming for more, or screaming for me to stop."

Oh god. Or maybe I'll be doing both. I don't know. I don't have a lot of experience with this.

Probably should have told him.

"And when I'm done using that little hole, I'll ask you again what you know. If you give me good answers, you'll get what you want and I'll let you go. If you lie…then we'll start all over again. You understand?"

That I'm about to be repeatedly and ruthlessly fucked? That Stone will ram that big cock into me over and over again?

Body trembling with both nervousness and anticipation, I nod. Nervousness starts tipping the scales, tension tightening my muscles when Stone climbs onto the bed, kneeling between my spread thighs, his heavy shaft jutting out and the thick head glistening with pre-cum.

Eyes locked on his dick, I pull desperately against the restraints.

"I'm not fucking you yet." He bends over me, his powerful arm braced beside my shoulder. "This is just playtime first. You'll know shit's about to get real when I grab that box of condoms over there. Because I ain't ever been in a girl without a rubber, and I'm not about to start with pussy used as bait."

Fucking pig. I snarl against the gag and his gaze flares hot.

"Hell, yes. Give me that rage. Just fucking burn me with it." His hand cups my jaw, fingers pressing into my cheeks, his voice hollow. "Spit at me all the hate that I deserve and no one else will give."

I…can't. My body shudders again as his teeth graze my neck. He wants to collect what I owe him. And I can give him a fight. I can give him anger.

But I can't hate him. Because he doesn't deserve that. No matter what he thinks.

Rage, though. Okay. As his tongue traces a hot, shivery path along my throat, he reaches down between my legs. I can't stop my moan when his fingers slick through my folds, delving between them to find my entrance.

His voice is a rasp against my ear. "Thought I'd have to play a long time to get this fuckhole ready. A girl tied up and paying what she owes. Figured you'd be dry as a bone. Instead you're real eager to be used, aren't you? Just fucking dying to pay up."

I hiss out a wet, furious breath. Fuck him for saying that. For making my reaction to him sound like something I should be ashamed of, instead of what it is.

He does this to me. The fucking asshole. He does this. From the first damn time I met him, he had me wet and squirming on that barstool. He has me wet and squirming now, then gasping when a blunt finger pushes past my entrance.

His mouth goes still against my neck, a ragged groan ripping from his throat. "Christing hell, you're so goddamn tight. Fuuuuuuuck." Harsh breaths burst against my skin as he presses deeper, as I helplessly moan and arch my hips.

"I take it back. You aren't wet enough. Don't know how I'm going to get my cock into you at all."

But he will. I know he will. Little sparks flare behind my eyes as my inner walls stretch and burn, adjusting to the thickness slowly working deeper.

And I'll burn hotter when it's his cock. I'll have to.

I want to.

With another groan, he begins pumping his hand, driving into me again and again. "Never felt a pussy this tight. No wonder they used it as bait. Man gets into this, he'd follow you anywhere. Probably why Crash was so damn calm when he decided to go. He'd fucked this tiny hole, so he already knew what heaven felt like."

The pleasure that was spilling through me sharpens to a painful edge and I spit a muffled *fuck you* into the gag, my body stiffening, my pussy tightening around the finger fucking into me.

"That's right." His voice roughens. "Get real pissed. Then remember it was Papa who decided to put him in that Cage against me, and tell me what I want to hear. You gonna tell me?"

With enraged, sobbing breaths shuddering against the gag, I shake my head—then cry out when he screws his finger deep before withdrawing and lifting his head. His eyes are hot when he licks my arousal from his finger.

"Your anger tastes real good, Cherry. Can't wait to eat it all up." Lazily he reaches down to jack his cock, my chest heaving and hollowing between us with every breath.

I watch his fist stroke his shaft, entranced as a bead of cum slides from that fat crown and drips onto my belly, then his voice has my gaze flying to meet his again. "But first I'll go back to that night at the tavern again, do every damn thing I wanted to then. And have a good taste of the rest of you first."

Beginning with my breasts. Stone bends his head, and he sets my nipples on fire with his mouth, sucking and licking the throbbing tips. Then rubbing his face against the soft mounds, his whiskers rasping my skin, as if not just tasting me but taking in every inch of me with every inch of him. Fingers wrapped around the straps tied to the bed, I try to brace myself against the onslaught of sensation—but there's no bracing. There's only being dragged along for the ride.

Then his hand settles between my thighs and his fingers begin teasing my clit, just teasing and teasing while his cheeks hollow and he sucks harder on my nipple. Head thrown back and spine arching, I try to fight this, too. But it's good. So good. My legs begin shaking uncontrollably. Each slippery pass of his fingertips over the most sensitive part of me seems to pull at every nerve until all I feel is Stone touching me, his tongue and his hands and then he pushes a finger inside my slick channel. The orgasm slams into me with it, and I scream into the gag when my pussy clamps down, my hips bucking wildly as I try to ride it out.

But all I do is ride his hand as I come. Thunder pounds through my head, Stone's harsh groan echoing with it.

Then his curse as he lifts his head from my breast. Voice sharp with irritation, he calls out, "The fuck is it?"

Over the storm of my heaving breaths, I barely hear the muffled reply. Through the door. Because someone was out there. Knocking. I can't make out the response, only the hiss of Stone's breath through clenched teeth. He abandons the bed, snatches up his jeans. But he doesn't put them on, just pulls the key from the pocket. From the duffle he digs out a pair of sweats and hauls them up to his hips.

I whimper, desperately aware that I'm tied spread-eagled on a bed, naked and flushed from my orgasm, with someone I don't know on the other side of that door.

Stone shoots me a fierce look. "Not a fucking sound."

He can't be worried about who's there. Not here on club property.

But I should have realized. He doesn't share. Not even the sounds I make. And not the sight of me. He only opens the door about six inches, then blocks the view into the cabin with his body. I can't hear any of the short conversation, but when he draws back and slams the door, he's holding a wad of cash. He drops the money onto the table, then digs around in his duffle again and pulls out a phone.

Whatever he sees on the screen make him smile. A genuine smile, as if it's good news. He types something out as he returns to the bed, then drops the device right next to my leg.

Oh, that bastard. Putting that phone so close to me. Putting escape so close. But I'm tied and can't reach it.

His lazy grin says he knows exactly why I'm glaring at him. But I can't keep glaring. Not when his fingers scratch at his broad chest, then slip down his washboard stomach and into his sweats. He drags out that thick cock, and everything inside me tightens again.

His big fist strokes his length from root to tip. "You remembering how it tastes?"

My gaze shoots to his again. He's watching me with narrowed eyes, no longer smiling, his expression hard and intense…and so hungry.

And I'm so ready.

"You think I'm going to fuck you now? Nah, not yet. We've still got a long way to go before that, making sure you get every bit of punishment you deserve." His hand jerks harder, rougher, and I can't stop watching. "This looks real fucking familiar, doesn't it? Except it was me tied up while you sucked on my cock. But what's *real* similar is how you're about to discover how goddamn hard you can come, even when you hate the fucking sight of the person who's getting you off."

He's all wrong. I don't hate him. Shaking my head, I try to deny it but go utterly still when he climbs onto the bed again…but lower this time. Settling his shoulders between my thighs.

Sheer need rocks through me like an earthquake, leaving me shivering and shaking. Just a little tease from his fingers made me come harder than I ever have from my own touch. And now he's going to lick me?

Oh god. Oh god.

His head dips toward my pussy, his warm breath wafting over my slick folds as he says harshly, "But here's the difference in this scenario: Men, we only come once. Twice, if we're real lucky. But you? You're going to come over and over again. Until you break and give me what I fucking want."

I'm not going to break. I'm not.

But I fight again, wildly pulling at the restraints and bucking beneath him, because I don't know how much I can take.

Hard hands clamp over my hips, forcing me to still. His thumbs spread me open, exposing my clit to his hungry gaze. The way he looks at my pussy is devouring me already, consuming every bit of my resistance from the inside out. Desperately I close my eyes, as if that will shut out everything that's coming.

It doesn't. It doesn't shut out anything. Not his mouth, so hot and hungry when he dives right in. Not his groan of pleasure when his tongue slicks through my folds. Not the shattering ecstasy when he begins sucking on my clit.

Oh my god, his mouth his mouth *his mouth*. Unable to move away from the devastating pleasure of it, not even able to writhe my hips, I can only take what Stone gives. And he gives so much. Or he's just so greedy. I don't know if there's a difference between taking and giving when his tongue slides over my clit again and again, if he's good or bad, I just know that I'm coming and coming, and that he groans in satisfaction while his mouth rides out the helpless convulsions of my flesh.

I'm still gasping, quivering when he bends his head again.

Each time takes longer, but Stone never seems to tire of eating my pussy. Instead each orgasm that he wrings from me only makes him hungrier, his groans deeper, his tongue rougher. But I reach my limit when he's sucking my clit to a fifth screaming orgasm, when coming isn't even a pure pleasure anymore but a hot agonizing release of the tension he'd built inside me. As my breath heaves in ragged little sobs, he kisses his way up my stomach, past my breasts, then looks down at me.

Gently he cups my face, his thumbs wiping the drool from the corners of my lips. "Done?"

Shuddering, I nod.

"You have anything to tell me?"

I shake my head.

"Then I'm going to fuck you real hard and real good." His gaze searches mine when I nod again. "You got any fight left in you?"

None. My entire body is limp beneath his.

His mouth quirks. "Maybe next time I'll let up sooner, then. But now that little fuckhole is so wet and soft, I could carry a tank between my legs and I'd still slide right in."

Into me. A shiver of anticipation works through my

depleted flesh.

"You want it, yeah?" His voice hardens, his fingers tangling in my hair, keeping my gaze direct on his. "Because I'm into rough but I'm not into rape. You nod so it's real clear. You want to be fucked?"

So much. My vigorous nod takes all the energy I have left.

Face stark with need, he leaves the bed. Another knock sounds at the door as he swipes the condoms from the fun bag, but he doesn't even glance that way before heading back. Eyes on me, he rolls on the latex sheath and climbs over my splayed form, his powerful thighs braced between my legs, one hand gripping his turgid shaft and the other sinking into the mattress beside my head as he lowers himself over me.

Aiming his erection to my center, he groans as the thick head parts my pussy lips. "Thought there was nothing better than your taste. But *this*. Just the fucking feel of you."

And the feel of *him*. His body so big and heavy above mine, his cock so thick and long between my thighs. Renewed pleasure sparks through me as he slides the crown up and down through my wet slit, my spent muscles coming back to life and quivering. Whimpering softly, I cant my hips upward.

"You asking to be filled with this big cock, girl?" The blunt tip of him teases my entrance. "I'll give it to you."

He abruptly surges forward—coming down over me, but not inside me, his body covering mine.

"Get the fuck out or I crack your head open." His voice is so cold, so dangerous. "Three seconds, brother."

Blowback. Who is inside the cabin. Looking at us with no expression—and no fear or apology, despite Stone's threat.

And despite the fact that I'm naked and tied to a bed and gagged, with Stone on top of me, his dick a hot iron rod against my belly. Heat rushes to my face. The muffled sound of panic I make is followed by Stone saying coldly, "Two seconds."

"We need to head out for that meetup."

"It can wait an hour. Or two."

"It can't. We arrive late, he'll be gone."

Stone's breath hisses through his teeth, a sound of pure frustration. "Turn your back until I cover her up."

Blowback doesn't, those empty eyes scanning the pair of us again. "This isn't who you are, brother."

Stone's body tenses to steel above mine. "It is now."

Blowback shakes his head but turns for the door. Stone rears up, grabbing the edge of the comforter and folding it over me before untying the straps around my wrists.

"Looks like you got a reprieve," he says harshly.

It doesn't feel like one. Not with this need aching so deep inside me. Lying on the bed and watching him go only feels like a punishment, not a reprieve.

He doesn't leave the key. Doesn't leave the phone. And a few minutes later, Bull comes through the door and clears away the turkey dinner and silverware.

I sigh in frustration, then search through Stone's duffle—just clothes, including a few items in my size with tags from Target still attached—before turning toward the fun bag. A whole lot of things in there to screw me with, but nothing to unscrew a vent frame.

Just my damn luck.

TWENTY-THREE

STONE

The meetup is a two-hour ride south, at a tiny casino outside of Klamath Falls. Blowback and I head inside, surrounded by cigarette smoke and the jaunty tunes coming from the slots. The entire place wouldn't fill up the lobby of a Vegas casino, and most of the seats are empty.

"Who we looking for?"

Blowback sits down at a penny slot. "He'll find us."

Fucking great. I take another machine, positioned so we can watch each other's backs, and feed the slot. A meetup with one of the Devil's Hangmen ought to be right at the front of my mind.

Instead I'm just thinking of how sweet Cherry's pussy tasted. How tight she was around my finger. How damn close I came to getting inside her.

And how all those jagged edges in me softened, even though I didn't let her touch me. Which means I should be thinking twice, three times about touching her again. But knowing I won't be able to stop myself, because she feels so damn good.

It also feels real damn good to be getting shit done. If this asshole ever shows up.

About twenty minutes pass before Blowback stands up, heads for the little restaurant at the back of the casino. All but empty here, too. A pair of senior citizens sit at a table near the front counter. There are more booths up in the back, and a man sitting in one of them, wearing jeans and a flannel and a baseball cap. I know that face.

Creek.

He ran with the chapter of the Hangmen who tried to take over the Eighty-Eight's territory after we burned down the skinheads' compound. The Hangmen's prez got real greedy, and tried to push the Riders into joining up or running off. They torched Blowback's garage and apartment, got their hands on Zoomie.

This fucker was a part of it all. But if he's got info, I'll listen. Then maybe do the same thing to him that I did to Sherlock in the Cage.

Blowback slides in across from him. I take the seat next to Creek and get real close, because I'm just pushy that way.

He's eyeing Blowback, jaw set and looking irritated as hell. "The fuck?"

"I trust him."

"Doesn't mean shit to me."

Blowback shrugs. "Maybe not. But I figured you two might get along."

Creek doesn't like that answer. And I don't know what the hell is going on. They're talking the way brothers do. Short and simple, with a lot more being said than what's coming out of their mouths.

"You left a fucking mess of those barns," Creek tells him now.

"The way everything burned, I didn't think we left much at all. You got any trace pointing back to us?"

"Not yet."

"You won't."

"If I do—"

"It'll vanish." Blowback pins him with a flat stare. "Yeah?"

"What have you got for me?"

"This."

Sliding his phone across the table, Blowback shows him a photo. Creek touches the screen and zooms in on the two people seated together. I recognize one—Paladin, the fucker from the Iron Blood who I fought before meeting Cherry. Don't know the other.

"Goddammit," Creek mutters, rubbing his face. "That's Gillam. Dirty fucking asshole."

"They met up before the Iron Blood went into lockdown," Blowback says. "I intended to have a conversation with Paladin. Saw this, instead."

And I'm catching up. Slow. But finally getting there.

Creek is a cop. Or a federal agent. Most likely FBI, if he's looking at the barns.

"That'll get you more than trace gone. I've lost too many agents because this fucker exposed them." Jaw clenched, Creek studies the photo another second before shoving the phone back to Blowback. "What do you want?"

"Papa."

"Papa who?"

"Don't fuck with me."

Creek's eyes sharpen. "Got more than a name?"

"That's why I'm looking at you."

A muscle works in the man's jaw before he sits back. "We barely have shit on the stable bosses. Just names floating around. Papa. The Greek. Caballo. Red Eye. A couple more. Though Red Eye's vanished—but I don't need to tell you."

Red Eye. The slick fucker who got Zoomie. I never asked how Blowback knew where she was, because she'd been taken by the Devil's Hangmen but he went after Red Eye's vehicle, instead.

Now I know. Creek tipped him off. Which makes me

feel just a little more generous toward the man.

Blowback tilts his head my direction. "He was in the Cage."

The cop's attention is suddenly all over me. "Did you meet him? Papa?"

"No."

"What'd you pick up?"

"Not much." Sure as fuck not anything I'll tell Creek. Not if it puts him ahead of me getting to Papa.

Blowback taps the table. "Here's the deal before I give you that photo. We share information. And if you flush out Papa first, you give us a head start."

Creek shakes his head. "I can't—"

"You can have all of the other stable bosses. And if you get one, the rest will unravel. We just want Papa."

"I can take Gillam down without the picture."

"Not as fast. How many more agents do you want to lose?"

"You're a fucking asshole." Frustration pours off the man. "What do you have?"

"Everything Stone saw. Vehicles they used, the setup at the fights, the men Papa hired as guards and whose bodies were in those barns."

Creek looks to me with a frown. "They weren't Iron Blood?"

I shake my head.

"And a girl," Blowback says.

My heart jacks into my ribs. "Hold up, brother."

"What girl?"

"Was in there three months. Met Papa, played the nurse and played bait, saw everything," Blowback tells him and Creek looks like he struck gold.

"And she's not on the fucking table," I snarl. "She's not."

Creek casts me a disbelieving glance. "That much information could bring down the whole operation."

"And get her killed."

"We'd give her protection—"

"While you've got a dirty cop on your payroll?" Any protection he provided would be pure bullshit. "That cop can't be the only one in Papa's pocket. So not a fucking chance."

His mouth presses into a tight line, then he nods. "All right. Give me a week. I've got a friend in the Marshals who can get her into WitSec fast and deep, without leaving a trace of who she is or why she's in."

Witness protection. Where'd she disappear for good. Chest tight, I tell him, "Not gonna happen."

"Then get what you can out of her and give it to me. For now. Eventually, I'll need her to come in, get everything on record, get her into protection. What have you gotten so far?"

Fucking hell. "Not much. She's scared. And lying her ass off."

Creek huffs a quiet laugh. "Smart girl, then."

Yeah, she is.

Blowback frowns down at his phone. "Did your teams move in against the Iron Blood?"

"Not mine," he says. "Why?"

"I've got eyes on them." Blowback sets the phone on the table, presses the speaker. "What did you see?"

Spiral's voice comes through. *"Three black Escalades roll up to the clubhouse. A dozen men in suits went in carrying crates between them. Looked real friendly at first, like the Iron Blood was looking to buy some shiny new guns to defend themselves."*

"License plates?"

"Covered."

"And they were still on lockdown?"

"Seemed like. No one else had been in or out until these guys. We don't know who started shooting, just heard the gunfire. Fully automatic. Went on for a while."

"How many came out?"

"Ten living suits, carrying two dead or injured. And they set off a big explosion and a fire behind them. Clubhouse is toast, along with everyone in it."

"Did you follow the vehicles?"

"As far as we could—which wasn't far. The explosion brought in the flashing red lights fast, so we figured that not bringing attention to ourselves and laying low was our best option."

"Good call. Lay low for another day or two," Blowback tells him.

"Will do."

When Blowback disconnects, Creek says dryly, "I'm going to need that gentleman's name and a witness statement from him."

Yeah, that's funny. "Handlebar said that Papa's security rode around in similar vehicles, wore the same suits, were just as professional."

His eyes narrow. "You think Papa took out his own muscle?"

"I think he's making sure there's no one who can point in his direction," I say, my gut knotted up. Someone like Cherry. I knew that her being out in the wild would be dangerous. But Papa just took out an entire fucking club to cover his tracks.

That's…I don't even know what the hell that is. Some next level shit. Most assholes who are afraid of the cops tracking them down would just go to ground, change their names. Then if the cops follow all the leads back to him, he's already a ghost.

So that means Papa has a personal life—or a public life—that he wants to hold onto. And he'll go to real extreme lengths to keep it.

Creek looks grim. "Does Papa know you have the girl?"

I shake my head. He wouldn't know to look at the Hellfire Riders, either. Or the Bedlam Butchers. We covered our tracks after the raid. And only Handlebar knows that I took her with me. Other than that, we were just random fighters who got freed with the others.

A short buzz sounds, and Creek glances at his phone. "Looks like there's a fire at the Iron Blood's compound. They're sending me in. Sure would be nice if an anonymous asshole sent me a photo showing a cop talking to a member of that club. Then maybe we can chat more about a head start on Papa."

"I've got audio, too," Blowback says. "Telling Paladin about a man you planted in the Eighty-Eight."

"You fucker." Creek's jaw clenches as he stares across the table. "If I give you a head start, it has to be clean. If you're still on site when we show up, I can't do a goddamn thing for you."

As long as Papa's dead, I wouldn't care. But I tell him, "We won't be there."

"Then give me the recording." He slides out of the booth. "And get something out of that girl."

Get something out of her. Then give her up to the feds.

Only one of those will happen. When I take out Papa, she won't need protection.

But she needs it now.

The knots in my gut don't ease up the entire ride back home. Which is real stupid, worrying so much. Those Escalades rolled in so easy because Papa was friends with the Iron Blood. But Papa's men couldn't just waltz into the Hellfire Riders' clubhouse—or the cabins. And the Riders are there, looking out for her. Protecting her.

But I thought the same damn thing about my sister. And those fuckers still got to Anna.

I'm not getting to Cherry right away, either. After hearing about the Iron Blood, the prez calls an executive board meeting of the club's officers. Everyone else on the board is already at the clubhouse by the time Blowback and I ride in. So I head straight up to the second level, because the faster we get this done, the faster I'm back with her.

And it needs to be done. This will all be about threat assessment and figuring out next steps. But walking into the conference room, instead of a dead serious group of bikers, I'm greeted with laughter and hoots of approval as Gunner shows off his new tattoos. One I've already seen in the picture Anna sent to me earlier—her name scrawled over his heart. But the one across his back is new: the Hellfire Riders emblem.

I've got one just like it. So that even without my kutte, I'm wearing my patch. But this asshole never tatted up his pretty, pretty skin before. His cult of a family considered marring their natural beauty sacrilegious or some shit. So it looks like he finally made a complete break away from them.

Gunner sees me, grins and calls out, "She said yes!"

I tell him the same thing I texted to her. "And it's about damn time."

"Yeah, it is." He laughs and hauls his shirt back on. "So let's get this shit over quick, because this is my engagement night."

I'm all for quick. So is everyone else, most likely. Usually these board meetings are on Wednesdays, and the veep's wife provides a spread for us to eat while going over the club's business. But there's only one bit of business for today and no vittles to linger over.

I head toward my usual seat at the conference table, stopping to bump fists with patchholders I haven't met up with since coming back—and pausing when I pass by Duke and Bull.

"Who's got eyes on the cabin?" We've got plenty of cameras on the property, one aimed straight at Cherry's cabin, and the video is monitored from the security station within the clubhouse.

"Grasshopper," Duke says.

Good. That patchholder won't fuck around in there.

"No prospects on security," I tell them. "Shit just got bumped up a level, so keep more experienced eyes on those monitors."

Bull nods. "Will do."

I clap my hand against his giant shoulder in thanks, then settle in next to Zoomie. She bumps my fist and glances at Gunner, then dips her blonde head close to mine and says, "Did you win the pot?"

For the wager that's been going on for years, placing bets on when Gunner and Anna will finally start banging.

"Yeah, I did. Beaver brought by a wad of cash earlier."

"Fucker. You should be disqualified. You've got inside

info and influence."

If that was true, they'd have gotten together when I put in my first bet years ago. "You're friends with Anna. That's influence and inside info."

"Not like family influence."

Maybe not. But instead of agreeing, I ask real quiet, "Did you know about Creek?"

She shrugs. "Know what?"

"Nothing." Because Zoomie won't ever say, but that shrug tells me she knew Creek was undercover with the Hangmen. If she didn't know, she'd lock onto my question and go after me for more. "Just thinking about inside info. And I heard you and Blowback got hitched in Vegas."

Her flinty eyes flare wide, then narrow dangerously. "You say a word to anyone else, I'll rip your tongue out. I don't need to deal with that 'wifey' shit from a bunch of insecure boy bikers."

"I ain't saying a word." I like my tongue. I especially like Cherry coming all over it. "I just thought it was real cute that you, a big tough biker, would go all softhearted and marry the club's resident psychopath."

She grins. "He tracked down the Desert Kings and we busted a few heads on our wedding night. It was so romantic. The best wedding present ever."

Then I've got a wedding present for her, too. "I put down Sherlock in the Cage."

Going still, she stares at me for a long second. Then bumps my fist again. "Good man."

Yeah, that was the one good thing. What came after sure as hell wasn't.

My throat closes up all at once and I stop talking. Just as well, since Saxon comes in and the meeting gets started. Blowback gives a rough sketch of what Spiral reported in from the Iron Blood's clubhouse, and how it means that Papa getting wind of the Hellfire Riders' involvement would be a real bad thing.

"The Butchers, too," Saxon says. "Anyone give them a heads-up yet?"

Not yet. Gunner leans in. "Hashtag's with them, chasing down that lead on the trucks moving the girls. He's due to check in about twenty minutes from now. I'll have him pass it along."

Not good enough for the prez. "Get him on now."

Cell reception out here is shit, so it's on the landline and speakerphone that Gunner rings him up. As soon as the brother answers, Gunner tells him, "You're talking to the board, so be on your best behavior. The prez wants an update."

"We found a stable full of girls," is Hashtag's quick response. "No fighters."

"You cut them loose?" the prez asks.

"We did."

"You still with the Butchers?"

"I am. Heading home tomorrow."

"You travel quiet," Saxon tells him. "And tell the Butchers to keep their heads down. Papa took out the Iron

Blood. Ain't a stretch to think that he'll take out anyone who's been around the Cage if he discovers who was there."

There's a quick exchange of voices in the background, the sound flattening out as if Hashtag turned on his speakerphone, then Handlebar comes on. "He took out the Iron Blood?"

The prez doesn't answer to anyone, so I take this one. "SUVs and suits rolled in, left nothing but ashes on the way out."

"Shit. You still got Cherry?"

"She's here."

"Cherry?" Hashtag breaks in. "Is that her real name?"

Fuck knows what her real name is. "Why?"

"Does she have that name branded on the back of her neck? These stables we found, that's how they marked their prize virgins."

"No brand." At least I'm fairly sure there isn't. Now I'll be looking again.

"That wasn't how Cherry came in," Handlebar tells him. "Lissa had a brand. But Crash and I figured that Cherry got nabbed, then they found out she was a nurse and so they used her for that. But since she's a virgin, too, they dangled her cherry as a prize for the fighters."

"What the fuck are you talking about, a virgin?" Her tight pussy itself had to be the prize because she can't be a virgin. "You said Crash was fucking her while she sucked you off."

"Nah, that was Lissa. She was an angel, too—and the

girl they usually used as bait. But Tusk got his hands on her just before you were brought in. So they made Cherry fill in for Lissa that time."

A thick roaring fills my head. "I'm the only one she pulled in?"

"Yeah. Why the fuck did you think they called her Cherry?"

Christ if I know. I don't know anything. "I figured they gave her a hooker name."

"No. It's because her entire worth to them was in that cherry." Handlebar's voice roughens. "You'll take good care of her, yeah? She might have brought you in, but she did right by Crash and me. Stuck her neck out for him again and again. So if you can't protect her from Papa, I will."

Burning steel hardens in my chest. Hand her over? Not a fucking chance.

Not to *anyone*. "I'll keep her safe."

Though I wouldn't have. I'd been on the verge of plowing into that hot little cunt. She'd been wet and eager but that wouldn't make a difference if I'd torn into a virgin pussy.

I'd have hurt her. Really fucking hurt her. If I'd done that, if I'd ripped her up... I can't bear to think about it.

Just thinking about how *near* to it I came tears new jagged edges around the hole in my chest. The rot's sitting thick and heavy in me as the call finishes up. But everyone else is real entertained by it, patchholders sporting a collection of bemused expressions around the table. Then Bull says, "A virgin is on Hellfire Rider property? Then it's time to start prepping for the zombie apocalypse, my friends, because I'm fairly certain this is how the end times begin."

That draws a laugh, and over the sound of it Blowback says flatly, "She's not a virgin anymore."

Saxon abruptly frowns, his steely gaze burning a path to me. "Are you fucking her?"

Not yet. But that's a technicality, because I will be.

"She offered payback for luring me in. I took her up on that offer." But because I know what's putting that fierce look in his eyes, I add, "She said yes real clear."

"All right." His tension eases. "Did you get anything out of her yet?"

"Not yet. But I will."

"Maybe not, if she's scared of you." Zoomie regards me with narrowed eyes. "You did threaten to pull a train on her."

During the raid. "She knew damn well I wouldn't let anyone touch her."

"It's still a bitch ass thing to threaten."

Yeah, it is. "And you think I give a fuck?"

Her gaze hardens dangerously.

Since the sergeant at arms is supposed to keep the peace between patchholders, Gunner jumps right in. "Hold up. Zoomie's got a point. You were pretty hard on this girl that night. So she might be afraid of you. So how about this? Let me go in and talk to her—"

Over my dead fucking body. "She thought you were

Strawman."

"Yeah, okay. Then send in Zoomie. She might respond better to a woman, anyway."

The rot starts boiling. "No."

"Why?"

"Because she's *mine*!" And I'm not handing her off to anyone. "Mine to protect. Mine to fuck. Mine to get answers from. Mine to do whatever the hell I want to do with her. She fucking *owes* me."

"And you owe this club," Saxon snaps, fury burning through each word like a whip. "First and foremost, you owe your fucking loyalty. Which means that whatever you do, you make sure it doesn't bounce back on us in any way, and you'd better not let a fucking virgin or your fucking payback make you lose sight of that. You went through some shit. So I'll give you some slack. But you better step real goddamn careful so I don't have to snap it tight. And if *I* say she talks to Zoomie, she talks to Zoomie. If *I* say we turn her over to the feds, we turn her over to the feds. Until then, we'll take care of her, keep Papa from touching her."

Rot pours right off my tongue. "The way you took care of Anna?"

Everything goes real fucking quiet. Real fucking still. The prez stares at me, knuckles white, jaw clenched.

With lethal calm, he lifts his forefinger. "One minute to say your piece."

Oh, I'll say it. "They got to my sister," I force out

through clenched teeth. "My fucking *sister*. You want me to say my piece? First you explain to my satisfaction how that happened. The only thing I trusted while sitting in that stall was that Anna would be safe. That the Riders would look after her. That was the only fucking thing to hold onto. But they got to her, they made her bleed, and I killed a friend to protect her. *To protect her*, because you didn't. I killed a man who was a brother to me because you let them get to her, and so I had to protect her from inside that fucking Cage. So don't you talk to me about loyalty when I've got fifty brothers who should have been looking after her and not one of them did."

By the end the rot has clogged up my throat so thick the words are barely getting through, each one sour and burning inside my chest.

Saxon's gaze never leaves mine as he gives a single nod. Gruffly he says, "We fucked up."

"Yeah." Christ, and I can't breathe. I shove my chair back. "So I'm not going to let the same happen to Cherry."

Concern furrowing her brow, Zoomie reaches for me. "Stone—"

I bat her hand away. "Just fuck off."

Every one of them can fuck off. I stalk out of the conference room, down the stairs, with goddamn fucking Gunner right on my tail.

"You want to blame someone?" He spreads his hands, inviting me to throw down on him. "Blame me. It was my family who put you in the Cage so they could get to me."

"Fuck off with that bullshit, brother."

"Then blame me because I'm the reason Anna went off alone. We were all out at Jenny's place after Red's funeral. Every Rider—and Anna, too. There was supposed to be someone who looked out for her when she left. But because we're all tight-lipped assholes about club business, no one told her she was in danger and that the Riders were watching over her." His voice thickens with emotion. "She got pissed at me because I'd been lying all week about you being missing, and I ended up saying that she didn't mean anything to me, except that she was your sister. And I hurt her so bad that she left without telling anyone. So Chef got to her. Because we fucked up. Me especially, because I meant to protect her and only ended up hurting her. So you blame someone, you blame me."

I can't do that. "Just fuck off," I tell him hoarsely.

His jaw tightens, and I know the stubborn bastard would chase after me forever if he thought it would help. But nothing will help. "Don't give up on us. We'll have your back. We'll help you watch over this girl. But— Christ, man. What the fuck are you even thinking of with her?"

What *am* I thinking? I close my eyes, throat aching. Because I don't want the sweetness. Don't want the softness.

But I can't stay away. "I'm thinking the only time this goddamn rot in my chest goes away is when I'm with her. I'm thinking it's the only fucking time that I'm not a walking corpse."

"Ah, hell." Gunner softly breathes the curse. He catches my face in his hands, his eyes searching mine. "All right, brother. You take whatever time you need. We'll be here on the other side. Yeah?"

I don't know if I'll get to the other side. But I nod.

"And if you need anything—"

"Yeah," I say, pulling away. Because the only thing I need right now is in the cabin ahead.

A girl who would have let me rip into her so she could pay up a debt. A girl who did me a wrong but who doesn't really owe me a goddamn thing. Not like these fuckers did. She didn't owe me her loyalty. And sure as hell doesn't owe me her pussy.

But she's offering. So I'm taking. I'll take anything she gives.

And I'm not letting *anyone* take her away.

I unlock the door. Wearing one of my shirts, she comes out of the bathroom in a rush, looking tousled and flushed and even prettier than the first time I saw her. My chest empties out, fills up again with all that fucking sweetness. Just from the sight of her. Her emerald eyes widen when I kick the door shut behind me and begin unfastening my belt.

Need roughens my voice. "Get on the bed, girl, and spread your legs real fucking wide."

Because it's payback time.

TWENTY-FOUR

Something's changed in the way Stone looks. I don't know what. He's still as big as ever, so tall and broad that his presence seems to fill up this entire cabin the moment he steps through the door. His dark blond hair's not as rumpled as before, but flattened as if he'd been wearing a helmet—and as he comes closer, the cold and crisp scent of the wind clings to his clothes. But that's not what's different.

My head tips back when he stops right in front of me, pulling his belt free and tossing it aside. Now that he's standing so close with his gaze locked on mine, I see what the change is.

It's not the way Stone looks. It's the way he looks *at me*. Still hungry. Still hot. But also *more*. As if he doesn't just want my pussy. As if he doesn't just want answers. As if he wants something else now, too.

I don't know what it is, but it does something more to me, too. Not just a shiver racing over my skin. Not just the anticipation quivering through my stomach. But a tightness in my chest, joined by the sweetest longing—and the need to give whatever it is he wants from me.

Eyes narrowing, he taps his finger against my up-tilted chin. "I see you got some of that fight back while I was gone."

Because I didn't rush to the bed and spread my legs. But I wasn't fighting. Just trying to figure out what had changed.

I'm glad now that I didn't obey that order when he abruptly snags his arm around my waist, lifting me straight off my feet and carrying me to the bed. Not just meekly complying. But being *taken*. By someone I feel absolutely safe with.

So much better than just giving in.

"Let me explain to you how this is going to go from now on," he says, tossing me down onto the mattress and unzipping his hoodie. "I come in that door, you tell me something about Papa. If you don't, I tell you to get on the bed—either on your hands and knees, or on your back with your legs spread. And then I'll use your pussy good and hard."

Hard, because he's got all that heavy muscle to back up that promise. I bite my bottom lip as he strips off his undershirt, revealing tanned and tatted skin. After so much time in the stables, the look of a big man like Stone should be nothing to me. Or even a turnoff. But it's not. Because I've seen his strength isn't only in his powerful body—and he's not just any fighter. He's the one whose fate was put in my hands, for better or worse.

So far it's been worse. But I think it's about to get a lot better.

His big hands go to the fastening of his jeans and he looks down at me. "Shirt off," he says hoarsely, eyes hot with need.

Breath trembling, I drag it up over my head. His gaze devours me when I throw it aside and lie back on the bed.

"Grab that headboard," he rasps out. "Legs spread wide. *Real* fucking wide."

Not tying me this time. My shaking fingers curl around the cold iron rail at the head of the bed. The arch of my back and the way the position lifts my breasts might have consumed all of my awareness if not for the effort it takes to part my legs. Not just wide. *Real fucking wide.* Until my feet are nearly hanging off either side of the bed. If they were spread any wider, I'd be doing the splits.

Which shouldn't feel sexy. Except for the way Stone's eyes go hooded when his gaze settles on my exposed pussy, and he rolls his tongue over his bottom lip. As if already tasting me.

But he shakes his head and mutters, "That's no fucking good," before reaching past me and snatching up two of the pillows by my head. I give a surprised little squeak, hands tightening on the rail when I'm almost upended and Stone wedges both pillows beneath my hips.

When he sets me back down, heat flushes my face. The arch in my back is deeper, and the spread of my legs and the height of my hips don't just expose my pussy, but put it on display.

Which must be what he wanted. Hunger suffuses the hard lines of his face. "Christ, yes," he groans, his big fingers spreading over my belly, sliding down between my legs. "This puts your little fuckhole right where my cock needs it. I'm gonna make your pussy pay up good."

Not just with his cock. His knee braced beside my upraised torso, he bends over, his tongue slicking over my clit. I cry out, my body jolting, then he grabs my hips and presses me down into the pillows, burying his head deeper between my splayed thighs. Hungrily he feasts, his mouth open and hot. My heartbeat fills my head with wild thunder. I can barely see anything past the arch of my own body and his broad shoulders, only feel the way he sucks and licks at my folds and clit until the sound of my wetness joins his harsh groans and my desperate breaths. Beside me, his cock juts from the open zipper of his jeans. So long and thick and I ache to stroke it, to taste it, to make him feel like he's making me feel, but keep hold of the rail because I couldn't bear to see him draw back from my dead fish hands. But the heavy shaft becomes my only focus beyond the delicious torment of his mouth, until even that recedes into a fog of pleasure when the orgasm nears, my body writhing and legs quaking.

Abruptly he stops.

I hold back my scream behind clenched teeth. Then nearly scream again when his fingers stroke between my legs instead, gliding past my clit—but only teasing.

He presses a kiss to my hip. "I learned something today."

I have to catch a breath before responding, "How to drive a woman to murder?"

I feel his quiet laugh against my skin. "Nah. Why you were named Cherry."

"Oh," I say, still breathless. "Does it matter?"

"Not a damned bit," he says, pushing up to sit on the edge of the bed and dragging off his boots. "I don't give a fuck whether you're a virgin or whether you screwed every man in the Cage. Except that it means you won't be running off to find any other fighters and offering to settle up with them, too. So I'll be the only one getting my pound of flesh."

I eye his big cock as he stands and shoves his jeans down his heavy thighs. "I think I'm getting more than a pound."

A short laugh barks from him. "Shut your damn mouth."

Because I'm making him like me. But it's not as if my mouth went anywhere. "You aren't gagging me again?"

"Not this time. I want to hear every sound you make." Naked, he heads over to the table and picks up a chair, then jams it up under the door handle. Preventing any more interruptions. My delicious view of his tight ass becomes a delicious view of his engorged cock when he makes his way back. "But you paying up this way makes a hell of a lot more sense now. You're a good girl who did a bad thing, and now you feel obligated to make amends. If I were a good man, I wouldn't make you follow through."

"I think you're a good man," I tell him huskily.

"You're wrong about that." The mattress sinks beneath his weight and he kneels between my legs, his voice roughening. "Because I'm going to use this little fuckhole until I get everything I need out of it."

What does he need? But I can't ask, only bite my lip against a moan when he strokes his thumb over my too-sensitive clit, my entire body shivering with anticipation.

Eyes narrowing, he asks in a dangerously soft voice, "Who were you saving that cherry for? You got someone waiting for you—is that why you're so eager for me to let you go? Because I'll tell you now, you saving it for someone else ain't going to save you from me."

"There's no one," I tell him, hips moving restlessly as he continues teasing my clit. "I was waiting for marriage."

He abruptly frowns. "You're religious?"

Not really. "It was just…something I decided was right for me."

"That's too damn bad, because fucking you is right for me." Gaze fierce, he moves in between my legs and braces one hand beside my shoulder, gripping his cock with the other. "I'll marry you after."

And he claims that he's not a good guy. A laugh ripples through me, following by a wake of longing that I absolutely will *not* examine right now.

"That's okay." And if he stopped now, it might kill me. "It's just like dessert. I don't want to spend any more time waiting for the good stuff."

"As tight and wet as your pussy is, this'll be the real good stuff," he says gruffly, dragging the head of his erection through my slick folds. Just like before. This time, though, there won't be anyone coming through the door. "But though I'll start easy, I don't know if this first time will be real good for you."

I know it won't be. Not right away. "Then use me for what you need."

"Sweet fucking Christ." A tortured laugh shakes through him. "Handlebar called you an angel and I figure he's not far off, because I've got you spread out beneath me and I'm about to break open your virgin cunt, but you're still trying to take care of me. Who the fuck are you, girl?"

"Cherry," I whisper.

His face hardens. "Not for long."

Only a few more seconds. With his jaw clenched,

Stone steadily presses forward. Despite preparing myself for it, I cry out when a sharp tearing pain blooms into a dark burning ache between my legs. My body involuntarily stiffens, stomach hollowing and hips tilting back, trying to ease the agonizing stretch when his thickness breaches my entrance.

Groaning, Stone wraps his arm around my waist, locks my lower body to his. His head bends to my ear and his voice is a strained rasp. "You're closing me out, angel. You want my cock inside you, keep those legs open wide."

Because I'd instinctively clamped my thighs tight to his sides, trying to push the pain away. With sobbing breaths, I spread them wide again.

The burning pressure inside me begins sinking deeper.

"Fuck, yes. That's my sweet girl." His breaths are harsh against my ear, the steely forearm behind my back anchoring me in place for his relentless penetration. "Your little virgin pussy is fighting so damn hard not to take what I'm giving it. But it ain't gonna win. So I'll get all the way up inside you, then we'll stop for a minute. Yeah?"

Wordlessly I nod, squeezing my eyes closed against the threatening tears. It doesn't even hurt as much now. It's just so…overwhelming. His cock looked big but *feels* enormous, wedging deeper than it seems like anything could go when his weight fully settles into the cradle of my thighs. As if I'm not even made of flesh and bone, but made to be filled by Stone.

"You took me in so good, angel. Your cunt's gripping

every inch real tight." His words are choked, his eyes closed and his expression close to agony when he raises his head, his hips pumping shallowly against me. "But I can't stop like I said I would. Christing hell, you feel too damn good to stop for even a second. Are you hurting?"

"No." Not anymore.

"Feeling good?"

No. Just so incredibly full. I don't give him that answer but his gaze rakes my face and he lets loose a harsh laugh, teeth gritted.

"I don't even give a fuck right now," he grinds out, those shallow pumps deepening. "Soon I'll need your pussy to come hard and suck me off, but for now I'll use this fuckhole as I was meant to. You stay real still. I'll go slow as I can. Just keep those legs open wide."

So wide. So he can use my pussy. Breath trembling, I nod.

Releasing my waist, he grips the bedframe, his hands on either side of mine. His height means that he's not stretched out like I am but looming over my upper body with his knees braced between my widespread thighs and his gaze fixed on my face. Our skin's not touching anywhere except when he presses forward again and his hips bump into my inner thighs.

And where he's touching me inside. So deep inside. A whimper escapes my throat when a full-length thrust rekindles the burning ache, but the hurt eases even as he pushes into my tight channel again.

Above me, Stone appears in more pain than I am, his lips drawn back in a tight grimace and his teeth clenched. As if the effort of fucking me slowly instead of hard and deep is sheer agony.

Because my pussy feels too good for him to stop.

A sweet pressure builds in my chest. Because that's pleasure I'm giving him. And I want him to feel *so* good. As my body rocks on a swaying thrust, I brace my heels against the mattress and spread a little more for him.

His head falls forward on a tormented groan. "Ah Christ, I can't fucking believe what you're doing to me, angel." His body over mine forms a bridge of steely muscles and tensile strength, his arms shaking with strain as he sinks into me again. "But I'll take everything you have to give."

He's the one giving, and I'm the one taking. Over and over, long and slow. Spikes of lust pierce me in the same rhythm as I watch ecstasy overtake the tight agony in his expression, as if a blissful drug surges through his veins with every stroke of his cock. Though he's looking down at me, his eyes slowly glaze over, his gaze feverishly hot and unseeing. His jaw unclenches, and his chest heaves as he drags in deep, ragged breaths through his open mouth as if he's drowning in the arousal between my thighs, the increasing wetness that I can hear with every thrust, the slickness that's easing his passage through the flesh he claimed was so tight, so good.

It still feels tight. But without the same discomfort

now, the delicious stretch as he pushes into me inevitably followed by the hollow ache of his withdrawal and the yearning clench of my inner walls, as if my body's trying to hold onto him. *All* of me wants to hold onto him, to wrap my arms around his neck and my legs around his thrusting hips.

But I can't bear to see his rapt, blissful expression vanish. So I keep still while my pussy takes every inch of his massive length.

Again. And again.

Pushing into me. So thick and long. So slow and deep.

A desperate whine builds in my chest. My thighs shake as I struggle to keep them spread wide, so wide, even though I'm unraveling inside.

All that effort is for nothing when his cock slides deep and an orgasm plows into me, ripping a scream from between my clenched teeth and jolting through my body like a stream of electricity. My spine arcs higher up off the bed, my heels digging into the mattress for leverage as I pump my hips and helplessly ride the heavy length lodged within me.

I'm still shuddering convulsively as my body eases back down—though not far. Stone is no longer holding onto the railing. Instead he's braced one forearm beside my shoulder with his hand cradling the back of my head, and his other arm is wrapped around my waist again, his cock still buried deep inside my quivering cunt.

My ankles are locked behind his ass. Not spread open.

But I don't want him to stop.

My thigh muscles tremble wildly when I unwind my legs from around him.

A deep groan rumbles from his chest, his forehead pressing to mine. "Hold up, greedy girl," he says raggedly. "Give me a minute to recover."

My body shakes on a breathless laugh. "*You* need to recover?"

Not from an orgasm. He's still rock hard inside me.

"The second I got into you, I thought I was in heaven. But I was only standing at the pearly gates, because when your pussy started squeezing my dick and you started thrashing around… Holy fuck." His fingers tighten in my hair. "I ain't never felt anything like that."

"You've never made a woman come before? That's sad."

His growl in response sounds mostly like a laugh. "You and your damn mouth." Then he kisses me, stealing the grin from my lips, a caress that's so sweet and far too brief. "But I should have known the tightest, wettest pussy in the world would turn into a fucking miracle when you come. Now you're going to do that again."

"I don't think I can." The last one just about wiped me out.

"No?" His eyes gleam. Letting go of my hair, he levers up on his straightened arm. I gasp as the movement shifts his weight between my legs and pleasure flares deep within me. "We'll see about that. Now open up those pretty thighs again."

Oh god. I do, every inch that I move them apart making me so much more aware of the pulsating length inside me, of the way Stone watches me with all that sharp, heavy-lidded hunger, of his forearm at my back still holding me so tight against him.

Then the slow roll of his hips that drags pure pleasure from my flesh and a moan from my lips.

"Knew it." His head hangs low, teeth gritted again. "You came so fucking hard and that was just on my dick. Wasn't even touching your clit. Now you tell me what you like best. Me screwing into you real deep like this?"

"Yes." My answer is a pleasured gasp. "Yes."

"Or maybe you just like me rubbing all the way up inside you, pushing in until I bottom out." He draws back for a slow, full-length stroke that presses so deep inside me. Another. "Maybe you like the way my cock stretches every inch of that tight little pussy."

Oh my god, that too. And I can't hold onto the rail anymore. My fingers twist in the bedcovers at my sides, anchoring me as if the next thrust might send me soaring.

Then he sits back a little more, the head of his cock wedged just inside my entrance. "Or maybe when I hit this little spot right here. Because that's what these pillows are really good for, angling you up so I can fuck into your cunt just right."

My G-spot. Of course he knows right where it is. And how to work that bulging tip into me with quick, shallow thrusts that strike the sensitive cluster of nerves again and again. The noise I make in the back of my throat doesn't even sound human, but more like a desperate animal cry—then a short scream bursts from my chest when he abruptly sinks deep again, stretching me, screwing me.

"Ah, Christ." He grinds into me, his gaze feral. "Your pussy loves all of it. Loves how I fuck it."

So much. I can't see anything but him, can't feel anything but him inside me.

His mouth dips closer to rasp against my lips, "And maybe you like a little dirty talk, too."

I laugh through my shuddering gasps. "Maybe."

Or maybe it's just Stone's voice, and all the gravel in it when he's buried so deep, when he's so hard and aroused and my pussy's giving him what he needs.

He bends his head against my ear and says gruffly, "Should we see if your pussy likes it rough? But not too rough. Not this time. Not with your cherry still painting my dick."

I don't care if it is. It doesn't hurt anymore.

"Do it." My inner thighs strain as I push them even wider. "*So* rough. Please."

"Christing fuck, that's a greedy cunt." With a grunt, he rears back, clamps his hands on my hips. "Gonna give everything you need."

Driving into me, hard and deep. Sending heat streaming up my spine to melt my brain, as he fucks into me over and over, the wet sound of my lust getting louder with every slap of skin against skin. I begin unraveling again, my control peeling away as he hikes my hips higher and makes me pay what I owe with each rough and deep stroke, then the slippery glide of his thumb over my clit turns me inside out, completely undone.

My head falls back and I choke on a silent scream, hips writhing against his powerful hold. He keeps fucking into my clenching pussy, bending over between my legs again, his features a tortured mask of pleasure.

"Nothing like it. Ain't nothing like it." His cock surges into me again, his mouth open wide and chest heaving. "Better than any prize. I'd have killed ten men for this. A hundred men. Will kill any man who tries to take you away. And I sure as fuck ain't letting you go."

A fist tightens around my heart. "You have to," I gasp out.

"Let this miracle of a pussy go?" All that glazed bliss vanishes from his eyes. "Not a fucking chance."

"Then I won't come anymore."

"No?"

He grinds against me, renewing the sparks of heat in my sensitized flesh. I grit my teeth against a moan and shove at his chest.

"You gonna fight me?" A hard thrust makes me gasp again, then he snatches my hands and pins my wrists over my head. "Go on and fight, then."

Oh my god. He meets my every struggle with a thrust and it's almost like I'm fucking myself onto him, and it feels so good.

"That doctor was real smart to put that little stick in your arm." His head bends closer, his voice harsh. "He knew that sooner or later a bad man like me would pin you down and fuck your good girl pussy full of his filthy cum."

Oh god, oh god. I cry out through clenched teeth and struggle harder, feeling his thick cock so deep. He's not moving at all now, but I can't stop pushing and writhing.

"You keep fighting me, angel, that's exactly what's going to happen." Hot breaths gust over my lips and he catches my jaw in his big hand, makes me meet his eyes. "But if you don't like what I'm giving you, just close up those legs."

And shut him out. Make him stop. If I don't like what he's doing…or saying.

I let them fall wider.

"That's my angel. Christ." Now he moves again, his swollen length pumping slowly into me. "You've kept those thighs open so damn good, keep letting me fill up this tight little cunt. First with my cock and now with my cum. Though maybe you didn't notice that I got into you raw."

I noticed. But it wasn't hard to guess why. I bare my teeth at him in a snarl of a smile. "Because it's not bait pussy anymore?"

"Because I know I'm clean. Now I know you're clean."

"Even when you didn't, you sure as hell didn't mind eating it!"

"I sure as hell didn't." He gives a hard laugh and his thumb presses between my lips to slide over the edge of my teeth.

My damn mouth. Making him like me.

I suck on the tip of his thumb.

He groans. "So you ain't gonna come?"

"No," I gasp, already so close.

"Yeah, you are." He surges deeper and pushes his hand between us, teasing my clit. "I need your pussy to suck me off, so I can empty out all this need into your hot little fuckhole. Because you made me need you so damn bad."

Yes. God, so much need. Back arching, I take his cock again, again.

"Your pussy's tightening up, angel." Above me his thrusts become more urgent, his breaths harsher and harder. "You still fighting your come? You want me to stop and pull out so you won't?"

"No!" The denial erupts as I begin to shatter, winding my legs around his back and holding him so deep inside me.

His eyes blaze down into mine and then glaze over as my inner walls begin convulsing around his shaft, a guttural curse ripping from his chest, his head falling back as he grinds into me, harder and harder. Abruptly he stills. His powerful body shakes, the tendons in his neck standing in sharp relief as his cock pulses inside me, so hot and deep.

"Holy fuck. Christing fucking hell." Skin slick with

sweat, Stone collapses over me, his weight partially braced on his forearms, his hips cradled between my thighs still wrapping him up tight. His forehead rests against mine. "The best thing I've ever seen is you chasing your come. That was the hottest fuck I've ever had."

"Me, too," I agree breathlessly. "Though I suppose it's also the worst."

He laughs on a gusting breath, then lifts his head to search my face. "You all right?"

Far better than all right. "Yes."

His gaze falls to my lips. Sweet emotion clutches at my chest when he lowers his head, brushing his mouth against mine.

"Let's get you cleaned up, then." Pulling me with him, Stone rolls to the side. That sweetness within me blooms brighter and tightens when he rises from the bed with me cradled in his arms and heads for the bathroom. "And don't look down, or you'll think you're dying."

Because of a few streaks of blood on the pillow and smears between my thighs? Hardly terrifying to anyone whose period often started while sleeping and then woke up to something out of a murder scene. But I don't protest, loving his strength as he carries me against his chest, then the tenderness in his touch when he sets me down and turns on the shower, holding his hand under the stream until it warms.

He urges me in ahead before following me, then seems to utterly fill the small shower cubicle. We're standing so close, face to face, and his gaze holds mine while he quickly soaps the blood from his cock, then reaches down to gently wash between my thighs.

"All right?" he murmurs.

Except for wishing that I could touch him. "Yes."

His eyes darken as he glances down between us. "If I remember Shakespeare right, when someone takes a pound of flesh, the rule is that they can't draw any blood with it."

"You remember right," I say. "But it was nitpicking bullshit, so that Antonio could wriggle his way out of paying the debt that he owed to Shylock."

His mouth quirks. "Seems you paid better attention in class than I did."

Steadily, I meet his gaze. "I don't want to wriggle my way out. I'd rather pay what I owe."

Especially if this is how I'm paying. His lathered hands move higher, soaping their way up my sides, before his right palm skims up my spine to clasp my nape.

"Sure would like to kiss you as deep and hard as I just fucked you," he says gruffly. Warmth spills through my chest as he tilts my head back, bending his mouth toward mine. "Take all the sweetness you have to give."

I want that, too. So much. But his fingers tighten in my hair as I rise up onto my toes, stopping my lips from meeting his.

His voice goes low and rough. "Then I remember how I landed in the shit after kissing you before. How I wanted everything that kiss said you had to give. So I'm sure as fuck not kissing you like that again. I just want answers and pussy."

A spear of pain lances into my heart. "I don't have answers."

"Bullshit. You're real smart, girl. Good memory, too. So don't tell me you didn't pay attention those three months, because I'm not letting you go until I get those answers from you."

"You have to," I tell him thickly, my throat raw. "That was the deal. I pay what I owe, then you let me go."

A muscle in his jaw works. I choke on a startled cry when he abruptly spins me around, pressing my upper body against the cold tile wall. His big body crowds up behind, one roughened hand palming my breast, his mouth hot against my ear.

"Then I'll be collecting for a long damn time, won't I?" His hard cock is a rigid brand nestled against the split of my ass. "Your little fuckhole makes me feel real good, but how many times do you figure your pussy will have to suck me off before I get rid of this rot in my chest? How long until we're even?"

"It'll never be even," I tell him on ragged breaths that fog the ceramic tile in front of me. It never *could* be even. "But I'll pay what I can—and you have to let me go soon."

"Not a fucking chance," he snarls.

With a scream of frustration locked behind my teeth, I shove back against his solid form. Stone doesn't budge an inch. Just laughs.

"Go on and fight, then. Get that cunt slicked up with your mad," he rasps, pinching my nipple between his knuckles, sending a sharp and unexpected zing of heat across my skin. His other hand angles down over my stomach. "And maybe if you don't come, I'll get tired of this pussy real fast. Want to try that?"

Oh god. Even as his fingers begin to tease my engorged clit, I nod and gasp my response. "I'll try that."

Though I'm already helplessly rocking my hips back against him, already arching my spine to press my breast more firmly into his hand. I feel him move, then white hot pleasure flares behind my eyes when his thick length surges deep, a powerful thrust that lifts me onto my tiptoes.

And I come twice before the hot water runs cold.

TWENTY-FIVE

STONE

Closing my eyes near a woman who once planned to kill a guard to escape probably isn't the smartest choice I ever made. But for five nights straight, I fall asleep while holding her close and wake up with her in my arms.

She hasn't slit my throat. But she sure is killing me slow.

Every morning, she wakes up long before dawn—still on barn time. Since I'm a real light sleeper, I wake up, too. Then I just stay quiet, because she doesn't get up, doesn't do anything except snuggle a little closer, lightly lay her hand on my chest, and slowly fall asleep again.

It's her hand that's killing me. And it's what I ought to push away. I've made it pretty clear: no touching me, no deep kissing. I'll take all the softness and sweetness that I can from her pussy, and leave everything else she has to give on the floor. So it'll be a whole lot easier to walk away when I'm done with her.

At least, that was the plan.

Now I'm completely fucked anyway. And every morning, she touches me. Lays her hand right over my heart. As if she wants more than my cock or to pay what she owes. As if she wants more than the one thing she's ever asked for.

Letting her go.

That's one thing I can't give. And I've told her why. If she's out there alone, Papa will get her. If she goes to the cops, some dirty bastard on Papa's payroll will get her. But it doesn't seem to matter to her that she'll be killed.

The only thing that seems to matter is going. Every day that I don't let her, her eyes become a little more haunted. Like the vulnerable girl I first met back in that tavern.

And this morning…she doesn't go back to sleep again. Just lies against me, real quiet, for a long damn time. I know the second she realizes I'm awake because she pulls her hand back and tucks it in between us.

But it doesn't seem like she took something off my

chest. Her hand gone feels like a heavy weight pressing down on my heart.

Pressing harder when she asks softly, "Do you think I could go outside today?"

"I don't know. You gonna try to escape?"

"Probably."

Yeah, she will. Because it's become a game between us—one that isn't really a game to either of us. Every chance she gets, she makes a break for it. And my heart just fucking stops until I catch her again. I've had to buy a lock box for the key because she started going after it every time my back was turned. Got the door open once before I got my hands on her and wrestled her to the floor. And she was still clutching that key in her fist when her pussy was squeezing the cum from me.

"You don't have any shoes," I remind her. "And it's damn cold out there."

"I could double up a pair of your socks."

Or I could just carry her. She wouldn't be getting away, then. "All right. This afternoon, if it's sunny. You need any more books? Or you want me to have them download some shows?"

Which are fine to put onto a device and bring out there, because there isn't any wireless or a way to connect to the outside. So she's been going through what she calls 'comfort reads'—which seems like a whole lot of Jane Austen.

"I won't have time to watch them," she says, her voice

going low and muffled when she presses her face into my shoulder. "Because I need to leave soon."

That weight on my chest makes it damn hard to breathe. "I don't give a fuck what you need. I'm not letting you go until I get some answers."

"You haven't even asked about Papa in two days."

"Because there's no point when you only pay in one way." I haul up off the bed. "So start rubbing that pussy and get it nice and wet. Gonna fuck it real hard in a minute."

She sits up, those emerald eyes looking so damn big. "And I'll love how you fuck it, because you make me come so hard when you do. But then you're going to let me go."

"Why the hell would I do that?"

"Because you're a good man," she says softly.

That bullshit ain't worth responding to. Especially with my throat closing up so damn tight. I head into the bathroom and stand in front of the john—my eyes on level with the evidence of how bad she wants to get away from me.

More tiny scratches around the vent screws today. And the fingernails that she kept so pretty in the stables are torn down to the quick. Because there's no fucking way she'll get it open like that, but she keeps trying.

I haven't said a damn thing about it, because if she's doing this, then she's not spending time trying to get out another way. I just don't know what I'll do if she starts making herself bleed.

Except I *do* know. I'd let her go…then follow her.

Because she can't be out there alone. Not while Papa's hunting down anyone who might point a finger at him.

But I know damn well where she'll be headed—straight to the cops. I'd have realized it the night of the raid if I'd known her better. Because she told me straight up that if she went to the police, I wouldn't have to worry. She wouldn't say anything to them about me.

And this girl, this fucking angel. She really does believe that she owes me. And she's *always* taking care of me.

Hell, maybe she thinks going to the police is taking care of me, too—so I won't end up killing another man and fucking myself up worse than I already am.

Which is sweet. Except killing Papa wouldn't do that. I've never had any trouble putting down the bad guys, the garbage people who the world would be a lot better off without.

But maybe her reason for going to the cops is simpler than that—and nothing to do with me at all. She's a real decent person. It might be that she believes in lawful justice for everyone, even for a bastard like Papa. Not the sort of justice that I intend to hand out.

I can respect a belief like that. But I still ain't going to let her go. Not when she's likely to end up dead.

And not when that would kill me, too. She's filled up this hole inside me with so much sweetness, so much soft-ness. But if that was gone? I suspect that her dying would tear open a hole in me that would rip out even more than

Crash did.

And I don't even know her fucking name.

I wash up and head back out to find her sitting on the bed, the comforter still tucked around her breasts, and trying out numbers on the key lock box.

"There's only ten thousand possible combinations," she says with a cheeky glance in my direction. "And I've got nothing but time."

"You've got a pussy that needs to be fucked," I tell her roughly, my chest pulling even tighter. Because this damn girl. She doesn't even have to touch me, doesn't have to kiss me. She just keeps on being so sweet and keeps fighting so hard, keeps on giving everything to me. "Hands and knees."

She must be gearing up for a hell of a fight. Because she just throws me another sassy look and rolls over onto her belly, lifting her pretty ass up in the air—her elbows braced on the mattress and her fingers still working that lock box combination, the numbers clicking rhythmically, steadily.

Christ, she gets me worked up. Stroking my stiff cock, I move in behind her. "What number you up to?"

"Eighty-seven."

"Tell me when you get to one hundred."

"I wi—"

Her gasp fills out the rest when I bury my face between her legs, the rhythm of that clicking coming to an abrupt halt. Then starting again, though so much more slowly when I spread her pussy lips and take a long lick through all that delicious heat, then groan and rub my face up in there before giving those sultry lips a deep kiss. She tastes so fucking good, but even better is how wet she gets, how it takes only a few thrusts of my tongue into her tight little hole before she's rocking back and demanding more.

I pull back with the scent and taste of her all over me. "What number you at?"

"Ninety…three," she pants.

Slowed way down. She ain't ever going to get to one hundred. Not after I open my mouth up over her clit and begin sucking. The muffled cry from up front tells me that she's got her face buried against the pillow, probably biting the shit out of it. Not playing with that lock anymore.

Stiffening the tip of my tongue, I tease her juicy clit until her legs start shaking. With a final lick the length of her drenched slit, I rise up behind her rounded little ass, my aching cock in hand.

One hard thrust buries me balls-deep in the sweetest, tightest heaven. She screams her fuck-me-hard scream, fingers clenching in the sheets, already wound up so good that a few rough pumps send her over and catapult me into the paradise of her convulsing cunt that is too incredible to be real. My girl's got a hair trigger, which is fucking amazing on its own, but the way she throws herself into her come, writhing and twisting like she's wringing every bit of pleasure out of herself, inside and out, is the hottest thing I've ever seen or felt.

I need to feel it again. Over and over. Her orgasm slowly releases its hold on her cunt, but I just hold onto her tighter, leaning over her trembling form with my cock still buried deep. Because the ache that was eating up my chest vanished the moment I got my mouth on her. All that sweetness just keeps filling me up—and will leave me with nothing if it's gone.

So I am *never* letting her go.

THE AFTERNOON SUN TURNS HER hair to copper and lights up her smile so bright. We're about five minutes into our walk by the stream when she whirls and races toward the driveway. Only a little more than a mile from the main road. My heart jackhammers and I sprint after her, and I'm a half second from tackling her to the ground when I realize there ain't no need for that. And she has to know it. She watched me run five miles on the regular.

So I settle in beside her, instead, and go for a little jog. A hundred yards later, she gets to the clubhouse lot and slows to a halt, bending over and gripping her side. Those doubled-up socks protecting her little feet are filthy and loose now.

"I'm…three months…out of shape," she wheezes.

I stop beside her, breathing easy. "I'd say you've had plenty of exercise this past—"

She takes off sprinting again. This fucking girl. I'd be laughing my head off if my chest didn't hurt so damn much.

This time when I catch her, I throw her over my shoulder and start carrying her back to the cabin, caveman-style—to the amusement of the brothers who've shown up early for today's club meeting. They shout encouragement my way, but my angel squirms and struggles and tells me to let her go. Then she tells me a whole bunch of lies: that she doesn't have anything else to tell me, that she'll be fine off the ranch and Papa won't find her, that she'll come back if I still want her to pay up more, that I'm a good man who knows what's right.

A note of desperation creeps in toward the end—and I just know that I'll lose my shit if she starts crying. She hasn't pulled out the tears yet, though I was stupid enough to tell her all of my soft spots. But something tells me the tears are close. And won't be faked.

That happens, I won't be able to hold out.

I can barely withstand those desperate pleas to let her go. So I pull out the ball gag and straps for the first time since our Thanksgiving dinner, get her tied up spread-eagled on the bed. All that struggling got her riled up and sopping wet, her hot cunt and her big eyes begging for my cock. I don't waste any time giving her what she needs. Like a man possessed, I ride that pussy until her juices and my cum are soaking the sheet, until she's orgasmed so many times that she's limp and quivering and so spent that she sure as fuck won't be running anywhere again. At least not real soon.

But I thought she was spent after a hundred yards, too.

So I keep those straps and gag in place while I get dressed again for the meeting, and consider leaving her tied up the entire time. Knowing all the reasons I shouldn't.

Also knowing that she's real close to making herself bleed while trying to get away. And that if she gets out, she'll be killed.

There's no good outcome here. No way to avoid the pain that's coming. But as long as she's alive, I just don't give a fuck.

A knock sounds at the door. Probably a prospect sent out here to remind me about the meeting. I yell that I'll be there in a minute, but a few seconds later, the damn knock comes again. I toss a sheet over my angel to cover her tits and pussy from prying eyes, then stalk to the door. I pull it open a few inches and a whirlwind shoves past my legs, barking and dancing in deliriously happy circles, the tags and bells on her collar jingling merrily. Daisy being Daisy, and so damn cute.

And outside, Anna being Anna, fiercely staring at me like I've got a whole lot of explaining to do.

I scowl at her. "Who the hell let you past the gate?"

"Ah, geez. So good to see you, too, you big—"

"Hold that thought." Because Daisy just figured out there's someone tied up on the bed and went to investigate a new playmate. I shut the door in my sister's face and haul ass across the room. Half up on the bed, Daisy's licking her cheek and snuffling her face, and my angel's eyes are squeezed closed as if she's afraid of being blinded by wet dog nose, but she's giggling against the gag.

"C'mere, Daisy girl. Ah, shit." I untie the strap on her nearest wrist, because as soon as that's free she can do the rest. Then I drag Daisy back, scratching at her ears and kissing her face. "Aw, you're a good girl. Such a good girl. But we leave naked ladies alone."

My naked lady snorts out a muffled laugh, reaching behind her head to unfasten the ball gag. Then she goes still and quiet, looking past me.

"Holy shit," Anna says from just inside the open door, staring at us with her hands covering her mouth, as if in horror. "Holy shit. It's true what they were saying. That you've a girl tied up in here and you're torturing her for information."

Fury spits acid through my veins. "Who is saying that?"

Eyes welling with tears, Anna shakes her head. "I don't care what happened to you. This is not okay. It is *not* okay."

"You don't know what the fuck you're talking about."

But I'm going to bust the head of every asshole who ran his mouth at the bar she tends. And I'm sure as hell not having this conversation here, with my girl still naked and tied.

"You all right to watch my dog for a minute?" I ask her. Her face is a fiery red, and she's not looking at me as she unfastens her other wrist. Real embarrassed. So as soon as she nods, I hustle Anna outside, locking the door behind me.

Watching me turn the key just sets her off again. "What the fuck, Aaron?" Anna hisses at me. "I mean, *what the actual fuck?*"

Shit, now she's using my given name. Only our parents do that.

But that's the least of my worries. Anna's Prius is parked out front and I know damn well it wasn't Gunner who let her show up out of the blue. I head over to the next cabin, where they store equipment for babysitting jobs, and snatch up a radio.

"Who the hell is on the gate?" I say into it.

"It was open," Anna tells me, just as Knucklehead comes on from inside the clubhouse's security room.

"Opened it up until the meeting," he replies.

"Keep it closed."

"You want me to open it up fifty times?"

Each time a brother comes through. Though it won't be that often—and doesn't matter if it were. "Yeah, I do. Unless you maybe want a couple of SUVs rolling in as easy as my sister just did."

"Not so much. Will do, brother."

Anna narrows her eyes at me. "What SUVs?"

"That's club business, pipsqueak."

"And *that* is a bullshit answer that I don't take anymore. Not after you went missing and everyone said 'club business,' like you weren't *my* brother, too," she says, her breath hitching as she comes closer to stab me in the chest with her finger. "Not after that asshole showed up at our house and made me give you a message that said you had to fight in a death match."

A message given while she was bleeding and bruised. Throat thick, I tell her, "That fucker got what was coming to him. Is that the business you want to know?"

"I don't give a fuck about club business. I care about *you!*" She blows her hands wide as if this is a big fucking revelation. "Because you get out of the Cage, but you're still gone. You don't ever come see Daisy. You don't go see Mom and Dad. Gunner says you went through some bad shit and I've just got to give you a little time to work through it. Okay. Sounds good. Except *that* is not an okay way to work through it." She waves wildly toward the cabin. "That."

That rot boils in my chest. "You think I'd rape a girl?"

"No," she says immediately, her breath hitching, her eyes going from fiery rings to big wet puddles. "I know you wouldn't. No matter what you're going through."

"She was the one who offered. And she said yes, clear. And she knew that if she ever said no, I'd back off."

"I know you would! But, Aaron, you've also got her locked up. And you know—maybe you know better than anyone now—someone might make choices while in a cage that they'd *never* make if they were free."

Like making Crash's spine pop apart in my hands. And the rot is thick, so fucking thick, I can't breathe.

"If you gave her a choice right now," she says in a gentle voice that ruthlessly tears me apart, "between getting into bed with you or going out that door—which would she choose? And that's all you need to know."

That's all I need to know. There's nothing but rot in me. I'm choking on it. "Anna—"

"It's okay." She wraps her arms so tight around me, buries her face in my shoulder. "It's okay. You'll be okay. And I'm so sorry. I know you're hurting so much."

Gonna be hurting more. I hold her close, my throat so fucking raw I can barely get the promise out. "I won't touch her again."

She nods.

"But I can't let her go."

"So it's like that?" Anna takes a deep breath before hugging me tighter. "Then maybe consider what they say about letting go of someone you love. If she comes back, then you know that love was meant to be."

"This ain't nothing to do with love," I tell her hoarsely. "She'll be killed out there."

"Oh." Anna leans back a little to frown up at me. "And she still wants to go?"

Jaw tight, I nod.

Sympathy deepens her gaze. "Well…I mean, I know you've got a thing for girls in trouble—but you can't save everyone from themselves."

"I know that. I just want to save her from Papa."

"And I just want to save my brother."

Too late. My short laugh feels like it rips my guts out. "I'm pretty sure your brother died in that Cage."

"No," she says firmly, reaching up to catch my face in her hands, her gaze holding mine. "I think he got hurt really bad. I think there will be scars. But it won't be the first time you got scarred up. And you were still my same brother after."

After scarring up my face. "A real stupid brother. Because the first time sure as hell didn't teach me a lesson about going home with girls who are trouble."

Her lips curve in an impish little smile. "Maybe second time is the charm."

"Yeah. Lesson learned."

There won't be any more girls. Not after this one. Can't imagine touching anyone else again.

But I sure as fuck wish now that I'd let her touch me a little more before it was over.

"Hey," Anna says softly, watching me. "I know you're not okay. But you *will* get through, yeah?"

Somehow. My throat's a fucking mess, so I just nod.

"All right." She gives me another tight hug before stepping back. "And don't shut us out. Not Mom and Dad, not me and Daisy. Or next time I'll send Mom—and if you think a gate will stop her…"

I give a thick laugh. "I'm not that stupid, pipsqueak."

"Good." She bites her lip. "Can you especially make the effort with Daisy? Mom and Dad and I, we all understand that you might need space. She doesn't. Now she's licking her leg constantly and the vet says it might be a self-comfort thing. So if you could just stop by more often, or I'll bring her out here more, or even if you do the video thing on the phone—"

"I will." I'm such a fucking asshole. "Thanks for looking out for her."

"Of course. Though it's Mom and Dad who are keeping her most of the time."

"You have her tomorrow morning?" At her nod, I say, "I'll stop by, yeah?"

"Yeah. Oh! Just don't be surprised by—" She wiggles her engagement ring, the diamond sparkling. "I'll have a visitor."

Gunner. But considering that neither of them banged anyone else for ten years, not real surprised they're making up for it now. "Is he moving in?"

"Kind of already has. Except I've got to figure out space for his books."

"I'll find another place. Then you can have the upstairs."

Dismay fills her expression. "You don't have to—"

"I know. But just…give me a little time to get it worked out. Don't just throw my stuff out on the lawn."

"Aw, man. There goes my plan to landscape the front yard with piles of your ratty sports shit from high school. Though I guess all your stuff wouldn't be much different than what Daisy leaves out there."

Ow. I grin and then all at once Crash's spine pops apart in my hands, and my girl's begging me to let her go, and I can't fucking breathe again.

"Aaron?" Concern sharpens her voice.

"Just…I need to walk around and clear my head." Because if I return to the cabin right now, my girl might destroy me if she asks me to let her go again. I press the key into her palm. "Lock it up again after you get Daisy. Don't look at me like that—I've got to figure out the rest first. Just don't let the girl go, no matter what she says. Because it'll kill me if she…" I can't finish that thought, because it kills me just thinking about it. "Just give the key to Gunner."

"Okay," she says softly. "I love you."

Throat in a knot, I head off. "Love you, too, pipsqueak."

One good thing to maybe get me through. Because the rest of this doesn't have a thing to do with love.

I don't even fucking know her name.

TWENTY-SIX

I haven't been giving much thought to the future. Not anything further than getting out of here and rescuing Matt. But one visit from a dog changes everything. Because I'm scratching her ears and giving her all the loving that she wants, and suddenly I am thinking ahead. That after freeing Matt…there might be a chance for more. If nothing else, at least giving Stone an explanation.

After my brother is safe.

I'm on the floor with Daisy when the key scrapes into the lock. I've dressed—in a pair of shorts and one of Stone's shirts—so I don't go scurrying for cover. And I try not to think about how I must have looked before, tied up and gagged and still flushed from sex. While his delicate fairy of a sister looked at me in horror. Because she'd thought Stone was torturing me.

And he does. But…not in a bad way.

To my surprise, she's the one with the key. She barely looks at me. "C'mon, Daisy. Time to go."

Wearing a happy grin, the boxer immediately races to her side. Like so many of her breed, Daisy's only got one speed: go go go. She's fun and silly and probably exactly what Stone could use right now.

And I hate the way his sister looked at him. "He's a good man."

"Oh, *you* think so?" Sarcastic fury burns through that reply, her gaze scalding my face. "You think you know *anything* about my brother? You don't. You're just another toxic piece of ass that he felt sorry for and tried to save."

My chest tightens. "Okay."

"And you don't get to talk to *me* at all. Not after what you did, playing bait. You're the reason he was in that Cage. You're the reason he's hurting so bad now." Her gaze swings around the cabin. "I don't agree with what he's doing here, but one thing is for damn sure—you should be locked up *somewhere*."

In jail. For what I did.

That's probably fair.

"Okay," I whisper past the clog in my throat. And I would have done what she wanted and not talked to her at all, but this isn't about her. Or even Stone. "Daisy's got a hot spot on her right foreleg. You should get it checked out."

"I know she does. That's why we're here. She misses him because he's stuck out here with you." She gives me a narrowed look. "As if you give a shit about a dog. Is that what you're doing? Taking advantage of all his soft spots so you can keep clinging to him? You need to just leave him alone. Because you're right, he is a good man. And you've done enough harm."

My head feels utterly numb when I nod. All of me is utterly numb as she leaves, slamming the door and turning the key.

Except my eyes and throat and heart are burning. I bury my face in my upraised knees, and every thought of a future turns to ash. Because what did I think, really? That I'd help rescue Matt, then triumphantly return and tell Stone everything? That we'd just pick up where we left off—or truly go back, to that night in the tavern. And I'd tell him my name instead of lying, and we'd have everything that might have been?

While his family hates me. While his club blames me.

While he still doesn't even want me to touch him.

There's no going back. I've done what I've done. There's no future beyond rescuing Matt. Not here.

And Stone *is* a good man. I always knew it, but now I have an even clearer picture of him. A man who loves his dog, and who stood in front of one of those do-it-yourself dog tag engravers, feeding coins into a slot and pushing a button so that if he ever lost her, it would be so easy to contact him and let him know she's been found. So he made a small tag engraved with Daisy's name and his phone number. Then put that tag on her collar.

I look at it now. Thin, sturdy metal. A diamond shape that will fit perfectly into a screw head. With one push of a button, a good man gave me a way to escape—and a way to contact him afterwards.

Even if it's only to say that I'm sorry.

I'LL HAVE TO APOLOGIZE FOR stealing from him, too. Two pairs of socks, a black hoodie, dark gray sweatpants—and a hundred dollars that I peel off the roll of cash on the table.

I'll pay it back. But I have no idea where we are now, or how long it'll take me to reach a police station. So I might need the money.

Getting through a hole in a wall ends up being a lot harder than getting through the bars over my stall. More painful, too. It feels as if I scrape away most of the skin over my hipbones—and scrape away the sweatpants, too. But I keep wriggling through, and it probably looks as if the cabin gives birth when gravity takes over and I land on the ground in a sweaty, bare-assed heap.

Oh god. I lay in the dirt, half laughing and half crying, then drag the pants back up my legs. I lift the hood up over my hair. The sun set a little while ago, so the dark clothes should help me get through this next part undetected. I saw security cameras on our walk earlier today, but they only seemed to cover the front of the cabins.

So I'll go behind.

Creeping, so quietly. I'm not afraid of being caught. Not in the same way as in the barns. I'm afraid of being *stopped*, but not afraid of any punishment afterward. Despite all that I've done, Stone has never hurt me. I suspect hurting a woman is a bright red line that he won't cross. Maybe something could shove him over that line. Like it did in the Cage. But it would have to be an immediate threat to someone he loved.

Behind the cabin nearest to the clubhouse, I flatten myself against the ground. A motorcycle rolls into the lot ahead, the headlight sweeping the side of the cabin. Not shining on me, but I remain absolutely still, watching.

I know they're having some kind of meeting, and the lot is completely full of bikes. A few are parked less than fifteen feet away from me. But the only biker I see is the one who just rode in, and he stops near the clubhouse entrance.

As soon as they're all inside, I'll steal a motorcycle and go. These bikes are a lot bigger than the dirt bikes that Matt and I used to mess around on while we were growing up, but the basics must be the same. Throttle, clutch, gearshift, brake. If I can figure out those, I'm golden. Even if someone on a security camera sees me leave, while I'm in these dark clothes they probably wouldn't realize right away that I'm not one of their own. They'd just assume someone was leaving the meeting early.

Oh shit. I flatten myself even closer to the ground, angling my face down so that only the dark hood points in the direction of the clubhouse. Because the biker who just arrived is heading this way—a big man with a short black beard.

Did he see me?

My heart thunders. I dare another peek. Oh god, and now he's not alone. I recognize the other biker who comes out of the clubhouse and joins him. The one who asked me all the questions.

Blowback.

Frantically I pull my sleeves down over my pale hands, bury my pale face in my crossed arms. Nothing here to see in the shadows behind this cabin. Nothing here to see.

Oh god, I hope they aren't heading toward *my* cabin. Let me get away before someone comes to check up on me. Just let one plan go right, just let me get away.

"You coming in?" the bearded biker calls out. "Or are you waiting for a fucking invite?"

Because someone is still out here, I realize. Maybe even sitting on this cabin's porch, and who would have seen me the minute I sneaked into the lot. Oh my god. Holy shit. That would have fucked up my plan really quick.

My breath catches when I hear the reply. Because it wasn't just someone. It was Stone.

"Planned to come in," he says, and my heart twists.

His voice sounds…dull, almost. Defeated. "Unless I need that invite?"

"I figure we're squared away. Unless you've got more to say?"

"I said my piece."

"And I heard it real loud and clear. We fucked up. But you can help make sure it won't happen again if you're all in."

"I'm all in, Prez." Stone's short, rueful laugh holds a bitter edge. "I'm just not all here."

"Fair enough. For now, we'll take what you've got to give. And Blowback's got something for you."

That man says, "Creek's ready for the girl."

My heart freezes. *What?* Is the girl me? And who's Creek?

"Is he?" Stone again, his voice flat and hollow.

"We've just got to set up a meet and hand her over. Then she disappears."

Disappears.

No. That can't mean— *No.*

Stone wouldn't hurt me, let alone have me killed. *He wouldn't.* He's a good man.

My pulse thumps sickly in my ears as the prez says, "The way I see it, Papa isn't going to be looking for anyone who isn't a danger to him. All those fighters came from outlaw clubs, so they aren't likely to head to the cops. Plus most of them killed someone in the Cage and they might have to confess to that. So they won't be thinking the outcome would be worth going to the law with what they know."

"From what I can tell, they don't know shit," Stone says. "Papa didn't exactly parade himself through the barns."

"So he'll just be after this girl. And if word reaches him that we've got her? Even if we handle whatever fire-power he throws at us, it'll put eyes on us that we don't need. Other clubs and the cops will be looking at us real hard. So our best option is just to get rid of her. Unless she's finally talked to you?"

"Not a damn word."

"But you think she'll talk to the cops?"

"Yeah." Stone gives a bitter laugh, and hot tears leak into my sleeves when he adds, "Pretty fucking sure that was her intention all along."

"So handing her over will be a win-win, sounds like. That deal Blowback made means you still get first shot at Papa. This girl vanishes into thin air and no one will ever know she was here." The prez's voice deepens. "Unless you've got another reason to keep her around? You've been spending a hell of a lot of time in that cabin lately."

There's a long silence, with my heart pounding so thick and slow. Then Stone replies with a flat, "No reason. She's just a girl I met in a bar—and I'm done trying to get answers from her. So set up that meet and we'll get this shit over with."

I don't hear anything more, desperately muffling my sobs against my arms while my shattered heart bleeds into the ground. Vaguely I'm aware that the three men head off toward the clubhouse, and that I'm alone out here, and I should get up and go. That I need to keep moving. Need to stop crying. Because Stone's not worth my tears and broken heart anyway. He's not the man I thought he was.

And Matt's waiting for me.

It's only the last that gets me going. Tears silently streaming down my cheeks, I get to my feet, trying to make my brain work again. To make anything inside of me work again. The bikes are even bigger than I realized, their consoles and controls more complicated. Until my gaze lands on a smaller motorcycle sitting in the shadows.

It looks older. And a lot simpler.

So that's the one. With my sleeves, I wipe the tears from my face—then toss away the dog tag engraved with Stone's number. I don't need to contact him again. He's not the good man I believed he was. So I'm not apologizing for shit. And as for what I've stolen…

I'm done with paying him back.

TWENTY-SEVEN

STONE

Unlike the executive board meetings, there's no alcohol allowed at the monthly club meetings. Afterwards, yeah. Pretty traditional to get trashed. And that's all I'm looking forward to while sitting and listening to Old Timer give a rundown of the club's finances. Just filling up this giant fucking hole with something else. Can't be my girl. Can't be any other woman. I don't even know if I give a fuck about Papa anymore.

There's just nothing left. Except getting real drunk.

Drunk enough that having nothing won't hurt so bad.

"What the fuck you doing, prospect?"

Gunner's rifle crack of a question cuts through the fog of misery in my head. Bottlecap's standing at the back of the room. Where he shouldn't be. Prospects aren't allowed to sit in on club meetings. Instead they were all assigned to security. Now fifty patchholders are staring him down.

The boy's looking real uneasy but lifts his hands, like there ain't no help for it. "Thought Blowback should know that Stone's girl is stealing his ride."

Holy fucking hell. I surge to my feet and start for the exit but no one else moves a muscle, except for fifty heads swiveling toward where Saxon is standing up front. The prez pinches the bridge of his nose like he's getting a headache.

"All right," he says. "Ten minute break."

Then I'm fighting my way through all the assholes trying to get to the door. Even at the front of the pack, I'm too damn late. The sound of an engine roaring to life greets me as I tear outside. Christ, she's all the way across the lot. Looking so fucking tiny on Blowback's vintage Sportster. My heart's up in my throat when she throttles it too high before popping into gear. The front tire rears up at the same time the back tire peels out. For a second it looks as if she'll eat asphalt right there, and I don't fucking breathe again until both wheels are down and the bike stops fishtailing.

Then she's nothing but a taillight heading down the

driveway. A bunch of fuckers behind me break into cheers, laughing it up. Because, hell. It ain't their ride. It ain't their girl. And that was a sweet display of gumption and a near-miss that any biker could appreciate.

"She wasn't wearing a helmet," Bull says beside me, frowning after her. "It's illegal in this state to be riding around on a stolen bike without one."

Maybe I'll laugh at that when I catch up to her—and if her fool skull's not cracked open. She's not going too fast yet, though. I can hear the engine whining hard in first gear before she manages to punch it into second.

Heading for my ride, I shout to Bottlecap, "Is that gate closed?"

It is. An answer that might have eased the tightness around my chest if I were more certain that she knew how to use the brakes better than she did a clutch.

Ain't no fishtailing here. I pull out smooth and fast, with Gunner falling in right behind me. I hear a few more engines fire up but all my focus is fixed ahead. I'm real familiar with this stretch. She isn't, and it's dark, and there's a million fucking deer just waiting to slam into her.

My headlight catches a bike lying on its side up ahead. Right in front of the gate. My chest hollows out until I realize that she isn't on the ground with it. Must have slowed down and bailed.

And climbed over. She's just a shadow racing ahead. I'm not waiting for the prospects in the security room to pull their heads out of their asses. I skid to a stop, leave my bike on the kickstand, and haul ass over the gate.

Then it's just a foot race. She's quick and had a small head start, but I've got longer legs and more staying power. My boots are also loud as fuck. As I start closing in, she looks behind and screams out a hysterical denial, putting on a burst of speed—while that sound she made nearly trips me over my feet.

Like she was really, *really* afraid. Of me. Though she never has been before. Not in all this time.

But she is. As soon as I catch up, get my hands on her, she starts screaming. And fighting. Really fucking fighting. Not sexy fighting. But desperately, crying and kicking at me, making me snag her wrists so she stops scratching and then pinning her to the ground when she goes for my balls. And she still keeps fighting, keeps sobbing.

"Angel girl," I tell her hoarsely, then narrowly jerk back in time to avoid a headbutt that would have busted my nose. "Stop this."

"Then let me go!" she screams, then breaks into sobs, turning her face toward the ground and begging, "Just let me go. Just let me go. You don't have to kill me, please please, just let me go."

"Kill you?" It's a gut punch. "Never in a million fucking years."

"I *heard* you!" she cries out, struggling again. "I heard you."

"What'd you hear?"

"That you'll make me…disappear." Her voice cracks

on the word and she goes still, tears sliding down her cheeks. "Please don't. Please. Just let me go."

"Ah, angel. No." Releasing her wrists, I slide my hands into her hair. I can barely get a word through my raw throat when I tell her, "You heard us talking about handing you over to the feds. Into witness protection."

A wary gaze fixed on my face, she goes utterly motionless, then shudders beneath me. Again. And again, sobs still hitching through her chest. "The feds?"

"The FBI. Who've set up something with the Marshals. They're all keeping it real quiet so it doesn't leak to anyone in Papa's pocket. It'll be like you'll just vanish, so he can't find you."

Her lips tremble, that wariness gradually transforming to hope. "Really?"

"Yeah." Gently I wipe the tears from her cheeks. "Really."

Her eyes close and she begins silently crying again, but her body softens beneath mine, and there's no mistaking the relief in her now.

Seeing her happy is the only thing that keeps my heart from tearing out. Though it nearly goes when she whispers raggedly, "Soon?"

"I told Blowback to set up the meet. We'll see if he has yet." I sit back, holding out my hand. "He might be a little pissed. You stole the bike he spent a whole lot of time restoring."

"Oh. Whoops," she says as I pull her up.

"He'll get over it."

If it ever really bothered him to begin with. He shows up with Zoomie, riding behind her, and hardly glances at his bike—which is no longer lying on its side, thanks to Gunner, who's got all the motorcycles out of the way and the gate open.

I tuck my girl in against my side as we walk back in that direction, then glance down. Double socks. "How are your feet?"

"Feeling like all those barefoot-running advocates are liars."

Good. Because it gives me an excuse to swing her up against my chest and carry her. My throat nearly closes up when she links her arms trustingly around my neck. "Give me a list of what you need before you go. Shoes, clothes, sizes. Because fuck knows what the cops will give you to wear. I'll have Bottlecap go pick it up."

And because the only way I'm going to get through this is by getting shit done.

Getting shit done for her.

"Thank you." She bites her lip, looking up at me. "I'm sorry that I stole some of your money."

"Don't you say sorry to me."

"I'm sorry that I believed you would kill me."

My voice is raw when I say, "I never gave you any reason to believe otherwise."

"Yes, you did," she says softly. "Everything you did said that you were a good man. I'm so glad that I wasn't wrong."

That fucks up my chest and ends the conversation there. With me carrying my girl, whose name I don't even know, to find out when I have to let her go.

I reach the gate and set her down. Just Gunner, Zoomie, and Blowback here. "She heard us saying that she was going to disappear."

"Ahh." Zoomie nods in understanding as she looks to my girl. "If that meant what you thought, there wouldn't be any conversation about it."

"Okay," she says. "Good to know. When people *don't* talk about killing me, that's when I run. I'm going to be in such good shape."

This fucking girl and her mouth. She just doesn't stop making me crazy about her. Even now. When it kills me to ask Blowback, "Did you already set up that meet?"

"But even if you did," she interrupts quickly, "can we set it up with someone else? I only want to talk to either George Martinez or Luke Harris, both out of the Las Vegas branch."

The fuck? Zoomie and Gunner exchange glances but Blowback doesn't blink. "The meetup is with Harris."

"You said Creek. I heard it."

"That was Luke Harris's road name when he was under. So it's the name that we all know him by."

"Oh. Okay." All at once those happy tears are in her eyes again, and she turns and throws her arms around me hard, so hard, pressing her face into my chest. "Thank you. Thank you so much for this."

"Yeah." Voice thick, I hold her close. But I don't know for how long. "Did you set the time yet?"

He nods. "Tonight at midnight. Motel in Klamath Falls. You taking her?"

Tonight. Fuck no. Ah, fuck no. I stare at him frozen, because I can't fucking do it. I can't let her go.

Then she looks up at me, those emerald eyes filled with hopeful tears. "Will you? I'd rather go with you."

"All right." Because I'll give her anything she needs. I take her hand, lead her to my bike. "Load up behind me. We'll head back to the cabin and get you packed up."

She laughs. "I don't have anything."

Yeah. Me, either.

TWENTY-EIGHT

STONE

Right now, some asshole out there is probably saying to someone else, "Be careful what you wish for." They maybe ought to have said it to me. Because just a little while ago, I was wishing that I'd let my girl touch me more.

Now her arms have been wrapped tight around me for two hours, but only because I'm taking her on the ride that'll end with me never touching her again. Never seeing her again.

Every mile, I think of heading in another direction. Taking her with me. Then I remember her happy tears, her relief. And I keep going straight.

The motel's about as nothing as nothing gets. Creek's in the room at the end of the building, bottom floor. I don't park right in front but a little ways down the lot. Like some pathetic high school fucker hoping to get a last kiss from a date, so he makes sure there's a bit of a walk between his ride and her front door.

She unwinds her arms from around me. And that's it. Got what I wished for. Won't be getting more.

She's the first off the bike, standing beside it while she pulls off her helmet. And Christ, she's so fucking pretty. It's a cold night, so we're both dressed for the ride, thermals and all. Her cheeks are flushed and she's got brown hair now, because that red is so damn noticeable. Her teeth are pinching into a bottom lip that's almost smiling…but those emerald eyes aren't smiling at all.

Her gaze searches my face. "Thank you again."

Fucking killing me. "Don't thank me yet."

I haul my ass off of the bike and unstrap her pack. A few changes of clothes are in there, some girly stuff for her hair and face. Aside from the new riding gear she's wearing, she's got nothing else.

She begins shaking her head when I pull a thick fold of cash out of my coat. "That's really not—"

"It's real fucking necessary. You got ID on you? Bank cards?" I shove the cash into her pack along with an untraceable burner phone. "You got *any* options if shit goes south?"

"No," she whispers.

"Yeah, you do. This cash, and me. You need any goddamn thing, you get in touch. You hear me?"

Her eyes are glittering when she nods. "I'll pay you b—"

"Don't. I don't want a fucking thing from you."

That was too harsh. But I can barely fucking breathe. And it just gets worse when she nods again, then takes the pack and holds it against her chest, her arms wrapped around it like she was holding onto me a few minutes ago.

"Okay." She looks past me, her chin wobbling before she firms it. "I know you just want to get this over with, and I can probably handle it from—"

"Who said I want to get this over with?"

"You did." Her voice is thick. "Because I'm just a girl you met in a bar. So you don't have to—"

"Hold up right there." Fucking hell. I'm not letting her go thinking that. I grab the pack, use it to drag her closer. "That entire conversation you heard wasn't what it sounded like. We weren't looking to kill you. And that shit I said at the end was just me trying to convince myself that you leaving wouldn't mean a damn thing. That it'd be easy to let you go. But it ain't easy, girl. It ain't easy at all."

That smile finally reaches her eyes, though her lips are trembling now. "Do you still intend to go after Papa?"

"Yeah, I do." Because she won't be safe until he's dead.

"Or they'll use me as a witness to put him away."

And to catch him. "They'll try."

"Then maybe…" She gives an uncertain, hopeful little shrug. "Maybe when this is all over with—whether he's in jail or whether you get him—we can meet up again. And compare notes about the Papa hunt."

That shit Anna said about letting something go and it coming back goes flying through my head, dropping a bomb in my chest.

"That ain't how it works, angel," I tell her hoarsely. "They'll give you a new name, a new life, maybe even a new face. Then they'll tell you real clear to *never* get in touch with anyone from before. Because that's always where witness protection falls apart."

Her brow furrows. "You think I'd still be in danger? Even after he's been put away?"

"Especially if he's put away." Just another reason to do this my way. "Rich fucker like that will keep appealing and trying to overturn any verdicts against him. Which means he'll never stop wanting to get rid of you or any other witnesses. So this step you're taking now is forever."

Maybe I shouldn't have told her. Because she looks so torn, eyes swimming as she looks toward the room where she'd be heading.

But a part of me knows exactly what I'm doing. Hoping she won't go through that door. Hoping she'll choose me.

Tears slip over her cheeks. "I have to take that step.

And I have a really good reason. I wish I could tell you now what the reason is, but I can't yet."

Christ. This big fucking hole in my chest. "You don't owe me an explanation."

"Maybe not. But I'd like to give you one. When I can." She wipes her cheeks on her sleeve and reaches into her pocket. Pulls out a little metal tag—Daisy's tag that she used to break out, and then went scrounging around behind a cabin to find before we left. A good luck charm, she said then. But now she tells me, "Maybe one day a stranger will call you up and say that she found your dog. And maybe you'll take that call, even if Daisy isn't really missing."

That hole in me fills up with so much sweetness. Not all the way full. But I'll take partial. "Don't lose that tag, angel."

And I won't ever change that number.

"I won't." She slides it into her pocket again, draws a deep and shuddering breath. "Will you go in with me? Just until I'm settled."

"Never planned to do anything else." I take her hand, lacing my fingers through hers. "Any reason you don't feel safe or you want to bail, you say the word and we're out of there. I don't leave until you're certain."

And fuck—after that, maybe just keep following her. Until *I'm* certain she's safe.

Her fingers squeeze mine so tight as we walk up to the door. Wearing only jeans and a T-shirt, in his bare feet like he was catching some sleep while waiting for us, Creek opens it up. He eyes her quickly before narrowing a look at me. "You decide to talk a little more, too? Or you're a package deal?"

Going into protection with her? That shouldn't sound so tempting.

Not the protection part. Just the part where I'm with her.

But it's also real stupid. "You couldn't ever hide this face good enough," I say, shouldering my way past the door and scoping out the room before leading her in. "Just you in here?"

"Just me." Creek holsters the gun he'd been holding behind his back. "And we could make those scars go away."

Nothing will ever make these scars go away. Still holding her hand, I head across the room. Two queen beds, still made up but one showing signs that a single person was lying on it for a while. Folders stacked up on the nightstands and table, a box of takeout and one empty water bottle in the trash. No one in the bathroom except maybe a cockroach or two, just a single hand towel used.

"All right," I tell him. "I know Blowback told you I was bringing her, and the deal was that we share infor-mation. So while you've got me in here, why don't you ask me what you want to ask. And while we're talking, that'll let her get a feel for the man she'll be trusting with her life."

"That'll work. Have a seat, then." He gestures to the

table, then looks her over again. "You're the one they call Cherry?"

Fingers tightening on mine, she nods.

"And your real name?"

She swallows hard. "Maybe a little later?"

"Fair enough." He grabs a few bottles of water out of the mini fridge, sets them in front of us and sits, notebook in hand. Looking over at me, he says, "How you want to play this?"

"Anonymous tip. And real dumb. I figure that I overheard two guys talking while I was trying to nap at a rest area. Didn't see who it was, don't know nothing else. It's just some shit your anonymous tipper overheard."

"So this girl will stick her neck out but you won't?"

My neck will be out there. But not for this fucker. "You think I don't know how that'll work? All at once, you'll be trading for everything. You say you'll ignore what happened in the Cage in exchange for my testimony in that witness stand. Because you know I'd get off if it came down to a trial, but also know the whole process would fuck up my life real good, and I'd do just about anything to avoid that. So you'll hold everything I say over my head, use it to jerk me around and make me do what you want me to do. Which is a whole lot like what Papa did. So all of this? It's just something I heard."

"You think we're like Papa?"

"You? Maybe not." Or Blowback wouldn't be talking to him. "But I ain't taking bets on the rest. How's your friend Gillam? Are they trading with him for info about Papa? And how many bodies will be swept under the rug so they can make that deal?"

His jaw tightens. "Gillam opted out."

Ate a bullet before they got to him. "Bad luck for you."

"Yeah, it was." He sits back, his gaze touching on my girl before returning to me. "I've got a pile of photos showing what was left in that barn, but it might put you off barbecue for a while. Long story short, we're running DNA, but that takes time. So no hits yet. But we've got plenty left to match up dental records—we just don't have any clue what records to pull, where to start. We know they were militia, but where were they out of? Where did Papa pick them up from?"

"No fucking clue." I look to my girl. "You?"

"The truck they used around the compound had Arizona plates. A black Silverado."

"There was no Silverado at the site," Creek says, frowning. "You got a tag number—even a partial?"

She shakes her head.

So maybe Victor had the pickup off-site. Or maybe one of the Bedlam Butchers or escaping fighters stole it during the raid. I'll ask around about that.

Still, Arizona's a smaller place to start looking for the militia than every-fucking-where is.

Creek looks pleased, too, as he asks me, "You were military. What was your sense of them?"

"Boys playing soldiers," I tell him. "Except for Victor.

You won't find him in those barns, though. Was on holiday leave. But he had a direct line to Papa."

"Victor?" he confirms while writing it down.

"Yeah. Six-two, one-eighty, brown hair and blue eyes. Forty to forty-five years old. Obviously in charge."

"Distinguishing marks?"

"Does a tight little sphincter for a mouth count? No?" Too bad. "I'd bet my left nut that he was Army once upon a time. Now he hates one-percenters—bikers, not billionaires—and anyone who steps outside the law. Sees the Cage as a way of meting out the justice that your boys won't."

"And hopefully wrote that on a message board somewhere," Creek says, scribbling in his notepad. "Victor. They used first names?"

"NATO alphabet. There was also a Bravo, Charlie, so on."

His eyes sharpen. "Did they go in order, Alfa to Zulu? If they got to Victor, that would mean at least twenty-two in their militia. Or random, maybe matching first letters of their real names?"

"There were sixteen—and no Alfa. At least not by the time I got there," my girl says. "In the east barn, those bodies are Hotel and Tango…and probably Charlie, though I didn't see for sure."

"It was Charlie," I tell her.

A sad look comes over her face, then her expression seems torn by confusion—as if she can't help grieving for the fuckers, yet isn't even sure if she should. Men she'd known for months and that she might have killed, too, if given the chance.

"It ain't easy for anyone to see what you saw," I say to her quietly. "Whatever you're feeling, don't you beat yourself up for it."

She nods, then says, "Hotel was five-ten, one hundred and sixty pounds, blond hair and blue eyes. Mid-twenties. Slightly chipped front tooth, tattoo of a crucifix on the nape of his neck. Tango was five-eleven and stockier, so probably one-ninety. Late twenties, early thirties. Brown and brown, a surgical scar on the back of his left hand that was probably only a year or two old." She traces a line up her own, demonstrating. "Charlie was six-one, one-seventy, dark blond and green, early thirties. I think he wore corrective contact lenses. Oh, and all of these guys were Caucasian, wore high-and-tights."

Christing fuck. "Are you a cop?"

That doesn't feel right but…the fuck? Combined with her asking specifically for Luke Harris by name, obviously she's got some connection to law enforcement. Which might explain a whole hell of a lot.

Biting her lip, she shakes her head. Her eyes are dark and apologetic when they meet mine. "But I *did* pay attention."

Knew it. I laugh and sit back. "Go on, then. He apparently doesn't need me for this part."

She gives him a list of guards most likely on duty in

the west barn—men that I'd only seen in the warehouse and whose names I didn't know. She's got names, descriptions, every damn thing. She fills out the remaining roster in the east barn, then tells him, "And there were five more, but they were already dead and buried out back."

"Out back?"

"You didn't find the graves?" she asks and when he shakes his head, tells him, "They're a couple of hundred yards behind the barns. The three newest are Delta, Mike, and Oscar." The guards that Tusk killed when he got out and went for her. "Rome's out there, too. He'll be the one with a broken neck. Because he had…an accident. And fell."

Into Handlebar's hands. But she isn't telling Creek that. The man's not buying the accident claim for a second but he doesn't press her, either.

So she's looking out for Handlebar. My chest feels real tight as I gently squeeze her fingers. She gives me a little smile, then it falters when she goes on, "And Bravo. They executed him after Lissa was…" She trails off, her throat working. "After Tusk dragged Lissa into his stall and killed her. And she's out there, too."

"Lissa?" Creek prods gently.

"Yeah. She was…I think a dancer in Vegas? She never really said for certain. But she had a little girl who was being looked after by her parents. That's how they made her do what they wanted. But she still tried to escape." Tears slip from her eyes before she looks to me, hard and angry. "You would have called her bait pussy. But she was so good and sweet. And helped me so much."

"And I'm so fucking sorry, angel." I bring her trembling hand to my lips, press an apologetic kiss to her fingers. Sorry she was hurt so bad, sorry I was such a fucking asshole. "Creek will make sure she gets out of the ground and home to her family. Yeah?"

"Yeah," he says softly.

She nods, still quietly crying, and I crack open her water bottle while Creek snags the box of tissues from the vanity.

To me, he says, "There was a fourth body in the barn. One of the rear stalls. Big guy. Bullet wound to the head."

"That was Tusk," my girl spits out. "A piece of shit murdering rapist asshole."

Surprise arches Creek's brows. "One of the fighters?"

"Yeah," I tell him. "And most likely you'll be getting a hit on that DNA. Either already in the system because he's been in prison for rape or murder, or waiting to be matched to some serial killer shit. That fucker loved what he did in the Cage. Fucking loved it."

"I'll keep that in mind. Any idea how he met his demise?"

My girl shakes her head. "It was really dark in there. And it was so loud. Bullets going everywhere. He probably got confused and just…accidentally fell into the path of a ricochet."

"'Accidentally fell into the path of a ricochet,'" Creek

echoes slowly as he writes that down, barely doing a better job than I am of not laughing. "Any idea who was pulling the trigger that started the ricochet?"

"No clue. It was so dark," she says again. "I was locked up in my stall. The next thing I know, someone picked me up and carried me out of there, and I saw Tango and Hotel on the ground as we went out. But other than that… nothing. Because I swooned."

"Swooned?"

"Fainted. But elegantly."

"Seems like a reasonable reaction," he says, lips quirking. "Maybe we'll come back to that. What can you tell me about the other fighters?"

"Nothing."

"Nothing?"

"Nothing." She regards him steadily. "I'll call it patient confidentiality."

"You can't claim that privilege if you aren't a doctor."

"Maybe not. But they were under my care. So if they want to come forward, fine. But I will *not* be responsible for doing more harm to them, if naming them puts a target on their backs. Or on their family's backs. They've been through enough. And I've got enough guilt to deal with." Beneath the table, she reaches for my hand again. "You want me for Papa. Ask me about him, instead."

This fucking girl. I don't know how I ever thought she was just saving her own skin. She doesn't say it was me who killed Tusk, doesn't say she saw Gunner and Zoomie coming into the barn and shooting the guards, and now she's protecting the fighters. She doesn't owe any of us a damn thing. Hell, she's probably got reason to make some of us pay. Yet she's not giving the feds any leverage over us.

Creek takes that explanation in stride. "All right. Give me Papa's basics first. Do you have a description?"

She does, and there isn't any more to it than what she already told me. A tanned, rich-looking asshole. Of course, the FBI will get her in front of a forensic artist and maybe have a portrait soon.

More interesting is what she says about his security. No names for the suits, but the general descriptions matching what Spiral reported from the Iron Blood's compound. No surprise that it was Papa's crew, but good to have confirmation. She describes sedans instead of SUVs, but likely they use different vehicles to escort Papa than they do when transporting crates of guns. And best of all is a state for those plates, too—Nevada.

Already narrowing him down. And this feels real fucking good again. Getting shit done.

Creek flips over a page in his notebook. "Tell me about your first meeting with Papa."

She hesitates for a long time, biting her lip—her fingers squeezing mine. Finally she says softly, "I'd like to save that for a little later."

A little later…after I'm gone. Because that meeting with Papa is part of the explanation that she can't give me yet, her good reason for walking into this motel room instead of leaving with me.

A silence falls as Creek looks at her, a quiet that feels so damn heavy. I can't fucking breathe again. And I'm thinking that maybe I would let them cover up these scars, if it meant never letting go of her hand.

But the best way of keeping her safe is staying out, and killing Papa when I get that chance. Not heading into another cage called witness protection.

For her, it's right. It's her choice. But she's got her good reason to go in, and I've got a million fucking reasons to stay out.

"All right," Creek says, closing his notebook and looking to me. "We can call it a night. We'll meet up again another time and get those details from the Cage."

After my girl will already have been handed over again to the Marshals and squirreled away. My throat a knotted wreck, I nod.

"One last thing, though," he says, reaching back to pick another folder out of the pile. "I've got photos of men who have been reported missing and who we suspect might be in one of the stables…or might have already fought in the Cage. I understand that you don't want to expose any fighters who are already free, Cherry. But some of these men are beyond harm. And others are still in danger. So if either of you can identify any who have been killed or who are in the other stables, we'll have a better idea of who we're searching for—and for the others, give their families some closure. Just as you wanted Lissa's family to have."

She meets my eyes, as if seeking agreement. I don't care what we do if it means staying here a little bit longer with her.

"Okay," she says softly to him. Maybe thinking what I am, because she's holding my hand so tight.

Or maybe she's just bracing herself against what's coming. A set of four pictures. Airbag's one, but she doesn't seem to even look at his. Instead her gaze settles on the second photo.

I know him. "That's the one Tusk killed in the Cage, yeah? Draft."

She nods. "The week before Thanksgiving," she tells Creek, her voice wavering. "The next one went by Zero. He was from our stable and he was killed in the Cage in, um…mid-October?"

"Killed by whom?"

"Papa," she says and Creek's eyebrows arch high.

"He was in there?"

"No. But that's who killed Zero by making him fight." Her breath trembles again and she looks to the fourth. "That one was…I'm sorry, I don't know his name. It was my first time at the Cage. And he was killed right after the first fight I saw and I knew they said it was a death match but I didn't really… So I wasn't— I couldn't— It was really hard to pay attention."

My chest aches for her so fucking bad. "It's all right, angel."

"We know his name," Creek tells her gently. "Was he

from Papa's stable?"

She shakes her head.

"Did you ever hear anything about the other stable owners?"

She shakes her head again, wiping her cheeks with a tissue.

"Okay." He lays out another set of four. "How about these?"

I can answer one for her. A fighter who was still alive, at least after the last bout in the Cage, in another stable. The one who killed Flack, though I don't say that. Then she identifies two more who were beaten to death in front of her. Then another set. Remembering their names, remembering when—even the ones who weren't in Papa's stables. And with each one, she looks more and more vulnerable, more haunted.

Creek begins laying out another set and her fingers clench hard on mine.

Fuck. "Do you need to do them all now? Can't you give her a fucking break?"

"It's okay," she whispers tremulously. "It's okay. That one is Pushcart. I don't know two of the others, but, um…" She lets go of my hand, her fingers trembling wildly as she reaches out to touch the final picture. "This one is still alive. In a clinic. Because his arm was broken."

Ah, fuck. Hatchet. I didn't recognize him in this photo, where he's looking like a Boy Scout fresh out of a seminary class. But she still thinks he was sent out for surgery after he saved her from Tusk. Now her face is full of so much hope, because after all of these pictures of dead men, here is one she believes she might save.

Fucking hell. Fucking hell.

Across from us, Creek is utterly still. "That one? You're sure?"

She nods, picking up the picture in her shaking hands. "In the doc's private clinic. And I don't know what the doc's name is, but if we can look up photos of licensed physicians or—"

"No, angel." As gently as I can, I stop her. "He's not in the clinic."

"Yes, he is. The doc said that—"

"The doc lied. And I'm so fucking sorry."

"What do you mean, he lied?" Her voice rises on a sharp note, her chest hitching wildly. "He told Victor to take him to the clinic. And Victor told him to go quietly. Because if Hatchet didn't…if he didn't… He *would* go quietly. He wouldn't give them trouble."

"Why do you say he lied?" Creek asks, though he sounds like he doesn't want to know. He's slumped back in his chair, eyes on me. "What did you see?"

"Victor walked him out behind the barns—"

My girl makes a sound like I gutted her with a knife. Shaking hands covering her mouth, she implores me, "Because they were walking to a vehicle? Please. Please."

Throat clogged, I shake my head and watch her shatter right in front of me, those emerald eyes turning to dull glass and breaking into glittering tears, face crumpling as she dissolves into heart-wrenching sobs. Utterly destroyed, I wrap my arms around her.

"I'm so fucking sorry, angel. I know he helped you. But this isn't your—"

"Puh…please. *Please*," she begs against my throat, her tears burning my skin. "You have to be wrong. You have to be."

"Did you see it?" Creek asks dully.

"Saw him on his knees." I hold her tighter with every quiet word. "Then heard it. A single shot."

My girl flinches at *shot*, the wild sobs breaking into gulping heaves of her chest. "No no no. Not Matt. Oh god, oh god no, please, not him."

"Ah fuck," Creek suddenly breathes, sitting upright. "You're the *sister*."

She chokes. Then bolts out of my arms, bumping into the table and sending the pictures flying as she races for the bathroom. I lurch after her. The door slams in my face but the sounds of violent retching make real clear what's happening on the other side.

Hands braced on the doorframe, I look over to Creek, who's rubbing his hands down his face. "What sister?" I ask hoarsely. "Who the fuck is Matt?"

"Hatchet," he says, a muscle in his jaw working. "He was one of mine. And we knew his sister had vanished around the same time, but her co-workers said she'd come into some money, and that she was either going back to college or traveling. We'd hoped it was just traveling."

Fuck. Stomach twisting hard, I open the door. Her head's hanging over the bowl, so I wet a washcloth before hunkering down beside her, holding back her hair. She's mostly just crying now, and when she gags again nothing comes up.

"Hey." Tenderly I wipe her face, her mouth. "I'm so sorry, angel. Hatchet's your brother, then—his name is Matt?"

She nods, tears coursing down her face. Rocking back, she crumples into the corner of the room, wedged up between the tub and the wall. I follow her down and give her a warm body to lean against instead of a cold tub. When I get my arm around her, she turns her face against my shoulder, still sobbing those heart-wrenching sobs.

Each one wrenching at my heart, too. Protecting her brother all this damn time, likely knowing that undercover agents with their covers blown have a real short life expectancy. Only to get here and learn this.

I don't know how long she cries with me holding her. Another wish of mine granted. To stay with her a little longer.

Didn't know it would cost her so fucking much.

Eventually she goes quiet. Just shaking against me with her chest hitching on every breath. I hold her, waiting for her to talk—or not. Words or silence, whatever she needs, that's what I'll give.

After a little while, it's words. Hers are thick and dull.

"Every horrible thing I did. Everything I *would* have done. Just trying to keep us alive long enough to get out of there. It was all for nothing."

I don't know if she's talking about playing bait and don't care. None of it was for nothing. "You're wrong there, angel. Because I can tell you right now that your brother didn't give a fuck about anything except getting you out. So all that you did, every step that got you to where you're sitting here now, safe from Papa and still breathing? That would mean *everything* to him."

That starts her tears up again. But I know I'm right. Anyone who loved this girl wouldn't care if he got out alive. As long as she was safe.

"He knew," she sobs quietly. "He knew what they were going to do. I didn't realize then but he told me not to wait for him to come back. But why didn't *I* realize? I could have...I could have done *something*."

There wasn't anything she could have done. Matt would have known that. Likely she knows it, too.

But that's cold comfort. "I'm sorry, angel."

"And instead of seeing what was right in front of me, I came up with another fucking *stupid* plan. Don't tell you anything that might send your club to that clinic, just get to his boss so we can mount a rescue. But it was just absolute shit. From the very start."

"Nah, girl. You did everything right. And you had the very best reason for staying quiet and fighting until you got here. You were so fucking loyal. You'd have made any brother proud."

"Whatever that's worth."

"That's worth everything."

"Then I don't have anything now." With a ragged sob, she presses her face into her hands. "Nothing at all."

Fuck. Throat raw, I hold her tight. Because I know exactly what's in her now. A big fucking hole.

As soon as she quiets again, I catch her tearstained cheeks in my hands, meet her shattered gaze. "You *do* have something, angel. You've got three months of information in your head. And with that, you'll help these feds nail those fuckers to the wall. Papa, the doc, Victor. Every single one of them. Pretty soon, you'll be looking across a courtroom at them, and making them *pay* for what they did to you. For what they did to Matt. Yeah?"

Though her lips are trembling, her face firms up and she nods. "Yeah."

"Your brother's the one who told you to remember all that stuff, isn't he?" Probably why she sounded like a cop reciting it. "So that everything you saw, you could tell the feds later. When you got out, he intended for you to burn the whole thing down. That right?"

A spark flares to life behind her eyes. "He did."

"Then that's what you have. I know you're hurting real bad, but you hold onto that. You're going to take these fuckers down. Say to me you will."

Her chin lifts. "I will."

"That's my girl." Softly I kiss those trembling lips, then

pull back to brush her tears from her cheeks. "Do you have any other family? Anyone they can bring in and—"

Those eyes fill with tears again, but don't shatter. "No other family," she whispers thickly. "I'm alone now."

"Nah. You've got an entire law enforcement agency about to bend over backwards for you. And you've got me. You keep that tag handy. And any fucking thing, you understand? *Anything.* I'll be there. You're not alone. I'll get another burner and send the number to that phone I gave you. Then you can text or call me any time and no one will be able to trace it. Okay?"

She takes a deep, shuddering breath before nodding. Steadying herself. "Okay."

This fucking girl. And my chest hurts so goddamn bad. But it's not rot anymore.

"C'mon, then. Let's get you off this floor."

I take her hand, but she shakes her head. "Thank you. But... I'm not ready to go out there and talk more yet."

"I'll tell Creek to keep his mouth shut."

"No. It's okay. I just need to...stop crying first."

"Might take a while."

"Yeah, well. I don't have any other plans for tonight." A watery smile curves her lips. "Mine fell apart."

Rescuing her brother. "I guess they did."

"But you should go," she says softly.

And leave her here. Throat feeling like it's shredded, I cup her face. "Is that what you want?"

"You've helped me so much." She swallows hard. "But

I can't ask you to be my shoulder to cry on all night."

"Yeah, you can."

She laughs as if I were joking before her mouth presses tight, her chin wobbling, her shimmering eyes searching my face.

"Thank you," she whispers, and I know a good-bye when I hear one. "But I just need to sit and figure out what to do now."

Yeah. Me, too.

It ain't rot in my chest now. But still hurts so fucking much as I nod and get to my feet. I'm at the bathroom door when she stops me.

"Stone." She's got her arms wrapped around herself, still all huddled up on the floor. "Are you still going after Papa, too?"

"Yeah," I say quietly. It's the only way she'll ever truly be safe from him. "Unless you want to get him first. I'll wait my turn."

She shakes her head, her eyes going distant. "But... let me know if you do?"

"Yeah. I'll do that."

"Thank you."

I can't bear to hear that even one more time. I force my feet to move. Creek's standing in the room, phone to his ear, face grim.

"—push the sweep back farther. Our man's in the dirt out there and I want him out, right fucking now." He tosses the phone to the bed and looks over to me. "She all right?"

"What the fuck do you think?" I grab my jacket. "She'll help you take down Papa. And if he ever gets to her, if he gets even a whiff of her existence, I will fucking end you."

He accepts that with a nod.

"And that deal with Blowback about the heads-up…I don't want Papa any more. If I get him first, I get him." Otherwise she can have first crack. "The heads-up I want now is Victor."

The fucker who pulled the trigger on her brother and is the reason she's crying now.

"All right," he agrees. "That suits me better, anyway."

I don't give a fuck what suits him. All that matters is that my girl is huddled up on the floor of a bathroom, hurting so bad. And that she told me I should go, and I'll give her anything she wants.

The cold air outside burns my eyes, my throat. Makes it hard to breathe. But this is the only thing to do. She had one real good reason to walk through that door. But for me, going through that door would mean cutting ties with my family and the club. I've got a million reasons to stay out—and only one reason to go in.

And I don't even know her name. But she's all that's inside me. Because there's no hole in my chest now.

There's just her.

I reach my bike, and my eyes aren't burning. Breathing is easier. Because the way ahead is clear. So many reasons to stay out.

But one real, real good reason to turn around and walk back through that door. And that one reason to go in is more important than a million others.

I turn back.

Up ahead, the door to the last room flings open. "Stone!"

My girl comes running out, clutching her pack and jacket, frantically looking in my direction. When she sees me, relief pours over her face before she races closer.

Swearing, Creek comes after her.

I head for her and she reaches me halfway, a light in her eyes that I've seen before—rage, burning like fire through that emerald. "When you go after Papa, you won't just have him thrown in jail, right? You'll literally be nailing him to the wall?"

Messy, but doable. "If that's what you want me to do."

Her chin lifts. "I want to do it with you. I want to make him really, *really* pay. I'll tell you everything I know. Just let me go with you."

"All right." Anything she wants.

Gratitude slips over her expression. "Thank—"

"Don't."

"Miss Faraday," Creek says, coming up slowly with his hands held out, as if thinking she'll bolt like a frightened doe. "Leaving is not a safe option for you. And if you're thinking of taking justice into your own hands, remember that is not what Matt stood for."

"I know what he stood for," she snaps at him. "I'll still

give you everything you want to know—just set up more meetings like this and I'll do my duty. I'll still sit in that witness stand. But I'm not going to sit in another cage until then."

Gritting his teeth, he pulls his hand through his hair, then looks to me. "Talk some fucking sense into her."

"She's making sense to me."

"I've given you a lot to go on already." She heads for my bike, straps her pack to the back. "But here's something more. At that town I was bait in. I don't know what it was called—"

"Cactus Gulch," I say.

"There was a sheriff who took a roll of cash from the Iron Blood. Baumgarten, according to his name tag. So if you're looking for someone who might be smoothing the way to these other stables, that might be a good place to start."

His eyes narrow. "While you start somewhere else."

She doesn't say anything. Just stands beside my bike with her helmet in hand. Waiting for me.

Creek meets my gaze. "This is grief talking. So when this anger passes, bring her back. Anytime, anywhere." He hands me a card. "For now, just keep her safe."

With my own life. I tuck his card away. "Be seeing you, Creek."

"Soon, I hope."

He can keep hoping. I'm done with wishing when it comes to this girl. I'll take everything she gives. But until she gives it, I won't ask for anything more.

I head back to my bike. That fire's still in her eyes, though a tremble has returned to her lips. "You sure about this?" I ask her.

She nods and pulls on her helmet, the faceplate still up.

"Then hold onto me, angel." I settle onto my bike. "We've got a ways to go."

"I know." Her hands briefly rest on my shoulders for balance as she straddles the seat behind me. "And it's Maxine."

My heart squeezes tight. "What's that?"

"My name." Her arms wrap around me. "It's Maxine."

My chest feeling real full, I fire up my engine. So there it is. The name of the girl I'd do anything for. The girl who's got me so damn deep in love with her. This fucking girl.

Maxine.

THE ROAD

TWENTY-NINE

STONE

That morning, for the first time since leaving the barns, my girl doesn't stir awake before sunrise.

My dog does. I hush Daisy's urgent whining and lead her downstairs, opening the side door to let her out. Anna's already up and in her kitchen, banging cupboards. Shit. It doesn't take a genius to figure out what set off her temper.

I open the door that leads from the stairwell to her kitchen and close it behind me. "Want to cool it for a bit? Maxine is still sleeping."

And that's the first time I've said her name. *Maxine.*

Fits her a whole lot better than Cherry.

Anna shoots me a look that's pure poison and slams her kettle onto a burner. Loud as fuck, but her voice is a low hiss. "I can't fucking believe you brought that girl here. You never bring anyone home. And when you do, it's *that* one?"

"And you don't know what the hell you're talking about," I tell her gently, because my sister's low view of Maxine is my own damn fault.

In sweat shorts and bare feet, Gunner comes into the kitchen. He gives me a single assessing glance before stopping behind Anna, leaning down to kiss her neck and to murmur something into her ear. And…yeah, that's a change. Holy shit. Knew it had happened between them. Seeing it is something different.

This ain't the first time we've all been in this kitchen together. Far from it. Yet always before, I was the link to both while they each pretended there was no link simmering between them. It was just Anna, my sister— and Gunner, my brother. But now, they've got their own link that doesn't have a damn thing to do with me. Something that puts me outside of what they are together.

All good. But it thumps me right in the feels.

Whatever it was Gunner said to her, Anna takes a deep breath. Then another. Settling down.

But emotion is still thick in her voice as she turns toward me. It's just worry now instead of anger.

Because that's all the anger was, anyway. Just worry.

"What don't I know?" she asks in a carefully even tone.

Gunner doesn't know, either. Not yet. When I brought Maxine home around four a.m, he woke up and came to check on me, but we didn't stop to chat.

So I tell them both. About Hatchet, who he really was, and what Maxine learned last night. By the time the coffee's ready, Anna's sitting at the table with Gunner rubbing his hand up and down her back, and my sister's lost all her anger.

"Holy shit," she says quietly. "That poor girl."

"Maxine." I fucking love saying it. "Maxine Faraday."

Gunner narrows his eyes. "What about the business last night?"

With Creek. "Finding out about her brother changed things up."

They both know me too well to doubt the rest, but my sister asks anyway, "Changed them up for her or for you?"

"For her." Learning about her brother didn't change anything for me. Except knowing she was hurting so bad made me face square on what I was trying hard not to see, and ripped away the blinders concealing how much she means to me.

"What next?" Gunner asks.

"Find Papa." I say it in front of Anna because this isn't club business anymore. Instead it's personal. "Finish it."

My brother nods, slides back his chair. "I'll get ready."

"No." I stop him. "Just Maxine and me."

Gunner shakes his head and Anna's already protesting before he says, "Hold up, brother—"

"She's in a real bad place," I talk over them. "Angry, hurt. So I'm going to help her."

Anna leans in, voice low. "Just a wild guess, but killing a man is *not* the kind of help she needs."

"I know it."

And it ain't the kind of help I'll give. Creek wasn't wrong. Her need to kill Papa is rage and grief talking.

If it comes to it, I'll kill Papa. But let Maxine do it— or even see it? Not a chance. Not a woman who said she almost puked while trying to psych herself up to kill a guard, even though it meant winning her own freedom. Not a woman who quietly cried over every man she saw killed in the Cage. Killing Papa would hurt her more than she already is hurting. So she shouldn't be killing anyone.

But if hunting him down is what she needs, if that's how her grief and rage are talking, then I'll let her scream that rage and grief until she's done screaming.

Anna sighs and leans back. "And whenever there's a girl in trouble—"

"No," I tell her. Maybe once upon a time, that might have been true. It isn't now. "This isn't like that."

They both know me well enough to see what that means, too. That she's a hell of a lot more than just a girl in trouble to me.

"Aw, fuck." Gunner rubs his hand over his face. "Let me come with you. I don't want to see you hurt."

"You coming wouldn't stop a damn thing." Wouldn't matter if he could, either. I don't care if I'm hurt. Don't care a bit. She's all that matters now. "And I owe her."

Gunner's eyebrows shoot upwards. "How do you figure that?"

"Because there was a big fucking hole in me, and Maxine got me through to the other side." Or maybe she just filled it up. Either way, the only hurt left in me is knowing that she's hurting, too. "Now it's my turn to help her get through."

They exchange a look. Daisy scratches on the door, so I get up to let her in while they carry on their eyeball conversation. Tail whipping everything in her path, Daisy careens her way to the table, sniffs up Gunner and Anna before returning to me.

And they've apparently finished their silent talk and come to an agreement.

"All right, brother," Gunner says. "Anything you need—"

"I know."

With a heavy sigh, Anna gets up and hugs me tight. "And be careful?"

"I will." Because Maxine will be with me. Being careful is just another way of keeping her safe. "I'll make those video calls for Daisy as often as I can."

"Okay." She tilts her head back. Her eyes are filled up with tears, but with a smile there, too. "It's good to have my brother back."

The man I was before the Cage. Not all the same. But closer than I was.

Not dead. Just wearing more scars.

Gunner claps me on the back, saying what Anna did without the words. "You heading out right away?"

"Depends on Maxine. Might be she'll need a day or two before she's ready to do anything. For now, I'll let her sleep."

"Sleep sounds good." Gunner takes Anna's hand, begins pulling her toward the hallway. "So we'll just head back to bed, too, and be real quiet down here."

Yeah, I think I'll be getting my own place soon. I reach down to scratch Daisy's ears, then she's on my heels all the way up the stairs. My apartment upstairs isn't much to look at. Anna's put some stuff up here to make it nicer but I just don't care beyond having what's necessary. Pretty sure Daisy's got more up here than I do. There's a couch and television in the living room; in the bedroom, there's the bed, a chair to pile up with my clean clothes and a basket for the dirty ones.

Last night, I took the pile of clean clothes and threw them in the empty basket, then settled into the chair while Maxine and Daisy curled up on the bed. About two seconds after we got here, my girl was all over my dog, petting her and kissing her furry face and crying again. Then she cried herself to sleep.

No signs of stirring yet. She's on her belly with her cheek turned against the pillow, her face and eyes puffy from all the tears. My throat's real tight as I adjust the blanket a little higher over her shoulders.

Daisy tries to snuffle around her, probably searching for all the loving that Maxine lavished on her while crying.

"C'mon, girl." Quietly, I pull Daisy back from the bed, then snag a few things out of the basket. Under my breath, I ask her, "Wanna go for a run? We're gonna stay real strong so we can take care of her, yeah?"

Daisy is all for that idea. In the living room, I change my clothes and lace up my shoes, and then my dog nearly rips my heart out when we're about to head down the stairs, and she looks back toward the bedroom, wagging her tail.

Waiting for our new friend.

I sit on the top stair, get her in close, scratching her ears. "We're going to let her sleep, okay? She's real hurt. The kind of hurt that I can't fix. And I'm so fucking sorry, girl, but I have to leave you with Anna again for a little while. But then I'll be back."

And this damn dog. Wagging her tail and loving me through all of this.

"But our girl ain't going to come back," I say through the raw ache in my throat. "And you oughta blame me for that. She's real angry at Papa now and grateful I can help, but pretty soon…pretty soon…she'll start thinking about all the shit I said to her. All the shit I *did* to her. And then— And then…I don't figure she'll ever let me see her again."

Whining softly, Daisy licks my face.

"You ain't gotta worry, though," I tell her hoarsely. "She loves you. She'll give you all the kisses while she's here. Because you're a good girl. Such a good girl."

Her favorite thing to hear. She grins up at me, tongue lolling.

"So you ready to go? Let's go, girl. We gotta be real strong for her."

Real fucking strong.

THIRTY

MAXINE

I don't want to get out of bed. But I do.

I don't want to take a shower. But I do.

I don't want to start crying again while I'm in there. But I do.

Then I turn the shower knob to full cold and let the icy water cascade over my face. It helps. A little.

I don't look into the mirror before I leave the bathroom. I don't know that girl, anyway. Brown hair and red eyes, and a brother who isn't alive. I don't ever want that girl to be me.

But I want that girl to be the last thing Papa ever sees.

I pack up my things and head downstairs. My steps falter at the bottom. I need to go left, but to the right is an open door leading to a kitchen—and Stone's sister, putting a bowl into the fridge, then glancing up and spotting me.

Shit. But I need to ask, "Where should I find him?"

Ah god. My voice sounds like a clogged drain.

"In the garage. But, uh, Maxine…" Sympathy pinches her expression. "I'm so sorry about your brother."

That doesn't help the mess in my throat, but I can't think about Matt now. Only what's ahead. Or else I'll start crying again. "Thank you. And, um…I'm sorry that you were attacked. And for my part in luring Stone."

Gently she says, "Honestly, it doesn't sound like you had a choice."

"There was a choice." The laugh that breaks from me sounds a little like a sob. "Bad options to choose from, maybe. But I still made the choice. So I'm sorry."

"All right, then. You want any coffee?"

Even if I did, I couldn't swallow past the lump in my throat. I shake my head.

"Okay." She points to the door behind me. "Garage is that way."

I get out as quickly as I can. The frigid air bites into my hot cheeks and stinging eyes. Frozen grass crunches under my boots as I make my way to the detached garage—

though now that I'm out here, I don't need the direction. He's got music playing, bass thumping hard enough that I'm not surprised he doesn't hear me open the side door. Inside are two motorcycles, including the one we rode last night, a workbench topped by an array of tools, and an area full of exercise equipment.

And this is *so* familiar. Yet not familiar at all. Stone's stripped to the waist, sweat gleaming over his skin as he pounds a heavy bag. But when he used to work out in the barn, he was so methodical about it. Controlled. Now he's just laying into the bag, each blow hard and vicious and fast, as if he's picturing Papa at the other end. The way he's going, though, it's hard to tell whether he's beating the bag or if the bag is beating him.

Daisy alerts him to my presence, looking up from where she's chewing on a rawhide strip and bouncing over when she sees me. Stone pivots away from the swinging bag, every muscle in his torso and arms jacked. His intense gaze is all over me, lingering for a second on my eyes before he strides over to a table, taps the screen of his phone. The music from the speakers falls silent, filling the space with his heaving breaths and Daisy's pants as I crouch and give her pettings.

"All right?" He's looking me over again, wiping the sweat from his face with the back of his forearm. "Figured you'd sleep longer."

"I can't."

Oh god, and my throat. That sounded as raw as I feel.

His face softens. "Feeling like you need to get shit done?"

I nod.

"We'll get started, then." He picks up a gallon jug of water—already half empty—still eyeing me as he chugs some more. "You got a driver's license anywhere?"

My chest tightens. "No. Matt tossed my purse into a trash can when he realized we were being taken. So they wouldn't know my real name—or learn his."

"Smart."

"He was." And shit. Shit. I bury my face in Daisy's neck, take deep breaths. Finally look up again. Stone's watching me, that intense gaze dark, his body utterly still. "Do we need ID?"

He nods before dragging a sleeveless T-shirt over his head. "The way I figure it, Creek will put someone on us. Watching everything we do, looking for any excuse to haul us in—and hoping for anything that'll give him leverage. So driving around without a license or using fake ID is a bad idea right now."

"Do I need to drive?"

"Shouldn't."

"What about a getaway car?"

Abruptly he grins. "If we get to that point, we've got bigger problems than no driver's license."

That's probably true. And getting a replacement license might take a couple of weeks—I don't want to wait weeks.

"Okay, well…I have a passport in storage. And a birth certificate. And some money, but that's in a bank."

His eyes narrow. "We're not using your money."

"But I asked you to take me, so I should—"

"You think I'm not after him, too? You think this is just a favor I'm doing for you?" His voice is low. Dangerously so. The same voice that I usually heard right before he ordered me onto my hands and knees, and simply hearing it sends little sparks of heat flying through my belly. "You contribute the info. I'll contribute the bankroll and the muscle."

That seems lopsided, but I don't want to argue about it now. "Okay."

"And new rule: We don't talk about *any* of what we're doing until we've got your passport, until we're in Vegas, and we're married."

"Ok—" *Wait.* My heart thumps like a fist slamming into a heavy bag. "What?"

"You heard right. Because it'll protect you, and it'll protect me." He comes closer, gaze fixed on mine as he crouches next to Daisy and me. "Last night, Creek let a whole lot of your lies pass, because he doesn't really want those fighters who were in the Cage. He's not looking to make them pay—he's just looking for as much info as he can get, because the more he has when he arrests Papa, the better the chance of a conviction. And you…you're just an innocent swept up in this. But what we're thinking of doing, you're not so innocent anymore, understand? Not in the eyes of the law. Killing Papa might be justified, but it's real fucking illegal."

A shiver works down my spine, but the mention of Papa chases it with fire. "I understand."

"And the thing is, the law can make you pay for not telling them something. Like for not saying what you and I were plan—"

"I wouldn't tell them anything."

"I know you wouldn't." His voice deepens and he brushes the back of his knuckles down the side of my jaw before giving Daisy's ears a scratch. "But they can make you pay for not saying it. Fines, contempt, jail time, all that shit. And if you lie, there's perjury. Unless we're married. A husband and wife have privileges a lot like a lawyer and client do. You can't be compelled to testify about anything we talked about. You can opt to say nothing at all."

"Really?"

"Yep. At least according to the internet research I did while I was out for a run."

I huff out a laugh.

His crooked grin flashes again. "Seems legit, though. If you saw me kill someone, that'd be one thing. But shit we talk about, any plans we make? They can't force you to testify about it, as long as we don't go sharing those confidences with anyone else. So you and me, we're going to Vegas, getting married, then having a road trip honeymoon that might just take us to wherever Papa is. You in?"

A marriage that doesn't just protect me. It protects

him, too. "I'm in."

"Good."

Despite that reply, though, his expression doesn't say *Good*. Shadowed, his hazel eyes search my face, and there's something troubled about the way he hesitates that tells me whatever he's going to add next will hurt.

Hurt *more*. Because the pain of losing Matt is a deep, constant ache. Yet…being in here with Stone has made it a little easier to bear.

It hasn't gone away. Hasn't lessened. It's simply easier to bear.

Just like last night, the only time I believed I might get through this was when I was riding behind him, holding him tight. Then holding onto Daisy, because as soon as we got to his house, all I could hear was his sister saying how I kept clinging to him. And thought maybe she was right. So I clung to his dog, instead. That was okay. But it wasn't the same.

Yet in the past few minutes, I've been able to laugh and smile, and not think so much about the giant part of me that's missing now. So instead of waiting for Stone to speak, I head him off, rubbing my face against Daisy's. "I don't suppose we can take her with us?"

"Nah. Motorcycle helmets look real cute on her but don't fit too well."

That image makes me smile, too. "I guess not."

"And she'd probably ruin any plans we made," he says affectionately, rubbing up under her jaw and making kissy noises. "Wouldn't you, girl? That's right. Because you're so cute but you're also real dumb."

I gasp in mock outrage. "Don't listen to him, Daisy. You just turn to him and say, 'If dumb means someone can't ride along with us, then who's going with Maxine?'"

"Shit." He shakes his head, a deep laugh rumbling from him. "Your damn mouth just… *Fuck.*"

Suddenly all that trouble returns to his face. I try to head him off again. "Don't you have work, though? Lumberjacking?"

"Widowmaker will give me the time off." His grave tone and steady gaze tell me that this time he won't be waylaid. "Until we're married, we don't talk about what's ahead for us. But before you hitch yourself up to me, we probably ought to talk about what's in the past."

"You mean those three months?" Of course we'll have to talk about that. I'm the info girl. "I truly don't have any names, but maybe we can find Papa through the doctor when—"

"Not Papa." A muscle in his jaw works, and he seems to struggle before saying gruffly, "You and me. Because I laid a whole lot of shit on you, and you didn't deserve any of it. Every damn thing I said to you. And…making you pay up, even though you didn't owe me a fucking thing."

His voice roughens more with each word, but I don't understand any of it. "Didn't owe you? Stone, I—"

"Did the same damn thing that I did. I was looking after my sister, and you were looking after your brother."

"Yes, but you didn't know that. I lied to you. Said I didn't have family. Said I was saving my own skin."

"It shouldn't have mattered. Saving your own skin or saving someone else, we were all being fucked over by Papa. He was the only one who needed to pay. But I took that shit out on you, made it personal." Something dark and desolate moves over his expression. "And by the time I got you into that cabin, I knew you didn't owe me anything. Knew it real damn well. All I should have gotten from you was answers. But you made me feel so fucking good, I made you pay up, too. Took the virginity that you were saving for a husband, then fucked you every chance that I could, even though you were begging for me to let you go. And I'm sorry for that, Maxine. For making you feel like you owed me anything, then for taking what you offered to pay. I'm so fucking sorry."

I can see how sorry he is in the bleak torment of his eyes, hear it in his voice. Sorry for the one thing from these past months that I want to hold onto. Sorry for the one thing that doesn't hurt me.

Or *didn't* hurt me. Until Stone said that he was sorry for it. And I don't know what to do now. Except shrug and tell him in a voice still raspy after a night of crying, "There's nothing to be sorry for. It turns out that I *will* be marrying the guy who took my virginity."

I was hoping for at least a smile, or for him to curse my mouth again, but he keeps watching me with that tormented gaze.

"I just want to be real clear that what's ahead of us ain't like that," he tells me, his voice all gravel. "You don't owe me anything. And I sure as fuck won't be asking you to pay up. So you don't need to worry that I'll touch you again."

"Okay." It's just a strained whisper. My eyes are hot, my throat aching, and the pressure in my chest so tight. Vision swimming with tears, I ask hoarsely, "Can I take Daisy out to play before we go?"

I only catch a blurry glimpse of his nod before I'm gone. Because somehow…the idea of a future with Stone had wormed its way into my head. After he said that letting me go wasn't so easy. After he agreed to meet up again when this was over. And after he held me so tight while I cried, encouraged me to keep fighting.

A part of me was still clinging to that future. Not actively thinking of it. Not on top of everything else. But feeling it out there, like a glimmer on the horizon. Something for *after* all of this. Something good and hopeful.

Something that promised I wouldn't be alone.

But I should have remembered that Stone wanted pussy or answers—and now he's getting answers. I should have remembered that he never wanted me to touch him or to kiss him. Now he won't be touching me, either.

So whatever future had been glimmering ahead… obviously I was wrong. There's nothing for me out there.

Nothing beyond getting to Papa.

It doesn't feel like much.

THIRTY-ONE

STONE

For most of my life, Maxine Faraday has only been a four-hour ride away.

Four hours on a motorcycle is nothing. For weekend rides, the Hellfire Riders make four-hour trips on the regular. From central Oregon, four hours can take you anywhere. The beach, the mountains, the desert, the forest.

Four hours can also take you to Redding, California. A city I've been to—and ridden through—dozens of times. It fucking kills me to know that Maxine's been so close and I had no damn clue. In a tavern, all it took was one look. If I'd have seen her while riding through, I'd have come down every weekend.

Because four hours is nothing. Barely any time.

And that's never been more true than when she's riding behind me, holding me so tight. For four hours.

Barely any time.

Her storage unit is at the edge of town. She called ahead, saying her ID was stolen and that she'll show them her passport after she collects it. Add in bolt cutters for the padlock, and we don't have any trouble getting in.

The unit is filled up mostly with rustic furniture. "From my grandpa's house," she tells me quietly as we head inside.

She hasn't said much else since leaving my place. Mostly because it's hard to hold any kind of conversation on a motorcycle. But I'm not sure she would have talked, anyway. Everything about her seems as if she's shut down.

But I know she's not. I know hurt and grief are roiling around in her. She's just not letting it out.

Or trying not to let it out. Because for a long minute she just stands and looks around, her eyes bright with tears that she's not letting fall. Every damn thing inside me aches with the need to go to her, to hold her close. But I swore I wouldn't touch her again.

A promise that might kill me. But hurting her would be worse than dying.

As it is, I'm waiting for her to take back her agreement to marry me. She still seems to think that she truly owed me back in the cabin. But I figure when this grief eases, she'll realize what a goddamn asshole I am and try to distance herself from me as far as she can. And maybe she'll realize our marriage isn't just to protect her—though it is that, too. But also because I'm a pathetic sack of shit who'll do anything to keep her bound to me, one way or another.

And help her, even if I can't hold her. "Do you need me to look for it?"

She shakes her head. "No." Her voice is hoarse. "It's just…it was hard enough when it felt like I was putting so much of my grandpa in here. But there's so much of Matt, too. His bed and his favorite chair and his dresser over there…"

So much damn hurt that I can't ease. "I take it that you lived with your grandpa, then?"

She nods, her tears spilling over, then chokes out a laugh before sending me a watery smile that says the joke's on her. "My parents drowned in a boating accident when I was eight and Matt was twelve. Not just them. My grandma and aunts and uncles, too. So Grandpa took us in."

Ah, fuck. My poor girl. "That's what happened to me," I tell her quietly. "But it was a car accident that killed my parents."

Confusion creases her brow. "But I thought your mom and dad were alive? Victor threatened them."

Yeah, he did. On top of what he did to her brother, just

another reason to kill him. "I was adopted. Anna, too. And I wasn't as old as you—I don't remember my real parents much. My adopted parents have always been Mom and Dad to me."

"Oh." She wipes her cheeks. "That's really sweet."

"They're pretty amazing," I say. "Sounds like you were close to your grandpa, too?"

"Yeah. Both Matt and I were," she whispers, but this time with more bittersweet nostalgia than painful grief. She takes a deep breath and heads toward a steel safe sitting on an old rolltop desk.

Pushy bastard that I am, I crowd in and glance through some of the other papers she pulls out and sets aside while looking for her passport, including a few leather-bound diploma covers. Her high school certificate, Matt's.

And a college degree. "You're a veterinarian?"

That makes her laugh a little and shake her head. "Just a vet tech. I originally intended to become a vet, but then…" She shrugs. "Grandpa got sick."

"And you took care of him." Don't even need to make it a question.

"I did. Matt had just started at the FBI." That sweet smile curves her mouth again. "His dream job. And it was easy for me to transfer to the community college here, start working as a vet tech while…" She trails off, biting her lip. "Grandpa could still work on the farm and get around. It was just better to have someone there. So I was happy to."

"You grew up on a farm?"

"Not a big farm. Just a couple of cows, goats, chickens—and right at the edge of town, so we didn't exactly grow up in the sticks." Her voice thickens. "It was a lot of fun. Grandpa made us do chores, of course, but mostly we were just…free. To do whatever."

"Like learn to steal motorcycles."

Another laugh breaks from her. "That was Matt. Not stealing. But he had a thing for dirt bikes. So of course I ended up with one, too."

Of course. There was no *of course* for me and Anna. Riding was my thing, not hers. But we also lived in a town, each had our own set of friends. Sounds like out on their farm, Maxine and her brother mostly had each other as friends. Though maybe losing their parents had something to do with that, too. Sticking together. "Is that bike stored in here?"

"No. After my grandpa… I sold the farm. Because I love working with animals but working a farm wasn't what I wanted. So I put some of the furniture and other stuff that I wanted to keep in here, but knew we wouldn't be using the bikes. Hadn't used them for a while, really. But I wish now that I had more of Matt's things." Those emerald eyes fill up again as she looks around the storage unit. "We got a really good sell price on the property. So there I was, with so much money and so many options. But Matt had already been under for a few years, and although I didn't know exactly what he was doing, I knew that I couldn't just move to where he was. So I thought that I'd go back to school, get that full veterinary degree. Or maybe travel for a year first. But I wanted to see Matt before making any big decisions. So I went to Vegas and…"

Her life went to shit. But there's no need to say that.

She pulls out the little blue passport booklet. Holds it in her hands for a long minute before looking up at me, eyes shimmering with tears. "When we stop for the night, can we go out and get really, really, *really* drunk?"

"Yeah, angel." I might not be able to help her with everything. But this is one thing I have plenty of experience with. "We'll get absolutely shit-faced together."

She smiles and sniffles. "Good. How far?"

"About four more hours."

Barely any time at all.

THIRTY-TWO

STONE

Reno's about halfway to Las Vegas, and it ain't hard to find a motel that'll take cash within stumbling distance of a bar. Both places are real questionable, so I fit right in. Maxine, not so much. But I'm pretty sure she doesn't give a fuck.

My girl gets plenty of looks when we go in. Then the people looking at her take a gander at me and return to minding their own business. A jukebox is playing some Kenny Loggins shit and no one's complaining, which tells me all I need to know about the owner.

She doesn't give a fuck, either.

I figure she's the one up at the bar. About sixty, brown hair going gray, an expression like rusty nails. I'd bet my right nut her name is Barb or Marge. She eyes Maxine, then me, then her lips quirk a bit when Maxine says, "Can I get a shot of tequila, please?"

Shit, that's cute.

"Hold up, angel. We've got to do this right." I scan the bottles. "What did your brother like to drink when it was special?"

"Um… Maker's Mark."

Can't argue with that. "Two shots of the whisky," I say to Barb. "And two more of that Don Julio Añejo."

Barb pours the tequila first. I slide one shot glass over to Maxine and lift the other.

"This one is for Crash, yeah?" I tell her, my throat going all fucking tight. Because he deserved a hell of a lot better. But this is what we've got.

Her gaze softens and she clinks her shot to mine. "For Crash."

And it burns so damn good. She throws hers back, eyes going real bright as she coughs.

I push the whisky in front of her. "You shooting this or sipping?"

"Shooting. Then sipping more."

Sounds good. "Then here's to Matt."

This time she can't repeat it. Only nods and clinks

before tossing it down. Those tears aren't all from the alcohol now.

"All right, then," I tell her gently. "You go and grab that booth in the back corner there, and I'll bring us something to sip on."

I watch her as she goes. Those two shots couldn't have hit her yet. Still, this is my only purpose tonight. Watching over her.

Barb's measuring me up with beady eyes. No need to guess why. I toss down a few bills to cover the shots—then add a few more.

"We're going to do a lot of damage to that bottle of whisky," I tell her, leaning in. "And you're probably already thinking that she's a lightweight and that you'll have to cut her off after this drink. You won't, though."

She purses her lips. "Is that right?"

"It is. Because that girl just found out her brother was killed in the line of duty. And the only thing she asked me for was to get drunk off her ass. So I'm going to help her do that." I lay a hundred-dollar bill on top of the cash pile. "You're going to let me help her, so that she doesn't ever think her only option is heading home with a bottle. Instead, she'll know the best option is going out with someone who'll look out for her."

"Fair enough," Barb says, sweeping up the money. "What's your sipping drink?"

"I'm guessing an old fashioned for her. Maybe with a little extra sugar and water. Straight up for me."

"Will do. You married to her?"

"Will be tomorrow." At least, I hope to hell that I will be.

"Hmmph." She begins muddling the old fashioned. "Well, honey—if you change your mind between now and then, I'm looking for husband number six."

Shit. With a grin, I ask her, "What happened to husbands one through five? Because you kinda look like a lady who'll eat a man alive."

"Chewed 'em up," she agrees. "Then had to spit 'em out."

"That settles it, then. You don't want me. I look real tasty, but I'm hard on the teeth."

"Oh, I know it. You tough boys are why I've got dentures," she says, popping them off her gums and clicking them together, and I'm still laughing when she puts the drinks in front of me. "Go on, then. Take care of your girl. Just wave when you need another."

Probably won't need too many more. Maxine's already got the flushed, slightly sleepy look of someone working a good buzz. Sexy as fuck, too.

But that ain't happening. Not tonight. Probably not ever again.

Though she might kill me in the meantime. Because I slide in right beside her, and she begins giggling.

"Look." She plucks the toothpick out of her drink, a maraschino skewered on it. "I got my cherry back."

She pops it into her mouth, still giggling. And yeah,

that's not a buzz. She's flat-out drunk off those two shots.

And so damn cute. "So you just ate your own cherry," I point out and she sputters, burying her face in her folded arms, shoulders shaking.

For a minute I wonder if she's just going to laugh herself to sleep right there, then she lifts her head and pulls the old fashioned closer. Then I nearly fucking lose it when she sips from the stirring straw, cheeks hollowing as she sucks hard, desperately trying to get more than a trickle through the little tube.

Torn between laughing and groaning, I ask her, "You're more of a margarita girl, aren't you?"

If she's a drinker at all. But I'm guessing if she is, it's party drinks with big straws, or sweet wines.

She nods, then stops sucking to say, "Or rosé. But this is good, too."

"Yeah, it is." To distract myself from her mouth, I pull out my phone. "So I was looking up how to get married—"

Maxine gives a little snort. "Internet research again."

"You got a better way?"

She nods solemnly, then grins and shakes her head before sipping from her straw again. Her eyebrows arch.

Waiting for me to continue. As if I can think clearly while she's teasing me. Or sucking on that straw.

But I try. "So we can pre-register for our marriage license. That way we don't wait in line at the county office."

Her brow furrows. "I thought you just had to show up at a chapel?"

"Apparently not. See? Internet research will save our asses. So we'll fill it out now, yeah?"

She nods, scooting closer, watching as I begin typing in my info. "Your name is Aaron?"

"Yeah."

"How'd you get Stone?" Then she giggles. "Never mind. I can guess."

She'd be guessing wrong. Except that my cock's hard enough to prove her right. "It's because of high school football."

Her eyes go wide. "You pulled your dick out during a football game?"

Oh shit. When I stop laughing, I explain, "They called me the stone wall. Because of my last name. And it stuck."

"Ahhhhhhhhhhhhh," she says like it's the most amazing story she's ever heard. "Stone Wall."

"Yep."

"Matt used to call me Mad Max. But it didn't stick."

"Mad?" I type my parents' info into the form. "As in angry or as in crazy?"

"Neither, really. More like…survived the apocalypse that took everyone else."

Everyone in her family except her grandfather and her brother. And now…even them. I hear when that realization hits her, the hitch in her breath.

Grief swims in her eyes. "I guess I really did."

"Hey." I set down the phone, cradle her face in my hands. "It's all right. I know it hurts. But they're real glad you survived. That you made it through."

"I'm not sure I'm through yet." Her tears slip over, and I can feel that hot salty pain in the back of my throat. "I'm not sure I ever will be."

"Yeah, you will. Because I'm going to help you."

Though that doesn't reassure her. Her eyes close and her voice breaks on a sob. "I probably won't even live through this. Everything always goes so wrong. Saving Matt. Saving you. This plan to get Papa probably will, too."

"No, angel," I tell her, chest aching. "Don't you think that. We'll do this together, yeah? And we'll both get through. Because I won't let anything happen to you. All right?"

She doesn't answer, eyes still closed, mouth trembling.

With more steel in my voice, I ask again, "All right?"

Finally she nods but doesn't look at me. Instead she sniffles and pulls her drink close again, then drains the glass with a long swallow.

All right. For now. I signal to Barb for another, then start in on the application again. "Middle name?"

I know it. Saw her diploma, her passport. But this way, she's talking.

"Abigail," she whispers.

I fill out the next bit and then hit the following section. My gut tightens up. "You want to take my last name afterwards? Or use your own? Or hyphenate? There's a list of options here."

"What options?"

I drop down the list and she begins reading them, sounding out the hyphenated versions under her breath. "Faraday-Wall doesn't have a nice enough rhythm, does it?"

Sounds real nice to me. "It's whatever you like."

"The only ID that I have says Faraday."

"That's true. But you could keep using that passport for a while and be fine." I gesture to the screen. "This mostly only matters if we end up in court."

"Oh yeah." She sits back. "Just use Wall, then. So we'll present a united front. A…stone wall."

Shit. I shake my head, but at least she's back to giggling again.

"Maxine Wall," she says, trying it out. "Maxine… Abigail…Wall. That's pretty good. You know who the most famous Faraday is?"

"Who?"

"A guy who invented the Faraday cage."

A cage? "You shitting me?"

She shakes her head. "But it wasn't a cage to keep people in. Or not really. It shielded whatever was inside from electromagnetic waves. You can shoot lightning at it, *pew!* And you'd be okay inside. A car is kind of a Faraday cage. That's why you're okay in one during a lightning storm. But motorcycles?" She sputters a laugh. "Just toast."

That's true. "I know a story of a biker who stopped to piss by the side of the road, got hit by lightning—and because his boots were insulated, it grounded through his dick and that stream of piss."

She sputters again. "Are you serious?"

"Dead serious. I bet I can find the news story once I'm done with this."

"Was he able to use it again? Or was it completely fried?"

Not something I ever thought about. Or wanted to think about. "Not sure."

"I just hope he changed his road name to Lightning Dick. Or—oh my god—Lightning *Rod*."

I mess up my social security number three times, trying to type it on the phone's little keyboard while laughing. Then ask for hers, while she's still able to remember.

"This is ready." I tilt the screen in her direction. "You press that submit button and we're good to go."

She doesn't hesitate, and makes a drunken 'boink' sound effect when she pushes it.

"So, that's it? We're married?"

"Not until tomorrow. This is just for the license."

I tuck my phone away. Barb shows up and trades out Maxine's drink for a fresh one before leaving again.

"Ooh," Maxine coos with a teasing grin. "Another cherry. You want this one?"

Fucking killing me. "Nah. It's all yours." And as she pops it into her mouth, I can't stop watching. Can't stop myself from saying, "But you've got to tell me why you decided to wait for marriage."

"Okay, but…" She leans in and whispers with sweet cherry all over her breath, "It's a really stupid story."

"And I want to hear all of your stupid stories."

"Then you're in luck, because I have a *lot* of them." She waggles her eyebrows. "Okay, so…when I was a sophomore in high school, there were three girls who got pregnant all at once. Not 'all at once' magically. But like…around the same time."

Not magically pregnant. "I got it."

"And one of them was a girl who was like…*the* girl. Smart and good at sports and everyone said she was going to Harvard or something. But she didn't. Instead she dropped out. One of the other girls did, too. And that one was really sad, because the guy said they always used condoms, so they broke up because he thought she was cheating. But it turned out to be just the condom failing. So I thought… Nope. Not going to risk any of that. And decided to wait for marriage."

"That's not a stupid story. Protecting the future that you wanted sounds damn smart."

"Real smart," she agrees with a slow, bouncing nod. "But I still had a few boyfriends. And made out with them. That was fun."

Lucky bastards. "I bet."

"And maybe in college, I might have eventually changed my mind. But then I transferred back and was living at home with Grandpa again, and even without waiting for marriage, I'm not built to just hook up with someone. Not that I met anyone who really tempted me. But even if I had, taking someone home might have felt…

disrespectful. Because he *was* really religious. But also not at all."

"What's that mean?"

"He was a pastor before the boating accident. Then he just…lost his faith in God. Still believed He existed, just didn't believe in Him anymore. So he stopped preaching. Didn't make Matt and me go to church, either. But he was still a really *moral* man. Still taught us good and bad. Just without the religious stuff. Does that make sense?"

"Yeah, it does. So he'd have been disappointed if you didn't wait?"

"No." With sadness darkening her expression, she shakes her head. "He told me once, 'Don't wait if something makes you happy. Because you don't know when it'll be gone.' That wasn't about sex, really. But I think he would have viewed it the same way if I'd met someone who made me happy. It took me a while to really learn that lesson, though."

"Not waiting for the good stuff." Dessert. Sex.

"Yeah." Her gaze lifts to meet mine, emerald eyes big and imploring. "Do you believe in God? Or that we'll be punished for the bad stuff we do?"

So damn cute. With my forefinger, I tap her up-tilted chin. "So drink number four is when you go deep and philosophical? That's good to know."

She catches my hand. "But do you, though? Do you think intentions matter?"

I can't resist those eyes. "Never thought about it much.

Why? You worried you'll be punished for not being a virgin?"

"No. I don't think sex makes anyone bad." Her lips tremble. "But after what I did to you? I really, really wanted to save you."

Ah fuck. "You *did* save me, Maxine. You truly did."

Filled up all that emptiness.

Eyes swimming, she shakes her head. "I meant to. But the entire plan went to shit."

"What plan was that? Because I guarantee you, whatever it was, it didn't go to shit. I'm right here. I'm fine."

"But you would never have been hurt or in the Cage. If I'd just…" Those tears slip over. "If I'd just looked at Gunner a little closer. Because I meant to get you safe with your friend and tell you everything, even though Victor was listening in. And I knew he'd kill me for it. Then I thought Gunner was that blue-eyed devil. So you weren't safe. But when I tried to get you out of there, Victor caught up to us and I just… I'm so sorry. *I'm so sorry.*"

My chest is real fucking tight. "What are you talking about?"

"At the tavern," she sobs quietly.

Yeah, I got that. "What do you mean, Victor was listening in?"

"To my wig. So I couldn't warn you off without him knowing." She bravely swipes at her eyes. "Though I was going to. I thought *someone* had to do something right. And it needed to be me. So I pretended to play along.

Pretended to spike your drink. But Victor caught up to us and drugged you anyway."

My heart's completely gone. Just a big mess left. "Was that why it took so damn long to get my bloodwork cleared to fight? He pumped me full of something else?"

"Because I didn't get you outside fast enough." Her face crumples again. "It just all went to shit. And I didn't save you. I just made it all worse."

"Hey." My throat's so damn raw, my voice is nothing but a croak when I cradle her cheeks between my hands—and search hard for something to say. "Listen. Maxine. Listen. It's not your fault. You've got nothing to be sorry for. Because those fuckers were going to get me anyway. They made a deal with Strawman to take me, so one way or another, they'd have gotten to me. And I'm not sorry at all that it happened this way, because I met you. I wouldn't trade that for anything. Okay?"

She just cries harder, so I pull her in and let her bury her face against my chest. Fucking stunned that my heart's still beating when it feels like it should be exploding.

I wouldn't have cared if she'd drugged me. I held onto that anger for a long time while I was so goddamn empty inside, looking for any excuse to keep her close. Telling myself she had to pay. But it didn't matter later. Not after that hole in me started closing up. After I started pulling my head out of my ass. Because I sure as hell couldn't blame her for spiking my drink if it meant saving her own life or avoiding the kind of punishments they'd have handed out to her.

But that's not what she did. Instead she tried to save me…knowing that she would have *died* for it. She'd been willing to trade her life for mine. A stranger who wasn't worth even one of her tears.

I can barely fucking deal with that. Except to let her cry. And think back to everything I can remember from that night. Of her tossing the wig while running ahead of me. Of looking down at her, feeling real pissed off and seeing her eyes filled with fear.

"I'm the one who slowed us down, wasn't I?" I realize. "You told me about Gunner, and I stopped you right there."

She hiccups against my chest. "But I should have seen that he wasn't—"

"Nah, there ain't no telling Gunner's brothers apart. So listen. You seem real determined to blame yourself for this. But let me share my part of the blame, too. We'd have made it out of there if I hadn't lost my temper and stopped listening to you." Already she's shaking her head, saying something about how of course I'd trust Gunner over some strange girl, but I pull back, make her meet my eyes. "See? You did your best with what you knew. I did my best with what I knew. Now you tell me: what more is anyone supposed to do?"

"I don't know." She wipes her face again. "There's probably an answer. But I'm too drunk to think."

Nah. Her drunk side runs a little silly and a little sad, but doesn't slow her thinking much. "That's what you wanted tonight, yeah?"

She nods. Then says in a whisper, "You don't have to be sorry, either. For the cabin. I liked making you feel good."

And she was also carrying a whole load of guilt over something that wasn't her fault. But I can't say that because it's *my* brain that's suddenly working damn slow, my cock hard as fuck and all I can remember is how she felt. How she tasted. Because *making you feel good* is a hell of an understatement about the effect she has on me.

That effect means I can't risk dwelling on how she liked it. Not while I'm still wrecked, knowing she'd have sacrificed herself for me. Not while I'm aching so bad and need's clawing me up inside. Because I just might ask her to make me feel so damn good again.

While she's drunk and grieving. And while feeling a guilt that she shouldn't be feeling.

Her waxing philosophical is a whole lot safer. So I tell her, "I figure that if there really is someone up there, they're telling me I ought to be sorry. But they aren't waiting to punish me. They're doing it now."

She scowls. So damn cute. "Punishing you how?"

"By letting me be so close to you." But not having her. It was only yesterday that I was last inside her but feels like forever. But it hasn't been forever. Instead, forever is what's stretching out ahead of me. "And getting a real clear look at how I don't deserve you."

Her chin wobbles. "Being with me is a punishment?"

Ah shit. Me getting philosophical is a big mistake, if that's what she comes away with.

"No, Maxine." I catch her face in my hands. "You're the best thing."

She pulls in a trembling breath—then goes utterly still, gaze fixed on mine. The flush drains from her skin, leaving her deathly pale.

"Maxine?"

She begins shaking. "Can we leave? Right now?"

"Yeah, but—what's got you spooked? Did you see someone?"

"No." Her eyes are wide, her pupils huge. "I don't know. I just want to go. I need to get out of here."

"Then we're going." Not trusting those whisky legs to hold her, I haul her up into my arms, gaze sweeping the bar. No one that wasn't here before. Yet she's shivering and her breaths are shallow, panicked as she buries her face against my neck.

Then I hear it. That fucking jukebox. Playing one of Elton's greatest hits.

"It's just the music, angel," I murmur against her ear as I'm carrying her out. "Just the music. You're safe."

Maxine lifts her head, listening. Then buries her face in the crook of my neck again, half crying and half laughing against my throat. "That stupid tiny dancer."

Tension easing, I ask her, "You want me to go back and get the rest of that bottle?"

"That's okay." Her reply is a laughing shudder against

my skin. "I think I'm done."

Yeah, she is. Nodding off by the time I cross the short distance to our motel room, and fully asleep before I put her to bed—then lay down with her, because I'm still watching over her. I shouldn't still be holding her, too.

But I can't fucking help myself.

THIRTY-THREE

MAXINE

Okay. I'm done crying. Mostly.

Stone is so wonderful, I don't know if that makes it easier or harder. If it was just me, alone, I would have no choice but to buck up and get through. But he's here taking care of me, giving me someone to lean on…and maybe I'm letting myself cry more than I would otherwise. Because I know he's here to hold me when I need him to.

But no more. Crying's over.

My head's a fuzzy mess when we ride out in the

morning, my stomach full of the greasy breakfast that Stone swore would help with a hangover. I don't know if the food helps anything, but holding him does—and so does sitting on that rumbling, powerful bike with the scenery flying by. For the first time since leaving the Cage, I feel both safe and *free*. And even though the hurt and grief are still a dull and constant ache in my chest…just being here with Stone—and knowing that we're doing something about Papa—makes it all so much easier to bear.

Then Stone has to go and ruin my pledge not to cry by being wonderful again. Because he didn't just pre-register our license. He also booked a honeymoon suite and a bridal package at a little chapel inside the hotel, complete with a beauty spa visit and a wedding dress for me. I assumed we'd be standing up together in our grimy motorcycle gear, but Stone says something about making this look good for the courts later, so that it appears we got married for all the usual reasons instead of planning a murder.

But it *feels* like all of the usual reasons. In the spa, I cry my makeup off when it hits me that Matt won't be there to give me away. Then I tear up again as I take the short walk down the aisle. Stone's waiting for me in a rented tux, and I laugh a little to see it—because the suit fits him perfectly, so perfectly, wrapping his tall, muscular body in those gorgeous threads. Yet it doesn't *fit* him at all. Nothing could truly contain him. I knew that from the first moment I saw him in that video fighting against Paladin.

Even then, noticing the sheer vitality and strength and *life* that seem to simply explode from him. For a while, in the Cage—after Crash—that vitality had dimmed.

No more. As Stone takes my hand, as he tells me that I look absolutely fucking beautiful, that vitality seems to shine from him again, warming me all the way through. Filling me with it, too.

I feel as if I'm glowing when I say my vows—to a man who, only a day ago, swore never to touch me again.

But he *does* kiss me when the officiant declares us husband and wife. Maybe only to make it look good for the courts and for the photos that come with the wedding package. Oh, but it must look *so* good—slow and deep and sweet, with his big hands cupping my face and his powerful body pressing close to mine. When he finishes, his kiss eases back into a smile against my mouth, and I laugh even as the tears start up again. But happy tears, this time.

I don't know why I'm so happy. But I am.

I can't stop smiling when Stone swings me up into his arms and carries me through the lobby. We receive small smatterings of applause—and in the elevator, we're given knowing looks that make me blush and turn my burning face against his shoulder. He carries me over the threshold into the honeymoon suite before setting me down.

The suite is decorated in the Vegas version of elegance, with gold and white everywhere. A huge four-poster bed has its own room. Rose petals are strewn across the duvet cover. My heart rate spikes when Stone tugs his bowtie free, regarding me with a hot look that I know so very well. My skin tightens with anticipation.

Then my heart flops painfully into my stomach when he turns away and says gruffly, "I'm heading down to the hotel gym. Blowback sent photos of doctors in Nevada who might fit the doc's description if you want to start going through them. I wrote the password on that notepad over there."

The password to his laptop. Because we're married now. And I'm the info girl.

"Okay," I whisper to no one. He's already in the bedroom changing into his gym clothes. I'm all alone, sitting down on a pretty white sofa in a pretty white dress, booting up a computer so that I can find the man who ordered my brother's murder.

But I'm not crying anymore. I'm not.

At least not until Stone is gone.

HE'S GONE FOR TWO HOURS, but I never end up crying. I'm just…numb. And Stone looks completely done in, sweat-soaked and beat, as if he spent the entire time pounding himself to exhaustion.

His gaze darkens as it slips over me. I'm no longer in the wedding dress. Just my jeans and tee. Because I'm not really a bride. Not really a wife.

And I can't remember why I was so happy.

Voice low, he asks, "Find him?"

I shake my head.

"Yeah, probably too easy. We'll tell Blowback to dig deeper. But first let me clean up and we'll order room service, since dinner comes with the whole honeymoon deal."

I don't really want a romantic wedding dinner, but I nod.

A muscle in his jaw works before he nods, too. "All right, then."

Ah god. As soon as I hear the shower start, I bury my face in my hands. Not so numb now. But hurting. So much. And I just want it to stop.

Throat aching, I put on my shoes and a baseball cap, pulling the brim down low. I'm not worried about being recognized by Papa or anyone connected to him. But I won't be stupid, either.

I knock on the bathroom door and call through it, "I'm heading down to the bar!"

"What?" The shower stops. "Maxine, hold up—"

"I'll be fine!" Physically.

Emotionally…I just don't know.

I shove the room's keycard into my pocket and head out. Stone calls my name again but I don't stop. I just need to make this pain go away. For a little while.

The bartender's quick to take my order. Stone's quick, too—sliding into the stool beside mine before my drink even arrives, his hair still wet and his damp shirt clinging to every thick muscle. Concern darkens his expression.

"Hey." His voice is low and gentle, and I can't stand it. "What's going on?"

I don't even know. Just that there's a knot in my throat and the whole fucking world is shit.

And I'm about to cry. But I won't. *I won't.*

Still, it's hard to get a single word out, let alone a string of them. "I just…want to be angry again."

Because that was so much easier. So much simpler. When it was rage that drove me away from witness protection and after Stone, when all that mattered was nailing Papa to the wall. But I've never been good at being mad for a long time.

"Instead of hurting?"

Lips pressed tight, I nod.

"That why you're down here? Maybe thinking you'll drink until it doesn't hurt so much?" When I nod again, he leans in, tenderly brushing the backs of his knuckles down my cheek. "Problem with that, angel, is we're on a mission now. You and I are a team—and our purpose is bringing down Papa. So we need to stay sharp. And remember how you felt this morning? That was the opposite of sharp, I'm guessing."

While I was hungover. Fuzzy and sick.

I pull in a shuddering breath. "It was."

"So we'll find another way for you to stop hurting so much, all right? Somewhere for you to put all of what's boiling inside you." His lips quirk. "Are you sure you can't find some rage for me? You've been there a couple of times."

"Because you're safe." My drink arrives but I don't reach for it. "You won't hurt me for getting angry. Or for lashing out. Or for fighting."

"I couldn't hurt you for any reason." His gaze moves over my face. "Is that what you want to do—fight? Because you can lay in on me anytime if you want to blow off steam. Or I'll teach you a few moves so you'll always feel safer. Or hit the gym with me, get those endorphins going."

Oh god. How selfish can I be? I hesitantly ask, "Is that why you were gone so long—because you're hurting, too?"

"Yeah. Though just in one spot." His crooked grin appears, a flashing curve that I feel straight through my heart. "But also because I'm the brawn on this team. So I gotta stay strong."

Just in one spot.

I reach for my drink, but only to have something to hold and look at. Because I can't meet his eyes now. Not when everything inside me is suddenly shifting around, hope and fear tumbling together.

Stone said that he'd never touch me again. And that felt like such a rejection. But he also thinks the only reason I slept with him was out of guilt and to pay him back. So he said that he was sorry, too.

He never said that he doesn't want me, though. That was what I *heard*. But it wasn't what he said.

If Stone says now that he doesn't want me, I don't know if I'll ever stop hurting. And I'm terrified, so terrified that he will. That I've misunderstood again.

But he's such a good man. And a good man who swears that he won't touch a woman would keep that promise. Even after he married her. Even after he carried her to a honeymoon suite. Even after he looked at her with so much heat in his eyes. That good man might leave as fast as he could, because a man hurting in one spot can't easily hide his want. Especially a man as well-endowed as Stone.

My heart pounds, so fast. So afraid. Because I might be wrong.

But I was so happy before. And I don't want to wait anymore for what makes me happy. Because I never know when it might be gone.

Thinking it was gone for a few days felt bad enough.

Clutching the glass tight, I whisper, "And there's sex."

Though I don't glance in his direction, I feel how tense he becomes. "What about it?"

"People use sex to blow off steam." I still can't look at him. "Or to feel good when they're hurting."

"Yeah, they do." There's a wry note in his reply, but no amusement. Instead each word seems taut and careful, as if he's crossing a tightrope over a bottomless pit.

As if he isn't sure whether I'm talking about what I need, or about how he used me the same way…or if I'm thinking of someone else.

But there could never be anyone else.

"I suppose they just walk into a bar and hook up with

a stranger. But that would be a bad idea for me. Because we're on this mission. So bringing in a random person might jeopardize the mission…and upset the team dynamics."

His voice roughens. "It would fucking destroy at least half this team."

My chest swells up with hope, until every breath is tight and painful. "So maybe—if I wanted to use sex to feel good—we could keep it within the team? Because I already know that you make me feel *so* good."

"Yeah," he says gruffly. "We can do that."

My eyes close with sheer relief. "Can we go back upstairs, then?"

"We can do that, too."

But when I slide off my stool, he doesn't move—except to snag his steely arm around my waist and pull me close against his side. Then closer, until I'm straddling his heavy thigh. I finally have the courage to look at him, but he's not looking back. Instead his eyes are closed and his jaw is clenched, his head slightly bowed. If he were any other man, I'd think that he was praying.

I bite my lip. "Stone?"

"I'm here." His broad chest rises and falls on a deep breath, his arm tightening around my waist. "But I need a second to recover from what you just did to me."

A laugh shakes through me. "You're such a lightweight."

"And you've got one hell of a punch, Maxine." But he

grins, reaching for my drink. "Maybe we'll have a sip of this now. To the team."

"To the team." I pluck out the garnish stick and its skewered maraschino, then take a sip. "And I'll be giving my husband a cherry on our wedding night, after all."

Stone chokes on a laugh while he drinks to the team, but his eyes burn into mine when he eats the cherry off the stick I'm holding out for him—then he downs the rest of the glass, gaze locked on my mouth. As if he's so hungry. So thirsty. My heart trips over itself, my breath trembling, my inner muscles tightening.

Setting the glass down, he tips his head closer, his firm lips only a breath away from the softness of mine. "Let's go make you feel real good, angel."

In so many ways…I already do.

THIRTY-FOUR

STONE

IF MAXINE EVER GETS TO A FOURTH DRINK AND GOES all philosophical again, I'll have an entire slew of different answers for her.

Do I believe in God? Fuck yes, I do.

Do I believe in miracles? Fuck yes, I do.

Do I believe in angels? Fuck yes, I do.

But I can't believe my angel is letting me touch her again. That she *needs* me to touch her.

Knowing that ain't all sweet, though. Because she's

hurting so bad. I'll give Maxine anything she needs. If the price of taking her pain away came at the cost of never touching her again, I'd pay it. Instead she just wants me to make her feel good. So I can't fuck this up, can't do anything that might hurt her more.

I've hurt her too much already. So much I don't deserve to touch her again. What I deserve is to watch her walk away with another man. Someone who'd treat her the way she ought to be treated from the start. Even though it'd kill me.

But that's not what she wanted. She wanted *me*.

I can barely fucking believe it. In the elevator, about every emotion a man can feel is twisting around in my chest, dominated by hope and need, all torqued hard and tight with the love I have for this woman.

All the want I feel for her is settling lower. My cock's a rigid ache when she leads me down the hallway to our suite, her fingers tangled with mine. She hasn't met my eyes much, but her nipples are stiff little candies beneath her pink tee, her breaths coming quick and shallow between her soft lips.

Chasing after her out of the shower earlier, I didn't grab a keycard. But she's ahead of me there, tugging one from her back pocket and glancing over her shoulder when the door unlocks.

Not looking so hurt and lost now. Just hot and eager.

She heads in, all sweet ass and swinging hips. And fuck me, I want to grab on. To lift her up against the door and take what I need, hard and rough and deep.

But this isn't about what I need. It's about what Maxine does. So I'll let her take the lead.

She's no longer holding my hand, but I follow close when she crosses to the bedroom, pulling off her baseball cap as she goes. Hair tumbling around her shoulders, she grips the hem of her shirt. My next few steps are awkward hops as I reach down for my boots and yank them off one at a time. The second boot hits the carpeted floor just as she stops beside the bed.

Dragging off her top, she emerges with flushed cheeks and rosy nipples that are begging for my mouth, and throws me an enquiring glance from beneath her lashes. A husky note of arousal lowers her voice when she asks, "Hands and knees? Or on my back?"

The emotions spinning in my chest wrench to a painful halt.

Shame clogs my throat. Maxine needs me to stop her from hurting. So she came up here, knowing I'd make her feel good…but not expecting me to give her anything more than I've already taken.

She deserves so much more.

"No, angel. This won't be like it was before, when I used you as a fuckhole." Voice hoarse, I capture her face in my hands. "This is for you. Whatever you want, however you want it. I'll give it to you."

Looking up at me, her eyes shine with anticipation and pleasure—and are shadowed by uncertainty. As if she isn't sure exactly what I mean. As if she still doesn't know how much she can ask for. Her teeth pinch her bottom lip as her gaze searches my face, and suddenly I know how to show her it's all different now.

I gruffly ask, "Can I kiss you, Maxine—kiss you real deep and real good?"

Her breath shudders and her eyes become glistening emerald pools. "Please."

Please. As if she's been wanting me to. Needing me to. And I can't even remember what stupid reason I had for ever denying her. I just know I'm a damn fool for letting all these days go by without kissing her like I should have.

Hands sliding into her hair, tilting her head back, I don't waste another second claiming her mouth now. And fuck, she's so sweet and hot. Tasting of whiskey and cherries, her body taut and trembling against mine when she rises onto her toes.

Maxine's not wasting time, either. A hungry sound comes from the back of her throat, then she shucks her jeans and panties with a rasp of her zipper and a shimmy of her hips that rubs her belly against my denim-covered shaft. All the while, I'm kissing her deep and slow, with my fingers tangled in her hair. Every moment, sheer bliss—and an agonizing exercise in restraint. I groan into her mouth when she unfastens my belt, each tug and pull an excruciating tease before she starts on the fly of my jeans. Primitive need clenches the muscles of my lower abdomen in anticipation of her soft hands gripping my cock and stroking the engorged length.

It's pure torture when she doesn't touch me. And pure heaven when she pushes closer, my heated flesh wedged against her bare stomach. Her arms come up to link around my neck, then she nearly blows my self-control to kingdom come when she just *climbs* onto me, hauling herself up and wrapping her legs around my waist—sliding her scorching wet pussy up the length of my shaft as if searching for the tip.

Wrenching my mouth from hers, I rasp against her lips, "This is what'll make you feel good, angel? You want to ride my cock?"

"I just want you inside me," Maxine pants, her thighs scrambling on my hips as she tries to lift herself high enough to take me in.

Inside her. So much need surges through my veins that it feels like a jet engine roaring through my head. Getting inside her, making her feel so damn good is all I want, too. But she shouldn't have to work so hard for it.

The bed's right behind me. Claiming her lips again, I fall back easy, sending rose petals flying up when I hit the mattress. Maxine gives a startled cry against my mouth, then huffs out a laugh that dissolves into a breathy moan when the new position puts the head of my erection right where she needs it.

Feels *so* fucking good. But just because she's wet doesn't mean she can take me in. "Sit up here on my face, angel, so I can get your pussy ready."

"I'm *so* ready," she breathes before slanting her lips over mine, kissing me deep. Her hips hitch up and down, working the fat tip through her drenched folds—but now she's *too* far up, straddling my stomach but her body's too short to take my cock in while I'm lying flat and she's kissing me.

With a soft groan of frustration, she sits up, bracing her hands on my chest and scooting back. I'm still wearing my jeans and shirt, but she's completely bare, and my eyes eat her up the way my mouth ought to be. The red's gone from her hair, except for a few crimson petals that are tangled up in the brown tresses. Her pink lips are swollen from our kisses, the tips of her breasts tight and rosy.

"You're so fucking beautiful, Maxine," I tell her hoarsely.

A blush stains her cheeks, those emerald eyes shining— just like they did in the chapel when she appeared in her wedding dress and I told her the same thing.

In the chapel. In her wedding dress.

She's not wearing the dress now, but she's not naked, either. Because she's wearing my ring. It's right there on her finger, gleaming gold as she guides my stiffened cock to her center.

Holy fuck, this is my wife. This sweet, gorgeous girl is my *wife*.

Poised over me, she abruptly pauses, teeth pinching her bottom lip. Uncertainty trembles through her voice. "You're all right with this?"

Probably asking because I'm lying here looking thunderstruck. If I weren't already on my back, I'd be flat on the floor. Because she actually fucking *married* me.

"I've never been better, angel." My voice sounds real thick as I gaze up at my wife. "You use me however you need to make yourself feel good."

Immediately, it hits me that Maxine said almost exactly the same thing just before I took her virginity—and which was also the last time I thought of her as Cherry. After that, she was just mine.

My girl, my angel. My wife.

My reply must have reminded Maxine of that first time in the cabin, too, because a giggle shakes through her before she lowers her voice to a mock growl. "Then get ready, boy, because I'm gonna use your fuckpole real good."

Christ, she destroys me. "You and your damn mouth," I tell her, then my laugh shreds into a ragged groan as she begins rolling her hips, working the fat head of my cock past the snug little entrance that I ought to have softened up with my fingers and tongue. Teeth gritted, I fight the need to take the lead, to grab her ass and hold her in place for a thrust that'll bury me balls-deep within her scalding wetness.

But it wasn't just Maxine's smart mouth that I fell in love with. She's also so sweet and generous. That first time, even with her virgin blood painting my dick, she told me to take what I needed. She held herself wide open, letting me fuck my way to the most mind-blowing orgasm I've ever experienced…and I wasn't even the one coming.

Instead Maxine stayed quiet and still while I used her pussy, though it must have been torture. Sweet torture, because I made her come so hard, but keeping still couldn't have been easy. Yet she did it. Because she was taking care of me.

It's my turn to take care of her. My turn to lie still while my wife takes what she needs.

Even if it kills me.

It just might. The heat and wet inside her threaten to shred my control when Maxine takes me in slow, so slow, her head falling back on a throaty moan and her hips swiveling as she drives my swollen flesh into her narrow channel. Christing fuck, it's so sweet. My every muscle goes rigid in my battle against the urge to thrust hard and rough, my hands fisting in the covers.

All that keeps me in check is knowing that this is what she needs. Ecstasy glazes her emerald eyes as she fills the glistening miracle of her cunt with my thick shaft—and then takes every inch. White flashes at the edges of my vision when she bites her lip, then wriggles and squirms and forces her way down until her slick inner walls grip my cock from root to tip.

So fucking hot. So fucking tight. So fucking *deep*.

I barely halt my tortured groan behind clenched teeth. Maxine kept so quiet. So still. Now all she's done is sink onto my dick and I'm about to lose it.

But Christ help me, she's so beautiful, her eyes blind with pleasure, hands braced on my chest. And her pussy feels so incredible when she tests out the seat of my erection with a roll of her hips.

"Oh my god, Stone." It's a gasping moan. "You feel *huge* inside me."

My dick would be swelling up bigger because of that if I'd had a chance to soften her up. Instead I make sure she still doesn't need me to.

"Hurting?" I rasp.

Wordlessly Maxine shakes her head, panting as she swivels her hips again, stirring my cock deep within her sultry depths. Pleasure surges the length of my dick like lightning that strikes again and again when she begins to ride. Slow and shallow, not rising up and down but sinuously rocking back and forth, her tight entrance working the base of my shaft while her inner walls suck and pull at every aching inch. Breath hissing through gritted teeth, I fight the orgasm that's building, all that need and heat stacking up like a brick wall that I'm trying so damn hard not to slam into. She's going to wreck me. Wreck me so bad. But I won't slow her down. Not if this is what Maxine needs.

But what she needs must not be what she's getting, because her hair trigger's not going off. Through all that bliss, frustration tightens her expression. She leans forward with her hands still braced on my chest, her hips still circling but her eyes squeezing closed and her teeth digging into her bottom lip. Then she just fucking kills me with a pained whimper, like she's reaching for something she can't touch.

"Tell me what you need, Maxine." Because I need to give it to her.

"I'm not tall enough," she pants. "Will you sit up so I can kiss you again?"

Fuck yes. I jack up to sitting, dragging my shirt over my head as I go. She gasps, moaning as the change in position pushes me deeper. Her body's shaking when I wrap my arm tight around her waist. My other hand grips her ass, begins lifting and lowering her onto my cock, making sure her clit's rubbing up against me just right.

"Want me to help out here, too?" I ask with my mouth against hers.

Her breaths trembling, she nods. "I love it when you hold me like this."

"Like what?" I'll make sure to always do it.

"When you're inside me, and you hold me against you so tight. Like you won't let me go until you're done getting what you need."

"If it means being done, then I ain't ever letting you go," I tell her gruffly.

Maxine makes a soft sound like something inside her crumples, then she's kissing me again, her mouth hungry and fierce. She slicks her hot tongue over mine and I'm done for, just fucking done for, barely holding back as I drag her up the length of my erection and grind her back down, rubbing up into her real good each time.

Christ, I ain't going to last. Ain't gonna last even another minute.

Raw lust clenches hard at the base of my spine. She's quaking against me, gasping and moaning into our kiss—then going still as her cunt constricts around my aching flesh tight enough to make my head explode. Groaning into her mouth, I fuck into her as she comes, and that goddamn miracle of a pussy destroys the last of my control, my release pumping out of me with every thrust.

But though my hips slow, I can't stop kissing her. It's Maxine who draws back a little, face flushed and her gaze searching mine—looking painfully shy and hesitant, though my cock's still buried in her cunt and I still haven't let her go. Though I made it clear I ain't ever going to.

"What is it you're needing now, angel? I'll give it."

Still she looks uncertain, and her reply is barely a husk of sound. "Is it… Is it okay if I touch you?"

Because she hasn't. All the while I've been kissing her, Maxine's hands have been fisted at her thighs. Even when she braced her palms on my chest, riding me, I was wearing my shirt. The rest of the time, she's been so damn careful not to touch my skin. Because I told her never to.

So she never has.

My heart fills with hot lead and I wonder if I'll ever pay enough for all I did to her. My angel. My wife. All this time, believing I don't want her touch, when the truth is there's not a fucking thing in this world that I want more.

Voice raw, I tell her, "I'd love it if you touched me."

A smile bursts across her face but as she lifts her trembling fingers to my jaw, the uncertainty doesn't vanish.

"But let me know if my hands are too cold, okay?"

"Ah fuck, Maxine, no," I groan as the hot lead in my chest turns to agony, catching her hand and bringing it to my lips, wishing I could unsay every fucking thing I ever said. She's not just thinking I don't want her to touch me but that I'm also revolted by her touch? *Like a dead fish.* Christ, I don't deserve her. Don't deserve anything from her. "I'm sorry. I'm so fucking sorry. You were an angel to me in the barn and I shit all over you, because every time you touched me, it felt so damn good. But I didn't want to feel good, not after Crash. And I sure as hell didn't deserve to."

Her smile becomes tremulous. "What about now?"

"I'm not in the same place." I still don't deserve her, but I'm sure as fuck never going to push her away again. "Now all I care about is what you need, Maxine—and what'll make you feel good. Nah, fuck. *Good* ain't good enough. So you tell me what's going to make you feel better than you did just a bit ago, because it seemed for a while there, you were having trouble chasing your come. Was there something missing? Or was it just thinking that I don't want you to touch me?"

Pink washes over her cheeks. "Nothing was missing. You felt *so* good. It was just…" Tentatively, she traces her fingers along my jaw, and her breath shudders when I turn my head to press a kiss into her palm. "I kept wanting you to take me like you used to. In the cabin."

I can't be hearing that right. "When I used you as a

fuckhole?"

Her blush deepens, but she nods. "Because I know you're a good man. But you needed me so much, you crossed that line into bad. Didn't you?"

"I crossed a hell of a line. One I shouldn't have."

"Why? I said you could." She bites her lip, her eyes searching mine. "You think that makes you the same as Tusk?"

Thinking he was owed something. "Pretty fucking close, yeah."

"You're not. The difference there is that I wanted you, too. And if I'd said no instead of yes, would you have stopped?"

"In an instant. But—"

"Because you're a good man," she says softly. "Did you ever cross that line with anyone else? Would you ever?"

Fuck, she's killing me. "No."

"So it was just me."

"Yeah."

"You think I don't know that?" She cups my face in her warm hands. "You think it wasn't thrilling to be wanted like that, knowing you were breaking all your own rules? Maybe that's my own bad coming out, too."

"No, angel," I say gruffly. "There's not a bit of bad in you."

"You sure? Because I liked you crossing that line. I liked you taking me as if you intended to collect what you were owed. All because you needed me so much." She looks suddenly vulnerable, her emerald eyes huge and dark. "Do you still?"

Need her as much as I did then? Hell no.

I need her more than I ever have.

"You have no fucking idea, angel," I tell her, my voice roughening with every word. "I'll cross every goddamn line to have you. To take what's mine. You want me to show you?"

Maxine's breath shudders as she nods, her eyes closing in relief—as if she wasn't certain what my answer to needing her would be.

So I'll make sure there isn't any doubt left.

"Go put on that wedding dress, then." I squeeze her ass before letting her go. "And I'll fuck you like I should have when I carried you in."

She kisses me hard before scrambling off my lap and snatching the dress from the closet. After coming, my dick's softened up some, but I ain't worried about that. By the time I'm ready to get into her again, I'll be aching just as much as I ever was. Maybe more. Because Maxine, god help me…she's just so damn sweet. So damn beautiful as she tosses me a blushing look before heading into bathroom.

I head over, bracing my hands on the doorframe so I'll be the first thing my wife sees when she comes out again. She must not have done more than clean up a bit, because in no time at all, that door swings open and she's there in front of me, wearing a silky white dress that I barely even see because the woman in it is such a vision.

Christing hell, she's stunning. It thumps me right in the chest how gorgeous my bride is, looking up at me with her green eyes alight with anticipation.

"You're so fucking pretty, Maxine," I tell her huskily. "Maybe I ought to put that tux back on, too."

She shakes her head, her fingers tucking into the waist of my jeans—which I zipped up but didn't do much more in the way of fastening. "This suits you better," she says softly.

So it does. But not as well as having this woman against me.

Now that I know she loves it when I hold her close, I snake my arm around her waist and draw her in tight. "Kiss me again like you did after they said 'man and wife.'"

With a delighted laugh, she throws her arms around my neck and rises onto her toes. That didn't happen in the chapel, but the happiness shining from her face is the same. So is the painful clench in my chest as I claim her mouth, long and slow and sweet. But the pain before came from believing that kiss was the only time I'd ever be touching her again. Now the ache comes from all the hope building up until my heart's as tight and as full as it's ever been—along with a hefty punch of terror, fearing that I might fuck this up and lose her.

So I'll give her a whole load of reasons to stay.

I swing her up into my arms, kissing her all the way to the bed. There I lay her down amid the scattered rose petals, then lean in with my hands beside her shoulders and my body braced over hers. "You like me needing you, girl? You like knowing you're the only woman in the whole fucking world I can imagine ever touching again?"

"I do," she breathes against my mouth.

"Then you must be feeling real good now. Because you've got me tied up in knots from needing you so bad."

"There's some payback, then." Her lips curve under mine. "You tied me up, too."

Damn this girl, always making me laugh. "You liked that?"

She gives a tiny nod before admitting, "Though maybe not the tied-to-the-bed part as much as I did the you-taking-what-you-wanted part."

That's the part I liked, too. And it wasn't a rope that held her still that first time. Won't be what holds her still now. I reach for her left hand, bringing her wedding ring up to my lips, watching the flare of her eyes when I press a kiss to the gold band.

"This ring is how I'm tying you up now, Maxine," I tell her in a voice that's pure gravel. "And I'll be taking what I need from my wife. *Only* my wife. Yeah?"

"Yes," she whispers.

"This ring means that anytime I want—and that'll be real damn often—you'll spread those pretty thighs for me. Yeah?"

She's trembling beneath me. "Yes."

"You ain't gonna fight?"

Maxine shakes her head, then pauses. "Unless you want me to?"

"Not gonna lie. It's sexy as fuck when you fight," I say, nipping her soft bottom lip. "But better you save the struggling for after I'm inside you, when you're pushing at me and crying that you can't come even one more time. Christ, getting the last one out of you while you're fighting against it is always the hottest damn ride."

She makes a small needy sound. "Try getting another out of me now."

"Not yet," I say, though my dick's already aching again. "Because you told me that you liked how I crossed lines to have you, but I don't think you know how wide of a line I crossed when I married you."

For a moment she looks baffled. "You think I don't know that planning to kill Papa is crossing a line?"

Well, shit. That wasn't what I meant. But probably best she knows this, too. "Crossing a line for you, maybe. Not for me. As far as I'm concerned, Papa's garbage—and I'm always happy to take out the trash."

"Oh." Her expression clears. "Tusk, too?"

"Yeah." Was *real* happy to take out that trash. "But that's not what I'm talking about. I told you this marriage is to protect you if we ever end up in court. But that's a load of bullshit."

Maxine goes real still. "How is it bullshit?"

"Because even though what I said about husband and wife privilege is true, I sure as fuck don't need a marriage license to protect you." And my heart's about to pound through my chest, because this might end up being a step too far over that line. "But I figured that as soon as you started thinking about all the shit I said to you and did to you, you'd take off. And I wanted to make it harder for you to get rid of me. So I told you that we ought to get married."

She stares up at me in disbelief. "But you lied about why?"

"Yeah, angel. I did. Though I didn't think you'd ever let me touch you again. I just knew that I had a big hole in me after I got out of the Cage…and that being with you filled it up, made me feel good again. But I also knew that if you left, it'd rip another hole in me. One I wouldn't ever recover from. So I locked you down with that ring."

"That's *so* wrong," she breathes.

"I know it." My throat feels raw all of a sudden. "But you oughta know that this is how bad I need you. And there's not a line I won't cross to keep you."

"Even if I try to run away?"

Ice splinters through my chest. Hoarsely I ask her, "Are you going to?"

In answer, Maxine begins wriggling beneath me. Not trying to get away. Instead she begins working her long skirt upwards, hitching the silky fabric up to her waist…so she can spread her legs.

Real fucking wide. Until she's lying open and vulnerable under me, her emerald eyes shining when they meet mine.

"Maybe one day I'll run," she says with a husky edge to her voice. "But only for fun, and only so you can catch me. Right now, I just want my husband to take what he needs. I just want to make him feel good."

That's what I want to do for her. But it sounds like me taking what I need is what she needs, too. "You want me to use your pussy real hard, angel? Want me to fuck you good and deep?"

She moans, her body moving restlessly. "Please."

"Nah, not yet." Roughly I tug down the front of her pretty white dress, baring her soft breasts and getting a handful of the left. "Because I'm gonna make sure your tight little fuckhole is real wet before I try getting into it again. And there's a whole lot of you that I like taking."

Starting with her mouth. Kissing her long and slow, with my fingers teasing her nipples until her breathless moans sharpen into needy whines. All at once, she seems to remember that touching me is allowed now, and her hands come up to cup the back of my head, her kiss deepening as she holds me tight. Then her fingers go roaming, and it turns out that I was right. All this fucking time, thinking Maxine's touch would destroy me…I was right.

Because no matter what she says, I'm not a good man. Not a man an angel like her could love. So I figure it's just pure luck that the woman I fell so hard for likes how I'll cross lines to have her—and even better luck that it makes her feel so damn good to let me take what I want, because otherwise she would never let me touch her. And if all I ever did was make her feel good for the rest of my life, I'd be a real fortunate bastard.

Yet here she is now, touching me like it's got nothing to do with sex. First she held me so tight, then her fingers went exploring—but although it feels damn good, it doesn't seem like she's trying to make this all hotter. She's not digging her nails into me, or pushing or tugging and silently telling me what she wants, or even mindlessly stroking her fingers over my skin. Instead it's as if Maxine simply wants to touch me. As if she's *wanted* to touch me, so now that she's getting her chance, she's taking it—and somehow it's separate from all the sexy shit we're doing at the same time.

And I remember how she used to put her hand over my heart when she thought I was sleeping. How that would destroy me, too. Because it made me wonder if she felt more than just guilt or that she owed me, made me wonder if she wasn't only taking care of me by letting me use her pussy. It made me wonder if my angel felt more than she was saying.

Now I'm wondering again. Fucking *praying* that she does. But not really believing that she could.

And I won't ask her. Won't ask for anything more than she's already giving. Instead I let her wreck me over and over and over with her fingers gliding across my skin, because the alternative is that she's *not* touching me…and I couldn't bear that again.

All I can do is give Maxine what *she* asked for. Making

her feel good. Making her so damn hot that when I leave the sweetness of her lips and lick my way down to her breasts, she spreads her legs wider and begs for my cock inside her. But I ain't done slicking her up. And she sure as hell doesn't seem to mind it either, moaning and arching her back when I suck one of her stiff nipples into my mouth. I move to her other breast, and as soon as she's panting and squirming, I keep on heading south, my breath skimming over white silk. Then she goes real still, her thighs trembling with the effort of staying so wide open as I draw in close, as if she's waiting for me to take what I want.

I want *all* of her. But no doubt, this tight pussy is one of my wife's most delicious parts. So fucking hot and wet, every lick making her hotter and wetter, each taste better than the last. Especially when she starts writhing and I have to hold her down so I can stay right on her juicy little clit. And this time when Maxine touches me…fuck yeah, she's pushing and pulling now, and chanting my name, but I don't stop until she's screaming it.

There just ain't no words for the taste of her as she's coming on my tongue. 'Delicious' doesn't even come close to describing pure fucking heaven.

I lick it all up, then shuck my jeans before rising up over her again. She watches me, her body flushed and languid, her lips swollen and her eyelids heavy.

'Beautiful' doesn't come even close to describing her now, either.

Her eyes flare wide as I grip the base of my shaft and

slick the fat tip up and down the drenched length of her slit. "You ready to be fucked, girl?"

"So ready," she says raggedly, holding herself so open, so still.

"I ain't so sure." Deliberately I run my gaze down her front, to the silk bunched around her waist. She married me in white, like the virgin she was before I took what I wanted in the cabin. But though I'm taking what I want now, what's between her and me is never going to be like that again. "Because I love the way you keep those pretty thighs spread for me. But if you want me inside you, you'd better wrap me up tight, like you're never going to let me go."

Holy fuck. I don't even finish before her legs cinch tight around my hips. Her hands come up to catch my face, kissing me fiercely as I drive my cock deep into her snug little cunt. She cries out into my mouth, then clings even tighter when I begin pulling back so I can fuck into her again. As if she thinks I might leave her. But there ain't a goddamn thing that could make me leave her now.

I give my wife what she needs, riding hard and rough into that slick velvet heat, feeling like I'll last a good damn while since I came earlier. Then she almost takes me out when her hips start thrashing and her cunt seizes up on my cock.

Nearly sucking me off right there. Christing fuck, her pussy. Ain't nothing else like it.

Chest heaving, I slow us way down, kissing her long

and deep. Then her hands go roaming again, sweetly destroying me with her touch.

I need Maxine to love me. Need it more than anything. But fuck if I know how to make her fall in love.

I just know how to make her come.

THIRTY-FIVE

STONE

I'm not sure yet when I'll be home, so I'm about to send you a link to a photo package that I'd like you to order for me. When you see the pictures, you'll want to call me. But you've got to hold off on that because I'm not talking to my mother on my wedding night.

Three dots telling me that my mom's typing a response pop up instantly. But she must visit that link and start over, because I've got time to let the room service waiter wheel our meal in and send him on his way again with a twenty in hand before her reply comes.

Congratulations, Aaron! You look happy. So does she. What's her name?

Maxine. And I'm real happy. She's the best thing that ever happened to me.

That's the right person to marry, then. Your father says congratulations, too. Though an invite would have been lovely.

Yeah, that would have been tricky getting you all here on my bike. Plus she recently lost her whole family. So if I had a crapload of people here and she had no one, it might have been rough on her.

I hear that you've had a rough time lately, too. How are you doing now?

Better than I was. Maxine got me through. Now I'm going to get her through.

I see.

Probably too much. Anna might be worried that Maxine's just another girl in trouble. But she's not.

I know.

Oh yeah?

Not since high school have you mentioned any other girl to me. I'm not entirely surprised that when you finally do mention one, you've already married her. I hope we'll meet her soon.

I'll bring her home after our honeymoon.

I won't keep you from it. Take care of yourself—and let us know if you need anything. We love you.

Love you, too.

"Good news?"

I look up as Maxine comes in from the bedroom, her hair tousled and sexy as fuck. I left her naked and tangled up in a sheet, while I dragged on a pair of gray sweatpants to answer the room service guy. But instead of putting her dress back on, she snagged the T-shirt that I tossed away earlier, and it looks a hell of a lot better on her than it ever did on me.

"What's good news?" Besides the way I'm getting an eyeful of her long legs.

"You." She gives my bare chest a blushing little glance before turning her attention to the covered plates on the table. "You were smiling at your phone."

"Ah, yeah. I figured that I ought to let my parents know that I got married. And I was telling my mom how I was a dead man inside until your miracle of a pussy brought me back to life."

She snorts lightly. "Is that what did it? Maybe I should use it on my brother, then—oh my god!" The metal cover clatters to the table as she slaps her palm over her mouth and looks to me in horror.

"Hold up." I catch her stricken face between my hands. "You're about to think what the fuck is wrong with you for saying that, but there's not a thing wrong with you, Maxine. Sometimes that funny morbid shit's going to pop out…and it's just another way to get through a bad situation. I know that real well."

Her lips are trembling when she uncovers her mouth. "Because you've been through it, too?"

"Partly." In the service, a bad situation turned us all into comedians. "But all my jokes are pretty bad."

That pulls a smile from her before she bites her lip. "So you told your parents?"

"That I married the most incredible girl in the world? Yep." Pleasure lights up her eyes, so I drop a kiss to her lips before letting her go. We worked up a hell of an appetite in the bedroom, so I want to get her fed before heading back there. "I told them they could meet you after our honeymoon. But you'll want to be careful of my mom."

"Really?" she says, suddenly wary. "Why?"

"No bad reason." I turn away from her to pop open the champagne. The stuff tastes like shit but I figure it's our wedding night and Maxine might like it. "Just that she'll have you spilling your guts to her after one or two conversations. She's good at that."

"Oh."

"That's why I didn't go home right after getting out of the Cage. She'd have taken one look at me and somehow I'd be telling her the whole thing. Not gonna lie, she's a little terrifying."

Maxine looks indecisively between her steak and the little wedding cake that was included with the dinner before cutting herself a tiny piece of cake. Still doing dessert first, but only a bite. "If you told her what happened, were you afraid of what she'd think?"

"Nah. That was the problem. I knew she'd love me anyway." I just didn't figure that I deserved it.

"That's a good problem to have."

No argument there. "I've got a couple of those good problems. My dad isn't terrifying, though. Instead he's quiet and small—and I know some people look at him and think he's small on the inside, too. And weak. But he's got the biggest fucking heart and he'll stand by you through anything."

"That sounds like my grandpa," she says softly. "Even after his heart broke into pieces, all the pieces were still so big."

"Your brother, too?"

She swallows hard and her eyes glisten as she nods. "Matt is—was—always looking out for me. And I looked out for him. We were like, I don't know…"

I do. "A team?"

"Yeah. Until he started at the FBI." Her eyes close, and her throat works before she continues all at once, "After Grandpa was gone, I didn't have anyone back home. I liked my job and had friends but…it wasn't the same. So that's why I went to see Matt before deciding what to do with the rest of my life. Because he was always part of everything important I ever did. So I let him know I was in Las Vegas, and we met at two in the morning at one of those casino restaurants where there are so many people always there for breakfast that it's easy to get lost in the crowd. But these big guys in suits show up right at our table, and Matt tells them to leave me there, that I'm just some hooker he picked up. But they take me with him anyway. They put us into a van, and they bring us to Papa, who says it's obvious we're brother and sister. And Matt's trying to talk his way out of the punishment they were giving him, and trying to talk Papa into letting me go—he's always been *so* good at talking his way in or out of anything. That's probably why they put him undercover. But I think he could see that punishment was coming no matter what, so he tells them I'm a nurse and would be useful. Papa says I can be useful on my back, and that could be part of his punishment. So Matt tells them I'm a virgin…and that's really what saved me." She opens her eyes again and I see the tears are gone and the anger's back. "Papa's a pig when it comes to women."

I'm real fucking glad that attitude saved her, because I've seen what happens to those other girls. "Where'd they take you to meet him?"

"It was a hotel room, I think. A really nice one. I don't know where, though. I was scared, and Matt was telling me to keep my head down as they were taking us there, so I did. I don't think it was a casino hotel, though. Or if it was, they took us in through an entrance that wasn't the lobby."

"But you didn't leave the city?"

"No. We weren't in the van long."

"Then you went straight to the barns?"

"Not right away. Papa wanted to make sure Matt wasn't lying about me being a virgin. So he had the doc come and examine me."

As she tells me that, humiliation edges into the anger in her voice and gets my own rage flaring, though I keep it carefully tamped down. "Was the doc already there?"

Maxine shakes her head.

"So Papa calls him up out of the blue in the middle of the night and says, 'Come here and look at this girl.' And the doc does." When she nods, I ask, "How long did you have to wait for him to show up?"

"I don't know." She looks real vicious as she cuts into her steak. "Maybe an hour or so."

"So the doc's likely here in the city, too—or one of the suburbs. That's good. That's real fucking good. The barns were nearer to Reno, so Blowback's been searching records in all of Nevada while trying to find the doc. But putting him within an hour's drive of Vegas will narrow it down." I study her for a long minute. She's eating, but seems stiff and focused, like she's got grief and anger tearing her up inside yet she's still trying to go through the motions. "A lot of these doctors have websites and pictures, but not all of them. When Blowback starts sending us names, are you gonna be up for driving around and taking a look at some of these guys? Or do you want me to take pictures and bring them back here for you to look at?"

"I'm up for it," she says quietly, then drags in a deep breath and sets down her knife and fork. "I'm sorry. We're supposed to be a team, but I'm obviously the weak link right now. Emotionally, I just… I feel like I'm all over the place."

"Don't you be sorry. Come here." I draw Maxine out of her chair and sideways onto my lap, loving the way she settles in so trustingly against me, her face buried against my throat. "We're here on a mission, but we've got this suite for a couple more days. So here's the plan—we aren't going to give a shit about anything Blowback sends us for a little while. While we're here, we're going to fuck each other stupid and watch all the *Die Hard* movies and eat cake or whatever the hell we want to do. That sound all right?"

With a shuddering breath, she nods against my neck. "Though I feel bad."

"Why do you feel bad?"

"Because it's almost the holidays, and you seem so close to your family, and the longer we take to find Papa… you already missed Thanksgiving."

"Yeah, and I missed a hell of a lot more when I was deployed. We all survived." Though maybe it's not me who needs to be surrounded by family when Christmas comes around—even if it's new family for her. "But I'll tell you what. Unless we're right on Papa's ass, we'll head home for a few days so we can open presents and be merry and shit. How about that?"

Another nod against my neck, then she tenses up. "Are you sure they'll want me there?"

"Why wouldn't they? You're part of the family now."

"But…your sister knows what I did to you."

"You didn't do shit to me. If you're thinking about

the way Anna reacted at the cabin, she knows better now. And remember what I said about their big hearts? They're going to love you, Maxine."

Just like I do.

"Okay," she whispers.

Good. "And I want you to promise me something, all right? When we're done with all this, you're gonna see someone. A therapist."

She starts giggling.

"I'm serious, angel. The shit you've been through, no wonder you're feeling all over the place. Any Marine or soldier will tell you that going home doesn't mean the shit goes away. Some things only need time to heal, but other things don't heal on their own."

"I know you're right," she says softly, and then sighs. "I just want to be tough and angry."

"Yeah, I tried that, too. It didn't work so well."

She huffs out a laugh before going quiet again. "I always fucked up when I got angry, anyway. First when I tased Tusk—"

"Hold up. You did what?"

"After Tusk killed Lissa, I got hold of Victor's stun gun and zapped his balls."

Shit. That was the root of all the fried ball jokes the other fighters were telling? "Don't kill me for laughing, angel, but that's pretty fucking amazing."

"Except I realized after that I could have used it on Victor. Maybe freed us all. And then when I had to give your reward, I got *so* angry again."

"As you should have."

"But I shouldn't have taken it out on you."

"Nah, that was pretty fucking amazing, too. The only good part about that whole fucked-up situation was seeing you so angry. Otherwise I never want to see you on your knees like that again."

She doesn't say anything for a second. Then, "Is that why you never made me suck your dick in the cabin?"

Pain clutches my chest at the mere thought of making her do that. "Yeah, it is. I won't ever ask it of you."

"What if I *want* to get on my knees?"

Christ, she kills me. "If you really want to, Maxine, you can touch me however and whenever you want."

"Okay," she says huskily, then slides off my lap and onto the floor, and gives me a hot look from beneath her lashes. "Though I'm not angry now. Do you think you'll still like it?"

"If I try real hard, I bet that I can drum up a little interest," I tell her, my voice already hoarse with need, my dick already bulging thick behind the heavy material of my sweatpants.

She grins and moves in, fingers curling around the waistband and letting that greedy fucker spring free. "Aw, look how happy it is. I really like your big dick, Stone."

That makes me laugh but all that comes out is a groan. "My big dick really likes you, too, angel."

"I'm glad." She rubs her soft cheek against my rigid

shaft while looking up at me. "If I had you tied up instead, what would you beg me to do?"

My fingers dig into the arms of the chair. "To suck me," I rasp out. "To suck me real hard and deep."

And this fucking girl. With an impish little smile, Maxine turns her head and teases my cock with the lightest flicks of her tongue, the softest kisses from her lips, the faintest touches of her hands. Over and over again. So that by the time she starts sucking the way I'm begging her to suck, I'm already about to come. And my dick, Christing hell—'like' ain't the word. My dick *loves* this girl.

And her damn mouth.

THIRTY-SIX

MAXINE

By the time we left the honeymoon suite, Blowback had compiled two lists of names. One was of licensed physicians in the area. The other named doctors who'd had their licenses revoked or suspended by Nevada's board of medical examiners, and it was as if a lightbulb went off in my brain. Because if Papa needed a doctor to treat his fighters, he wouldn't go after someone who was secure in his position or financially sound, and who was respected in his community and could afford protection for his family.

No, he'd go after the guy who was barely holding on. So I told Stone that was the list we needed to look at first.

Some of the names we could look up online to find pictures. None of those were the doc. For the others, the plan was simple: drive to the addresses listed, wait until the person who lived there comes out. If it wasn't the doc, Stone would go talk to him to make sure it actually was the person named on the list.

Claiming a motorcycle was too noticeable and no good for stakeouts, Stone bought a silver Honda Accord off a used lot—and used a fake identification to do it, so apparently he was more concerned about not leaving a paper trail than the possibility that the FBI was watching our every step.

Each day, we checked a few names off the list. Then we returned to the motel room that he paid for in cash—using a fake ID again—and it didn't matter that we weren't in a nice hotel, because it was like the honeymoon suite all over again. As if there wasn't anything in the world except Stone and me, and our bed.

On the fourth day of tracking down the names on the list, we found him.

Gerald Johnson, who'd had his license suspended for administering a controlled substance to himself. With my heart thundering, I watched him leave his big house and get behind the wheel of a Maserati. My reaction probably told Stone all that he needed to know, because even before I said a word, he muttered something about pervert hair and followed the doc's car. Then he got on the phone with Blowback and told him to look deeper into Gerald Johnson.

So even before we arrived at his clinic, we knew where he was headed. He wasn't currently licensed to practice medicine. Instead his clinic was a weight loss and lifestyle spa, a facility which could *never* have been capable of treating Matt's broken arm. Not that he'd ever intended to. Yet still, I'd believed that order to kill Matt had really come down from Papa and the doc had just been too afraid to do anything except obey. Because he'd always been kind to me, helped me. And all this time, I assumed that the doc was just like the rest of us—forced to do what Papa said, or his family would suffer for it.

But according to Blowback's info, the doc doesn't have a family. And I wouldn't have blamed him for saving his own skin. But after comparing the relative shabbiness of his clinic to the grandeur of his house and the gleam of his car…obviously the incentive to help Papa had more to do with money.

"You're looking real angry, girl," Stone tells me softly, parking the Honda in an adjacent lot. "You need me to take you into the backseat again?"

A laugh huffs through the rage. Stakeouts have never been boring with him. And that backseat has gotten quite a bit of use the past couple of days.

But I shake my head, angry tears blurring my vision. "I just want to go in there and *scream* at him. Just to ask why. Why why *why* was that fancy car worth more than Matt's life? Or more than Crash's and Lissa's? Because do you see any sign that he's being watched? Any of Papa's security?"

"No tails that I can see," he says softly.

And Stone *would* see them. Just like he spotted Victor and Hotel in the tavern that first night.

"So at any time, he could have gone to the police. He could have asked for protection, and told them who Papa was, and freed all of us…but he never did. And I just don't *understand* it."

"Because you're a decent person, angel." Stone turns in his seat, cupping my face, thumbs gently wiping away the tears. "And he's a garbage person. It's that simple. But here's the good thing about that—we've got some options here. One is contacting Creek and letting him know we've identified this fucker. They'll make a deal with him in trade for Papa, most likely, but it'll take the rest of this out of your hands, except for when you're in court. Second option is the original plan—sit tight, watch him, see if he leads us to Papa. Or maybe after watching him, if he doesn't lead us anywhere, then I go and ask him a few questions. Which one you want to do?"

"Original plan." I draw a shuddering breath. "But it should be a team decision."

"I don't figure you'll ever be really safe until Papa's dead, so I'd rather have him lead us to Papa, too." His fingers tighten slightly, the intensity of his gaze sharpening. "But listen—this is the part where we start being real careful."

"I thought we were being careful."

"We were. But now *real* careful. The doc doesn't know me but he might recognize you. So those big sunglasses go on and you don't look his way if he's outside. And you always had your hair brushed out all big in the barn, so now you keep it tied up or under a hat."

Biting my lip, I nod. Then narrow my eyes. "Are you making fun of my big nurse hair?"

Stone grins. "Nah, girl. That big hair made me want to get my hands all tangled up in it while I was drilling into you from behind. I loved that hair." With a tug at the braid I'm wearing now, he sobers a bit. "Even if we don't pull Creek and the feds into this, we might soon want to pull in help from the Riders. Someone to watch the doc at night and also to watch our backs. If we stay low and don't call any attention to ourselves, we oughta be all right for now. But Papa's security took out the Iron Blood, and they are not fucking around. So if you ever start feeling uneasy or thinking for a second that you've been made, we get the fuck out of here. Yeah?"

"Yes," I whisper, my stomach roiling at the thought of him being hurt. And wondering if I should just call this off now.

But I know it wouldn't really change anything. Because Stone is determined to get Papa, too. He would just go it alone, instead. No team necessary, especially now that we've found the doc. He doesn't need me for info anymore. I'm the one who needs him.

So much.

Stone must sense my worry, because he brushes his thumb over my lips, says in a reassuring voice, "It'll be all right, angel. Finding the doc is a huge fucking leap closer to Papa. We're getting there."

I know we are. So I should be feeling hopeful. Instead all I feel is terror and dread, because when it comes to believing that I'm getting somewhere, when it comes to being hopeful…my track record is pure shit. I was hopeful that Lissa would escape, and Tusk killed her. I was hopeful that my plan to slip laxatives to the guards would work, then Crash was killed. I was hopeful that we'd be able to rescue Matt…and discovered that he'd been killed.

But it's never me. It's always the person I love.

So instead of being hopeful now, I'm just terrified that I'll lose Stone, too.

THIRTY-SEVEN

MAXINE

Two days later, Stone trades in the Honda for a blue Toyota and we switch up our pattern, doing a few drivebys past the doc's house and his business, but parking at a long distance when we're just waiting. We begin driving by his house at night, too—and I can see why Stone said we might want to bring in help. I'm getting more than eight hours of sleep between naps in the car and at the motel, but I'm still worn out. Even though I'm basically doing nothing except sitting on my ass, it's as if the constant battle of hope and dread is wearing me down.

The fourth night after we locate the doc, we drive past his house around midnight. I don't see anything, but I sense Stone's sudden tension, and know there's something wrong when he asks me, "Did you leave anything back at the room?"

"No." We never do. Every day, we toss our packs into the trunk of the car. "What was it?"

"The power to his security camera was out. Fuck. Tag Blowback, tell him to put in an anonymous tip that'll make the cops check out the situation at Johnson's house. Maybe it's nothing, but I want to know."

But he's not waiting around to find out. We drive to one of the big casino lots and leave the car, then take a casino shuttle to where he stored his bike at another lot.

Minutes after that, we're on the road home.

SNOW STOPS US IN RENO. It's around eight in the morning when we get another room and tag Blowback again. Standing by one of the double beds, I watch Stone with my arms crossed and my pulse racing.

"Fuck." Jaw clenched, Stone shakes his head and puts away the phone before looking to me. "Gerald Johnson died of an apparent accidental overdose last night."

My heart drops. "What does that mean?"

"Don't know yet, except it wasn't accidental."

So they killed him. Sour fear coats my tongue. "Do

you think it's because of us?"

"Don't know. Blowback's good at covering his tracks, but it might be that digging around online tipped them off that someone was looking at Johnson, and they took him out just in case. Or it might have nothing to do with us and they killed him for another reason. But they'd have to work real fucking hard to connect those cars driving by his house to us and where we are now. So we'll sit tight for a bit and rest up. You all right?"

I nod. "I think so."

"Tired?"

I shake my head. "Too wired."

"Yeah, you'll crash soon. Come here." He draws me in against his big body, kisses me hard. "You want me to wear you out?"

I throw my arms around his neck. "God, yes."

HE WEARS ME OUT *so* well. I can barely move later, lying in bed and half sprawled across his chest, feeling wonderfully sleepy and deliciously sore in all the right places… and my worry gone. But then, he always does this to me. I've spent so many days recently dreading and fearing the worst. Yet the second he touches me, it all goes away.

"So what's the plan now?" I ask drowsily.

He kisses the top of my head. "Sleep."

"But after that?"

"It's supposed to stop snowing tonight. So we'll try to get a flight out tomorrow morning and get our asses back to the ranch."

And back to the protection of the club. "What about your motorcycle?"

"I'll sort it out."

"Are we going to tell Creek about Gerald Johnson?"

"Pretty sure Blowback already has. Because if Papa's looking for us, but federal agents hop right on Johnson's death…maybe it'll distract him and his security."

"Do you think he's looking for us?"

Frustration roughens his voice. "I don't know."

And he obviously hates not knowing. "You said Blowback was good at covering his tracks. And we did a good job covering ours, too. Didn't we?"

"Yeah, we did."

But Stone must not be depending on that alone to keep us safe. His gun's on the nightstand, within easy reach. And I have no doubt that he's proficient with it. That he's trained with weapons and knows exactly what he's doing.

But that might not save him.

I sigh heavily. "I wish we were still back at the cabin, wallowing in your cum."

"Wallowing?" A laugh shakes his big body beneath mine. "Why?"

"Because I didn't know about Matt yet," I say and his laughter quiets, his arms tightening around me. "Do you know what I think about most?"

"What's that, angel?"

"The way Victor did it. How it was such a waste of how hard Matt fought to get where he was. All that training, all that work. And in the end, he couldn't do anything, because I'm the gun they're holding to his head." My throat constricts unbearably. "He deserved so much better than being forced to his knees and put down like a dog who couldn't even bite back."

"Yeah, he did," Stone says gruffly.

My tears leak onto his shoulder. "Crash must have been so grateful to you."

He stiffens. "Why would you say that?"

"Because that's what he was going to do, wasn't it? He wasn't going to fight you. He'd have refused and then the guards would have shot him. Isn't that true?"

"Yeah, it is." His voice sounds raw, as if his throat's burning like mine is.

"It would have been the same as what happened to Matt. To save you, Crash wouldn't have fought. Even though not fighting must have gone against everything he was. You gave him another way out, though. And I know...I know it hurt you so bad. But the Cage stole the dignity of every man who died in there—and you helped Crash keep his."

"Doesn't feel like I did."

"I know. Just like you say that Matt would have been glad just to keep me safe. It doesn't feel like that's worth much."

"It is," he tells me. "It's everything."

"It must have been to Crash, too. To do the one thing he could that mattered. And that was saving you."

"Fuck." His voice sounds so thick, and his arms wrap so tight around me. "Don't wreck me like this, Maxine. Not while I'm naked and sober and supposed to be on guard."

I give a watery laugh against his skin. "Okay. Next time we're drunk."

"Sounds good." His mouth presses to my temple. "Sleep now."

I do. Throughout the day I'm vaguely aware of Stone sitting near the window, where he can see anyone coming or going without exposing himself. Watching over me. He smells like coffee and toothpaste when he begins kissing me gently awake, stretched out on the bed beside me and fully clothed.

"You've been sleeping all day, girl," he says while nuzzling my neck. "Let's go out and get something to eat."

"Nah," I say like he does. "I've got something real meaty to eat right here."

While he laughs, I push him onto his back, begin kissing my way down his shirt-covered chest. Then I hear the soft *click* of the door unlatching behind me, and feel his body stiffen—and there's no thinking about what comes next. Before I even met this man, saving him is what I intended to do…but now it matters more than anything else could. Because Stone's fast, but his gun's on the nightstand and they're already coming into the room.

So I just need to give him that extra second so he can protect himself.

Even as Stone tries to shove me aside, I throw myself across his chest. Behind me, it only sounds as if someone coughs twice, but it feels like two bricks slam into my back and shoulder before tearing through my skin and exploding. Then Stone's got his weapon in hand and my ears are ringing from the gunfire. His heavy weight smothers me into the bed and then another muffled shot reaches my ears. In the next second he's off me, and in the distance I hear tires screeching and shouts coming from other guests. But I can't get up and can't stop hurting.

"Angel girl, no no." Stone's stricken face swims into view as he turns me over, and then pain nearly blinds me. Blood coats my tongue and I can barely breathe without choking. His hands are all over me, sitting me up and pressing into my back and everything goes distant as I'm carried away on a black wave of agony, except I hear him screaming *"Help me!"* and for someone to call a fucking ambulance and I would, I would call one, but I can't.

But I need to know I did enough. I have to spit blood out of my throat. "Saved…you?"

"Yeah, girl. You saved me. And I'm sorry, this is going to hurt so fucking bad," he says raggedly, and shoves something against my back and ties it with the sheet, his jaw locked and the muscles in his arms straining as he pulls the sheet tight tight tighter and it does hurt so fucking bad, agony shredding up and down my body, but I can only choke silently when I scream.

He gathers me up against his chest. "I'm sorry, I'm so sorry, but we've got to stop the bleeding. Ah fuck, angel. Why'd you do it? I can't fucking…I can't…" His voice breaks. "You didn't owe me that. You hear? You don't owe me *anything*. But especially not ever this."

"Not…payback." Everything's going numb. It doesn't hurt so much now to talk, but I can barely draw a breath and each one I manage is thick and wet. "Couldn't lose… someone else…I love."

"And I can't bear losing you." His forehead presses to mine, and he holds me so tight, his strong arms nearly crushing my back. "I love you, Maxine. So you can't leave me. You can't, because it'll destroy me. So if you want to save me, you fucking *fight* to stay with me."

Okay, I mean to say.

But I can't when everything slips away.

THE GRAVE

THIRTY-EIGHT

STONE

THE RAGGED HOLE IN ME NOW IS THE SIZE OF THOSE two bullet wounds that Papa's men put in Maxine's back. So fucking small. But big enough to kill me.

"Stone!"

I look up as Anna flings herself against my chest, holding on hard before sliding into the seat beside mine. Tears drip down her cheeks, and she grips my hands tight. "We heard on the news coming to the hospital. They didn't give her name but said that a woman who was shot at a motel succumbed to her injuries…and I'm so sorry. So sorry."

Gunner's behind her, echoing, "So fucking sorry, brother."

Me, too. But not for that. And since it's just the three of us in this waiting room, there's no one to overhear when I tell them, "Maxine's not dead. They're just saying she is."

Anna and Gunner exchange a worried look. "The doctors are saying she is?" she asks carefully.

"The feds. They're going to write Christina Miller on the death certificate." I swallow past the thick knot in my throat. "Maxine made it through surgery. They're closing her up now."

"Oh, thank god," Anna says softly. "So this is to throw that Papa person off her trail?"

I nod, barely able to fucking breathe.

"And she's all right?" Gunner asks.

"Not sure yet. Good chance." But still a chance she won't be. And until I know for sure, those two fucking holes are killing me.

"That's good, then." Anna's fingers squeeze mine. "Have you been here since they brought her in?"

"Where the fuck else would I go?"

"To piss, to breathe some fresh air, and get something to eat," Gunner tells me. "It's been about fourteen hours, brother, and you're no good to her if you collapse on your feet. Take ten minutes with me. Anna can stay here. If there's any updates from surgery, they can tell her since she's family, too. She'll text us right away."

No good to her. That's fucking true enough. But I need to be.

I couldn't choke down a bite right now, so I tell Gunner to fuck off when he suggests the cafeteria. Instead I head outside. The sun's glaring up high and the snow's melted—and I should have tried to get a flight out of here earlier. Should have done every goddamn thing different.

"How'd they get a trace on you?"

"They put a fucking tracker in her arm and told her it was birth control." With a range that was weak as hell, so it wasn't picked up while she was on the ranch, where we can't even get a cell signal. "But it must have blipped in Vegas. Don't know when. Maybe they picked it up right away and waited to see what we were doing. Or maybe it was recent, and they saw she'd been near Johnson's house and business, so they tied off that loose end before coming after us."

"You never noticed anyone on your ass?"

Chest aching, I shake my head.

"Then they weren't on your ass. You'd have noticed." He frowns at me. "How'd you find out about the tracker here?"

"They were scanning for bullet fragments and realized the thing in her arm wasn't what it was supposed to be."

"Not birth control?" Gunner says and hesitates before asking, "Could she be pregnant, then?"

"They checked. She isn't." And thank fucking Christ,

with all the drugs they'll be pumping into her after the surgery. I tilt my head back, and the sky's so fucking bright, my eyes burning. "She threw herself in front of me. Took the bullets so I could get to my weapon."

Gunner doesn't say a damn thing because there's not a damn thing to say. Nothing that can ease the agony of knowing your woman put herself in harm's way for you.

But there's a hell of a lot to say about pride. "She's so fucking brave. And an angel. Has been since day one. Took care of me. And wasn't the one who drugged me—she tried to get me the hell away from those fuckers, though they'd have killed her for it. Then she threw herself in front of me. So if I ever hear the brothers say a single goddamn word about her being bait, I'll rip their throats out. You let them know before I get home."

"I will." Then he shakes his head. "You really think I'm going home before you are? I'll take down Papa with you. The whole damn club is gearing up to ride this way."

"Yeah, well…tell them to hold off," I say and it feels like there's a knife lodged in my chest. "Because I knew the brothers would come, but I needed protection for her faster than that."

He frowns at me. "What the hell does that mean?"

It means I made a deal with the fucking devil.

THIRTY-NINE

STONE

I'VE BEEN CARRYING AROUND CREEK'S CARD SINCE THAT night Maxine almost went into witness protection—and a good thing, too. Because when the cops showed up, asking who the fuck the three dead suits in the motel room were, a call to Creek smoothed shit over real fast. He's the one who arranged for the fake announcement of her death, and who arranged for the guards watching her hospital room now…but it all came at a price.

And that price is me. I'll be a consultant or some shit,

which means I'll be the eyes and ears heading into places that his investigative team can't legally go, gathering info that'll help bring down all the owners of the stables. That end result is something I'd love to do anyway. Didn't think I'd be doing it like this, but fuck it all. Whatever keeps Maxine safe.

Maxine's out of surgery and the doctors are real certain that she'll pull through. But she's not awake yet. Instead they intend to keep her under for a few days more. And she's hooked up to a million goddamn machines. At least she's breathing on her own, though, and that heart monitor is steadily beeping.

My parents arrive not long after Anna and Gunner, and my mom and dad sit with Maxine when Creek texts me to meet.

I figured he'd know better than to come to the hospital and try to collect payment before my wife even opened her eyes. So I'm fucking pissed when I see him waiting for me at a booth in the hospital's cafe.

"You got an ID on the three assholes I killed?" I ask, not bothering to sit. Because right now, the suits who hunted Maxine down and shot her are all I give a shit about. "Or you got the bastard who ran away?"

"Not yet. But I'm not here for that."

"That's all I'm here for," I say and turn back the way I came.

"We think we found Victor."

I take a seat. "Where?"

"Got a hit on that missing Silverado. Looks like he's been

holed up in a squatter's cabin in the middle of nowhere ever since the raid on the barns."

"But you haven't gone in yet?"

"The deal was you get a heads-up. I'm giving you the heads-up."

Fuck. I can't go while Maxine's still out. But I can send Gunner. "Where?"

"You go in with my team, we get a feel for each other… you wouldn't be gone more than a half day."

So this is some fucking bullshit. "I go in with your team, I can't kill him."

"He's got a self-righteous streak wider than Texas and he's holed up in a cabin with fuck knows how many weapons," Creek tells me. "There's a real good chance that he's not gonna let us take him alive. You want in or you don't? But before you answer, let me tell you something else. We can't find Faraday's body out in the big grave behind the barns. Found everyone else and a whole lot of other shit, but not Faraday."

I go still. "What did the fucker do with him?"

"You come, you can ask the fucker," Creek tells me. "And then your wife will get a chance to bury her brother like he ought to be buried, instead of rotting out in the desert somewhere."

Fuck. *Fuck.* Any other goddamn reason, I wouldn't even be thinking twice. But she loved her brother so damn much. I can do this for her.

Then put a bullet in Victor's head.

* * *

WE LEAVE LONG BEFORE DAWN and Creek's team catches me up to speed along the way. Victor's cabin is in a box canyon with only one access road, which means getting in there without being seen will be near fucking impossible. But the canyon walls offer a vantage to scope out the place before we head in.

There's snow everywhere, so we suit up in some winter whites, and any other time I'd be loving this shit. But I just want to get back to Maxine. So when day breaks and Victor trudges out of his cabin toward his outhouse, if I hadn't needed to ask about her brother, I'd have snagged one of the rifles and put that bullet in his head then and there.

He heads back to his cabin and we start scanning for snares and traps. Most likely he's laid down some kind of defense.

Then we hunker down as his cabin door opens again and he comes out carrying a rifle. But he's not alone. Another man is walking ahead of him, arm in a sling and Victor's weapon trained on his back as they head for the outhouse.

"Holy fucking hell," Creek breathes beside me.

Suddenly, I'm real goddamn glad I came. "Seems to me that Victor's holding a federal agent captive and has a gun aimed at his back. We charge in there, you risk spooking that fucker and him pulling the trigger. Which means the best time to take Victor out is when your man's in the shithouse and Victor's alone outside. So give me that sniper rifle," I tell Creek. "And I'll get your man back for you right now."

And get Maxine something even better.

FORTY

MAXINE

Everything hurts. But it's a deep, muffled hurt… as if the pain's there, but I'm floating right above it. Which probably means that I'm full of painkillers.

Which means I must be alive.

And Stone, too. My eyelashes feel as if they weigh a ton, and everything's fuzzy and bright when I finally open my eyes. But he's right there sitting beside me. And I don't know if it's a sob or a laugh that tries to rise up through my chest, but it hurts to do it. Hurts so much that everything around me goes even fuzzier, and I don't see Stone move. But suddenly he's leaning in closer and grinning his crooked grin at me, and I can feel his hand on mine.

"Merry Christmas, angel," he says in a thick rasp, then brings my fingers to his lips. "It's so fucking good to see you. No, don't try to talk yet. Your throat's probably going to feel a bit raw for a while."

A bit? I show him my middle finger and he kisses it.

"Christmas?" I mouth the word.

"You've been out a week, but healing up good while you've been sleeping. And the doctor doesn't think you'll be up to doing much today, so the second you feel tired, tap out. Yeah?"

Might be soon. Already I'm feeling the weight of my eyelids again. But I don't want to let go of him yet. I squeeze his hand.

"So I should tell you, I know you were worried about me missing another holiday with my family. But you made sure that didn't happen by jumping in front of those bullets. And they're all here now, celebrating how the magic of Christmas can bring a family together."

Oh, even a little laugh hurts. And exhausts me. But Stone's suddenly looking at me so seriously that I still can't let go.

"But this family get-together is even bigger than we thought it would be, Maxine," he says quietly. "We weren't sure whether to tell you right away, because you'll likely get real emotional, and you're still in rough shape. But I figured this will do you more good than anything else in the world. Except you've got to promise to try to hold it together, all right? Because I've got you the best goddamn Christmas present ever…and I found it in a toilet."

What? But Stone steps back, and someone's behind him—sitting in a wheelchair, wearing a hospital gown and with his arm in a surgical cast.

And maybe I'm not alive, after all, because dead is the only way that Matt could be in front of me. Or maybe I'm just drugged and dreaming. But the tears spilling down my cheeks are hotter than dream tears should be, and although they blur everything in front of me, I can hear his familiar voice so clearly.

"Hey, sis." And I know that touch, his fingers squeezing mine. A sob shreds up my chest and then my big brother's hushing me in the same way he always did. "Shh, don't do that. I'm all right."

He's all right. Another sob tears through me. "How?"

I can't manage more than that painful whisper.

"Victor wouldn't have thought twice about executing one of the Eighty-Eight. But when I told him that I was an undercover agent…I guess cop-killing is where he drew his line in the sand. Took some fast talking to convince him that I was telling the truth, though. After I did, he pretended to put me down and then he didn't know what to do with me. Couldn't let me go. Couldn't kill me. So we went glamping out in a cabin for a while."

A cabin? He couldn't have received the medical attention he needed there. My gaze moves to his arm.

"Noticed that cast, huh? Holing up in a cabin didn't do it much good, but the doctors say it'll be all right after a few more surgeries."

More tears spill and a nurse clicks her tongue from the other side of my bed. "We've got to let her rest now."

I can't. But I don't think I'll have a choice. My gaze moves from Matt to Stone, who's watching me with concern darkening his hazel eyes.

"Thank you," I mouth to him.

"Best damn thing I ever did," he says gruffly. "That and marrying you."

As I drift away again, I think I'm smiling. Because although I was only awake for about ten minutes of it… that was the best Christmas ever.

FORTY-ONE

STONE

FOR THE NEXT TWO WEEKS, I'M AT MAXINE'S SIDE nearly every minute—and for the first week, a few minutes of wakefulness at a time is all we get. By the end of the next week, she can stay awake for a couple of hours at a stretch. She still tires quickly, but she sits up a little better now, and the doctors are saying that it won't be too long before she's able to head home…or in this case, to my parents' place, because they'll be able to look after her full time.

And me…I'm heading out tomorrow. Which means I can't put off telling her about the deal I made with Creek any longer.

But it's so fucking hard. Even harder when I'm in there while the nurses are showing my mom the best way to bathe her, and as they're changing the bandages I get a look at the scars forming on her back.

Scars that are there because she threw herself in front of me. And yet I'll be leaving before she's completely healed.

So even after the nurse and my mother are gone, and it's just Maxine and me, I'm having trouble getting the words out. No fucking surprise, she picks up on it. Though not the reason why.

She's half-reclining in the bed, her face pale with strain and her emerald eyes dulled by exhaustion. "It's true that neither of us got out prettier than we went in."

Sitting on the chair next to her bed, I have to shake my own thoughts out of my head. "What's that?"

"Your new scars from Crash." She brushes her fingers over her eyebrows. "The scars on my back. You said once that no one gets out of a place like the Cage prettier than they went in."

"You came out prettier," I tell her hoarsely, realizing exactly when I said that to her—when I was accusing her of saving her own skin. "You're more beautiful than you ever have been, Maxine. And that's really fucking saying something, because my first look at you about knocked me on my ass. But that was never about how you looked on the outside, anyway…and inside, you're still the most beautiful woman I know."

That curves her lips into a smile but it doesn't reach her tired eyes. "And you're a good man. Which is maybe why you've been putting off what you need to tell me."

Shit. "I was that obvious?"

She gives a little nod, her chin wobbling. "But it's okay. We were in what Matt would call a really extreme situation…and those always produce extreme reactions. So I understand that you might have said something that you didn't really mean, and now you need to take it back."

"I'm not taking anything back." I frown at her. "What exactly do you think I said that I didn't mean?"

"That you love me," she whispers, closing her eyes. "But it's okay—"

"Bullshit if that's okay." I take her hand, lean in with my elbows braced on the bed. "Are you taking yours back? Because if you do, I'm telling you right now, Maxine, you'll kill me. And you'll just be *okay* if I take mine back?"

Tears glitter on her eyelashes, and she gives a tiny shake of her head.

"All right, then. Because I love you. I'm absolutely fucking crazy in love with you." I kiss her fingers, my voice roughening. "But I didn't say anything before you were hurt because I didn't figure you'd feel the same way. Not for me. Now that you've said it, though, I ain't ever letting you take it back."

Her eyes are shining now, partly with tears, partly with a true smile. "Matt might be right, though. It has been an extreme few months for both of us. So when this is all done and I'm just a regular girl again—"

"You think it's going to fade?"

"Not the way I feel for you," she says softly. "Because you'll be the same. So vibrant and alive and *such* a good man. But me… You said you have a soft spot for damsels in distress. And I'm usually not ever in trouble. Really, I'm not."

"Yeah, that's not how it works. Sure, you being vulnerable caught my attention. But what *kept* my attention, Maxine, and what I fell for is that you were so damn smart and funny and sexy. Is that going to fade? Fuck no." I drag in a deep breath. "And I'm going to be able to prove it."

Her brows pull together. "What do you mean?"

"I made a deal with Creek to help him hunt down Papa." My chest aches so damn bad. "But you'll be going home with my mom and dad while I'm under."

"Under?" Her lips part as if in disbelief while her gaze wildly searches my face. "For how long?"

"Until it's done. Maybe a few months. Maybe a year."

Her eyes squeeze shut and a little sob hitches through her chest. "Let me come with you."

"You can't, angel."

Her voice breaks again. "But we're a team."

"We always will be." I cup her cheek in my hand, my heart raw. "But right now, your job as part of this team is to rest and to heal, while I take out these Cage fuckers so you'll always be safe. And our team is going to be just fine. If I'd met you when I was younger, I'd have married you then, too—and likely would have been deployed at some point for the same stretch of time as I'll be gone now. This is no different than what thousands of husbands and wives go through."

Except I'll be leaving when she's not even healed yet.

Tears slip over her cheeks. "I'm so afraid of losing you now."

Groaning, I lean in and kiss her trembling lips. "You won't. I swear to fuck you won't. All right?"

And this fucking girl, so steady and strong. She's already steeling herself for it. Wiping her eyes, she nods. "All right."

"Good." Though I know this is killing us both. "I'm going to make a few videos for Daisy before I head out. And I'm hoping you'll do the same for me while I'm gone."

She gives a teary laugh. "Sexy ones? Might have to be hospital-gown sexy."

"Nah, girl. Just messages that tell me you're okay. My club will be protecting you, and I trust them to keep you safe…but it's not the same as seeing it for myself. So I'll have Blowback set up an encrypted site where you can send messages from your phone, and he'll make sure no one but me ever accesses them. And I'll send messages to you when I can—those will probably be from burner phones that I'll destroy as soon as I send anything. Those won't be coming often. Because if anyone starts looking at me real hard, I don't want to give them a way to find you."

"Okay," she whispers, lips trembling, her hands coming up to clasp my face in her hands and drawing me down for a kiss. Even that effort strains her so damn much—and probably hurts her, too, though she'd never say it.

"I miss you already, angel."

"I miss you, too." Tears falling, she kisses me again. "Come back to me."

There's nothing in this world that could keep me away.

I DON'T GO UNTIL AFTER she's asleep again…and then I have to force myself to leave. There's still a big hole in me, but this time it's the size of Maxine. I don't know how all those married fuckers in the military do it. Leaving like this.

Except I *do* know. Because going means protecting her. It means making sure she's safe. It means she won't always be in witness protection, running or hiding. It means she'll be free. And I'd rip my heart out a million fucking times to make sure she is.

Just wish I wasn't hurting her, too. But that would mean she didn't love me…and I can't wish for that. Because I wouldn't trade her heart for anything.

I head out, slowing as I see that my sister's got her arms around a dark-haired woman. Jenny. Anna's best friend, a girl I've known forever, because our families have been close over the years. Though I didn't expect to see her here. Not considering how she must still be grieving.

Jenny turns to me, takes my hand before drawing me in for a tight hug, then pulling back again. Her pale green gaze searches my face. "I'm so sorry she was hurt. And so glad she's okay." A sudden little smile curves her lips. "And Anna says some congratulations are in order, too."

Throat feeling rough, I nod. "I was so damn sorry to hear about Red," I tell her, since I haven't seen her since it happened. "Your dad was one of the best men I've ever known. You all right?"

Her smile wobbles a bit, but she nods. "I'm doing okay. And…we've brought you a present."

We. Not her and Anna. Her and Saxon. The prez is standing over by Gunner, obviously waiting for me to finish up talking to Jenny. I head over there, the prez watching me come with steel in his eyes.

"I don't like this shit," he tells me with a muscle working in his jaw. "These fucking feds dragging you into this like you owe them a favor. That's some goddamn bull-shit. They want her as a witness, so they'd have done all this for her regardless—and instead they pulled you in, too. So if you want out, you say the word. We'll get you and your woman out. And we'll hunt down this fucker Papa with you."

Chest feeling real swollen, I shake my head. "If it was just bringing down Papa, maybe. But they're going after the whole fucking Cage, all the owners. That's a whole lotta resources they'll be pulling in…and I'd rather spend the government's time and money and blood than my brothers'." My voice thickens real deep. "What I need from you is to keep my woman safe."

Jaw clenched, he nods. "We will, brother. And I swear to you—we won't fuck up again. They'll have to go through every goddamn brother to touch her."

I know it. And if I didn't believe it, didn't trust it, I wouldn't be leaving her tomorrow. Or ever.

Throat burning, I nod.

"And we've got something else for you," he says gruffly. "You might say it's a present from Blowback. Because he heard they found a whole bunch of shit in the holes out behind those barns."

I frown. "The graves?"

"Yeah." He turns to Gunner, who hands him a folded leather bundle. "And apparently Creek gave him some shit about tampering with evidence, but Blowback must have had something Creek wanted real bad, because he traded for this."

My kutte. That burning in my throat turns into a big fucking lump when I see the vest I've worn since patching in. The vest that's been like a second skin to me ever since.

"Turn around, brother," Saxon tells me.

So the Hellfire Riders' president can put it back where it belongs. The familiar weight settles on my shoulders. Straight out of a grave. Worn by a man who was all but dead not too long ago. And I sure as fuck can't leave Maxine yet. I'll have to wait until she wakes up again, show her this. Let her see the man who'll be coming back to her. Let her see the man who'll be destroying every fucker who ever hurt her.

"All right, then." Saxon turns me back to face him, gives me a once-over. "Looks real good."

Fuck yeah, it does. Looks real fucking good. I'm a sexy motherfucking beast in these colors, and Maxine's going to cream her little hospital gown when she sees me. Just picturing it makes me grin like a jackass, and Saxon gives a short laugh before regarding me seriously again.

"You need *anything*…you just say the fucking word," he tells me.

I just need to get this done. Then get back to the club. And back to Maxine.

THE CLUB

FORTY-TWO

JANUARY

I hope this works! Gunner says he's been leaving messages this way to tell you how I'm doing. So you probably already know that I'm at your mom and dad's house… as you can probably also see from the room behind me. They put me in their bedroom for now, because walking up the stairs was… Well, it didn't happen. Oh, and Daisy says hi! She loves your videos. I do, too, honestly. The way you say 'good girl' makes me all tingly.

Oh, wait. Should I say that I'm tingly while I'm in

your parents' bed? That's either really weird or really hot. So…yeah.

Anyway! You probably know about the interviews I already did with Creek, and the sketches they made from my description of Papa. I can't think of anything I left out…but if I do think of anything, I'll let you know. I hope you're safe. Gunner tells me not to worry, that you're one tough motherfucker, and I know that. But I miss you. And… Oh shit, I'm not going to cry. I swore to myself I wouldn't cry in these videos. So I'm going to stop now, and I'll see you again tomorrow.

FEBRUARY

Look, I'm finally upstairs! They put me in your old bedroom…and I'm not going to lie, I've been going through all your stuff. Your senior yearbook photos are *amazing*. And I don't believe for one second that they called you "Stone" because of football. It was probably just that "Stoned Wall" didn't sound as good. Also I read all the things the girls wrote in your yearbook and you were such a player! So bad! I'd cry for all the hearts you broke except all those hearts were used up dotting the 'i' in their names.

And Daisy says hi! I went for a walk with her today. Not very far, just to the end of the block and back. But I noticed that I had an escort who was wearing a vest just like yours. I'm guessing that was something you arranged, and thank you. I already felt safe…but that does make me feel safer. It's you I worry about. So I hope you're okay.

MARCH

I'M GOING TO START SEEING SOMEONE. JUST LIKE YOU said I should. I wasn't deliberately putting it off, but kind of waiting to see what would heal on its own, and then your mom and I were talking and she gently suggested it, too. Then she gave me the names of a few therapists who she thought would be a good fit for me. So that starts next week.

Also I told your mom everything! I didn't mean to. And you warned me. But it happened anyway. I didn't give her all the sexy details but pretty much everything else. And she said that she's more proud of you than she's ever been. Just so you know.

Oh, and Daisy says hi! She was just up here with me…I should have started recording then so you could see her, too. Crap. Next time. And Matt went back to work today. Maybe you already know, though. He said he's not going to be in the field right away, so not to worry. But I still do. I miss him, and I miss you. And I'm *not* going to cry, so I'll see you tomorrow.

* * *

APRIL

Ooh, I got flowers delivered to me today! Aren't they gorgeous? And they smell so good. They were sent by a mysterious handsome stranger, because there wasn't a name on the card saying who they were from. Just someone who wrote, 'Happy birthday, angel.' So I think I have a secret admirer.

I also went to lunch with Anna today, and I'm happy to report that she's completely repressed the memory of how she saw me that first time. I like her so much. Gunner, too. And we all miss you.

And Daisy says hi! Say hi to Daddy! Aw, that's a good girl. Oh… Oh, wait. No, we don't eat the pretty flowers. Oh god, hold on.

Ah, okay—I'm back. I'm not sure if this was a birthday present, too, but I just got the message about the piece of garbage you took out. I know it wasn't the piece of garbage that you really want to clean up, but any garbage gone is better for everyone. And I suppose it's selfish of me to hope that you do take out the right one soon, not even because of what he did…but just so you come home.

MAY

So the other day when I mentioned looking at the veterinary programs nearby…I've thought about it a little more, and I think I'll put off applying to school for another year. I'm stronger now, but some of the work will likely involve bigger animals. So I think waiting will be the right thing to do, and in the meantime, maybe just volunteer at the animal shelter or something.

And Daisy says hi! Aw, she's sleeping. Look at her. She gets excited whenever I take out my phone because she thinks I'm going to play one of your videos. So when I began recording, she was so disappointed that my face was on the screen instead of yours that she started pouting and then went to sleep. I'll make it up to her in a bit.

Oh! This is also important. Since I'm getting around more easily now, Anna asked whether I wanted to move into your place. And I hope it's okay with you, but I told her that I'd rather we get our own house. I have the money from my grandpa's farm and all that stuff in storage, so I was thinking about looking around for a property to either rent or buy. I know that's a big decision for one person to make for the whole team. So if you *really* hate the idea, will you try to let me know? Otherwise I'll start looking for a place that will hopefully suit us both.

JUNE

DAISY SAYS HI! AND LOOK! WE FOUND A HOUSE OFF Newberry Road. Here's a picture of it, if you can make any of that out…but Anna says to just tell you that it's the old Roberts' place. I loved all the open space inside and the yard for Daisy, and Gunner says the garage is perfect for you, so I hope you'll like it.

Saxon's arranging for Hashtag to move in to the guest room downstairs, because he says you'll trust Hashtag to keep his hands to himself. Apparently that's an issue with some of the brothers? I haven't noticed. They've all been really polite to me and no one's ever tried anything. So Hashtag will be there every night and then I'll have my usual rotation of escorts during the day. Plus they're setting up a security system before they let me and Daisy move in.

So don't worry about whether I'll be safe. Everyone has been taking such good care of me. I just hope that you're okay, too.

JULY

Gunner moved in all your things from Anna's today. I didn't know what to do with some of it, so now you have a mancave. It's full of boxes that you can sort through when you get back.

And Daisy *would* say hi! Except she's in your mancave sniffing all of your boxes, so I'm guessing that some of the stuff must still smell like you. Which makes me super jealous of a dog, because I sniffed some of your shirts when I was unpacking them and I didn't smell anything.

Oh, and there's other exciting news. I think Gunner and Anna were holding off on announcing a date for their wedding because they weren't sure when you'd be back, but they've finally settled on October. I forgot the exact day that Anna said, but I'll get it for you next time—so even if you aren't done, maybe take a few days leave if you can, because they want you to stand up with them as best man.

AUGUST

So…today is the anniversary of when Matt and I were taken, and of the day that I stopped being Maxine and became Cherry. A whole year gone by.

And the Cage just doesn't feel real anymore. Or the barns. Which is stupid, because every day I see the scars on my back. And I have really strong flashbacks sometimes. But most of the time, like right now…it just feels like something that I heard happen to someone else. I guess that means some of what Matt said about extreme situations is true. And that even the most extreme reactions and emotions can fade.

If I needed an answer about how I feel about *you*, though…it's still so real to me, Stone. Nothing's faded. Instead it's just a big ache. Like there's a giant hole inside me where you're supposed to be. Because I'm happy, and I'm surrounded by your family, your friends—and I love them so much now. But you're not here, so there's a huge part of me missing.

And oh my god, I'm sorry. I should delete this one, because maybe it isn't fair to dump all these feelings on you, especially if you don't feel the same way anymore. I just want you to know that there was a point when I'd lost every bit of hope, when I didn't even *dare* to hope because then everything would turn to shit, when it seemed like Papa and the others had taken everything from me. But they didn't. So here I am…truly Maxine again. And when this is done, and you come home, I don't want you to feel obligated or worried that I won't be okay. If there's one thing this year has taught me, it's that I can survive just about anything.

But I'm also going to warn you…if you don't feel the same way as you did when you married me, I will chain you to our bed and rock your world until you fall in love with me again.

SEPTEMBER

OKAY, SO…I DON'T KNOW WHY I HAVEN'T DONE THIS before. Maybe it's because I was at your mom's house for so long and that would have been awkward. But now we've got our own place and lookie here! I got a new toy! This part right here is supposed to suck on my clit while this other part is supposed to vibrate my G-spot, so I'm going to pretend this is your tongue and your fingers.

So, um. Let's do this. I don't think this other part can go in until I'm wet, so I'll start with the clit sucker. Whoa, that's a bad angle for the camera. Yikes. That is not sexy, either. Oh god, how do people do this? I think I'll just hold the camera pointed at my face, because otherwise I'm not coordinated enough for this.

Now I'm supposed to press this button until it starts… Oh. Oh. Oh my god. This was the best idea ever. Oh shit. Sorry, I just dropped the phone on my face. But oh my god, Stone. I should have been doing this every day. It's not at all like your tongue but it's… *Mmmmm.* So I'm going to close my eyes and pretend you've got me all tied up and you're sucking on my clit. Holy shit, it feels *so* good. Oh god. And then you're like 'Open your legs real wide, girl' and I fight because I know you're about to hold me down and fuck me with your big cock and make me come and oh my god you're still sucking my clit and this is so—

Oh shit. Daisy, no! Off the bed—it's not a toy for you! No! Give it back! Oh my god, shit. Hahaha, oh my god. Oh, Daisy…oh no. That's a lot of slobber. No, that's okay, girl. I don't want it back now, just let me turn it off first. Yes, you're still a good girl. It's okay. You're such a good girl. It's Mommy's fault because I didn't close the bedroom door all the way.

Um, okay. I'm back. So…that was fun.

And Daisy says hi.

OCTOBER

I JUST GOT BACK HOME AFTER TASTE-TESTING *SO MUCH* wedding cake at our girls' night. And I had some champagne, too. But don't worry, because Lily brought me home. Should I call her Lily or Zoomie when I'm talking to you?

Also Jenny told me the story of how you once set your dick on fire at a party and you would have been a legend except the stench of singed pubic hair made everyone gag and bail.

And— Oh my god. That made me laugh when she was telling it, but now that I'm thinking about it again… I'm begging you, please please *please* don't ever risk your beautiful cock again. I *need* that cock.

Oh hey, Hashtag! Wait, where are you going? Hold on a sec, Stone. Hashtag just came into the kitchen and then left again without saying anything. Hey! I brought some cake for you! Do you want to say hi to Stone?

He doesn't want to say hi. I guess bikers are too manly and tough for that. Instead you all just punch each other hello. But Daisy wants to say hi! Come here, girl, and say hi to Daddy! Do we miss him? Do we miss him? Yes, we do. We love him *so* much. You're such a sweetheart. Yes, I'll let you out.

So…Anna was asking if I know whether you'll make it to the wedding, and I told her that I haven't heard from you yet. But I really hope you can come. And today I was thinking about how long it's been since you sent a garbage update. For a while there were so many, it seemed like most of the trash must be gone. Except that one.

I really hope you get him soon.

FORTY-THREE

MAXINE

"It doesn't look like Hashtag is back yet," Jenny says when she pulls into my driveway.

"It's okay," I tell her, gathering up my purse and turning to glance through the rear window of her pickup. Two Hellfire Riders have tailed us from her house, where we've been putting together the last of the decorations before tonight's rehearsal and dinner. "They'll hang out until he gets here."

Picasso and Beaver again today, but after all these

months, I think every club member has been rotated in a few times to serve as my bodyguard. Even Saxon. But some are scheduled in more often than others. I'm a little surprised that they're still so good-natured about it, but if any have been complaining or impatient for the guard duty to end, they never let me see it.

"Thank you so much for your help! And I'll see you tonight," Jenny says, then laughs and shakes her head. "We'll see if we can pull this off."

"It'll be amazing," I tell her. She's put so much work into Anna's wedding, there's no way it wouldn't be.

I head into the house, where Daisy greets me with wild kisses and her tail wagging her entire body. I grin, kissing her back before letting her out. As soon as she's back inside, I'll play one of Stone's videos for her…and for me. They're the best part of every day—several times a day—when Daisy and I listen to him say she's such a good girl.

Because aside from a few brief messages—and the flowers for my birthday—I haven't heard anything else. Just a "We got Caballo." Or "We got the Greek." Stable owners who weren't Papa. There have been six so far. But it's been a while since more names have come.

But it's got to be soon. It has to be.

I let Daisy inside again and we head to the kitchen at the back of the house, where she goes wild and dances happily while Stone's deep voice rumbles from my phone. Maybe I spoil her a bit when I play it a second and third time. But she's so cute she deserves to be spoiled.

Especially cute is how she pouts when it's done, heading over to her favorite bed, and curling up in the late afternoon sunlight that streams through the patio door.

Then it's my turn. After so many months, it seems like I'd run out of things to say every day. But the truth is…I'm constantly stopping myself from saying too much. Because this is hard enough for both of us. Stone knows that I miss him. So if every day was just me pouring out my heart, all it would do is lay a heavier burden on him.

I *am* okay. I am. I just…really wish he was here. And I was hoping that we would hear something about him coming back for the wedding. Anna's his sister and Gunner's his best friend. If he *could* come, he would. Even if only for a day. So I'm guessing he can't. But I'll do everything I can to share their wedding with him, so that Stone feels like he was here, too.

Flipping the camera so my face is onscreen, I start recording. "So everything is pretty much ready to go at Jenny's house. I spent most of the day there and we finished up the decorations, so now there's only…" The loud rumble of a Harley-Davidson engine slows me down for a moment. "That must be Hashtag coming in. I'll wait for a second, because it's just going to get loud again when Beaver and Picasso take off. In the meantime, look at Daisy sleeping over there. She's so cute. Oh, whoops, she sees the phone and— It's not your Daddy on here, girl! Sorry!"

Because the dog is up and barking and dancing wildly, racing across the kitchen and spinning back toward me. Laughing, I record that for him, instead. "Aw, she gets so excited whenever she thinks she's going to see you. I'll play Daddy's video again in a minute, girl." I hear Beaver and Picasso finally leaving. "Okay. Now we just have to wait for her to calm down. Daisy, give me just a minute! Go say hi to Hashtag because I just heard him come in and…and…"

It's not Hashtag.

The phone clatters to the table and I stand with my hands covering my mouth and sudden tears swimming in my eyes, staring at the big man coming into the kitchen.

Stone. With his hair a little shorter and his face a little harder, but everything about him still bursting with vitality. Bursting with *life*. The sight of him fills up every dark and aching place inside me with light, and with a joy that overflows into the tears that are streaming down my cheeks. Daisy launches herself at his legs and Stone crouches to pet her, scratching her ears and kissing her and saying she's a good girl—but all the while his eyes are on me.

"There's a good girl," he says gruffly as she dances and wags. "You've been so good and I've missed you so much. But let me go say hi to Mommy now."

He doesn't say hi. The way his throat's working, I'm guessing he's got a lump in there to match the one in mine. Instead he cups my face in his big hands, and his touch is enough to break me, to put me back together again. A laugh and a sob burst out of me at the same time, then his mouth is on mine. His kiss is long and slow and deep, like the kiss when he married me, then *so* hungry. Need tears through me with each lick of his tongue past my lips. My fingers fly to his belt and he doesn't stop kissing me as his strong hands grip my ass and lift me up onto the counter, doesn't stop kissing me as his fingers find me so hot and ready. His groan into my mouth roughens when I eagerly guide his stiffened cock to my entrance, and I cry out when he surges deep. So deep. And it's been so long.

For a long minute he doesn't move, just kisses me slow and sweet while my body remembers how to take his massive length, with his arm wrapped around my back and holding me so tight against him.

As if he'll never let me go. As if he remembers how I love that, too.

Slowly he begins to thrust, and pleasure sparks bright with every long slide of his cock, with every breathless kiss. With my legs cinched around his hips, I urge him harder, faster, then the sparks burn brighter and brighter until I'm gasping, crying into his mouth while my inner muscles clamp down on the thickness inside me. He groans and plunges deep, and I can't remember him ever coming so fast, either. So I'm laughing against his lips even as I feel the hot pulse of his cum within me, then he's kissing me and kissing me, before finally drawing back the barest distance.

His gaze caresses my face. "I know you're worried that I don't feel the same way that I did when I married you. And what I feel for you *has* changed, Maxine," he says thickly. "Because I love you more than ever."

I give a watery laugh, that joy filling up my eyes with tears again. "You just want me to chain you to our bed."

"That, too," he says and hauls me off the counter with my legs still wrapped around his hips and his cock buried deep inside me. "Now steer me to our room. I've got ten months of loving you to catch up on."

Ten months without him. But the pain of missing him doesn't even feel real now. Because it vanished with a single touch.

Now there's only Stone. For however long I get to hold him.

"I THINK WE MISSED THE wedding rehearsal," I say sleepily. He's holding me with my head pillowed on his shoulder and my fingers tracing through the hair on his chest, because I can't stop touching him.

"Yeah, and they better get used to me being late and missing things. I've got a wife with a pussy made of sugar and who squirms like the hottest fucking thing while she's chasing her come. And why the hell do we need to practice walking down an aisle? It's not like you can get lost on the way. You and I managed all right without a rehearsal."

"We did." I smile, remembering, but his *better get used to me being late* forces me to ask the question I've been avoiding, because I'm so afraid of the answer. "Are you staying for a while?"

"Forever, I hope."

Sheer happiness swells through my chest. Except that last part doesn't seem so certain. "You hope?"

He sighs heavily. "We didn't get Papa. We figure he must have gone to ground—and since we got the rest of those fuckers, and most of the Cage's network is dismantled, they didn't want to keep paying for all the manpower. But I suppose if they get wind of him, maybe they'd pull me back in. Maybe they wouldn't, though."

"Oh," I say softly. "You sound disappointed."

"Just disappointed we didn't nail that fucker to the wall. Sure as hell not disappointed that it was time to come back home."

"I'm sorry, too. About Papa. Not about you here. That's the best thing."

"For me, too." He brushes his thumb over my lips, his gaze searching my face. "How you doing? You're looking real good, and you seem to be moving all right. But I probably ought to have been more careful down there in the kitchen."

I shake my head. "There's still a twinge now and then, but otherwise I'm a hundred percent. I've been doing yoga and some other things the doctors recommended."

"Good." Gently he kisses me. "And what about the rest of you? Your heart, your head. They're doing okay, too?"

"Yes," I whisper, my throat tightening up. "I really am.

Especially now. And you?"

"I ain't never been better than I am now, angel. Though I might be even better than this in about five minutes, when I'm inside you again."

Unsurprisingly, that's even better for me, too.

FORTY-FOUR

STONE

Maybe I ought to have gone to the rehearsal. As the best man, I assumed that I'd be escorting the maid of honor. But Saxon isn't about to let any other bastard ever walk Jenny down any aisle, and it's me and Zoomie instead. So aside from nearly getting an asskicking from the prez before he led Jenny up near the altar, the rest of the ceremony seemed to go all right. Not that I was paying a whole lot of attention. My heart felt real big while I watched my dad bring Anna down the aisle and give her to Gunner, but after that, I just kept eyes on Maxine, who's looking so fucking pretty sitting between my mom and my cousin Penny. Her hair's back to red, her emerald eyes are bright, and she looks so damn happy.

Life just ain't never been better.

"You back for good, then?" Spiral asks me at the reception, then looks real disappointed when I say that I am. "Well, goddammit. Glad to have you back, brother, but I was *this* fucking close to getting your enforcer patch."

Yeah, that patch ain't going anywhere. "Sorry, brother."

He snorts. "You're not a bit sorry."

True. And not gonna lie, it was a fucking knife to the gut when Saxon sent me a message saying that I'd been gone so long that he needed to give my patch to someone else. I didn't blame him. The club needs an enforcer who's present and accounted for. And I wasn't.

But keeping my patch isn't why I'm so glad to be back.

Instead my reason is in my arms a little bit later when the dancing begins. I ain't much of a dancer. But I'm real good at holding Maxine against me, so I just sway a bit while I do, nuzzling her soft hair, loving the smell of her.

Hell, loving all of her.

"You doing anything this week?" I know she volunteers at an animal shelter and also helps the VP's wife out at their stables, but she hasn't taken up a steady job yet… and probably won't before heading back to school next year, so she can take as much time as possible to heal. And that cash from her grandpa gives her a nice cushion, but I don't want her to have to use it. So now that this job with the feds is over, I'll need to figure out my own situation pretty soon. I don't think I'll be going back to work as a lumberjack for Widowmaker—or any other job that'll take me away from her for days at a time. But I've got enough money socked away that I won't need to sort that just yet. "Because I sure would love to spend every minute with you."

She looks up at me, those emerald eyes dark. "I assume you'll be trying to find Papa."

The one thing I needed to do for her. The one thing I didn't get done. The whole fucking reason I left her alone for so long. "I won't stop looking, angel. But until we get some kind of—"

"No, I mean…" She trails off uncertainly for a moment before continuing, "I think I know how to find him. Or at least figure out who he is."

I stop swaying. "How?"

"Well, while I was watching the ceremony, I remembered something about Papa. Something that I didn't think to tell Creek, because it was when Papa was in the farmhouse and sending me to be bait, and we were more focused on describing his security team and talking about the Iron Blood. But Papa has a daughter."

"You told him that." I saw those interviews she did with Creek…while she was still barely able to sit up in bed. *Hours* of fucking interviews. "You said that you thought Papa arranged her marriage to one of his business associates."

"Because he said all that creepy shit about her being a virgin and taking to her new role as a woman. Her *new* role," she emphasizes, "because her marriage had taken place in the past month."

She says that like it means something, but I'm pretty sure she mentioned it being a recent marriage to Creek, too. "And?"

"Well…look at all this." She gestures around us, at the big heated tent set up in Jenny's backyard, where everything's dripping with fairy lights and flowers. "Jenny put a lot of work into it herself, but still there's so much preparation. And so much money spent. That's got to leave a trail. But we're not talking about a small town wedding. I *met* Papa. And that man did not marry off his virgin daughter to his business associate in a tiny ceremony in a Vegas chapel. No, I bet anything that it was a big church wedding, because he was so focused on her being pure. And there was something about him that was just…old world and old money and steeped in tradition. So I bet it wasn't even a church, but more like a cathedral of some kind. And there have to be records. A big wedding, last October…and a fuckton of money spent on a reception afterwards. All paid for by the father of the bride, because that's traditional, too."

I bring her in tight against me and start swaying again, my heart thumping. Because she might be right.

She's *probably* right. And she's not talking about finding one marriage out of the hundred thousand that happen in Las Vegas each year. The way she's talking about Papa would narrow that down to a real small number.

"All right, angel," I tell her gruffly. "This will be your choice. We pass on all of what you just said to Creek…or we give it to Blowback."

"Blowback," she whispers, and I clench my fist in celebration behind her back.

Fuck yes.

"But I want to come, too."

"Hold up—"

"Not to fight. I'll stay in a car or wherever is safe." She pulls back to look up at me, her gaze steady on mine and shadowed with remembered pain. "But…I can't bear to wait here again while you're so far away. And we'll be with your club. I know you will all protect me."

"Yeah, we will." With our lives if we have to. But she won't be getting that close to any action when it goes down. "All right. I'll get Blowback started. It might take a while, because that's still a shitload of information for him to wade through…and that'll give time for Gunner to come back from his honeymoon."

Suddenly she laughs. "Yes, please. Or your sister might kill me."

"Nah, it'd be me that she went after." But it won't be an issue, because we aren't rushing into this. "And until then?"

Her smile turns impish. "We've still got ten months to make up for. And since we're here anyway...Jenny's house has a whole lot of rooms."

I fucking love the way my wife thinks.

FORTY-FIVE

STONE

When Blowback finally nails down Papa's name and location, Gunner and Anna are still on their honeymoon and won't return for another week yet. Which means I've got time to do something that needs to be done.

Maxine insists on coming with me. I ain't real sure about that at first, especially since she doesn't know all of why I'm going. But I can't leave her behind again.

And we're a team, she reminds me. But so were Handlebar and Crash, which is partly what'll make this so fucking hard. And partly it's because I've never begged a man for a reprieve before. As far as Maxine knows, we're just riding to New Mexico to give Handlebar the heads-up about Papa and to invite him along. But I owe Handlebar. And after we take down Papa, the time will come for us to settle up.

For a while there, I didn't give a fuck if he killed me. I give a fuck now. And not just for myself. I can't let him do that to Maxine. But I don't want to kill him, either.

So I'll ask him to wait a while. Maybe about eighty years. Then we'll settle up in a nursing home or some shit.

Before we hit the state line, I contact the Bedlam Butchers to let Handlebar know we're headed his way. He tags me not long afterward with the address of a truck stop where we'll meet up the next morning.

Maxine and I get a room nearby and I spend pretty much the whole night inside her. By morning, coffee and pancakes at the truck stop cafe are a real welcome sight. We're in a booth with a view of the door and the lot, so we get a good look at the brother before he comes in.

"He's lost a lot of weight," Maxine says softly.

"Yeah." He's such a big, barrel-chested bastard that he'll never be thin, but in the year since we've seen him it's like any softness he had was pared away, giving his bearded face a rawboned look. "A giant fucking hole eating at him."

She sighs heavily, then nudges my side—and it takes me a second to realize that she wants me to scoot out of the booth so she can get past me. I always put her in the seat next to the wall so I can protect her with my body if I need to, and it isn't easy letting her out when it feels like a threat is approaching. But she wasn't just *my* angel.

And Handlebar wasn't expecting to see her here. He's a few tables away when the scowl he's wearing drops away into surprise and breaks into a huge grin. "Cherry! Holy fuck! Get over here, girl."

She throws a hug around his waist and he gives her a good squeeze in return, while over her head he's measuring me up and down—and stopping at the wedding band on my left hand, eyes narrowing. Then glancing at her ring, too, when she takes his hand and leads him to our table, saying she's not Cherry anymore.

"Maxine, huh?" Handlebar says, taking the seat opposite. "And you look real fucking good. Freedom suits you."

"I think so, too." She grins at him and slides in beside me. "And I know you don't appreciate bullshit, so I'll just say it: You look like you're still going through hell."

"Then I look how I feel. Probably because I don't have a pretty nurse making me take my vitamins anymore."

"I'm sorry. I miss Crash, too." Maxine reaches across the table to take his hand. "How is his mangy cat?"

His mouth quirks. "Had a mangy litter a month ago. You want a kitten?"

"We already have a dog who's the equivalent of ten cats biting an electric wire."

"For the best. I keep asking if people want them, but I'll never fucking give those kittens away. Some days, I figure that damn cat's the only reason I'm still here." His gaze moves over to me but he's still talking to her. "You married this asshole?"

She smiles. "I did."

"He treating you right?"

"*So* right."

"Fuck. I was hoping you'd say otherwise, because I'm just looking for an excuse." Now he's addressing me. "But I don't need an excuse, do I?"

Not when I can still feel Crash's spine popping apart in my hands. "You don't."

"I figured you were coming to settle up, not to tug at my heartstrings."

"I'm here to talk about that, too. But also that we found Papa."

He goes still. "You put him in the ground yet?"

"Not yet. We're hoping you'll join us."

Then I shut my mouth as the waitress swings by to give our coffee a warm up and take Handlebar's order. When she leaves again, Maxine asks quietly, "Settle what up?"

Her troubled gaze is going from Handlebar's face to mine, and despite her asking, I can tell that she knows what it means. She knows damn well.

"Well, it's pretty fucking simple," Handlebar says, sitting back. "He killed my ride partner. And I know the reason he did it. Saving his sister. I understand that real damn well. But it doesn't fucking matter. So at some point, we settle up. And one of us won't get up again."

Maxine's eyes are real bright and glittering with tears. "But—"

"No, angel," I tell her gently. "He's right. And this is between me and him."

"And between you and Crash," Handlebar adds with a rough catch in his voice. "Which makes it not so fucking simple anymore. If you'd showed up a year ago, I'd have already put that bullet in your head. But now I've had a long damn time to think on it."

"Think on what?" Because it still seems pretty fucking simple to me.

"That he had a purpose, and it wasn't saving your sister. No, he was saving a brother. So that you could do this"— he gestures between me and Maxine—"get married to an angel, start popping out kids, have a full fucking life. So if I took that life now and made his sacrifice worth nothing, I'd be betraying him worse than you did. So instead you're going to fucking *live* that life, yeah? You making those fucking kids yet?"

My throat's real damn tight. "Not yet."

Because she's mostly recovered, but pregnancy is a hell of a strain on a body. So we're still putting that off a bit—and her birth control is real this time.

"When you do, maybe you name the first one after him. And you and me, we'll consider this shit settled." He leans forward, eyes burning into mine. "We ain't ever going to be brothers again. But there's a life he should have had, and maybe that goddamn tumor would have taken it from him, maybe it wouldn't have. All I know is, he put that future in your hands. What could have been his life is now yours, so you take care of what he gave you."

A life with Maxine. "I'll take real fucking good care of it."

"Good." He sits back, then looks to her. "So that's done."

"No," she whispers, eyes brimming. "Because Crash would have wanted the same future for you, too. And for you to take care of it—and yourself."

"I know it. I'm just getting there the long way around." His voice is real thick. "So let's talk about something we'll all be looking forward to, and tell me: Who the fuck is Papa, and how are we taking him out?"

His name's Elliot Pearce. Which doesn't mean shit to Maxine, Handlebar, or me—or probably anyone outside of casino construction. His grandfather broke ground on some of the old, big name casinos, his father carried on the tradition, and Papa came up into the world with a whole lot of contacts in Las Vegas and a whole lot of money. The kind of Vegas royalty that isn't the glitz and glamour but sheer power in the labor unions…and in the dirty underbelly, too.

We figure that's where he got the bright idea to start up his own high-stakes game in the Cage, along with all the contacts he needed in Caballo, the Greek, and every other cartel- and mafia-connected piece of garbage that I spent the last year taking down.

The best fucking part is that Elliot Pearce looks real good on paper. So at first glance, it seems like we'll be heading into a war with his security on one side and us on the other. But when we get eyes on him at his big oasis villa about fifteen miles west of the Strip, turns out the fucker hasn't been having a good year. Apparently he got real damn lazy on some projects and his company's barely afloat, getting outbid left and right. His security's down to a team of four, and word is that Papa hasn't been paying his bills. I'm guessing because all the money that was supposed to come in from the Cage didn't come in.

Ain't real sorry about that.

Still, this won't be a simple thing. His villa's up on a high ridge looking out over the city and it's a goddamn fortress. So we pay real close attention to his comings and goings. Likely that'll be how we have to get him. But even that won't be quick and easy. Maybe that asshole has a whole bevy of people looking to kill him, because he only travels in armored sedans with bulletproof glass. Which means an ambush or a sniper rifle won't do much good.

It's frustrating as hell, but there's only one way to do this: real patient and real smart. Because all this time, Papa's been patient and smart, too. And although I want Papa—and I *really* want his fucking guards, because they put bullets in my girl—better to spill their blood than ours by rushing in too quick.

That patience pays off a few days later. My phone lights up with a message from Zoomie, who's currently got eyes on him.

He and his security just left his house.

At four o'clock in the morning. Which could be any number of reasons.

Then she follows up with, *Just got onto the freeway. Looks like he's headed north out of town.*

Maxine's sleeping beside me after a long night of watching the villa. We only got back to our room about two hours ago. But she can sleep on the way.

I kiss her awake, but even as she smiles and gives a sexy little moan, reaching for me like she usually does when I wake her up this way, I have to tell her, "Get dressed, angel. I'm tagging the others and we're heading out."

She blinks and sits up. "Did Papa realize we're onto him?"

"Nah. This ain't like when they took out the doc and we had to run." I kiss the worry from her brow and haul my ass out of bed. "He's heading out of town."

Frowning, she glances at the clock. "Why?"

"That's what we're going to find out." And if this gives us an opportunity, we're going to take it.

We knew we might be in for the long haul, so the entire club isn't here—though they're on standby and ready to ride this way if we come up with a plan that needs a hell of a lot more manpower. But right now it's just ten of us spread out over four vehicles. No bikes, no vests. Nothing that'll point fingers at us later.

From the interstate, Papa's car turns onto the Great Basin Highway, which passes through a long stretch of nowhere. Zoomie and Blowback back off a bit so the fuckers won't spot their tail. Anyone else but Blowback driving, that might have worried me we'd lose them. But that brother's like a dog on a bone and Papa won't be slipping away from him.

The way the rest of us are hauling ass, when Zoomie tags us to say they turned off onto a smaller road, we're only about ten minutes behind. All around us, there's just desert scrub—a different part of the state but reminding me a whole lot of where the barns were. Just the middle of fucking nowhere. But that makes it a little easier to figure out where we might be headed. In the vehicle Saxon's driving, Gunner's looking through online maps for anything that might draw Papa out here.

He sends me a screenshot. *Look at this shit, then zoom in. That the van you were talking about?*

The communications van they used to broadcast the fight from the Cage. The van itself isn't real clear, but the shadow cast by the satellite dish is.

God bless fucking Google Earth. Those photos might have been taken any time in the past few years, and that van might not be there now…but it *was*. And that's a real clear connection to Papa.

I show it to Maxine, who sucks in a breath. Then in the backseat, Handlebar takes a look. His face goes real grim. "And is that another farmhouse and a fucking barn?"

"Looks like."

"I thought you said the Cage was done."

"It is," I tell him. "But he's out of money and probably real desperate. So it might be he's starting it up again." And it wouldn't be the first time greed made even a smart and patient man careless. "The feds never found that van. If he's got it, he can still broadcast. There's nothing stopping him if he can put a few new stables together."

"There's something stopping him," Maxine says with that rage flaring in her eyes.

Yeah, there is. "Get everyone on that map. We need a way in that doesn't have us rolling up the driveway with our dicks flapping in the wind."

That way in is a reservoir road that cuts around behind the property on a ridge running east. We'll be hoofing it for about a half mile, but the lay of the land and the barn itself will keep us out of sight of the farmhouse and give us some cover. We just have to make sure Papa is out of that armored car before we start lighting shit up.

Ideally, we'd take longer to scope out the territory and the property. Can't be patient now. Fuck knows how long he'll be here—or when a chance like this will come again.

We pull off the reservoir road and meet Zoomie, who points up toward the ridge where Blowback's seeing what he can see. As I'm gearing up, I tell Maxine, "You'll be staying here with Hashtag and Bull."

She nods. Her face is pale and expression taut, just

like I remember how it was when we were watching her brother fight in the Cage.

I hate that she's afraid. But there's nothing that can fix it except getting this done, so there won't be anything left for her to fear. "You're gonna hear some gunfire, maybe an explosion or two. But I fucking swear to you, I'm coming back. We're all coming back."

"I know," she whispers, and I kiss the hell out of her before heading out.

It's a sunny, cold morning. The air's clean and clear and just the right temperature to take out the trash.

We move in quick and low, Blowback taking the lead since he already scoped out the path that'll give us the most cover. Handlebar, Gunner, and me are right on his ass—just like old times, except that Crash isn't with us. Otherwise this shit's like slipping on a real comfortable boot. Right behind us comes Saxon and Zoomie and Duke. If we need it, they'll lay down suppressive fire while the four of us cross the stretch of open yard between the barn and the house…and then make sure that if Papa runs for it, he doesn't reach his car. But I don't want him to run for it. I want him to hole up and trust his security to protect him.

We split up approaching the house, Gunner and Handlebar heading for the back entrance, me and Blowback taking the front. We pause at the side of the porch, because we haven't had eyes on the front of the building— and his security would be real fucking stupid not to have at least one man out there. But that's why Gunner and Handlebar and a hand grenade are going to provide a real nice distraction out back.

The explosion means it's go time. The bang of the grenade is still ringing in my ears when I slide around the side of the house, where a big fucker in a suit did what any human would and looked in the direction of the boom. It ain't the suit who escaped that night, but they all fucking drop the same when I pull the trigger. The airy cough of my silencer is buried under the noise Handlebar and Gunner are still making, shooting out the windows at the back of the house. One of two things will happen now: the security guards will rush Papa out the front door, or they'll hunker down in the most secure room.

They hunker down. And this is turning into a hell of a good day.

Three guards left. They'll make sure Papa's secure, then leave one guard with him while the other two go see what the fuck is going on and to clear us out.

No shouting from inside to give away their position. These suits know their shit. I crouch near the dead guard and take a look at his radio earpiece. No good to us. My bullet clipped the receiver and the whole thing fucking shattered. The others are likely asking him for a sitrep. When he doesn't answer, they'll know we're out front, too.

I look to Blowback, then glance to the narrow windows peeking through the foundation. There's a basement. He nods, motions me ahead.

I go in low through the front door, sweeping the living room, then cover his six as he moves swiftly into the dining room. Gunner and Handlebar come in from the kitchen, both silent as fuck. I gesture to what I'm assuming is the basement door set into the kitchen wall. Gunner nods, then points upward.

Shit. Stairs are the worst goddamn thing, and the suits have the advantage for both. No doubt two of them are on the second floor, one guard ready to blow the head off anyone who comes up the steps while the other checks the windows, from where he can sweep the yard and fire at anyone outside. And the basement, hell. Even the stupidest guard can shoot someone who comes down the stairs.

Good thing Gunner came with goodies.

He passes a few flash grenades to Handlebar, gives us all a pair of combat earplugs, then looks to Blowback. Time to switch dance partners, because the basement will be just some blunt force shit, while taking out the fuckers upstairs requires a little more stealth.

Handlebar and I are the blunt force. He smirks a bit as he looks to the basement door...which can't even be locked from the inside. Yeah, yeah, yeah. He gets the fun part. I get the shitty part, going blind into a hole. But I'm more accurate with a handgun than he is, so that's the way it's gotta be.

We both put in our earplugs using the unblocked end that'll muffle loud explosions while still letting voices through. We wait just long enough for Gunner and Blowback to get where they're going, because the flashbang down here will probably be like poking a hornet's nest upstairs.

Standing to the side of the door, Handlebar reaches for the knob, swings it open. No shots. So either nobody's down there, or Papa's guard isn't some impulsive dipshit.

Then Handlebar yells, "FBI! Come out with your hands up!" and I about lose my shit trying not to laugh, but hoping they're dumb enough to fall for it.

They aren't. He shrugs, because it was worth a try, and tosses down the flashbang. I cover my eyes with my hand. Now the shout comes, a guard yelling to get down—then the percussion slams through my chest and pops in my ears.

I charge through the door, down three steps with my gaze scanning through the swirling smoke below. Unfinished basement. Support columns. A furnace. Lots of shit to hide behind but the suit's only partially behind cover, still wobbling a bit as he aims my direction. And that's the fucker. The fucker who hunted down my girl. I put two bullets in his chest but he must be wearing body armor, because he gets knocked back but doesn't go down.

Bullet in his face gets the job done.

"Guard's down!" I call up to Handlebar. Smoothly I take the rest of the stairs, making a sweep—and find Papa cowering behind the furnace.

Fuck me, and Maxine was right. He *does* have rich people hair.

"Let's go, asshole," I tell him, then realize his ears are probably still ringing and he's probably half deaf. Shit. I grab his collar, haul him out. And maybe because he's not dead yet, the cowering stops. Now will come the negotiation when he'll offer us money, maybe threaten us.

Before he can start playing the rich asshole, I give his cheek a friendly little pat. "I ain't gonna kill you!" I yell at him.

Relief fills his expression. Then his eyes narrow on my face, and I'm guessing he recognizes the scars from that demonstration Crash and I gave.

More important that he recognizes me from somewhere else. Grinning, I shout, "All them money troubles you've been having?" I point my thumbs at my chest. "You can thank me! I took down *all* your fucking buddies and dismantled your Cage!"

His expression hardens and he begins shaking his head. I catch his face again, make sure he registers every word that comes next.

"And it was Cherry who figured out how to find you! You remember her? Tased your prize bull's balls?"

I can see he remembers her—and is real fucking irritated knowing that a little redheaded virgin took him down.

Though I'd love to smash his goddamn teeth in, I give his cheek another friendly pat. "But like I said, I ain't going to kill you! Nah. I'm going to walk up those stairs, and lock that door for…oh, maybe fifteen minutes. Because this basement seems a hell of a lot like the Cage. And if you refuse to fight—well, shit. Your choice is to fight or else get a bullet in the head. So which will it be?"

Jaw clenched, rage reddening his face, he tells me, "I will *not* fight. And you will pay for this."

I laugh. That's the best he's got? "All right, man."

Turning, I head for the stairs.

"Wha— Where are you going?"

"I told you that I'm not killing you!" I call back, then bump Handlebar's fist as he comes down. "But I *am* starting that clock. And you know the rules, Mr. Pearce— two men enter, one man leaves."

And Crash gave me a future. Now I can give Handlebar this.

I head up to the kitchen and don't bother to lock the door. Blowback and Gunner are waiting there.

"All done?"

"Except for the cleanup," Gunner says, then eyes the basement door. "What about Papa?"

"There won't be much left to clean up." I pull out my phone, tag Bull and tell him to bring Maxine in. I'll need to get the body off the porch.

But I think she'll want to see the rest of this.

FORTY-SIX

MAXINE

Bull drives me to the farmhouse, but my heart doesn't stop pounding until Stone meets me at the truck and pulls me in so tight against him.

"You aren't going anywhere near that house," he tells me. "But I want you to see that it's done. We're just waiting for Handlebar to finish up."

I nod against his chest, then he turns me around to hold me against him, both of us facing the farmhouse. Every breath I take smells faintly of fuel.

Carrying a gas can, Hashtag comes out of the barn. "That van in there must have a million dollars worth of equipment in it," he says, sounding awed. "Are we burning that, too, or should we break it down and sell it off?"

"Burn it," Saxon orders. "If we start selling equipment that might be traced back to us, that million dollars won't be worth shit."

"It's been a lot longer than fifteen minutes," Zoomie says, frowning toward the house. "Do we need to go in and pull him out?"

Behind me, Stone shakes his head. "Give him another minute."

My heart jumps into my throat when Handlebar emerges from the house, fists covered in blood. I make a sound and take a step forward, but Stone pulls me back.

"That's not his blood, angel. And he's all right."

That seems true. Though the big man isn't exactly smiling, somehow he looks a hell of a lot happier than he did only an hour ago.

Duke and Gunner head into the house carrying more fuel, and Handlebar comes closer, wiping down his hands with a cloth that Hashtag douses with more gas as soon as he's done with it.

Handlebar pauses in front of us, his gaze locked on Stone. "I appreciate that, brother."

"I figured you would," Stone says gruffly, then takes my hand. "So let's finish this."

Handlebar walks with us closer to the house. We stop

at the end of a trail of fuel that Blowback pours for us...a trail that leads back to the farmhouse. Stone pulls out a lighter from his pocket.

"Ready to watch it burn?" he asks me.

I've been ready for *so* long. It seems like forever since the moment I stood inside a tavern, preparing myself to meet a fighter that I didn't know but was determined to save, and realizing that the next step I took would be the one that lit the match to burn down the nightmare I'd found myself in.

But I had no idea how far that step would take me.

"Can I do it?" I ask him, my throat aching.

"Fuck yes, angel," he says, then kisses me before handing over the lighter.

And finally, *finally*—I burn down the fucking Cage.

EPILOGUE

STONE

"Show of hands." At the head of the table, Saxon calls for a vote. "Those in favor of establishing a new chapter of the Hellfire Riders?"

Every hand on the executive board goes up. No surprise there. Our numbers are getting too damn big for this little town, and after all the shit that went down a while back—the Devil's Hangmen gone, the Iron Blood gone, the Eighty-Eight weakened without Papa and the other Cage-fuckers to provide all the shit they were running—there's been a huge power vacuum in the region. And the Hellfire Riders aren't looking for power, but we'd sure as fuck like to take up some more territory and flex some muscle when more skinheads or skin traffickers try to move in.

And do it real quiet, just like we've always been.

"All right, then. Record that vote, Widowmaker, and then all you fuckers go home."

Zoomie smirks. "Aw," she says to me. "I think the new daddy is cranky."

"Probably hasn't slept in about two years," I agree. Not since his first boy came along. Now the second's only three months old. "Jenny always looks real well-rested, though."

Saxon narrows that steely glare at me. "Laugh it up, fucker. Your turn is coming."

I grin. Yeah, it is. And I can't fucking wait.

Groaning, Zoomie shakes her head. "This new chapter shouldn't be called the Hellfire Riders. Just call it the Happy Fuckers Club."

"And make you the president?" I ask her.

"I can't be a member. You have to be real sappy to patch in. Jack could be prez, though," she says, looking toward Blowback, and his dead flat stare lights up when he grins at her.

"I'll be prez," he agrees. "But it sounds like we also need to have a baby."

She snorts. "We have a dog. That's close enough. So you'll be prez, then we'll throw both these happy fuckers in there, too"—she waves toward me and Saxon—"and also you, and you, and you."

She points to Gunner and Duke and Bull, who all missed the beginning of the conversation but look real worried now that she's singling them out.

"What club are we joining?" Duke asks.

"The Happy Fuckers Club," I tell him.

Bull seems to consider that before nodding. "Yeah, all right. Next executive meeting, I'm bringing Nadia in that little lamb pajama set she's got, and we're going to spend the whole time coloring rainbows. Because I'm a real happy fucker when we do that."

"And that's just too damn cute." Zoomie pushes back from the table. "So I'll leave all you dick-swingers to this sappy shit, while I go have a real good time out drinking with your wives."

Yeah, maybe I'll be going that way soon, too. I look to Gunner as she heads out. "Where are they meeting up tonight?"

"The prez's place."

"House or bar?"

"Bar," Saxon says.

"No offense, brothers," Duke tells us as he gets to his feet. "This happy fuck club sounds like good clean fun, but I'm thinking Zoomie's got a point. I can stay here and look at you all, or I can go look at Olivia, and I know which one sounds like a real good time."

"Shit, I don't know." Bull looks real torn. "Gunner's so

pretty."

"Prettier than Sara?" Gunner asks dryly.

The big man shoots out of his chair. "Not even close. Sorry, brother. Maybe there's an Ugly Fuckers Club you can join."

Scowling, Saxon drums his fingers on the table. "Does anyone else have any real funny jokes to tell before we get the fuck out of here?"

Blowback's expression doesn't crack a bit. "Lily's pregnant," he says.

The prez closes his eyes like he's in pain. "And now I'm gonna go see my wife."

AND I'M GONNA GO SEE mine. It's been over four years since I first saw her in a tavern and then had to keep staring—and that hasn't changed a damn bit. She's up at the bar, looking so fucking pretty…but not a bit vulnerable.

She catches sight of me in the mirror behind the shelves of liquor, and spins on her stool, her emerald eyes shining and her smile bright. Then she brings me in with a crook of her finger.

I push in close, dropping a kiss to her mouth. "I missed you, angel."

"I missed you, too," she says softly, though it's only been a few hours since we last saw each other, when her last class of the day ended and I finished up the final coaching session at the gym that me and a few of the other brothers own. I made enough of a reputation for myself fighting in the biker circuit that the training slots are always filled up, and I'm enjoying the hell out of it. But there's always a Maxine-sized hole in me when I'm not with her.

"How'd your meeting go?" she asks. "Saxon came in and then he and Jenny went back to his office, but I can never tell if he's in a good mood or bad."

"We established that we're all happy fuckers. Why's Anna working the bar?"

Which is why I'm assuming that the women are sitting up here instead of at a table. Anna used to bartend at Saxon's joint, but cut back her hours as soon as she started selling paintings on the regular, then quit altogether when her and Gunner's adoption paperwork finally went through.

"She just stepped in while Lacey went on break, so we're keeping her company." Maxine takes a sip from the glass in front of her and then gives me a little pout. "No cherry for you tonight."

Because she's drinking water instead of a cocktail. Grinning, I glance down at her rounded little belly, then let my gaze drift lower. She's wearing a white dress that flirts around her knees and some sexy-as-fuck red heels. "I bet I can still find something sweet to eat between those pretty thighs of yours."

"Are you sure you want to?" Gripping my vest, she tugs me closer and brings my gaze back to hers. "I'm trouble. I'll take advantage of all your soft spots."

"I fucking hope so," I say real low. "But I don't have

any soft spots right now, angel. They're all real damn hard."

"What about your soft spot for dogs? Because I've got one of those. And I've got a kid coming. And I'm also a damsel in so *much* distress," she adds breathily.

Killing me. "You hurting?"

"Mmm-hmmm."

"You need to be fucked, girl?" I push in real close. "Want me to just tug those panties aside and get into you right here in front of everyone?"

"Oh god. I don't even care. Yes."

"Nah," I tell her. "I ain't sharing you with anyone."

But I'm a man who likes to get things done. And there's something that needs doing.

She lets out a laugh when I scoop her off the barstool, then winds her arms around my neck as I cradle her against my chest and head for the employees' door.

"Saxon and Jenny are already back there!" Anna calls after me, and Maxine starts giggling.

I head through the kitchen instead, carrying her out behind the building and into the warm spring night. There I back her up against the brick wall, and she looks up at me with her eyes shining with need—and so much more.

All that emotion just grabs me by the throat. "I love you so fucking much, angel," I tell her hoarsely.

That emerald glistens. "Show me."

Always. I lift her up, tug her panties aside, and slide deep. So fucking deep, while her legs wrap me up tight. Never letting me go. And as I start pumping into her, she's kissing me, touching me, wrecking me. This girl, this fucking girl, who's got me so crazy in love with her. Maxine. My wife, my angel, my everything.

And she just about takes me out with that hair trigger and her miracle of a pussy, but I ain't done.

Kissing her panting mouth, I tell her gruffly, "Hold on tight, angel. We've still got a ways to go."

Not just tonight. We've got a lifetime ahead of us.

And it's gonna be a long, hot ride.

THE END

GOING NOWHERE FAST

The brakes are off in this sizzling-hot new adult romance from the author of the Hellfire Riders MC Romance series…

One promise.
Two hearts.
Three rules.
Four weeks to break them all.

When Aspen Phillips' best friend invites her on a month-long road trip, she has serious mixed feelings. Sharing their tight quarters will be Bramwell Gage, overprotective brother and all-around jerk. Bram may be ridiculously sexy, but he's made no effort to hide how he feels about Aspen—that she's trash who's no good for his sister. But Aspen is determined to get along with the uptight millionaire—and to keep her promise, concealing a secret about his sister that Bram can never know.

But after a scorching kiss reveals that Bram's feelings toward her run much hotter than she believed, Aspen's emotions swerve into a complete 180. Suddenly the girl who has nothing has everything—but only as long as the truth about his sister remains hidden. Because when all the secrets and promises unravel, she risks losing it all…

AVAILABLE ONLY IN EBOOK!

A NOTE FROM KATI

TL;DR version of this long author's note: Phew, this was a long time coming, and now it's done! Thank you for sticking with me, and I hope you loved it! Next up is Sheriff's Bad Bear and Midsummer Bride — and more discreet cover editions!

So...this has been a long road. I intended to finish this book in late 2016/early 2017. But between contracted work, 'real-life' stuff, and just personal and emotional reasons (and then the story not being exactly what I wanted) writing Stone's book was a lot harder than I expected. But it's finally here!

A few quick notes about the timeline for *Stone (Losing It All)* and other books (and if you are skipping ahead to read this author's note first, there are spoilers!): originally this book was going to be a part of a crossover between Ella's Death Lords and Ruby's Bedlam Butchers. That plan never quite pulled together for various reasons, but you can still see where we planted a few seeds of that crossover through a few of our books, beginning with Jack & Lily's story and the first mention of the Cage. The strongest crossover element was of course Crash & Handlebar disappearing off the pages of the Bedlam Butchers, then showing up in Gunner's story … and now in this story, we see exactly what happened to them. I'm super grateful to Ruby for letting me take on Crash and Handlebar, especially since she knew what I planned to do. When I told Ruby and Ella that I needed Stone to fight someone in the Cage who'd have a deeper emotional impact on him (as well as the Riders and the Butchers…and our readers) and it couldn't be just a random fighter, she graciously offered me her characters.

She also wrote *Double Dare You*, which tells the story of one of the girls who was branded as a "cherry" and is eventually rescued by two Bedlam Butchers. Those events take place at the same time as *Gunner* and *Stone*… but we did have a little timeline bobble there. My books are set primarily in November/December, whereas her heroine is about to begin college (which would be early autumn, unless we pretended it was the rare freshman who started during winter term.) So if you are going from one book to the next and scratching your head about the timeline, it's just a mix-up on our part, and not something we caught at the time of writing. Just pretend it's the same month!

Also my new adult romance, *Going Nowhere Fast*, features Stone's cousin as a heroine and has a few chapters where the Hellfire Riders show up. Although Maxine isn't mentioned (because I was trying to avoid spoilers for Stone's book) — and Gunner is also missing because it would have been weird if he was there and Aspen didn't remark on how pretty he was, and so his presence would have been too distracting, story-wise — that romance takes place the summer after Gunner & Anna are married.

The final timeline note is from *Bull*, when Stone returns to help the Riders hand out a punishment. Originally, I'd planned to have Maxine in a long coma after being shot (seriously, that version was so much darker and a more depressing, with Maxine still believing Stone hated her even up to the point where she was shot, and with Matt staying dead and I'm so glad I rewrote the second half) — so when I wrote both *Bull* and *Duke*, part of the reason Stone was still away for so long was because he was chasing down bad guys but also always checking in on her in the hospital. Since I changed that part of the plot, however, now it means that in *Bull*, he showed up in Pine Valley while Maxine was waiting for him to come home. I thought about forcing a scene into this book that would explain that, because it really doesn't make sense that Maxine would be so close to him and he wouldn't go see her. (And pushing their reunion ahead to that moment would have then completely messed up a larger plot element in *Duke* when Stone is still gone and his enforcer's patch is up for grabs.) So there are one of two options there: I go back to revise Bull's book and take out the mention that Stone was there … or Stone did make a very quick trip home to take care of Club business, and looked longingly in at Maxine at some point without alerting Daisy to his presence or Maxine knowing he was there, but had to leave again right away to take down one of the stable owners.

And I don't really like the idea of going back to change Bull's book, so I'm okay with that second option. Just picture a heart-wrenching moment when Stone is about to go see Maxine — and it's probably pouring rain, so it looks like tears are dripping down his cheeks — and he sees that she's lonely and she's playing with Daisy but still a little sore from her injuries, and he's fighting his guilt that she was shot but he LOVES HER SO MUCH HE HAS TO SEE HER, and is just about to go knock on the door…but then he gets that call saying that maybe there's a lead on Papa. So he goes, because taking Papa out was how he'd protect her. Awww.

Also, we are going to pretend that there is a good veterinary school near where Pine Valley is supposed to be (if you're familiar with Central Oregon, you might be scratching your head about where she's going to enroll in a veterinary program.) In Oregon, only OSU in Corvallis offers a doctorate in veterinary medicine, but we'll just say that by the time Maxine had finished her undergraduate work, they also had a program at the OSU Cascades campus in Bend. Make-believe is fun!

WHAT'S COMING NEXT?

SHERIFF'S BAD BEAR AND *THE MIDSUMMER BRIDE*! *SHERIFF's Bad Bear* will come first, simply because I have the audiobook under contract with Tantor Media and so there's an additional obligation there (plus it's shorter, so it'll come out faster!) I have another 'other job' project about to hit, too, so I can't give any concrete dates for either book. Just know that it'll be as soon as I possibly can.

After that … I'm not sure! It's funny, because when I started out with the Motorcycle Clubs, I was very focused on just one type of sexy, contemporary MC story — but knowing myself a bit better now, I really need to let off creative pressure in different ways. So that's why you've been getting all these different things from me: holiday contemporary, paranormal werewolves, barbarian fantasy, and motorcycle clubs. I probably won't have any more Hellfire Riders for a while (at least not in the sense of "I'm writing a motorcycle club romance") but we might see them show up again in stories I've been tossing around in my head for Creek, Hashtag, and a few others.

So I have a ton of ideas, but which one will come after *Midsummer Bride* mostly depends on which one grabs me the hardest! For right now, though, I'll just focus on getting those two stories done.

If you'd like to stay on top of Kati news, my website is always a good place to go. And as always, if you'd like to be notified of a new release, you can sign up for my newsletter. I won't spam you; I typically only send out newsletters when I have a release or other important news, and I never share your information with other authors.

Again, thank you all so much for picking up Stone's book after all this time (or if you're a new reader, thank

you for giving it a try!) I hope you loved it as much as I do.
Happy reading!
Kati

ABOUT KATI

Kati Wilde is a tight-lipped, loose-hipped
woman of indeterminate age and low breeding.
She writes romantic fiction to assuage her
darker urge to write Transformers erotica.
You can reach Kati at kati@katiwilde.com or any
of the Club authors (Ella Goode, Ruby Dixon,
and Kati Wilde) at 1theclub1@gmail.com.

www.katiwilde.com

Facebook: www.facebook.com/authorkatiwilde
Instagram: www.instagram.com/authorkatiwilde
Twitter: www.twitter.com/katiwilde

www.katiwilde.com/newsletter

CONTENT WARNINGS

- **Disturbing Violence:** The situation my hero/heroine are in (the Cage) is bad enough, but one of the fighters is especially horrible. I try not to go into gory detail about what happens, but some detail is there, and the implication about the rest is clear enough.
- **Sexual violence/rape:** The heroine lives under a constant threat of rape, and is assaulted in an attempted rape (we saw part of this attempt in *Gunner*). Rapes also occur during the story—one is off-page (but the rapist gloats about it on-page) and the other is on-page but non-explicit. Neither the hero nor the heroine is raped.
- **Consent:** In a very narrow sense, all of the interactions between my hero/heroine are consensual. More broadly, their situation adds clear noncon and dubcon aspects. SPOILERS: For the noncon, the heroine is ordered to perform oral sex on the hero after a traumatizing event. Under non-Cage circumstances, neither one would object to the act itself/being sexual with each other, but they object to the situation. She eventually agrees because the alternative is horrid. He initially says 'no', then agrees when he realizes what the consequences for her might be. Later in the book, the hero holds her prisoner in a cabin while he gets his payback; although she enthusiastically consents, obviously the situation adds a dubious aspect.
- **"Good guy" character deaths:** The hero & heroine live, of course, but usually in my books only the bad guys are killed. That is not true in this book.
- **Grief & trauma:** All of the above means that the hero and heroine have considerable grief and trauma to work through.